ENTIRELY EMMIE

ENTIRELY EMMIE

TERRI LIBENSON

STORYTIDE
An Imprint of HarperCollinsPublishers

Storytide is an imprint of HarperCollins Publishers.
Entirely Emmie
Copyright © 2025 by Terri Libenson
All rights reserved. Manufactured in Beauceville, Quebec, Canada.
No part of this book may be used or reproduced in any manner whatsoever without written permission except in the case of brief quotations embodied in critical articles and reviews. For information address HarperCollins Children's Books, a division of HarperCollins Publishers, 195 Broadway, New York, NY 10007.
www.harpercollinschildrens.com

Library of Congress Control Number: 2024952224
ISBN 978-0-06-332098-7 (hardcover) — ISBN 978-0-06-332097-0 (pbk.)
ISBN 978-0-06-346417-9 (special edition) — ISBN 978-0-06-346420-9 (special edition)

Typography by Terri Libenson and Laura Mock
25 26 27 28 29 PC/TC 10 9 8 7 6 5 4 3 2 1
First Edition

To all my readers, I'm entirely grateful

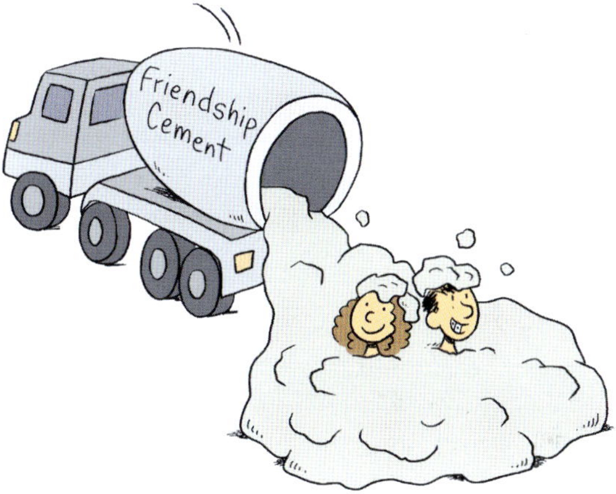
Friendship Cement

PROLOGUE
EMMIE

Really?

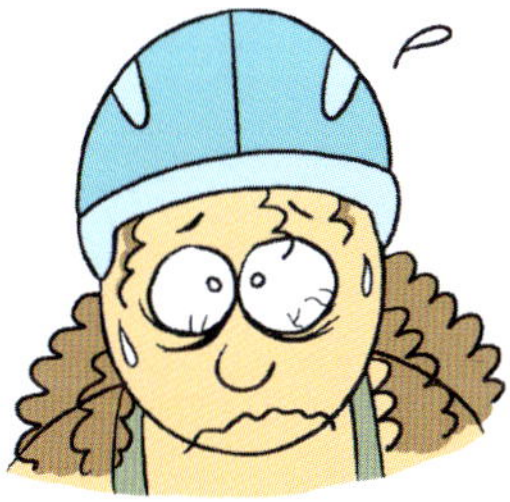

How, how, **how** do I get myself in these situations?

I am about a hundred feet from the ground (possibly exaggerated) and I can't move. Totally frozen. Pretty much the story of my life.

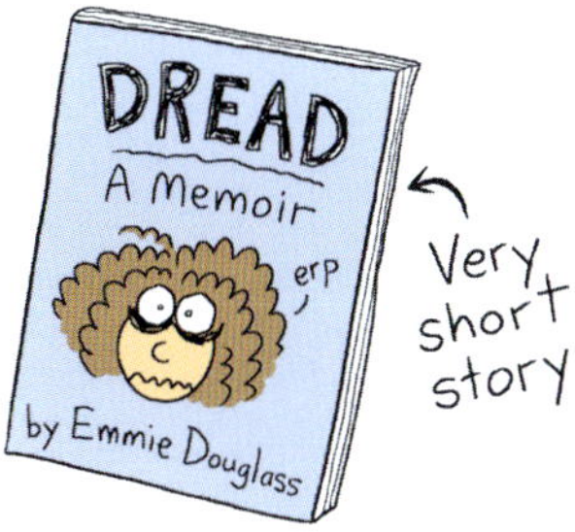
DREAD
A Memoir
erp
by Emmie Douglass
Very short story

But I can't say I ever felt like I was in actual physical danger before.

Now I want out.

For someone who usually flies under the radar, it feels like I have the world's largest spotlight on me. It's always at the wrong time, you know? Instead of shining on me during my finest hour . . .

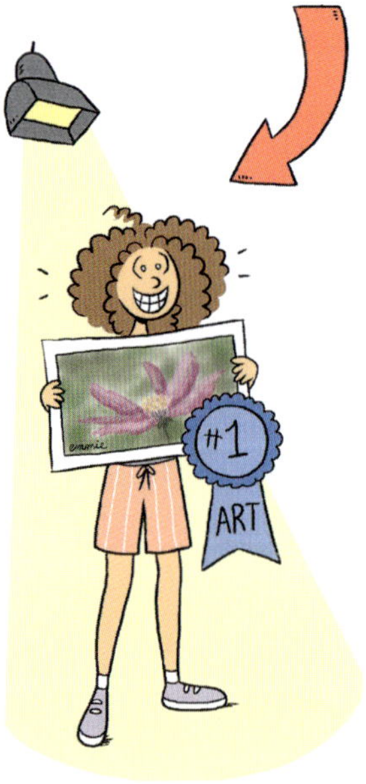
#1
ART

. . . it's pointed at me during my imminent* demise. A cringey one, too.

*Winn** Word of the Week

**English teacher

Things sure didn't start out this way. I was having a pretty good year till now. Everything was looking up.

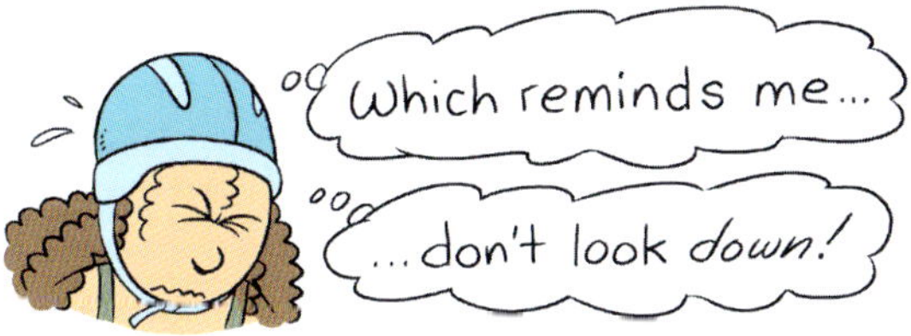
Which reminds me...
...don't look *down!*

Okay, here's how it all started. . . .

EMMIE

Things have changed.

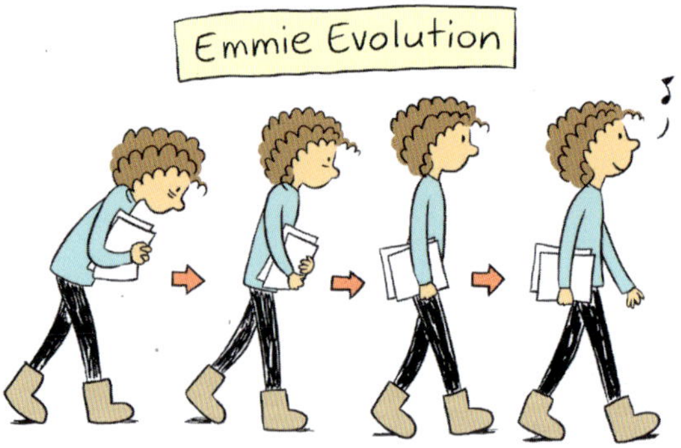
Emmie Evolution

That's an understatement. Since winter, I've made a ton of new friends.

Okay, fine, just two. But that's a lot for me. They are Sarah and Tyler, to be exact. And they aren't just your regular old acquaintances or friendly classmates. They're friend-friends. Like, **good** friends.

And if you wanna know just how much I've changed . . . well, here are two portraits of me. One from the beginning of seventh grade and one from now:

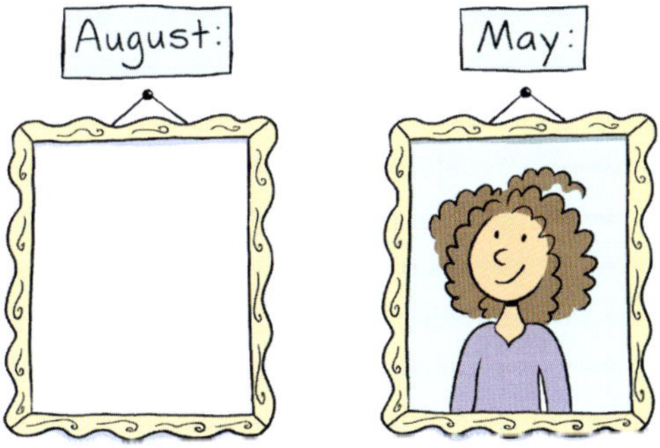
August:
May:

Kidding about that first one. But that's how I really felt. Like I wasn't there. The only person who ever made me feel like I wasn't alone was my best friend, Brianna (Bri for short).

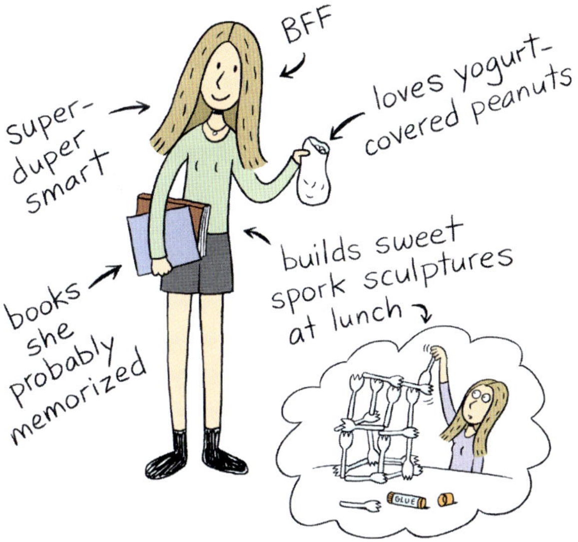
BFF
super-duper smart
loves yogurt-covered peanuts
builds sweet spork sculptures at lunch
books she probably memorized
GLUE

She's not perfect or anything. She can be a know-it-all and super bossy. But at least she thinks for herself and knows who her friends are (mainly me). Also, she's a good person and a fun BFF. I used to think I was lucky to have her, but now I think we're lucky to have each other. I try not to take our friendship for granted.

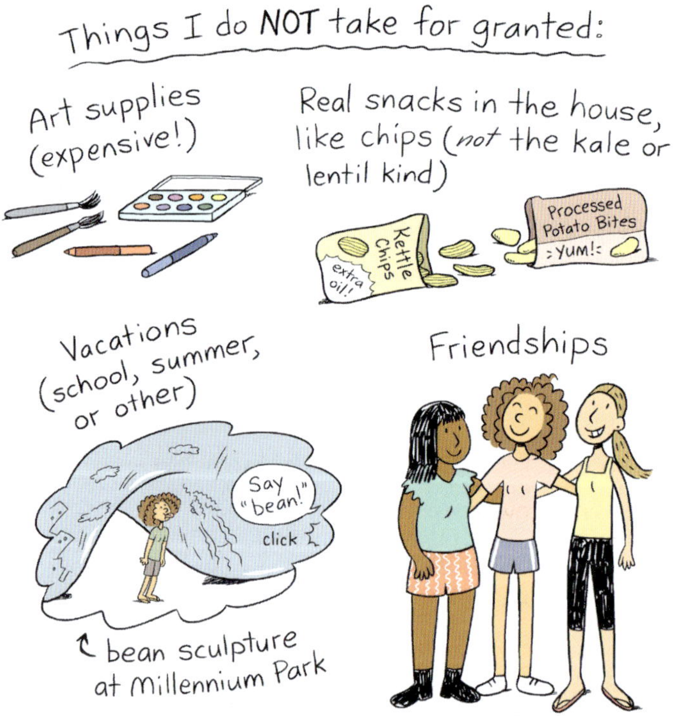
Things I do NOT take for granted:
Art supplies (expensive!)
Real snacks in the house, like chips (*not* the kale or lentil kind)
Kettle Chips
extra oil!
Processed Potato Bites
:YUM!:
Vacations (school, summer, or other)
Say "bean!"
click
bean sculpture at Millennium Park
Friendships

I know Sarah mainly from art class. We became friends there. Same with Tyler. No wait, that's not true. Tyler and I got to know each other through a veryveryveryveryveryvery embarrassing incident (very). It involved a missing note. I won't go into it here, but, trust me, it could've ended badly. Luckily, it ended in a really important collaboration and friendship. The collaboration was a comic book we created together for an art project a few months ago. Which cemented our friendship.

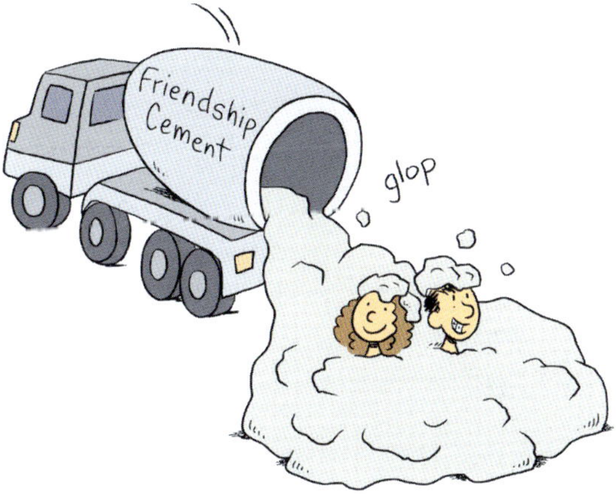
Friendship
Cement
glop

Okay . . . so, I kinda haven't mentioned my crush. Actually, that's how our friendship **really** started. I've had a HUGE crush on Tyler since fourth grade.

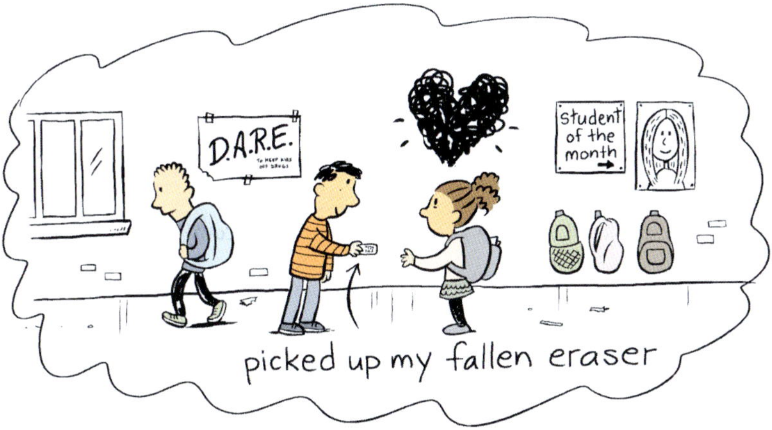
D.A.R.E.
student of the month
picked up my fallen eraser

It continues to this day. But it's not a sad, woe-is-me kind of crush. It sorta gives me a butterflies-in-the-stomach, buzzy feeling. It makes me energetic and happy to see him.

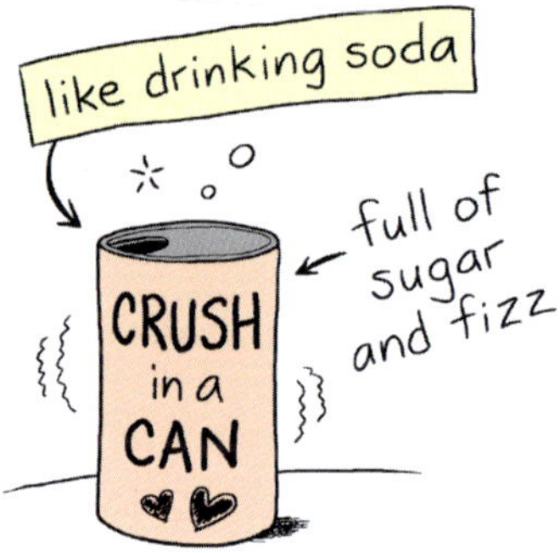
like drinking soda
CRUSH in a CAN
full of sugar and fizz

Other things that have changed:

1. I got a phone upgrade.

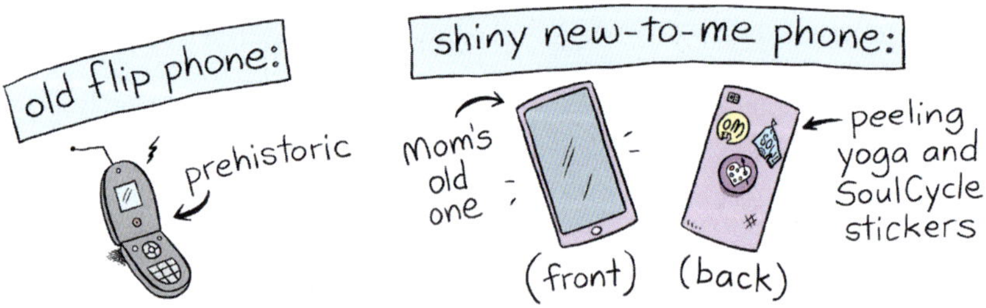
old flip phone:
prehistoric
shiny new-to-me phone:
Mom's old one
(front)
(back)
peeling yoga and SoulCycle stickers

2. I no longer get **the knots**: a tight, squeezy feeling in my stomach that flared up whenever I'd walk into school. The only thing that helped were some breathing exercises. My mom is a health fanatic and has all these ancient yoga DVDs from the '00s. That's where I learned my breathing techniques (aka how to "bloom my diaphragm" and "unclench my chakras").

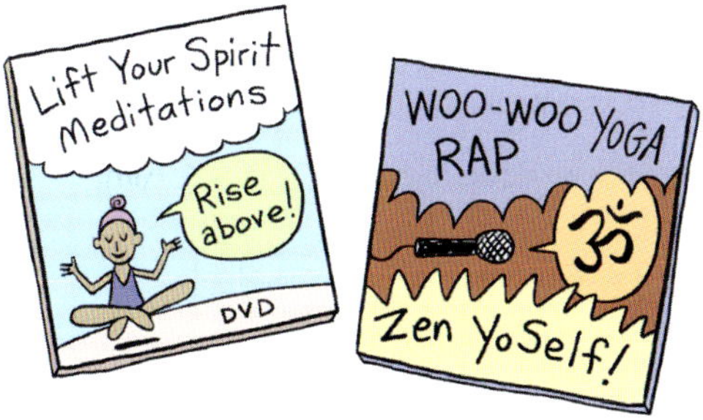
Lift Your Spirit Meditations
Rise above!
DVD
WOO-WOO YOGA RAP
ॐ
Zen YoSelf!

On a related note, I also no longer feel the need to rest my head on the top shelf of my locker (number 322) to escape the overwhelming chaos pit that is the school's main hall. To sum up, I just feel . . . **better**.

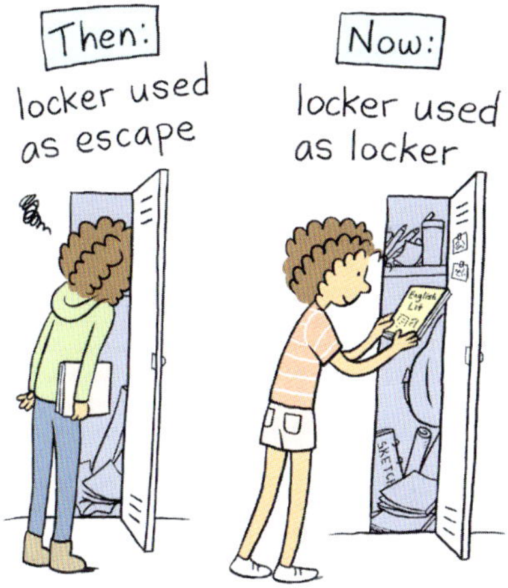
Then:
locker used as escape
Now:
locker used as locker
English Lit
SKETCH

3. Remember how I said that Bri was bossy? Well, she used to order me around all the time.

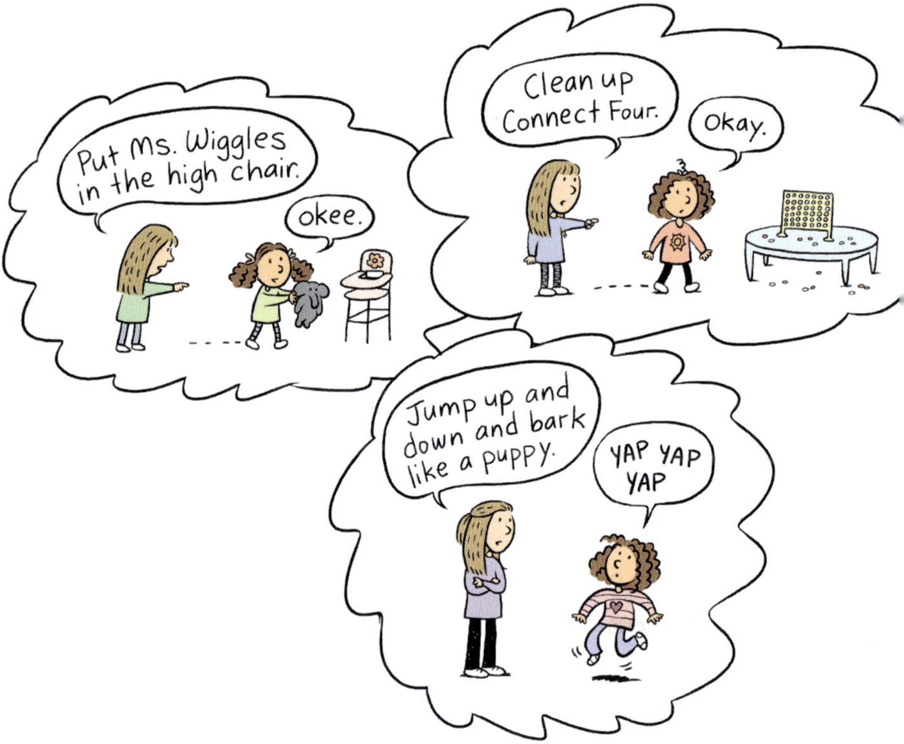
Put Ms. Wiggles in the high chair.
okee.
Clean up Connect Four.
Okay.
Jump up and down and bark like a puppy.
YAP YAP YAP

Now she doesn't . . . as much. We both came to an agreement: if she starts up, I let her know and she stops. This has worked wonders for our relationship. **And** it's taught me to stand up for myself more.

Anyway, I feel like I've grown a lot this year. It hasn't been easy; my dad said growing pains aren't always physical—and I can get **bad** physical ones. In my knees especially.

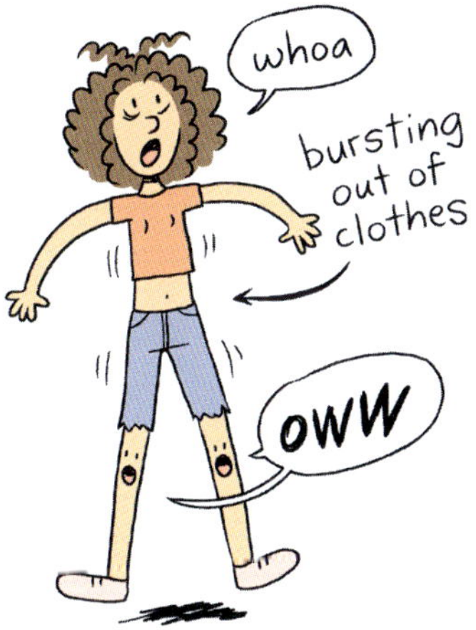
whoa
bursting out of clothes
OWW

And yeah, the emotional growing pains have been . . . something. But I guess that's middle school. I've watched my friends (all three) go through stuff, too. Luckily, seventh grade is almost over, which means one year closer to graduation.

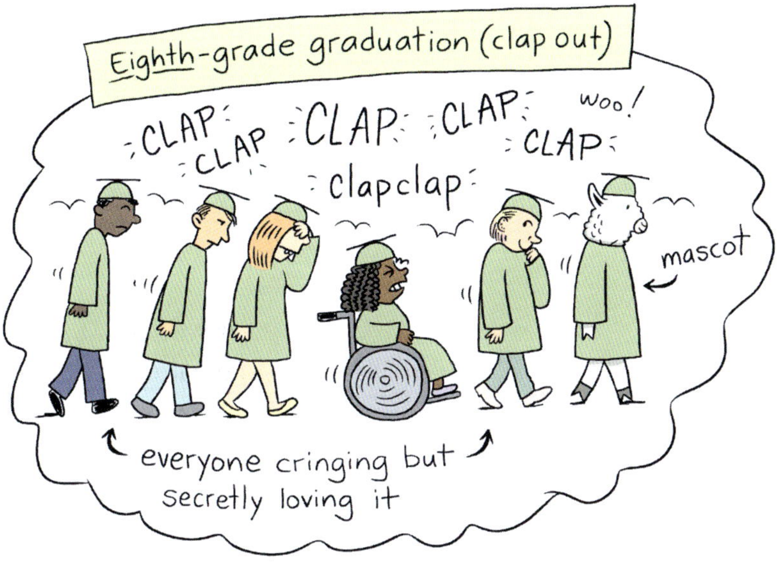
Eighth-grade graduation (clap out)
CLAP
CLAP
CLAP
CLAP
woo!
CLAP
clapclap
mascot
everyone cringing but secretly loving it

In the meantime, I'm sitting in my room, FaceTiming Bri and Sarah. We're looking at a flyer that was passed out at the end of the school day.

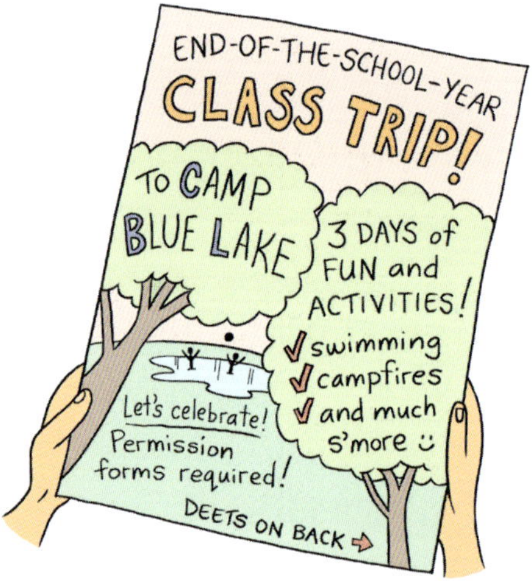
END-OF-THE-SCHOOL-YEAR
CLASS TRIP!
TO CAMP BLUE LAKE
3 DAYS of FUN and ACTIVITIES!
swimming
campfires
and much s'more
Let's celebrate!
Permission forms required!
DEETS ON BACK

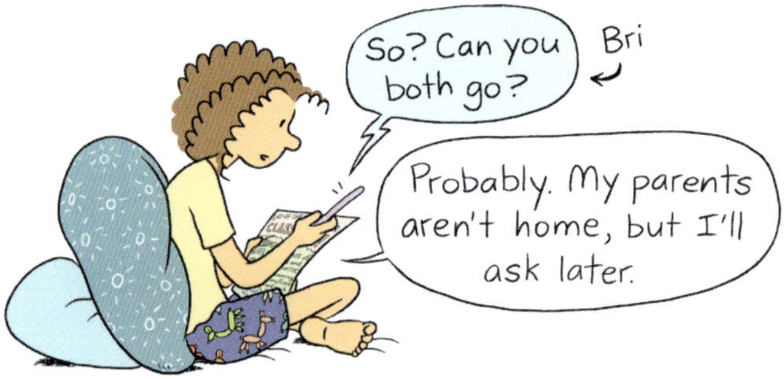
So? Can you both go?
Bri
Probably. My parents aren't home, but I'll ask later.

My parents are at work. My mom is a part-time receptionist and part-time cardio instructor at a local fitness club. She puts the rest of our family to shame.

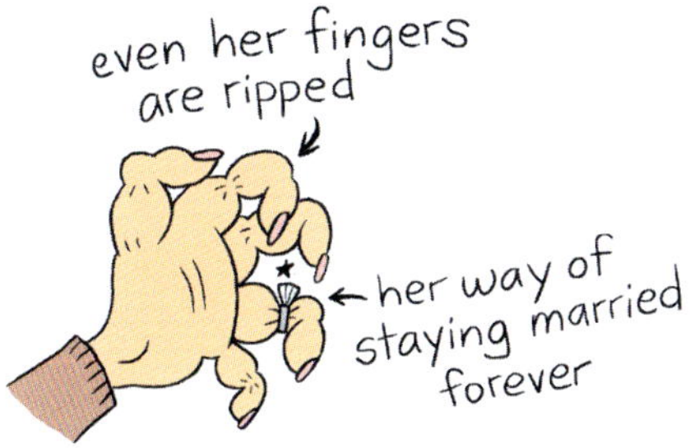
even her fingers are ripped
her way of staying married forever

My dad is an IT manager, and I won't bother to explain what he does because I have absolutely no idea.

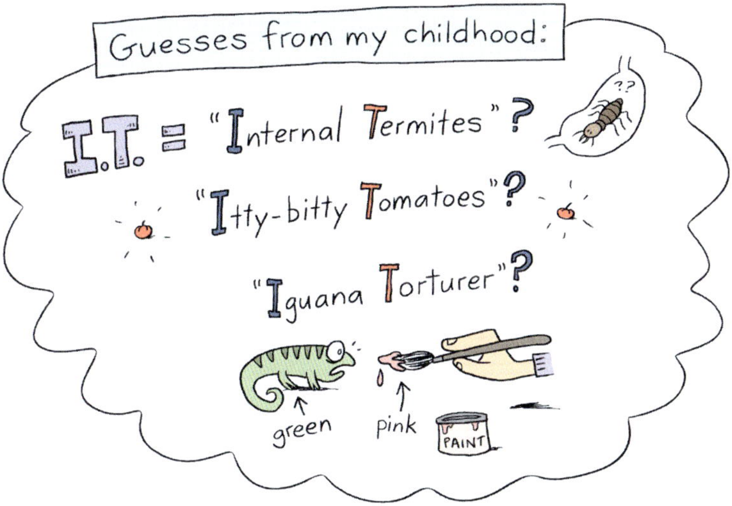
Guesses from my childhood:
I.T. = "Internal Termites"?
??
"Itty-bitty Tomatoes"?
"Iguana Torturer"?
green
pink
PAINT

Anyway . . .

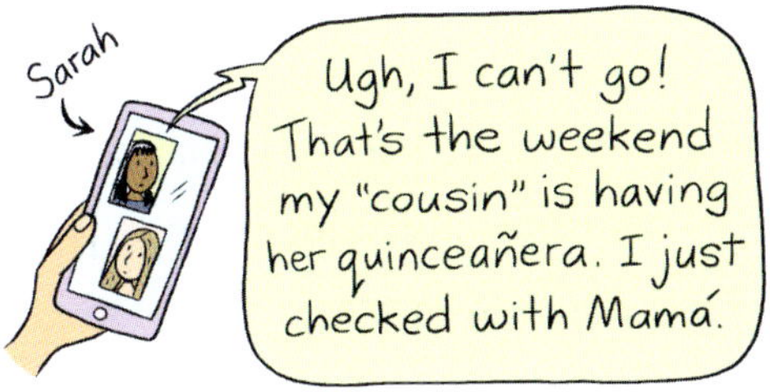
Sarah
Ugh, I can't go! That's the weekend my "cousin" is having her quinceañera. I just checked with Mamá.

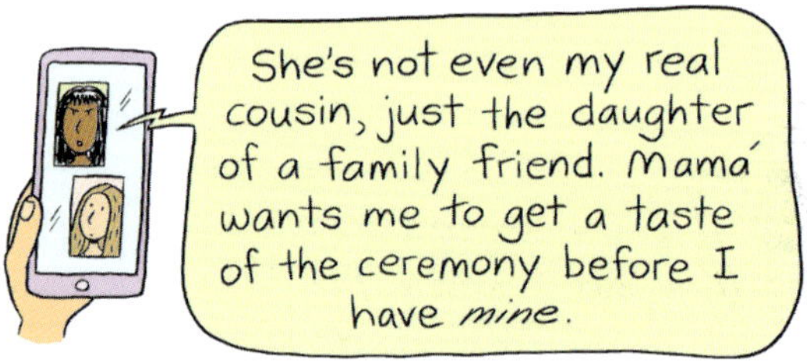
She's not even my real cousin, just the daughter of a family friend. Mamá wants me to get a taste of the ceremony before I have *mine*.

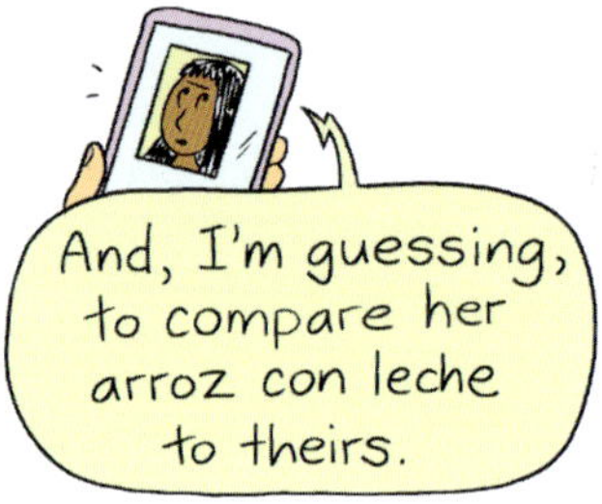
And, I'm guessing, to compare her arroz con leche to theirs.

Sarah's mom is an amazing pastry chef. Bri and I use any excuse to go to her house.

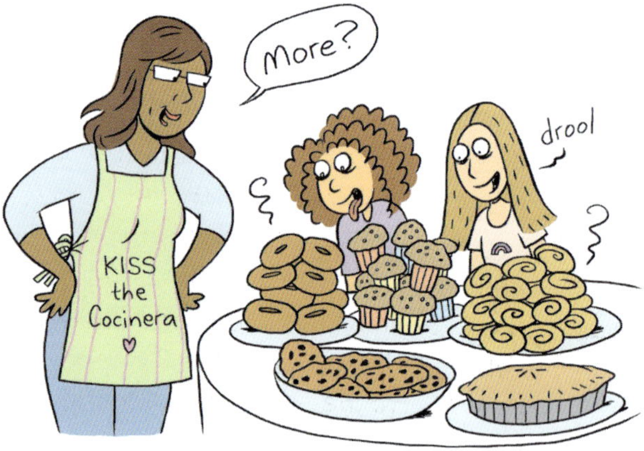
More?
drool
KISS the Cocinera

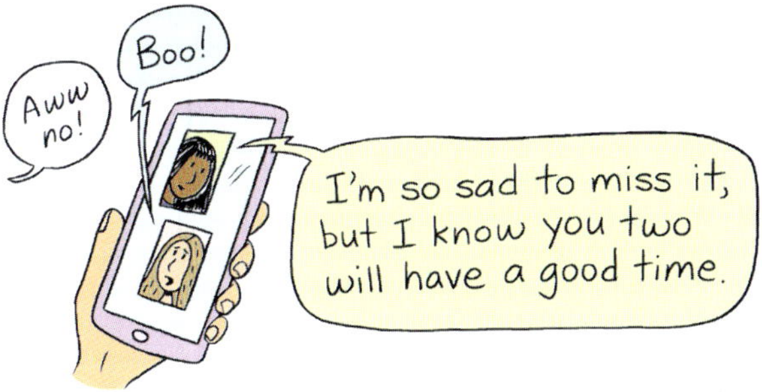
Aww no!
Boo!
I'm so sad to miss it, but I know you two will have a good time.

That's Sarah: total optimist. Unlike Bri and me.

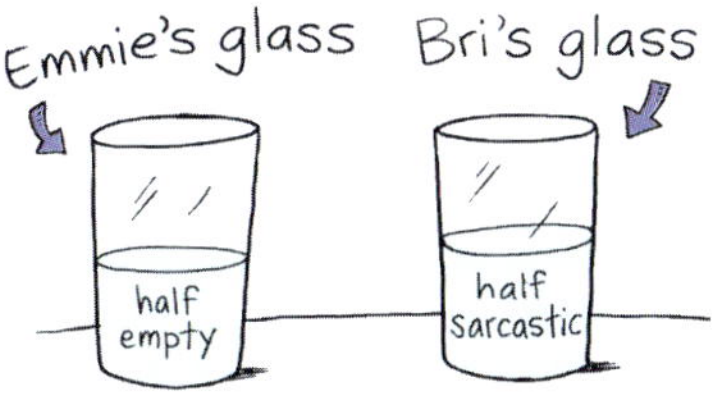
Emmie's glass
Bri's glass
half empty
half sarcastic

Sarah gets off the phone to do chores, so it's just Bri and me.

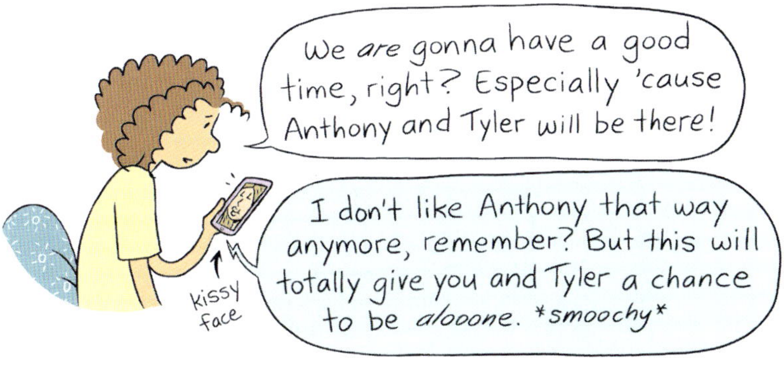
We *are* gonna have a good time, right? Especially 'cause Anthony and Tyler will be there!
I don't like Anthony that way anymore, remember? But this will totally give you and Tyler a chance to be *alooone*. *smoochy*
kissy face

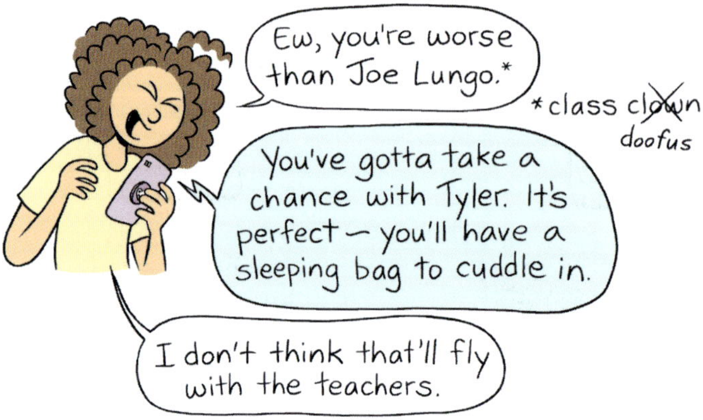
Ew, you're worse than Joe Lungo.*
*class clown doofus
You've gotta take a chance with Tyler. It's perfect—you'll have a sleeping bag to cuddle in.
I don't think that'll fly with the teachers.

Soon, Bri has to do homework (and I have to eat something), so we end the call.

I know Bri was joking around, but she's right—this will be my big chance to get close to Tyler. I mean, close-close. I feel like there's something there already. Sometimes he throws me these weird looks . . . especially in art class. Like, admiring looks. Not because I'm pretty. I'm okay, but I'm not in Celia Thomas's league or anything.

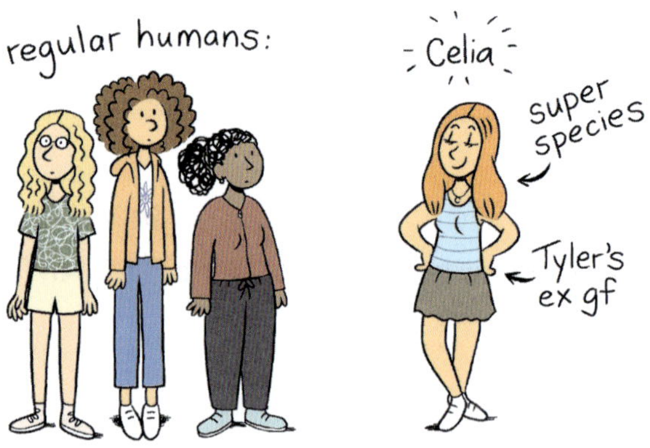
regular humans:
Celia
super species
Tyler's ex gf

It's mostly 'cause I think we have this kind of . . . connection. We both like and hate a lot of the same stuff.

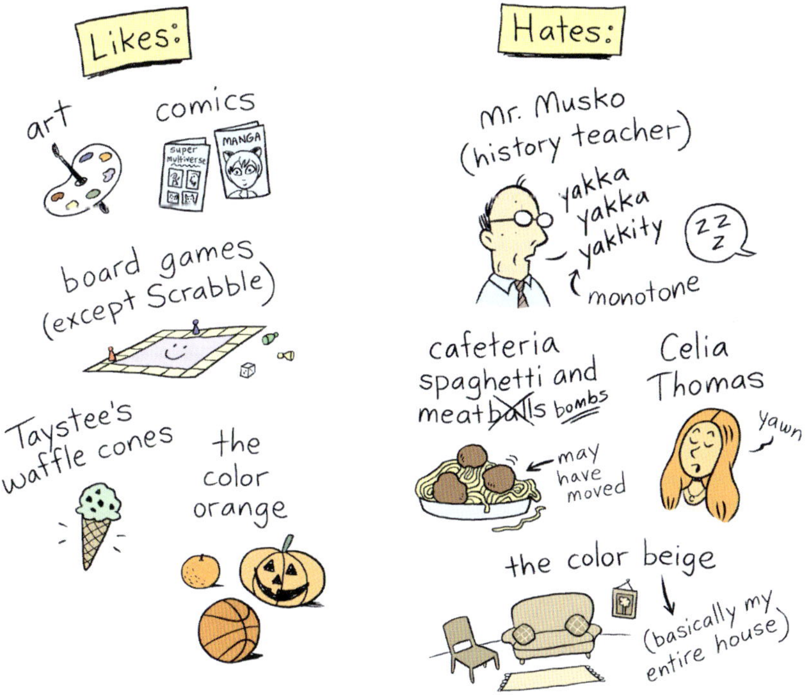
Likes:
art
comics
Super Multiverse
MANGA
board games
(except Scrabble)
Taystee's
waffle cones
the
color
orange
Hates:
Mr. Musko
(history teacher)
yakka
yakka
yakkity
z z
z
monotone
cafeteria
spaghetti and
meatballs bombs
may
have
moved
Celia
Thomas
yawn
the color beige
(basically my
entire house)

And we can talk. Like, a lot. I've never been able to talk to boys. Especially popular boys. But Tyler's always been super nice, which helps.

Anyway, that's how I'm looking at this class trip: as an opportunity to have fun with Bri and get closer to Tyler. I'll worry about all the campy stuff later.

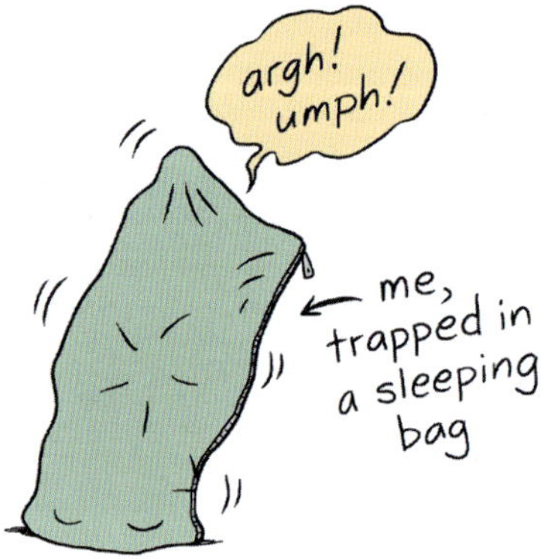
argh! umph!
me, trapped in a sleeping bag

Much later.

Joe

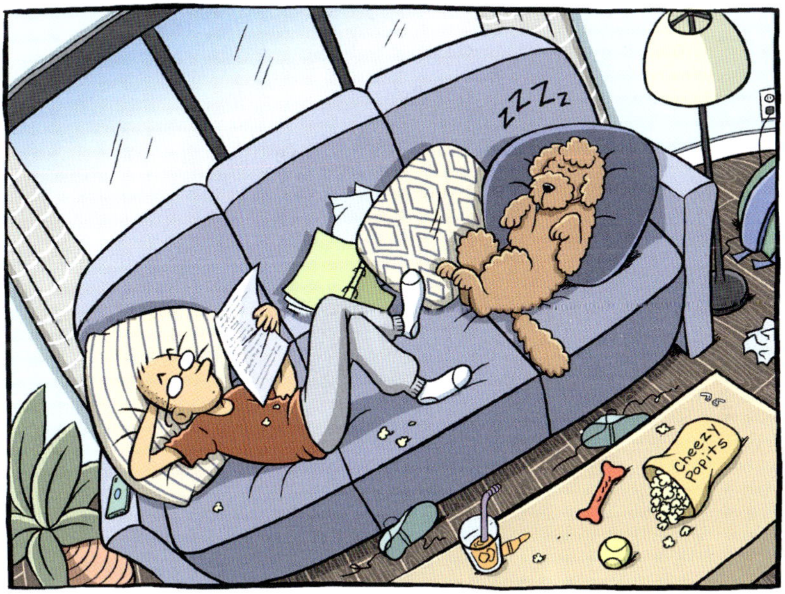
zZZz
Cheezy Popits

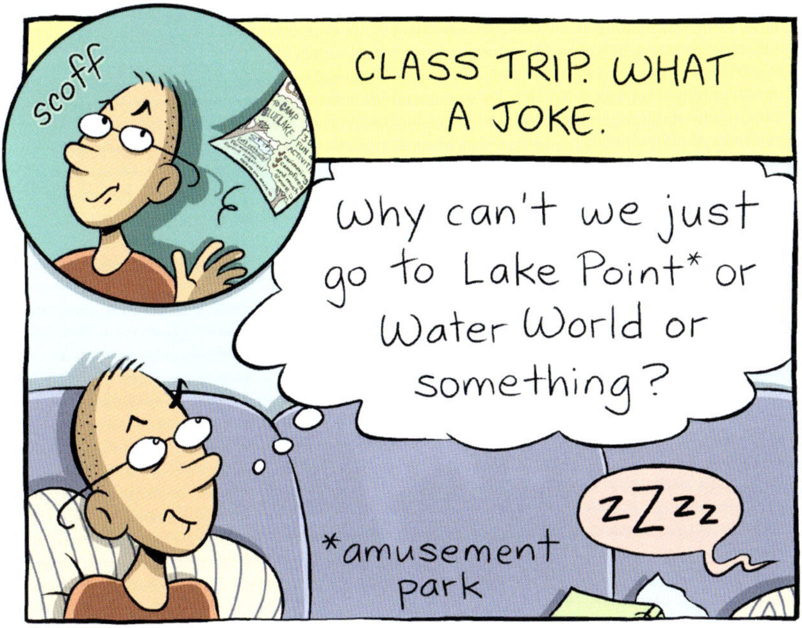
scoff
CLASS TRIP. WHAT A JOKE.
Why can't we just go to Lake Point* or Water World or something?
*amusement park
zZzz

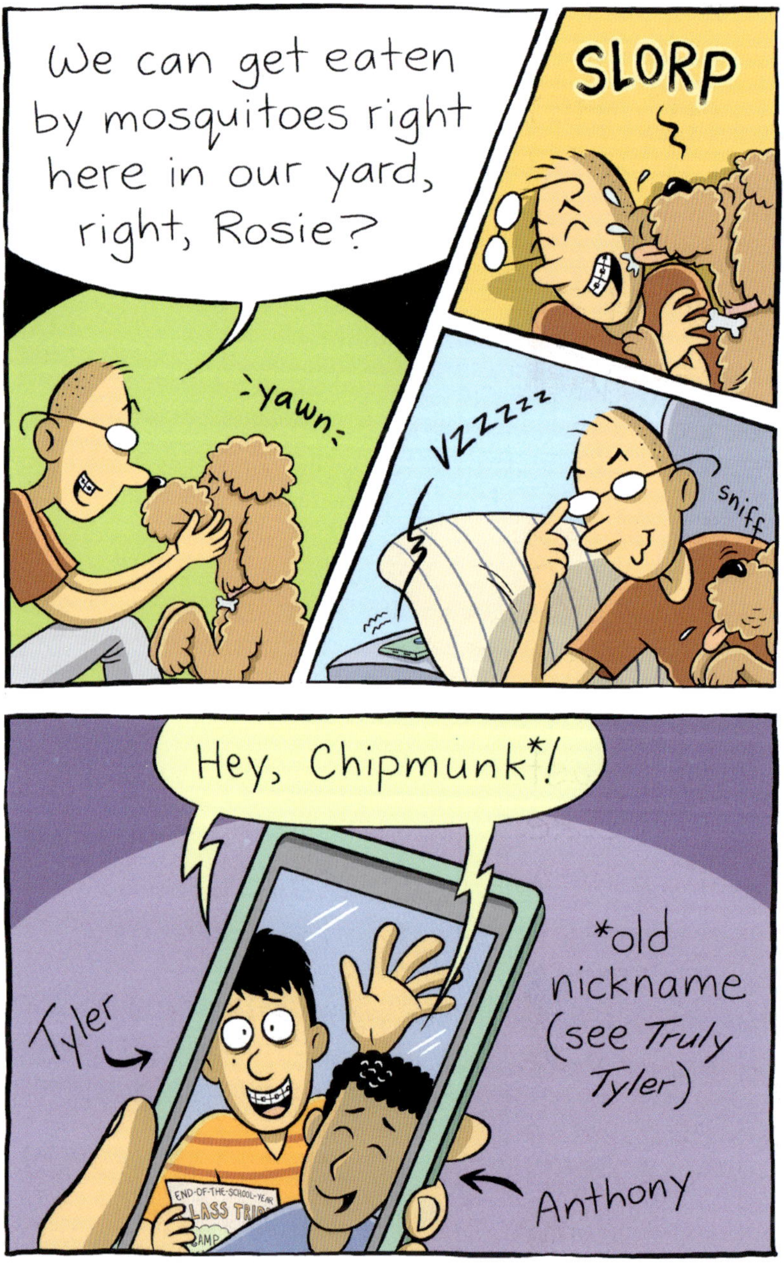
We can get eaten by mosquitoes right here in our yard, right, Rosie?
yawn
SLORP
VZZZZZ
sniff
Hey, Chipmunk*!
Tyler
Anthony
END-OF-THE-SCHOOL-YEAR CLASS TRIP
*old nickname (see *Truly Tyler*)

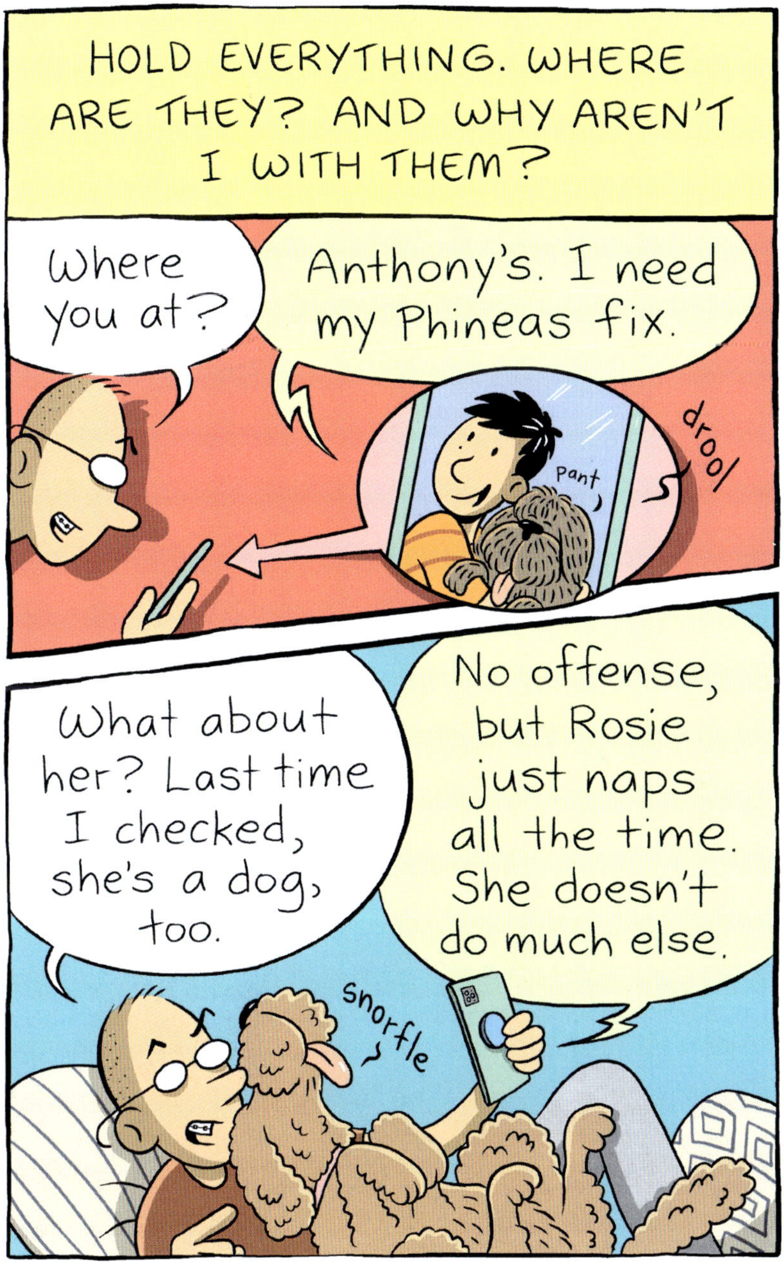
HOLD EVERYTHING. WHERE ARE THEY? AND WHY AREN'T I WITH THEM?
Where you at?
Anthony's. I need my Phineas fix.
pant
drool
What about her? Last time I checked, she's a dog, too.
No offense, but Rosie just naps all the time. She doesn't do much else.
snorfle

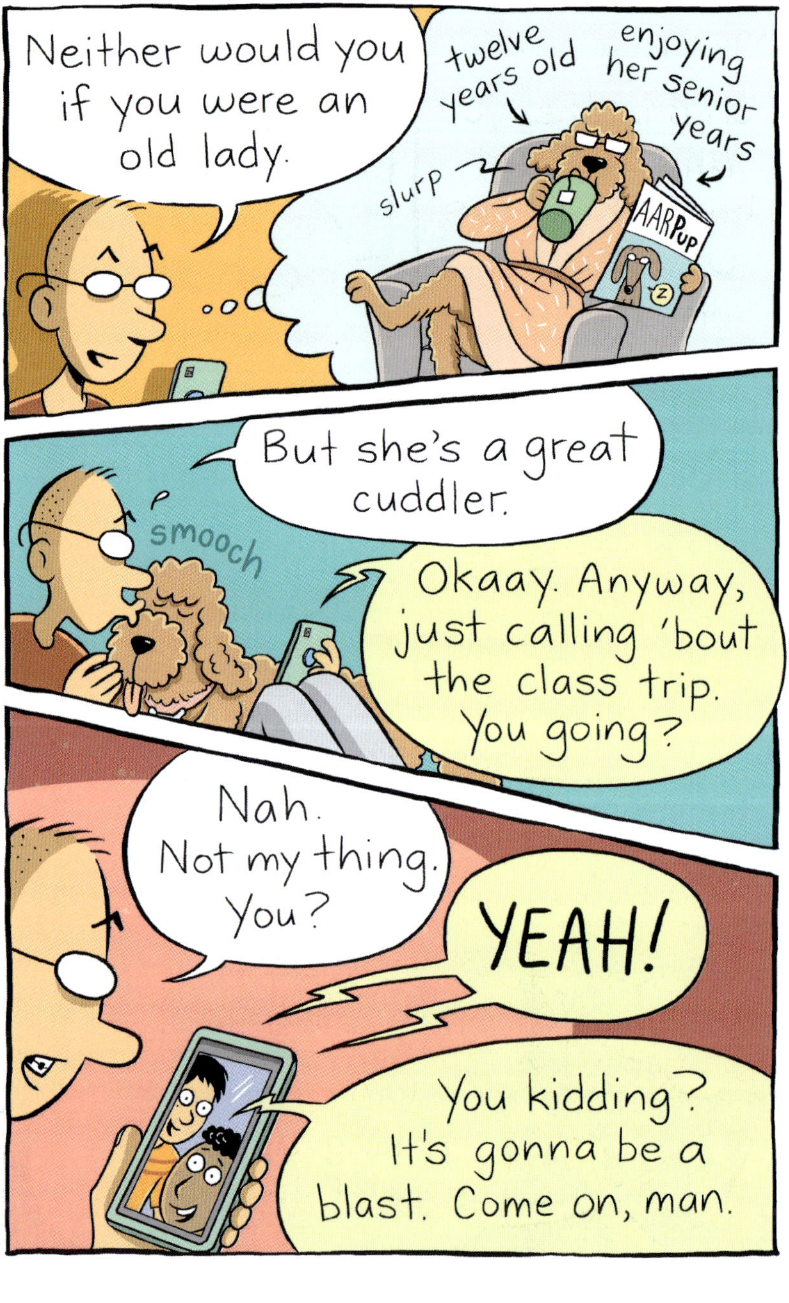
Neither would you if you were an old lady.
twelve years old
enjoying her senior years
slurp
AARPUP
z
But she's a great cuddler.
smooch
Okaay. Anyway, just calling 'bout the class trip. You going?
Nah. Not my thing. You?
YEAH!
You kidding? It's gonna be a blast. Come on, man.

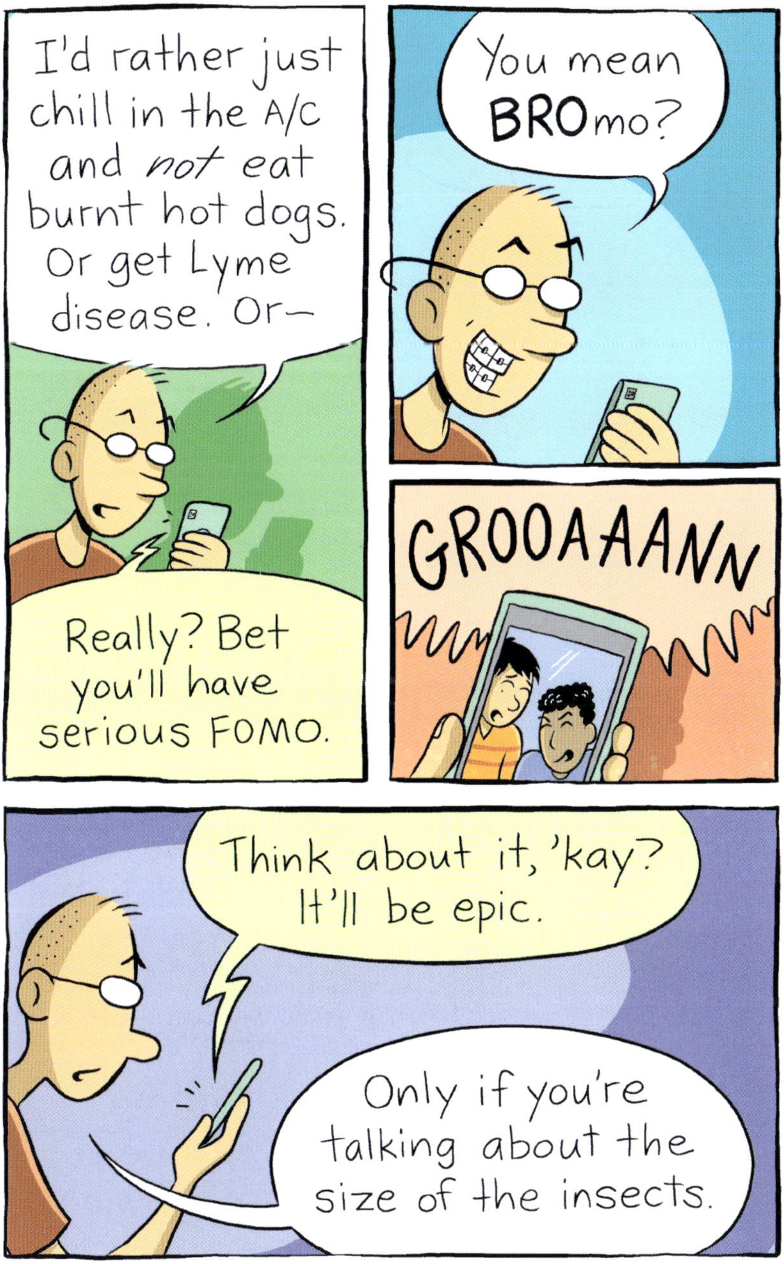
I'd rather just chill in the A/C and *not* eat burnt hot dogs. Or get Lyme disease. Or—
Really? Bet you'll have serious FOMO.
You mean BROmo?
GROOAAANN
Think about it, 'kay? It'll be epic.
Only if you're talking about the size of the insects.

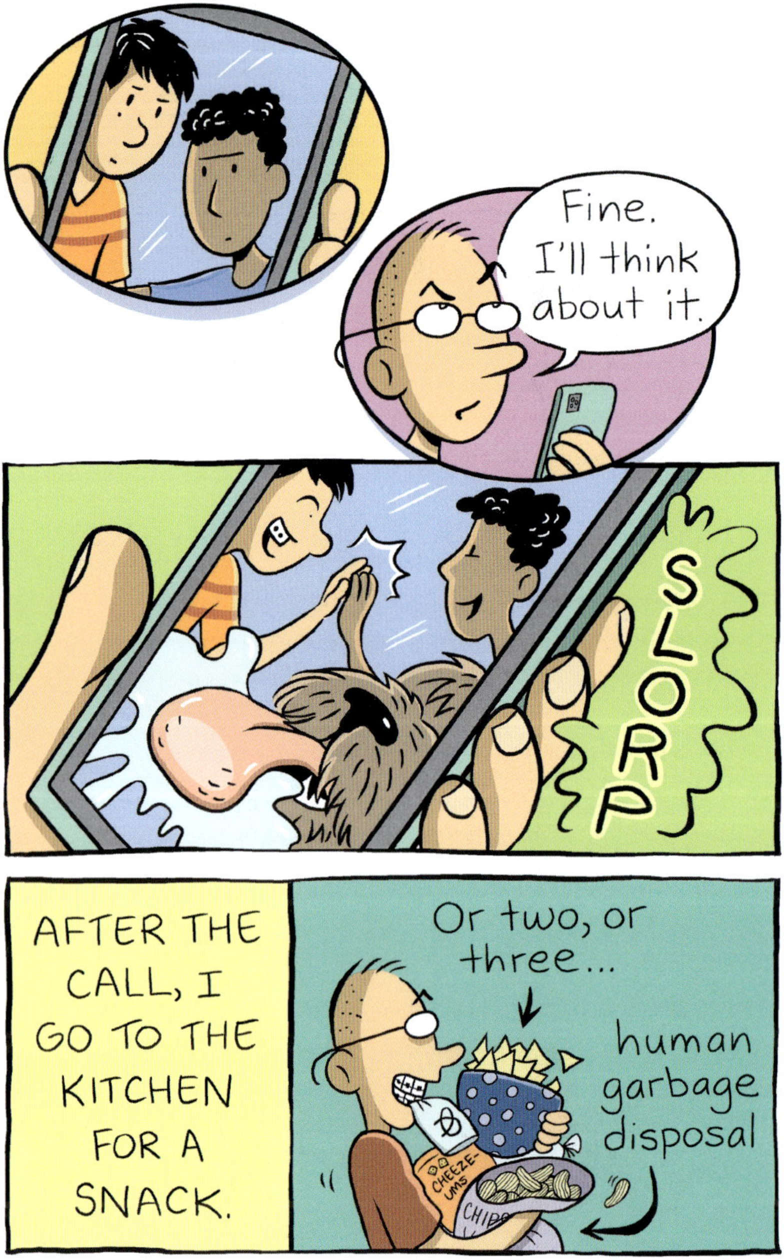
Fine. I'll think about it.
SLORP
AFTER THE CALL, I GO TO THE KITCHEN FOR A SNACK.
Or two, or three...
human garbage disposal
CHEEZE-UMS
CHIPS

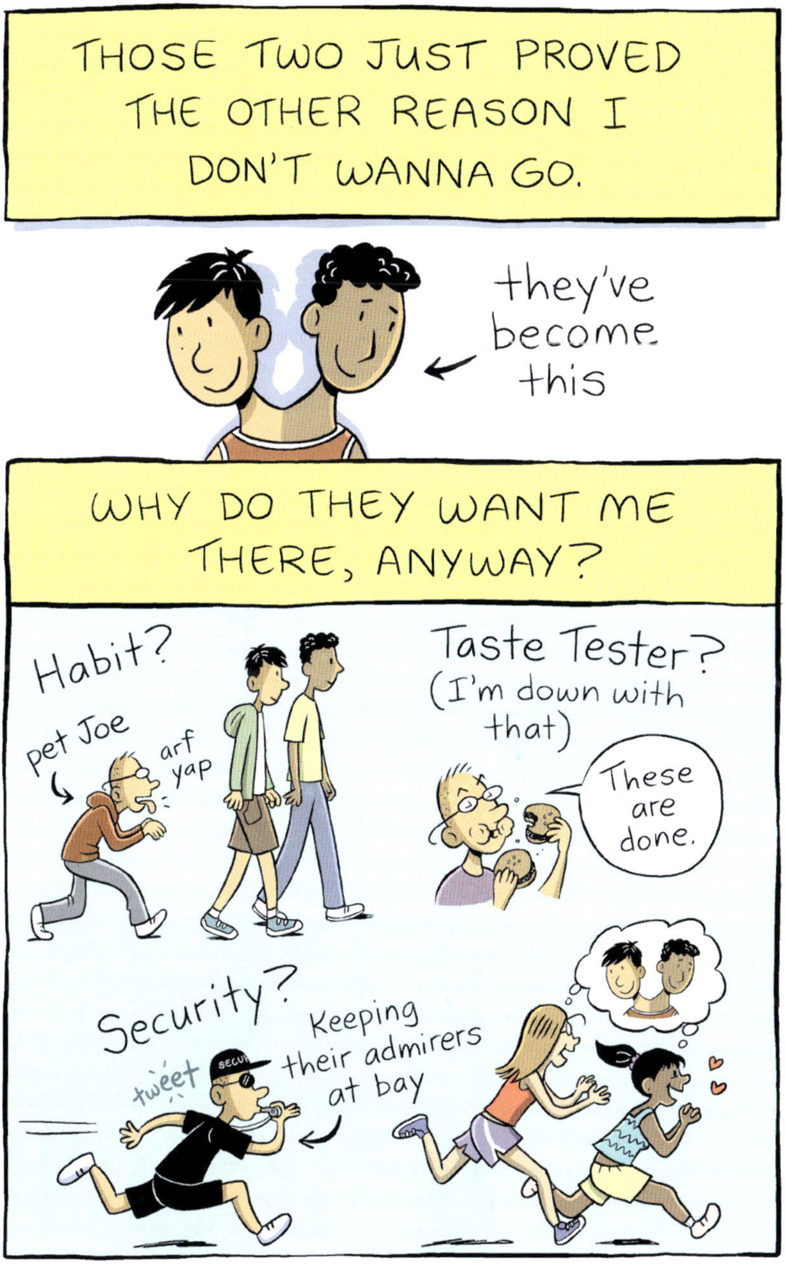

THOSE TWO JUST PROVED THE OTHER REASON I DON'T WANNA GO.
they've become this
WHY DO THEY WANT ME THERE, ANYWAY?
Habit?
pet Joe
arf yap
Taste Tester? (I'm down with that)
These are done.
Security?
Keeping their admirers at bay
tweet

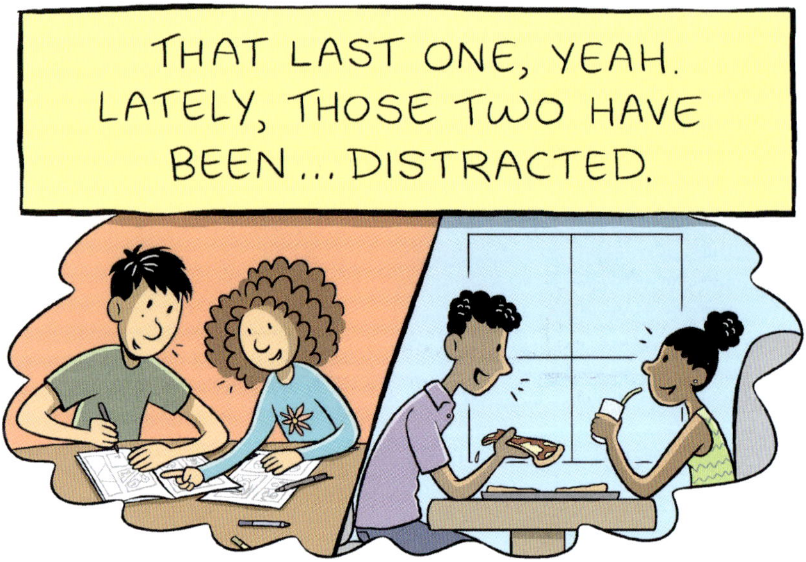
THAT LAST ONE, YEAH. LATELY, THOSE TWO HAVE BEEN... DISTRACTED.

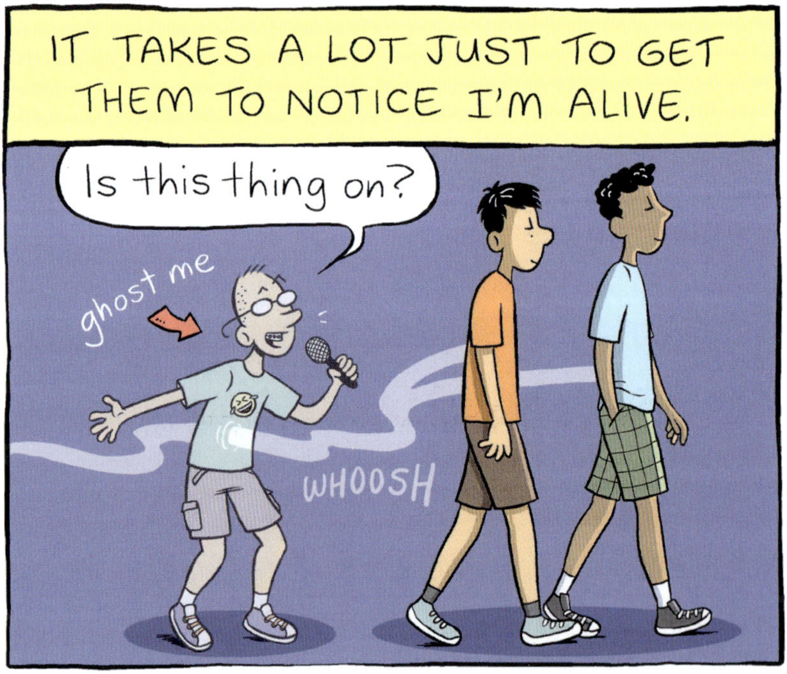
IT TAKES A LOT JUST TO GET THEM TO NOTICE I'M ALIVE.
Is this thing on?
ghost me
WHOOSH

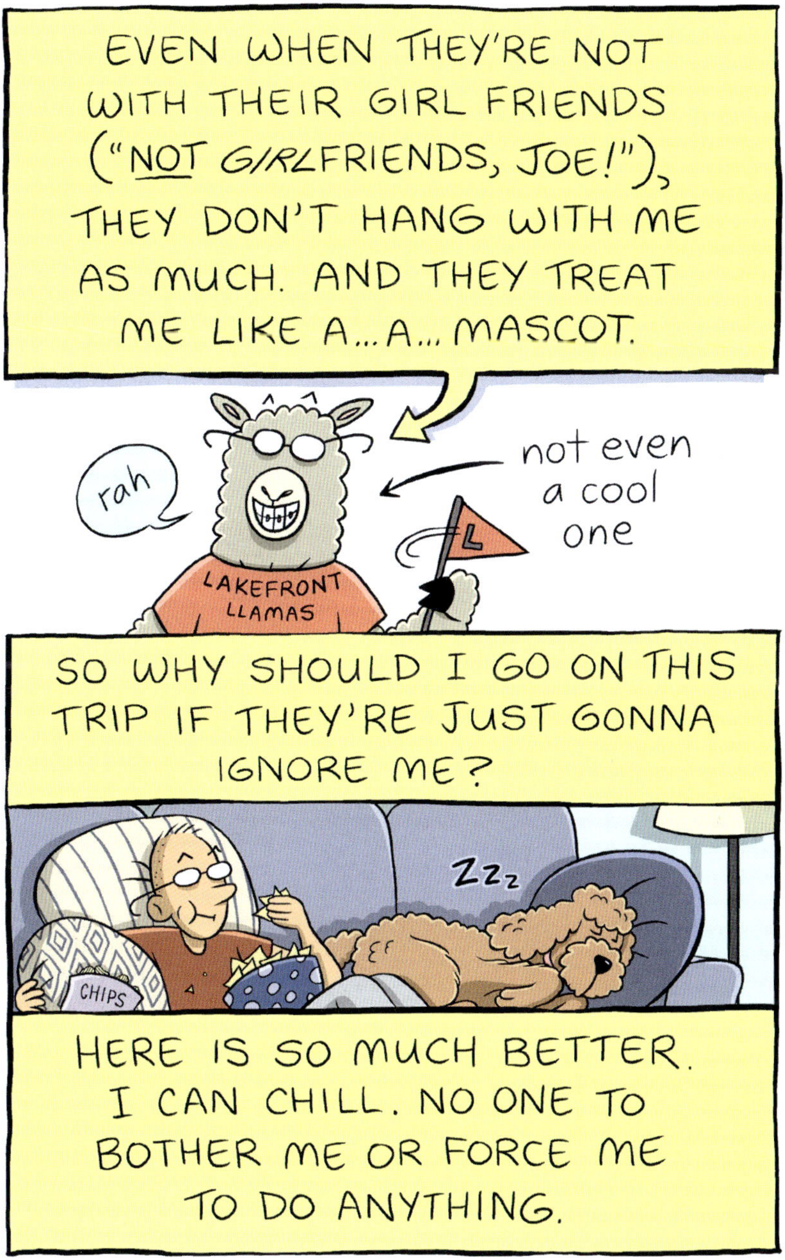
EVEN WHEN THEY'RE NOT WITH THEIR GIRL FRIENDS ("NOT GIRLFRIENDS, JOE!"), THEY DON'T HANG WITH ME AS MUCH. AND THEY TREAT ME LIKE A... A... MASCOT.
rah
not even a cool one
LAKEFRONT LLAMAS
L
SO WHY SHOULD I GO ON THIS TRIP IF THEY'RE JUST GONNA IGNORE ME?
ZZz
CHIPS
HERE IS SO MUCH BETTER. I CAN CHILL. NO ONE TO BOTHER ME OR FORCE ME TO DO ANYTHING.

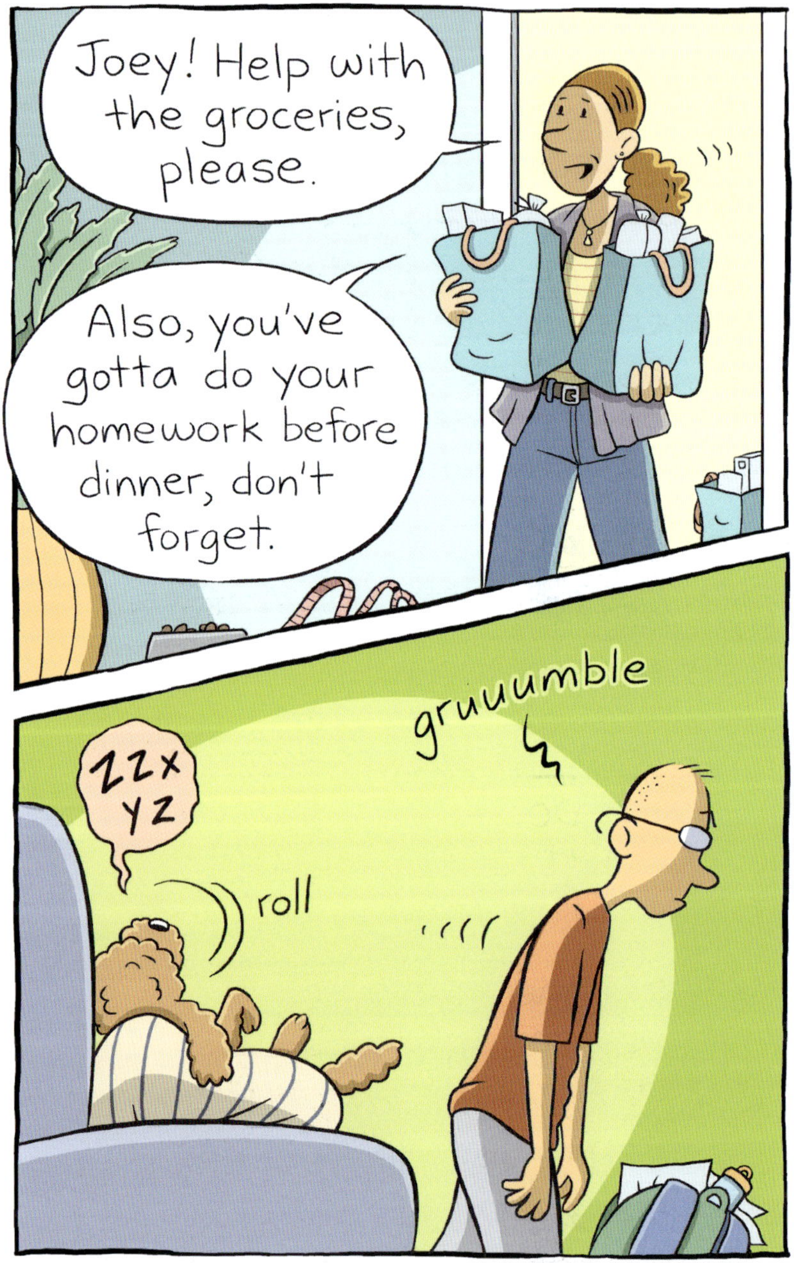
Joey! Help with the groceries, please.
Also, you've gotta do your homework before dinner, don't forget.
ZZX YZ
roll
gruuumble

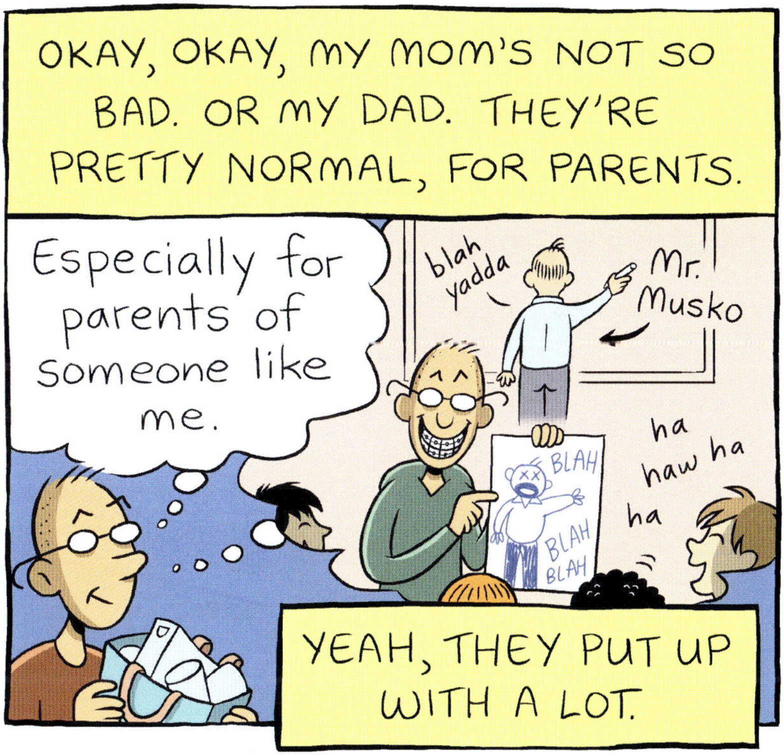
OKAY, OKAY, MY MOM'S NOT SO BAD. OR MY DAD. THEY'RE PRETTY NORMAL, FOR PARENTS.
Especially for parents of someone like me.
blah yadda
Mr. Musko
BLAH BLAH BLAH
ha haw ha ha
YEAH, THEY PUT UP WITH A LOT.

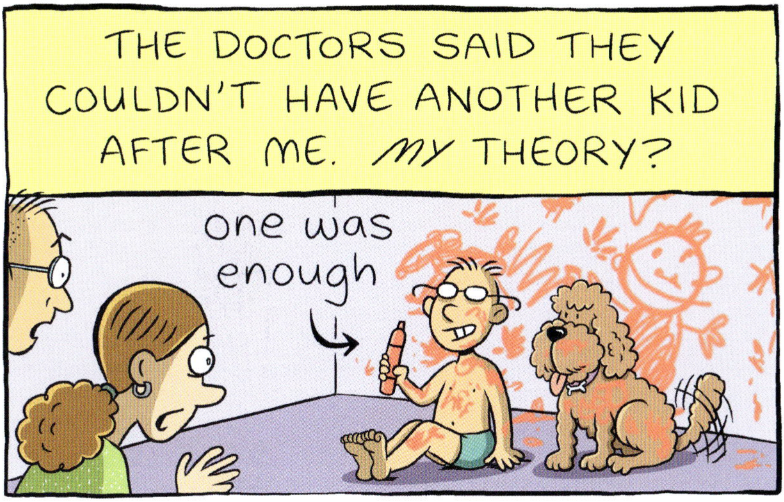
THE DOCTORS SAID THEY COULDN'T HAVE ANOTHER KID AFTER ME. *MY* THEORY?
one was enough

I'VE GOTTA ADMIT I DO LIKE ATTENTION. IT GETS ME:

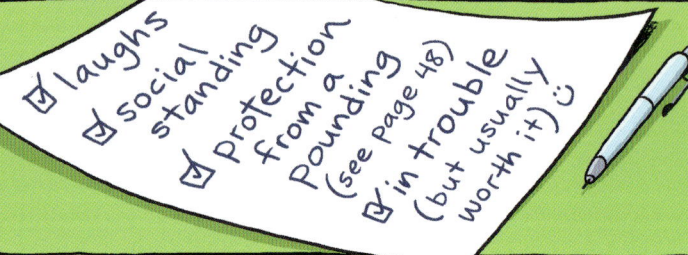

- ☑ laughs
- ☑ social standing
- ☑ protection from a pounding (see page 48)
- ☑ in trouble (but usually worth it) ☺

BUT WITH ANTHONY AND TY THESE DAYS... I CAN ONLY TRY SO HARD.

SO YEAH... I'M GONNA STAY HOME.

EVEN IF IT (LITERALLY) KILLS ME.

EMMIE

It's been an exciting weekend. Dad signed my permission form for the class trip (yay!). And my mom bought me a cute dress for Bri's bat mitzvah next month (yay x 2!). But the best part of the weekend?

big sis
home from college
seven piercings (that I'm aware of)

I wish my brother, Brandon, was home, too, but he has a few more weeks of school and is staying at his college apartment until graduation next month. In fact, he graduates the week after the bat mitzvah, so I get to wear the dress twice.

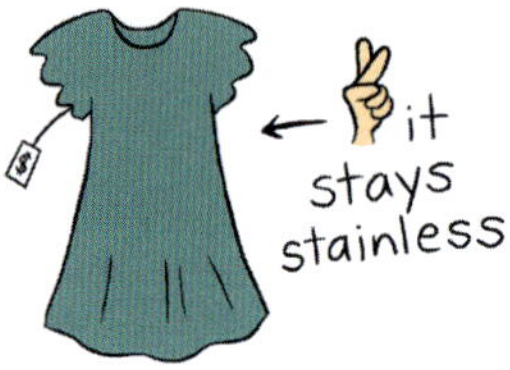
it stays stainless

Trina is—I mean **was**—a sophomore in college. Technically, she's a junior now that she's done with classes. It's hard to keep up. My sibs are sooo much older than me* and I can barely remember what it was like when they were still living here.

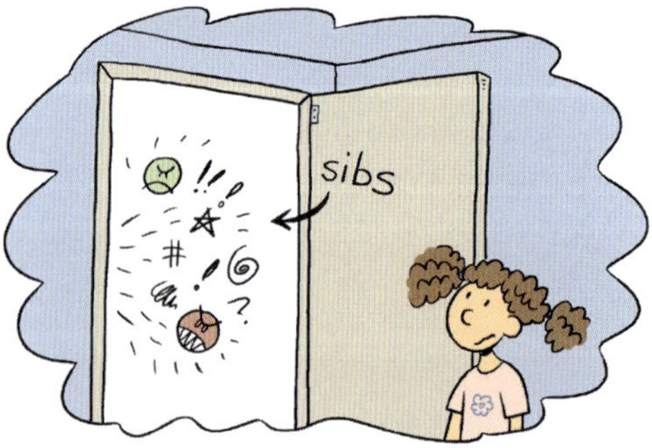
sibs

I do remember it was louder.

After Trina unpacked and settled in, she and I gabbed over snacks. I told her about the class trip.

*I was a "happy accident," which I try not to think about.

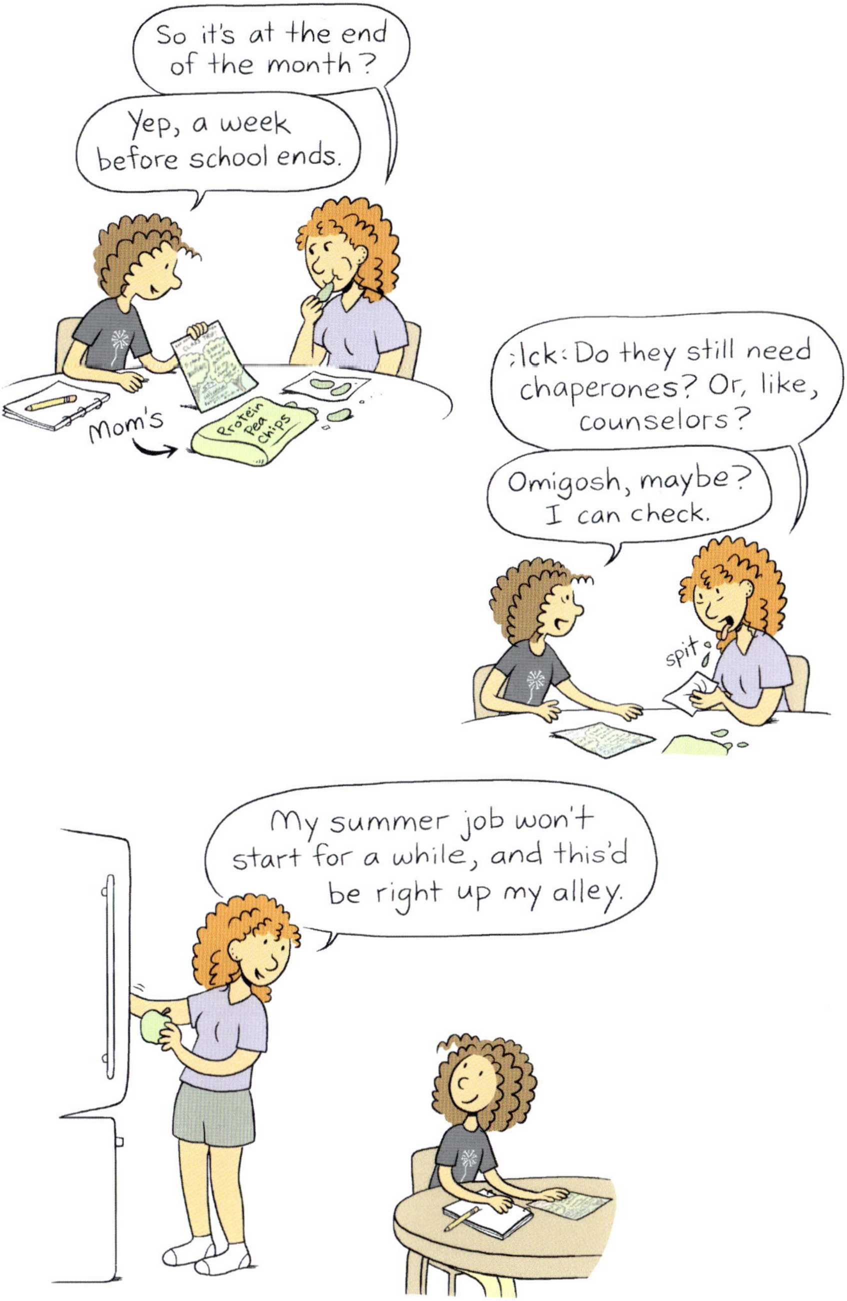
So it's at the end of the month?
Yep, a week before school ends.
Protein Pea Chips
Mom's
:lck: Do they still need chaperones? Or, like, counselors?
Omigosh, maybe? I can check.
spit
My summer job won't start for a while, and this'd be right up my alley.

Up her alley is right. Trina will be a lifeguard at Lakefront Day Camp this summer. She's done it on and off since she was sixteen. She was also a camp counselor there twice. Trina loves kids and wants to teach someday.

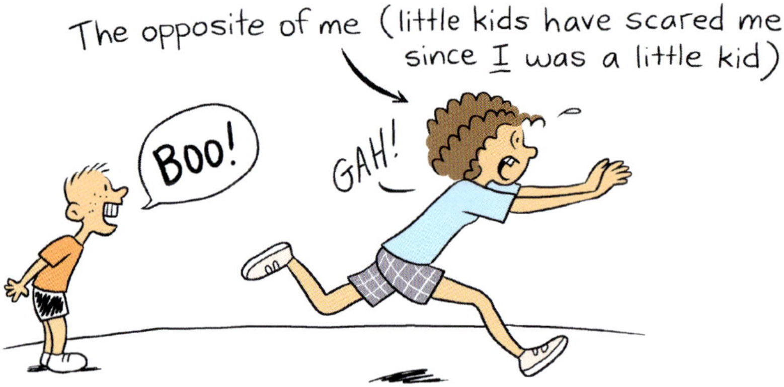
The opposite of me (little kids have scared me since I was a little kid)
BOO!
GAH!

Today at school, I asked my health teacher, Mr. Bauman, if they're still looking for chaperones. He's in charge of the trip. He told me they were "indeed" looking for cabin counselors. He said they usually recruit kids from Lakefront High School, but he thought Trina sounded perfect.

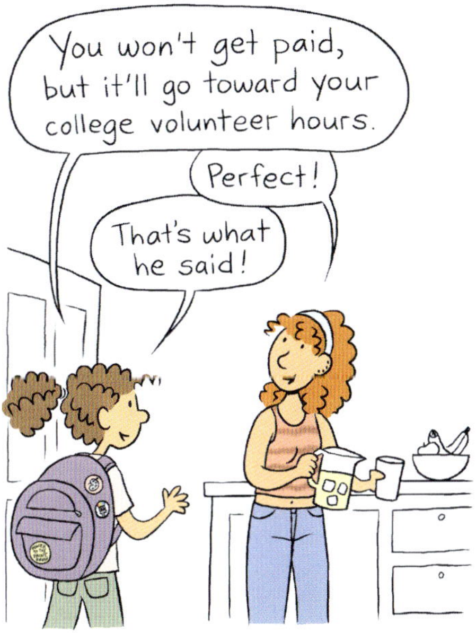
You won't get paid, but it'll go toward your college volunteer hours.
That's what he said!
Perfect!

She fills out the online application, has a quick interview, and within the week, gets accepted!

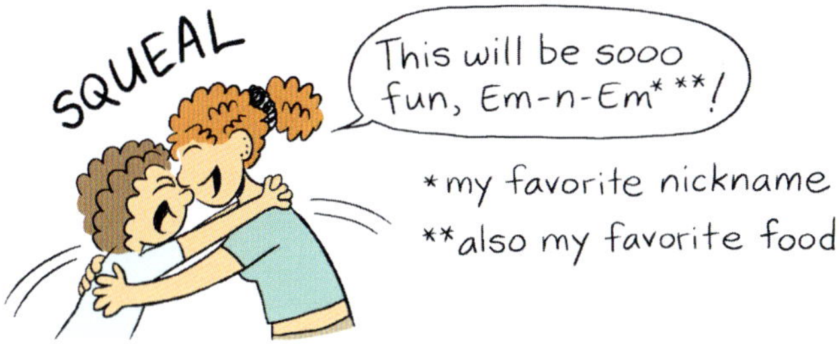
SQUEAL
This will be sooo fun, Em-n-Em* **!
*my favorite nickname
**also my favorite food

Now I **really** can't wait! I'm SO looking forward to spending time with Trina, packing together, and showing off my cool big sis to my (disbelieving) classmates.

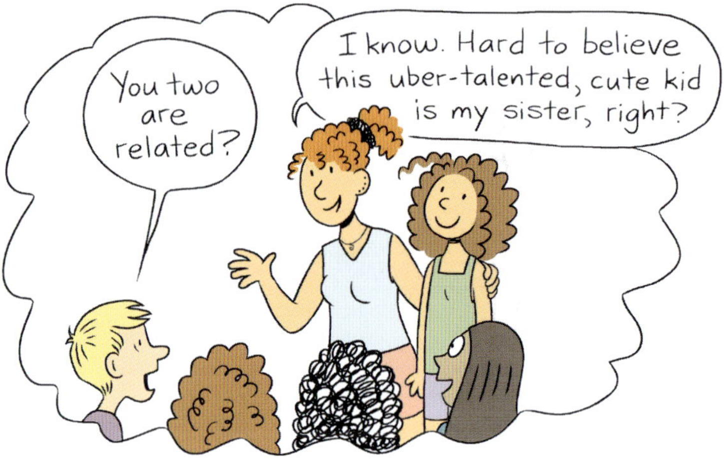
You two are related?
I know. Hard to believe this uber-talented, cute kid is my sister, right?

Another cool thing: Trina's good at water sports and taught me how to paddleboard last summer. She's planning to ask permission to teach a mini lesson at the campground lake. I'm actually pretty good (shocking, right?). This could be the one and only sport where I'd (kinda) shine.

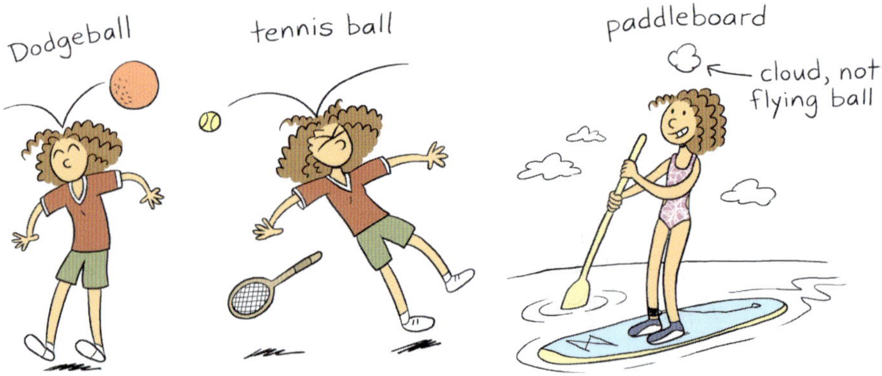
Dodgeball
tennis ball
paddleboard
cloud, not flying ball

I count down the days until the trip. So does Bri.

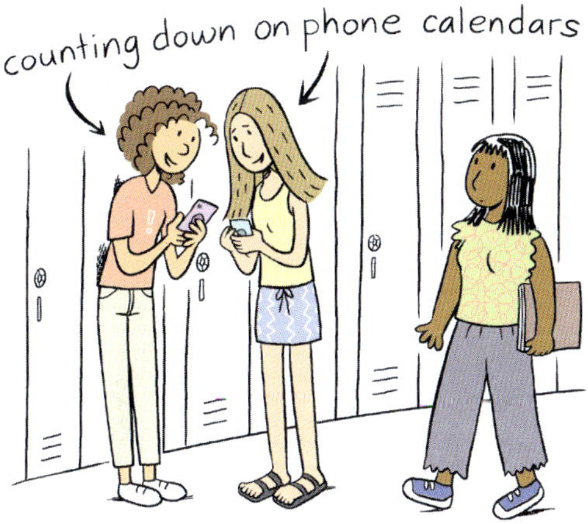
counting down on phone calendars

Sarah tries to be excited for us.

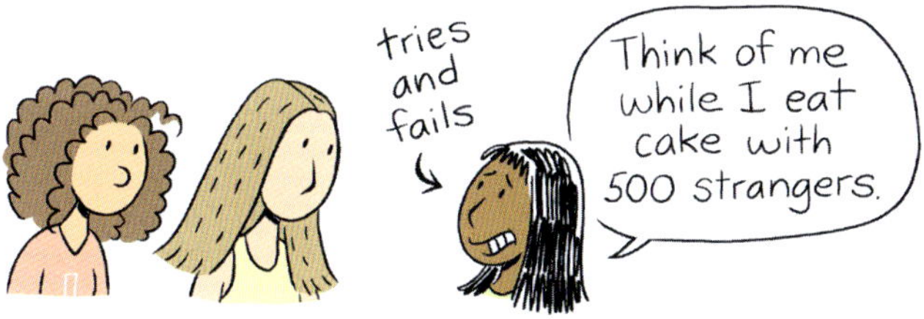
tries and fails
Think of me while I eat cake with 500 strangers.

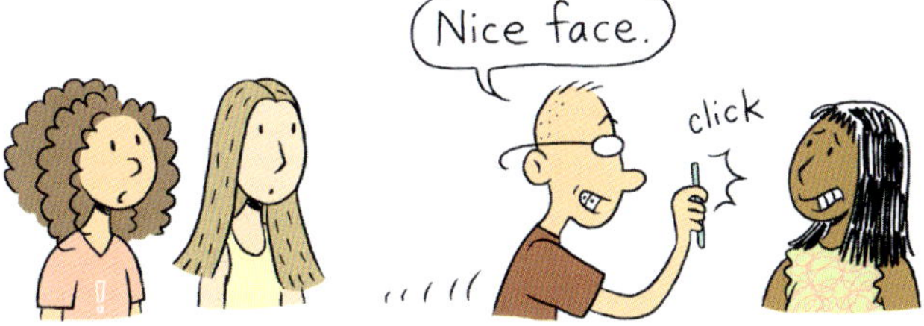
Nice face.
click

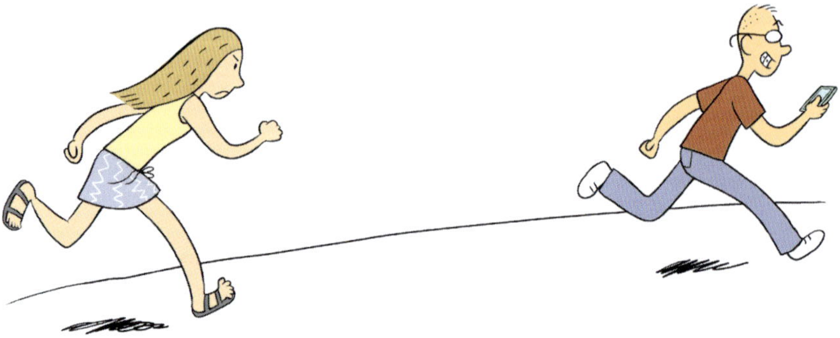

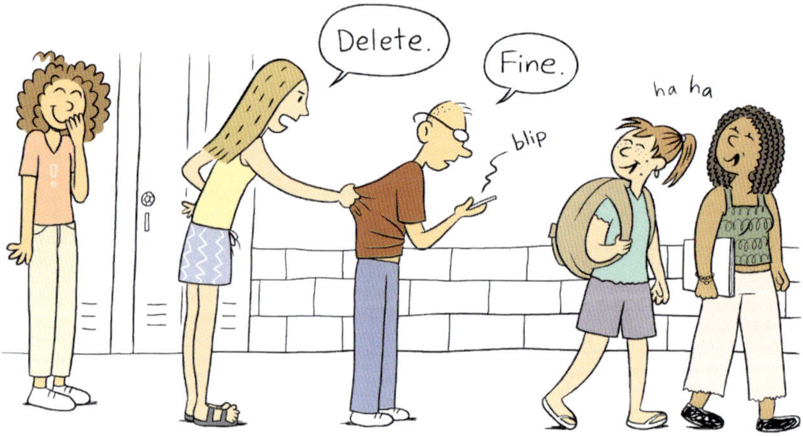
Delete.
Fine.
blip
ha ha

The next three weeks go by super slowly.

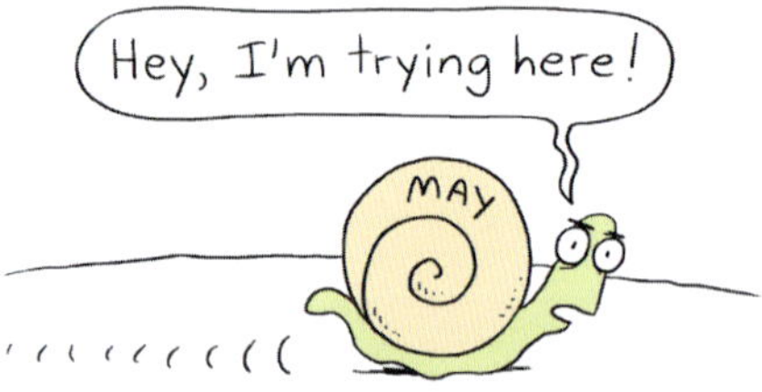
Hey, I'm trying here!
MAY

In the meantime, I'm constantly scanning the packing list and obsessively checking the weather. I pack, repack, and repack again. **And** again.

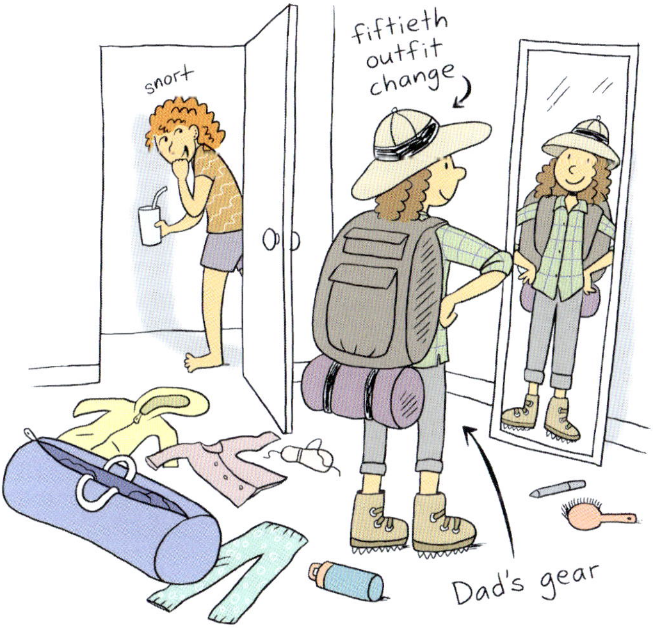
snort
fiftieth outfit change
Dad's gear

Bri and I are pumped because everyone is partnering up (yeah, even seventh graders have to use the buddy system). We'll get to sit on the bus together, do activities together, eat s'mores together, and bunk together. Bri and I would do it anyway, but this kinda makes our bestie time even **more** official. **And** . . .

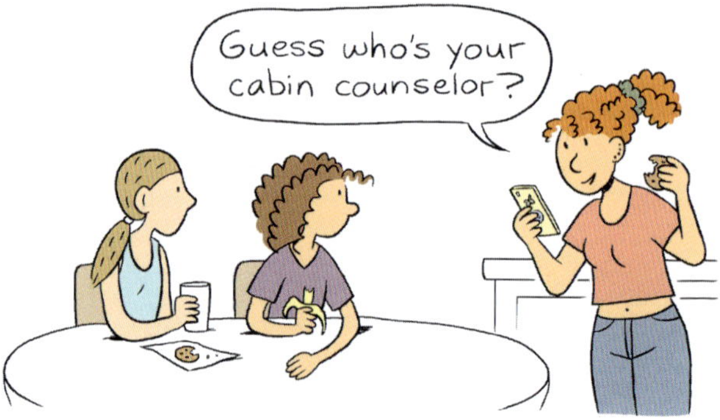
Guess who's your cabin counselor?

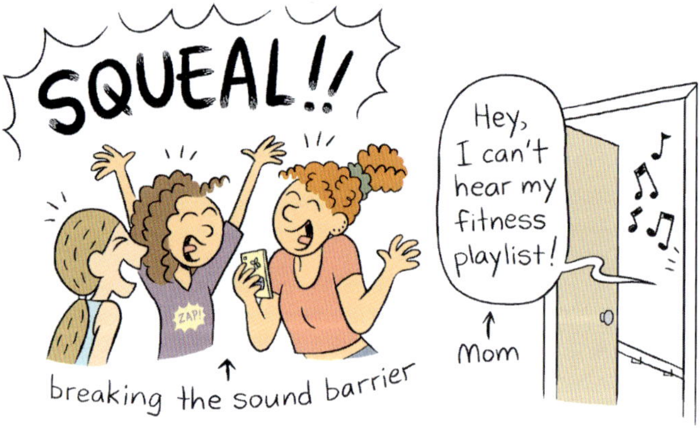
SQUEAL!!
ZAP!
breaking the sound barrier
Hey, I can't hear my fitness playlist!
Mom

The night before the trip, I'm all packed up and ready to go—for real this time. I'm daydreaming about Tyler (while drawing him). We've been chatting about the trip in art class. I can't wait to see him outside of his "natural environment" (aka school).

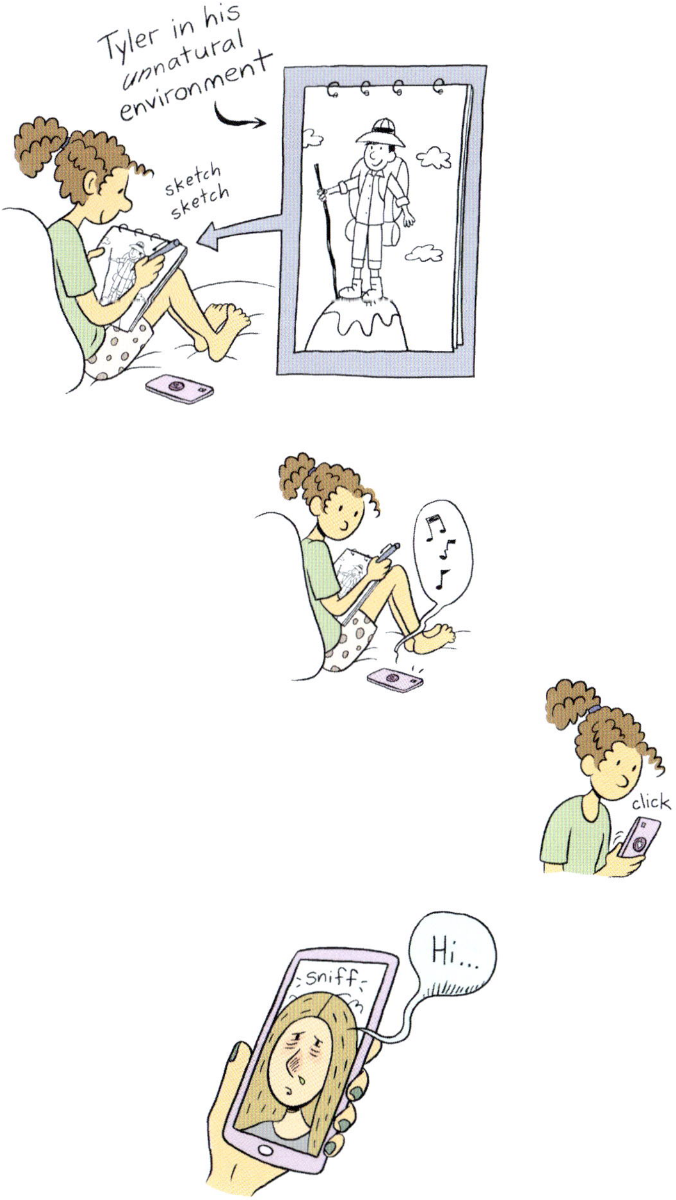
Tyler in his unnatural environment
sketch sketch
click
sniff
Hi...

Joe

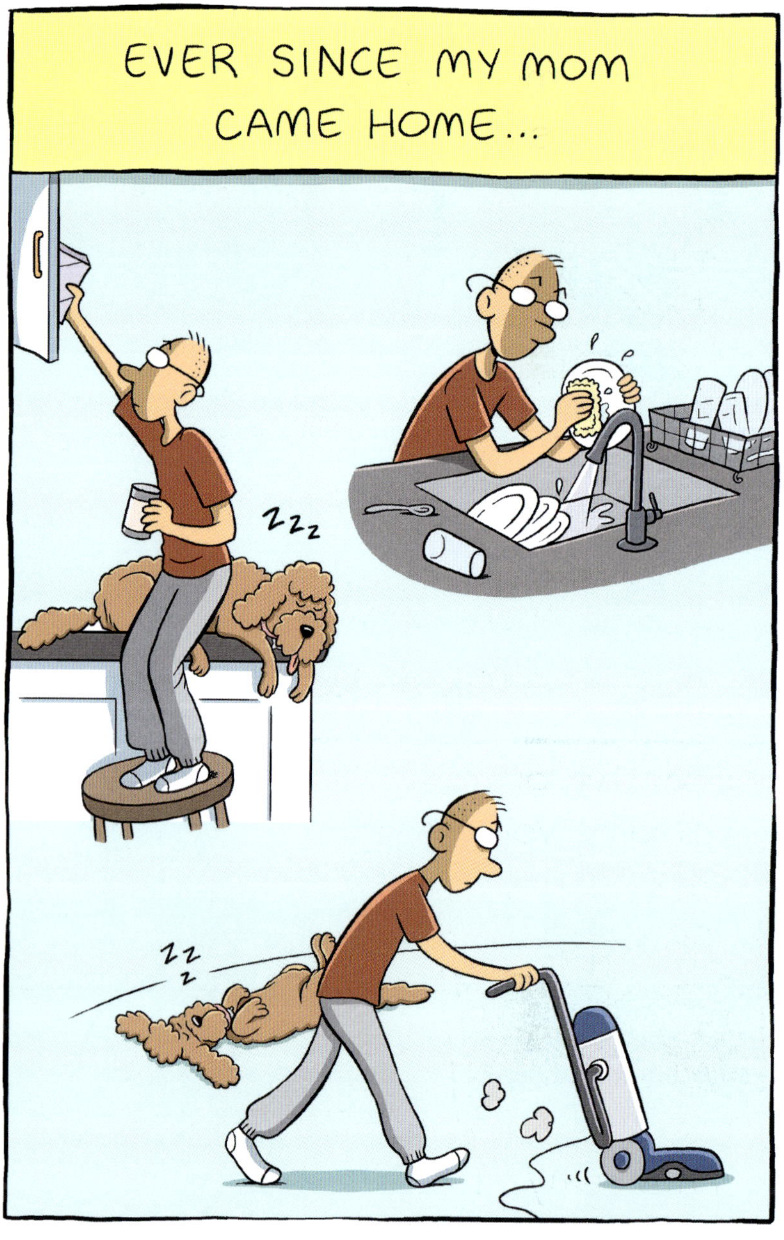
EVER SINCE MY MOM CAME HOME...
ZZZ
ZZZ

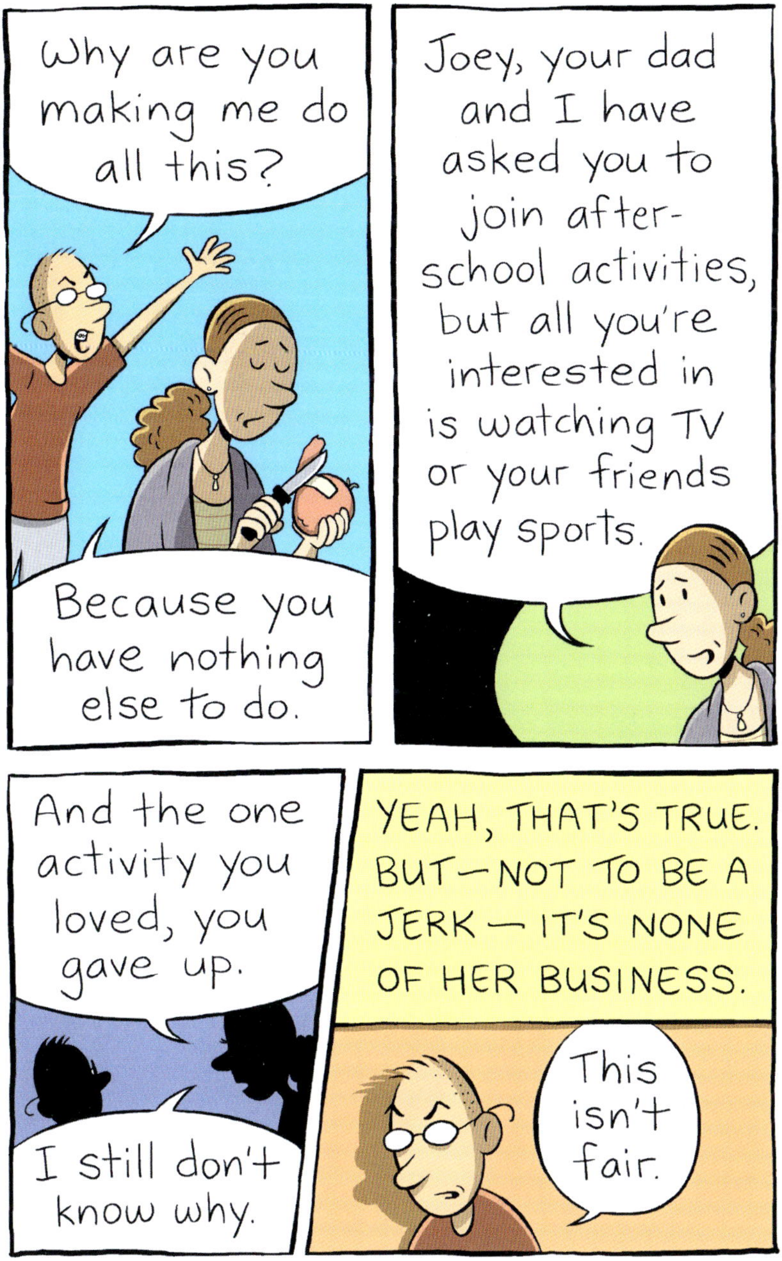
Why are you making me do all this?
Because you have nothing else to do.
Joey, your dad and I have asked you to join after-school activities, but all you're interested in is watching TV or your friends play sports.
And the one activity you loved, you gave up.
I still don't know why.
YEAH, THAT'S TRUE. BUT—NOT TO BE A JERK—IT'S NONE OF HER BUSINESS.
This isn't fair.

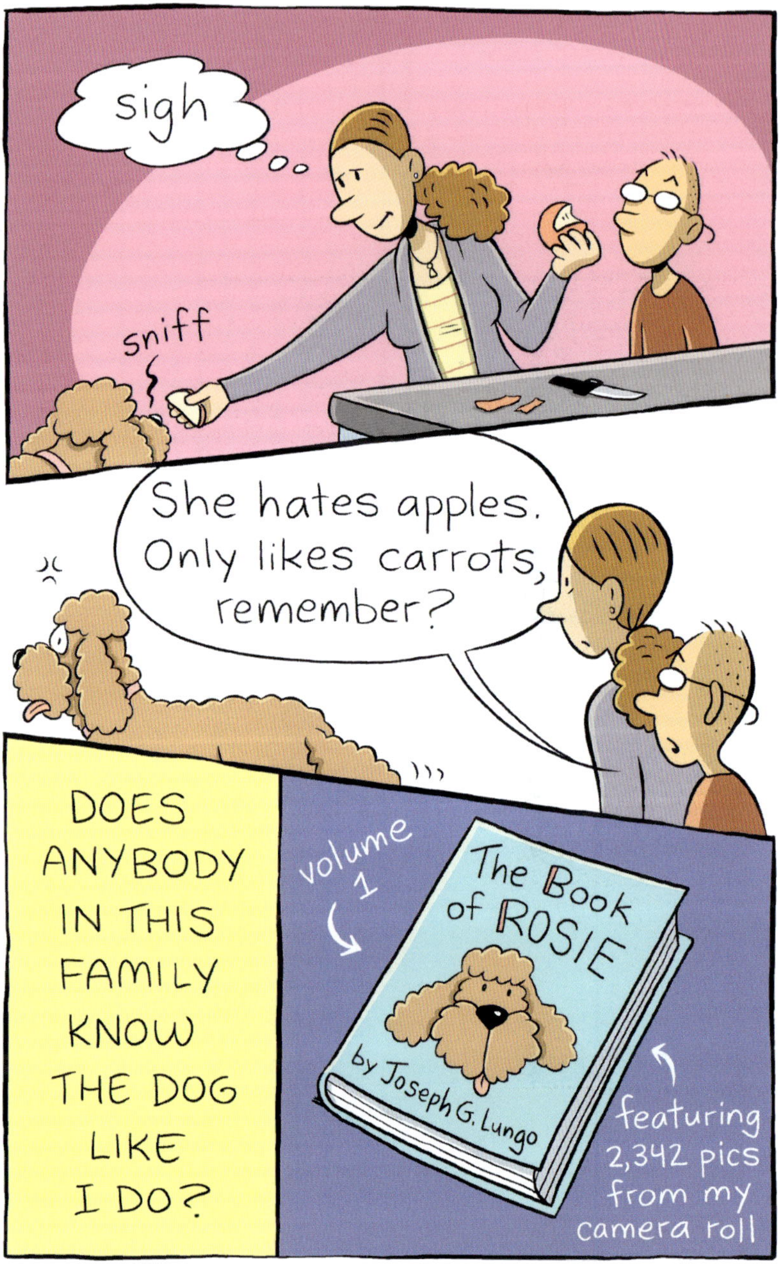
sigh
sniff
She hates apples. Only likes carrots, remember?
DOES ANYBODY IN THIS FAMILY KNOW THE DOG LIKE I DO?
volume 1
The Book of ROSIE
by Joseph G. Lungo
featuring 2,342 pics from my camera roll

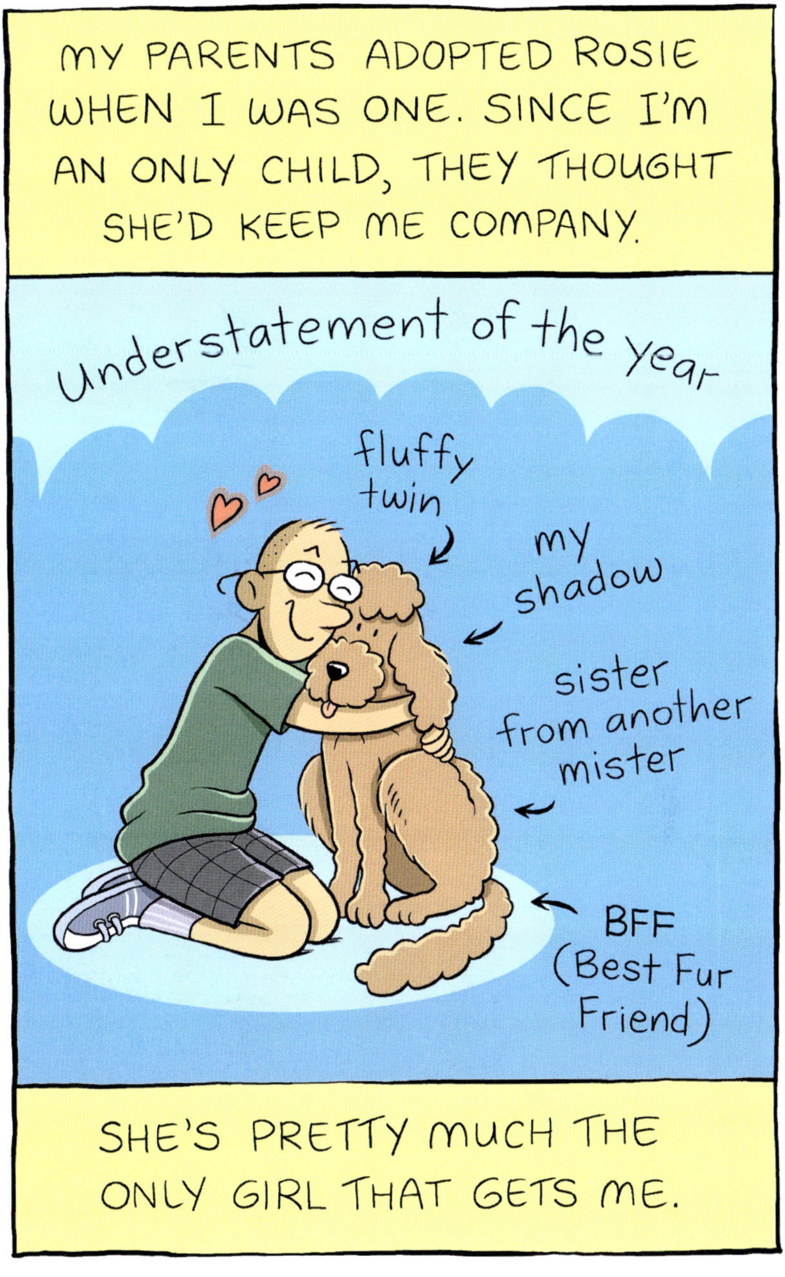
MY PARENTS ADOPTED ROSIE WHEN I WAS ONE. SINCE I'M AN ONLY CHILD, THEY THOUGHT SHE'D KEEP ME COMPANY.
Understatement of the year
fluffy twin
my shadow
sister from another mister
BFF (Best Fur Friend)
SHE'S PRETTY MUCH THE ONLY GIRL THAT GETS ME.

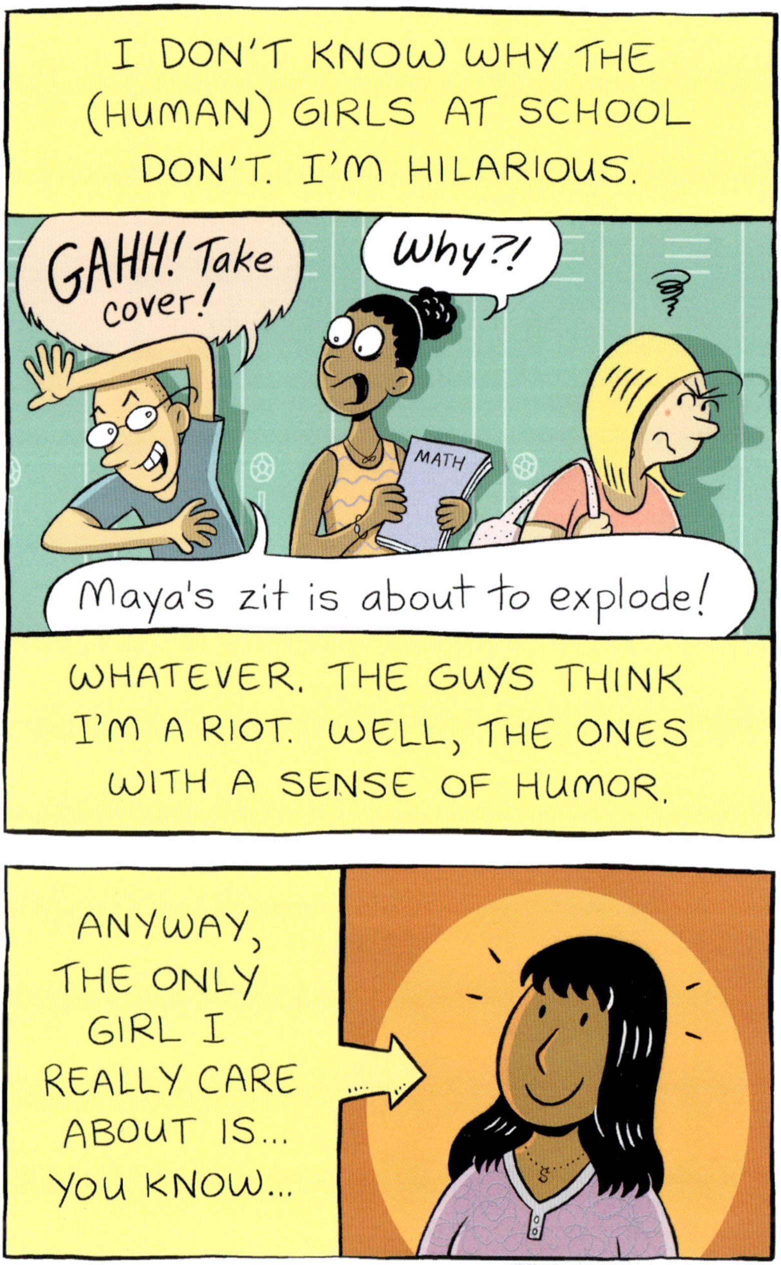
I DON'T KNOW WHY THE (HUMAN) GIRLS AT SCHOOL DON'T. I'M HILARIOUS.
GAHH! Take cover!
Why?!
Maya's zit is about to explode!
WHATEVER. THE GUYS THINK I'M A RIOT. WELL, THE ONES WITH A SENSE OF HUMOR.
ANYWAY, THE ONLY GIRL I REALLY CARE ABOUT IS... YOU KNOW...

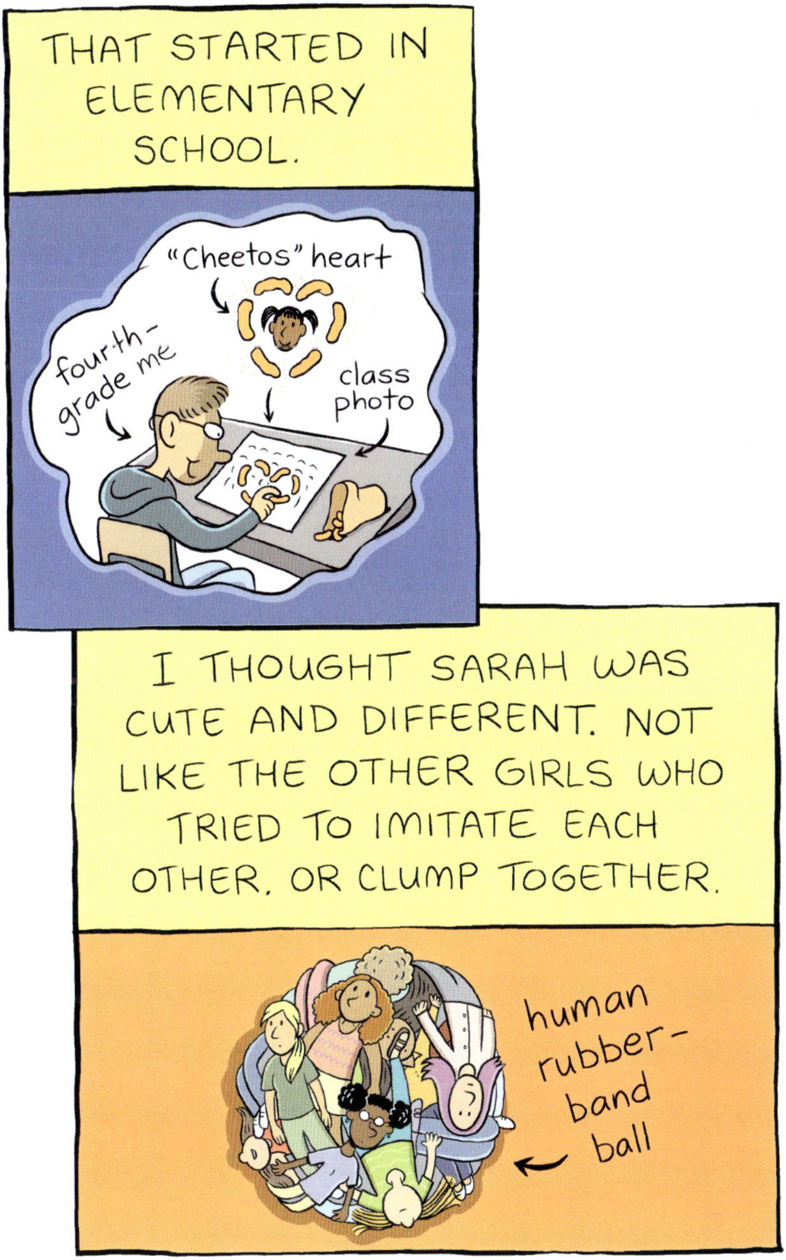
THAT STARTED IN ELEMENTARY SCHOOL.
"Cheetos" heart
fourth-grade me
class photo
I THOUGHT SARAH WAS CUTE AND DIFFERENT. NOT LIKE THE OTHER GIRLS WHO TRIED TO IMITATE EACH OTHER, OR CLUMP TOGETHER.
human rubber-band ball

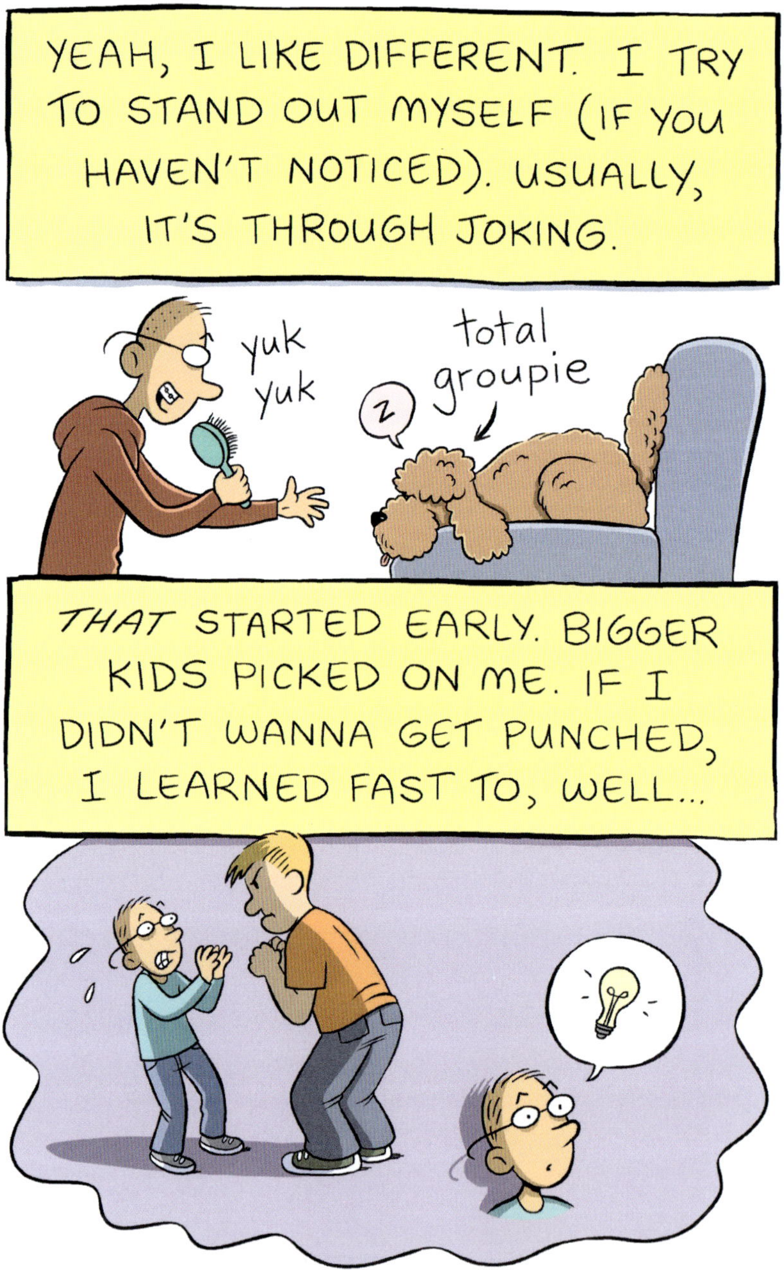
YEAH, I LIKE DIFFERENT. I TRY TO STAND OUT MYSELF (IF YOU HAVEN'T NOTICED). USUALLY, IT'S THROUGH JOKING.
yuk yuk
total groupie
z
THAT STARTED EARLY. BIGGER KIDS PICKED ON ME. IF I DIDN'T WANNA GET PUNCHED, I LEARNED FAST TO, WELL...

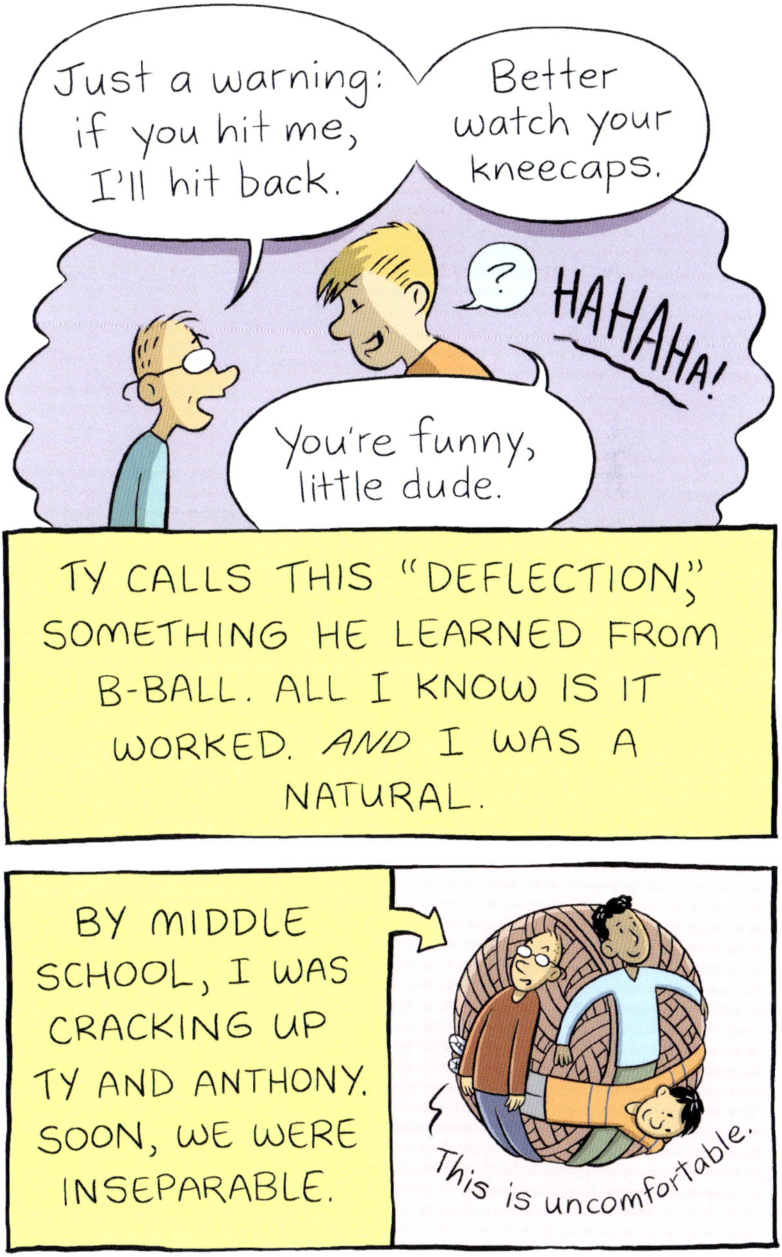

Just a warning: if you hit me, I'll hit back.
Better watch your kneecaps.
?
HAHAHA!
You're funny, little dude.
TY CALLS THIS "DEFLECTION," SOMETHING HE LEARNED FROM B-BALL. ALL I KNOW IS IT WORKED. *AND* I WAS A NATURAL.
BY MIDDLE SCHOOL, I WAS CRACKING UP TY AND ANTHONY. SOON, WE WERE INSEPARABLE.
This is uncomfortable.

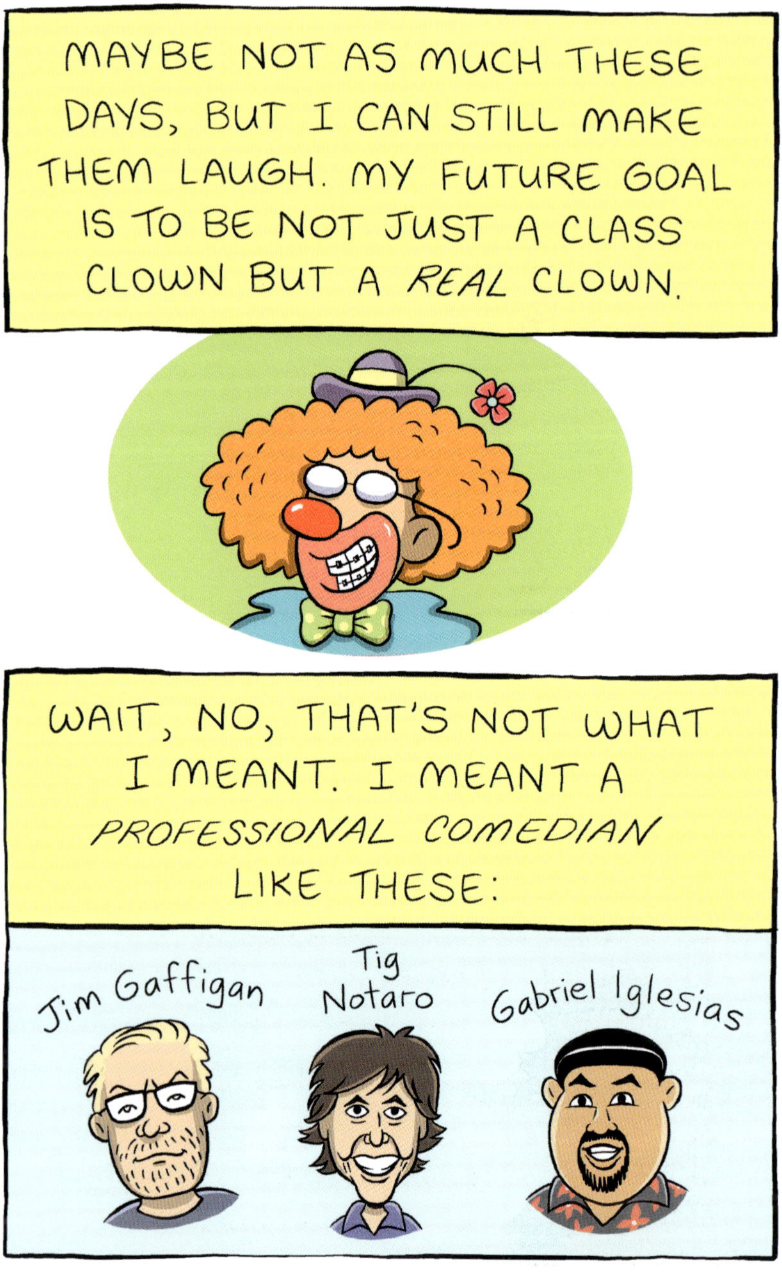
MAYBE NOT AS MUCH THESE DAYS, BUT I CAN STILL MAKE THEM LAUGH. MY FUTURE GOAL IS TO BE NOT JUST A CLASS CLOWN BUT A *REAL* CLOWN.
WAIT, NO, THAT'S NOT WHAT I MEANT. I MEANT A *PROFESSIONAL COMEDIAN* LIKE THESE:
Jim Gaffigan
Tig Notaro
Gabriel Iglesias

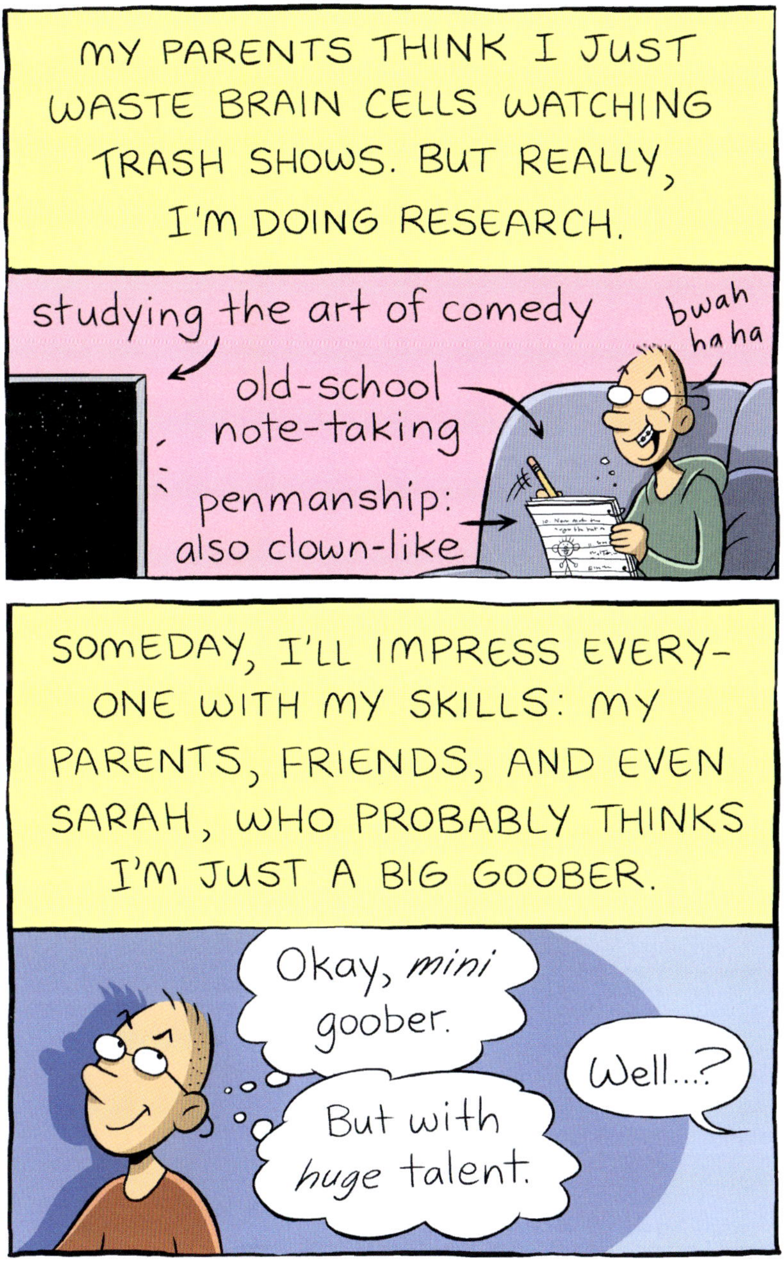
MY PARENTS THINK I JUST WASTE BRAIN CELLS WATCHING TRASH SHOWS. BUT REALLY, I'M DOING RESEARCH.
studying the art of comedy
bwah haha
old-school note-taking
penmanship: also clown-like
SOMEDAY, I'LL IMPRESS EVERY-ONE WITH MY SKILLS: MY PARENTS, FRIENDS, AND EVEN SARAH, WHO PROBABLY THINKS I'M JUST A BIG GOOBER.
Okay, *mini* goober.
But with *huge* talent.
Well...?

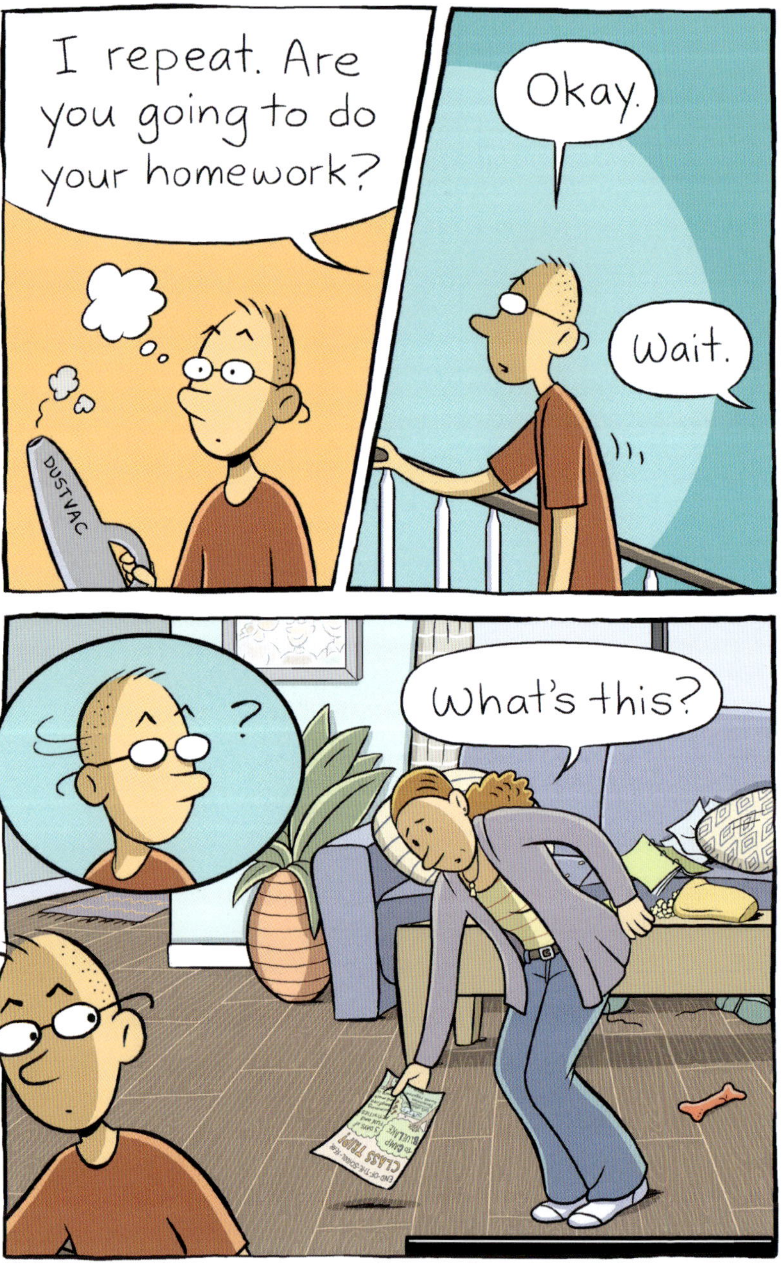
I repeat. Are you going to do your homework?
Okay.
Wait.
DUSTVAC
What's this?
?
END-OF-THE-SCHOOL-YEAR CLASS TRIP! TO CAMP BLUE LAKE

EMMIE

Oh nooooooooooo!

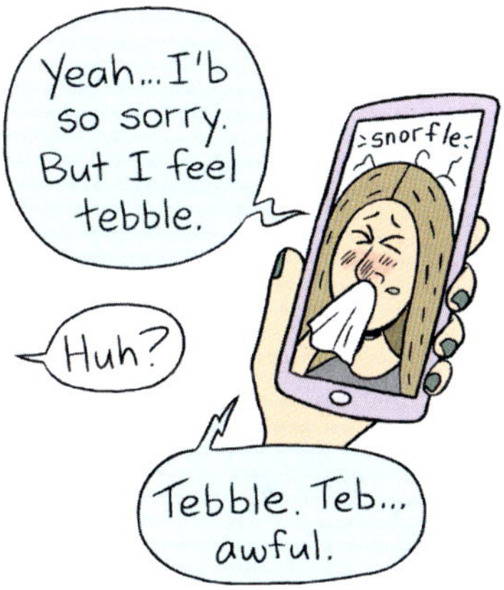

Yeah... I'b so sorry. But I feel tebble.
:snorfle:
Huh?
Tebble. Teb... awful.

Nononono! Bri has to come! I can't go alone, there's no way!

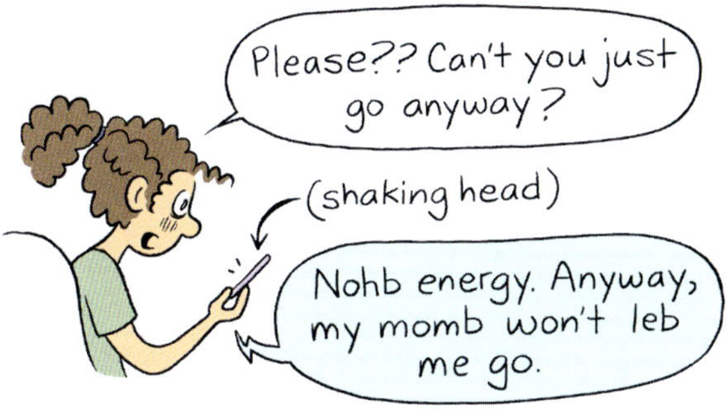

Please?? Can't you just go anyway?
(shaking head)
Nohb energy. Anyway, my momb won't leb me go.

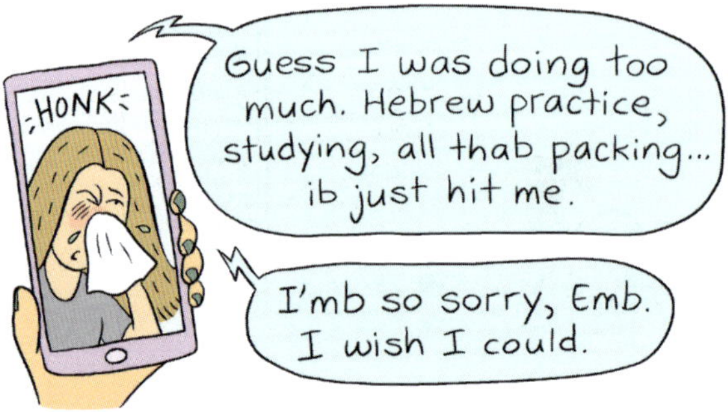
HONK
Guess I was doing too much. Hebrew practice, studying, all thab packing... ib just hit me.
I'mb so sorry, Emb. I wish I could.

We talk for a little bit longer, but I really don't have much to say. I tell Bri to feel better, and then I get off the phone and just sit and stare at the Paul Klee poster on my wall.

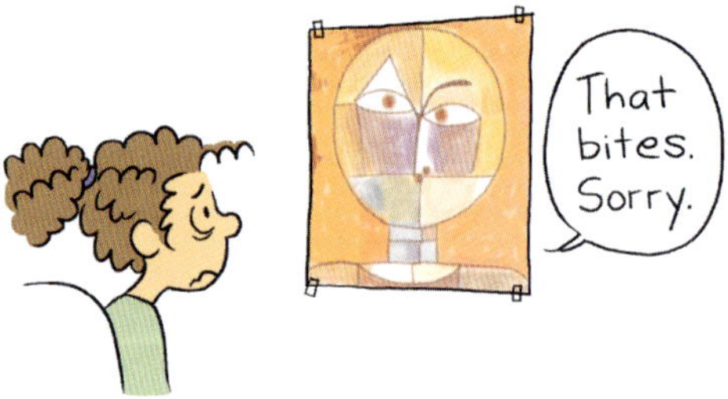
That bites. Sorry.

How am I gonna go on this trip alone?? Should I play sick, too? My parents—and Trina—would kill me.

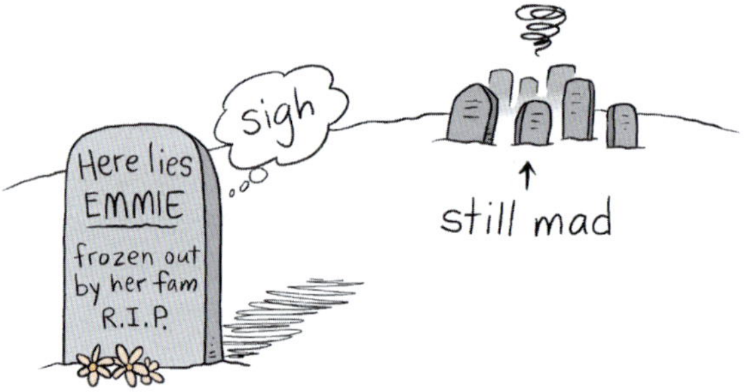
sigh
Here lies EMMIE frozen out by her fam R.I.P.
still mad

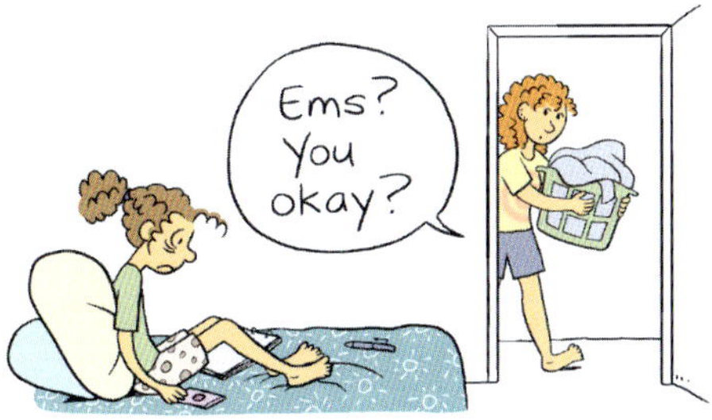
Ems? You okay?

OMG. Trina. My cool big sis is gonna see me alone and pathetic! All. Weekend. Long.

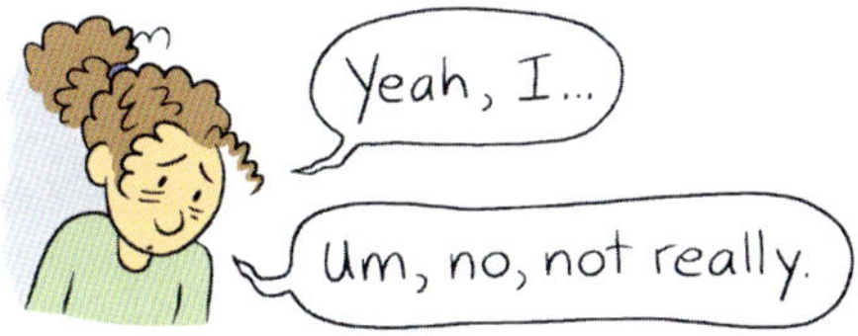
Yeah, I...
Um, no, not really.

She comes in and sits on the bed beside me.

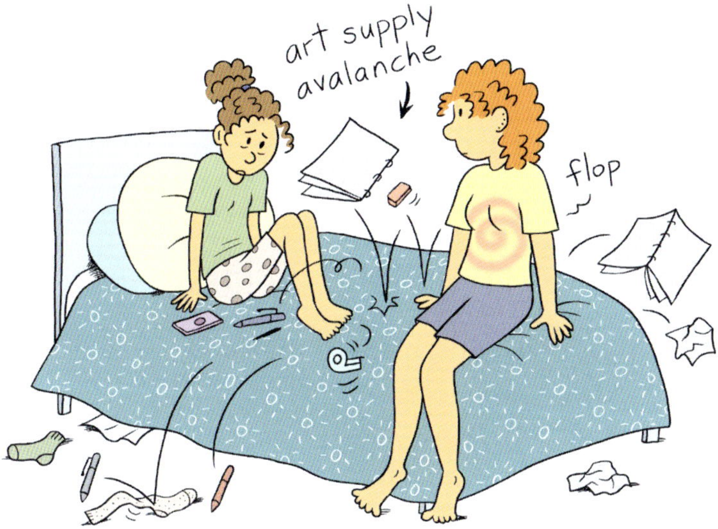
art supply avalanche
flop

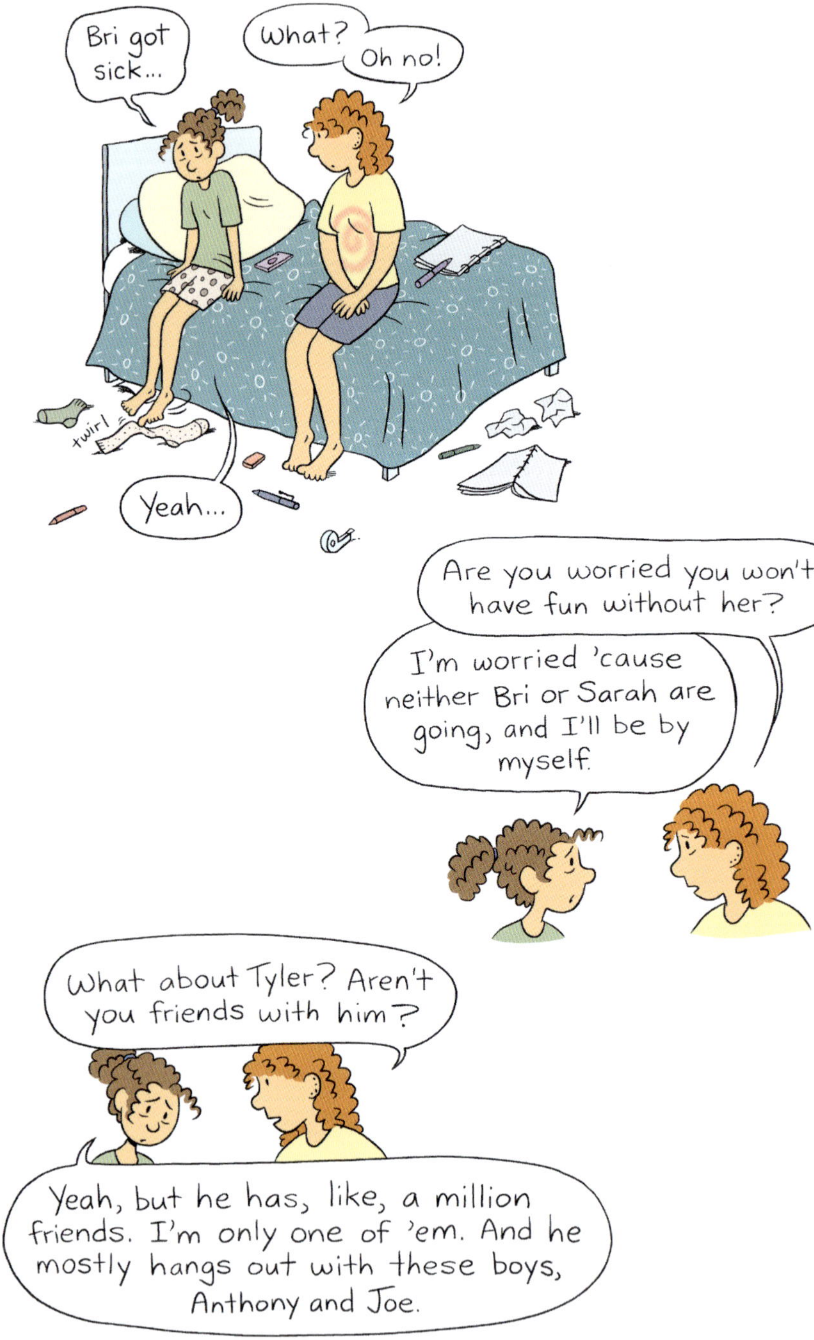
Bri got sick...
What?
Oh no!
twirl
Yeah...
Are you worried you won't have fun without her?
I'm worried 'cause neither Bri or Sarah are going, and I'll be by myself.
What about Tyler? Aren't you friends with him?
Yeah, but he has, like, a million friends. I'm only one of 'em. And he mostly hangs out with these boys, Anthony and Joe.

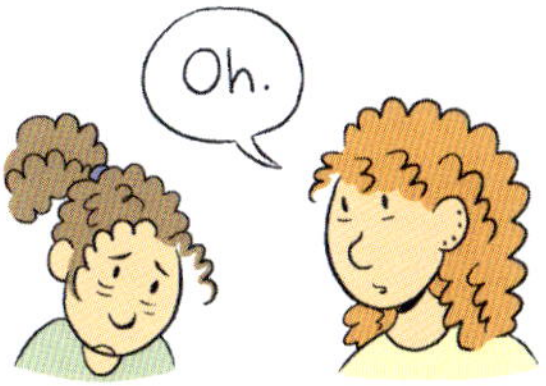
Oh.

We just sit there in silence for a minute. I try not to cry, but it's really hard.

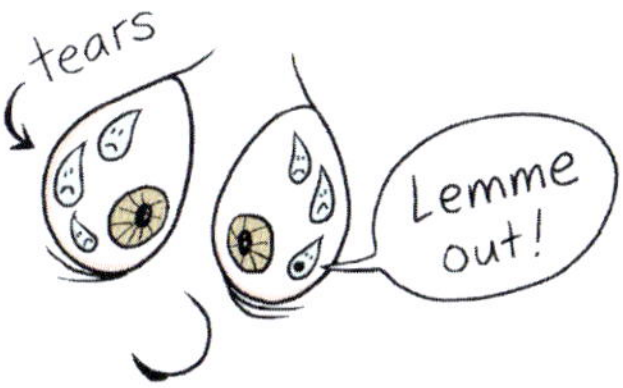
tears
Lemme out!

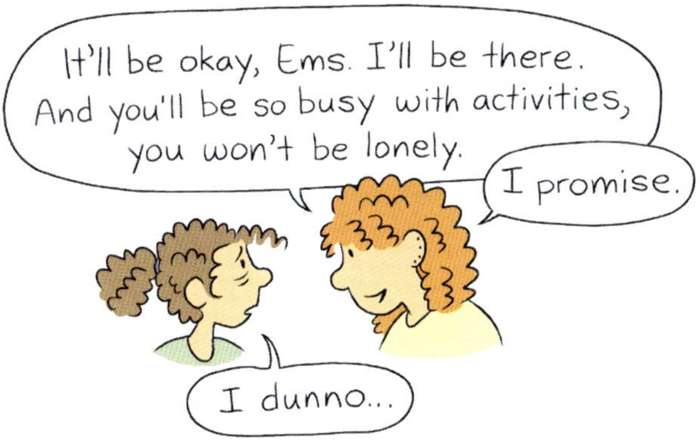
It'll be okay, Ems. I'll be there. And you'll be so busy with activities, you won't be lonely.
I promise.
I dunno...

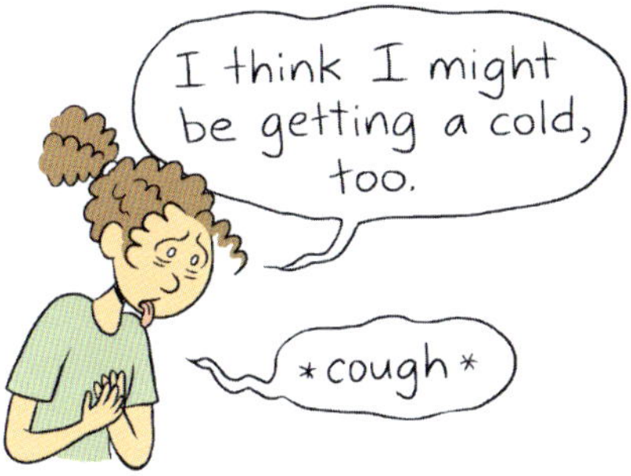
I think I might be getting a cold, too.
cough

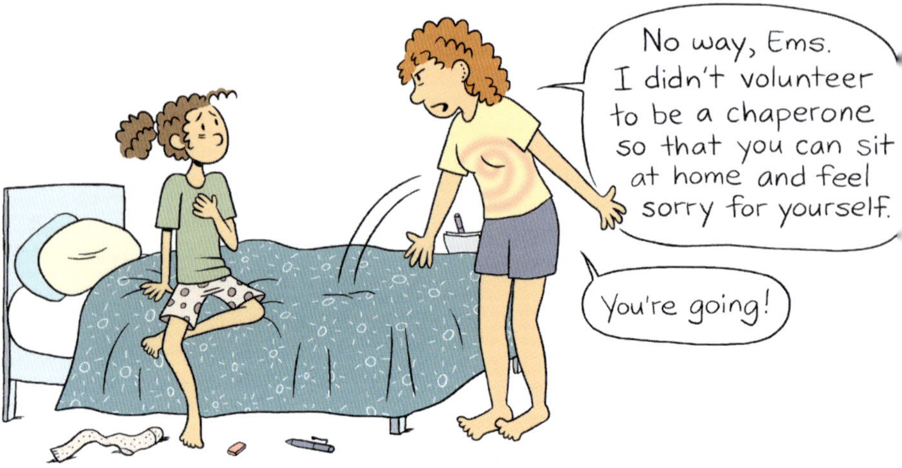
No way, Ems. I didn't volunteer to be a chaperone so that you can sit at home and feel sorry for yourself.
You're going!

I sit there, frozen.

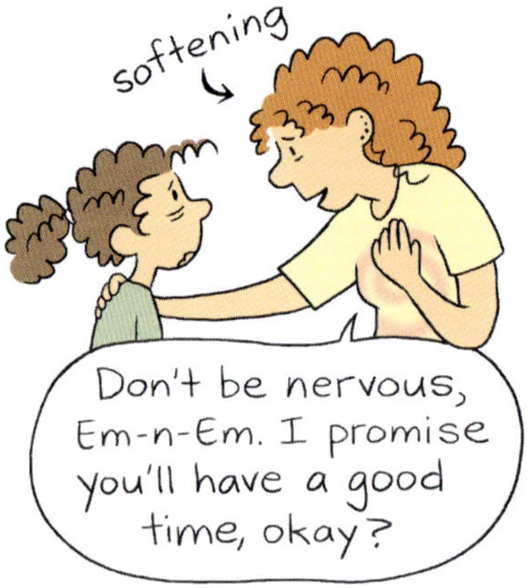
softening
Don't be nervous, Em-n-Em. I promise you'll have a good time, okay?

I don't believe her. At all. But I nod.

Besides, Trina's always been there for me. I'll call or FaceTime her at school with problems and she usually drops everything. Especially when I'm having boy (aka Tyler) trouble. And she's great with advice.

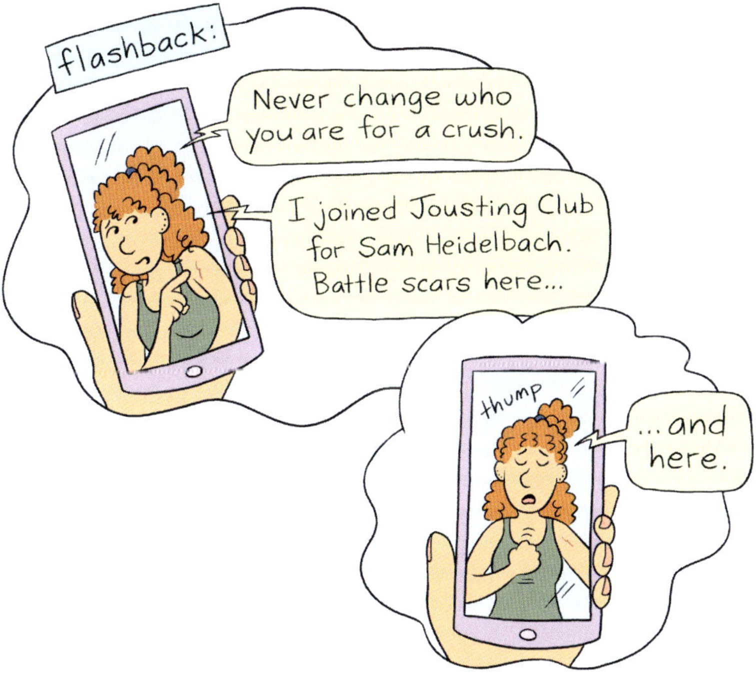
flashback:
Never change who you are for a crush.
I joined Jousting Club for Sam Heidelbach. Battle scars here...
thump
...and here.

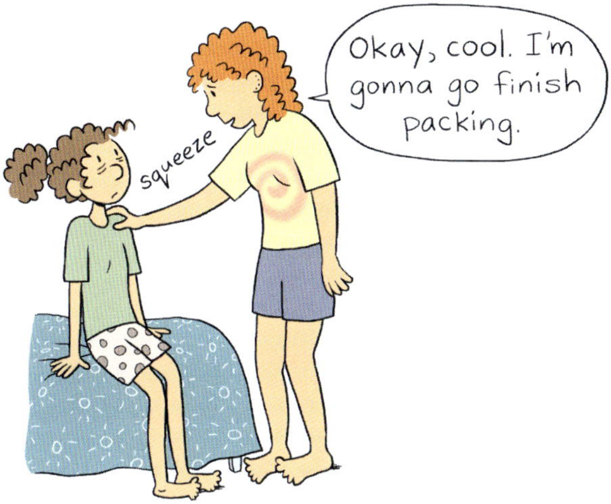
squeeze
Okay, cool. I'm gonna go finish packing.

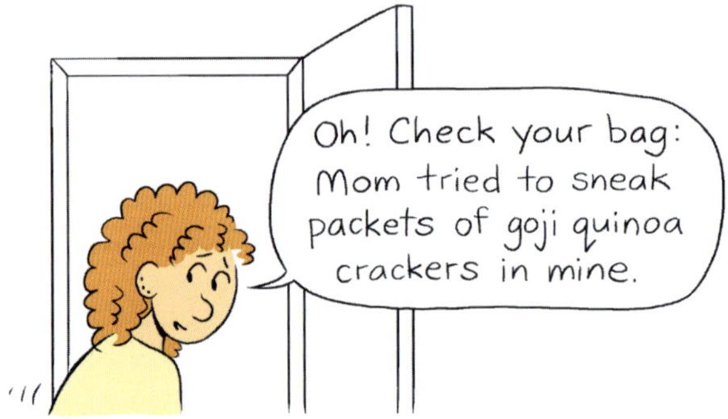
Oh! Check your bag: Mom tried to sneak packets of goji quinoa crackers in mine.

She leaves and closes the door. I bend down and rummage through my duffel, still amazed that the tears haven't started.

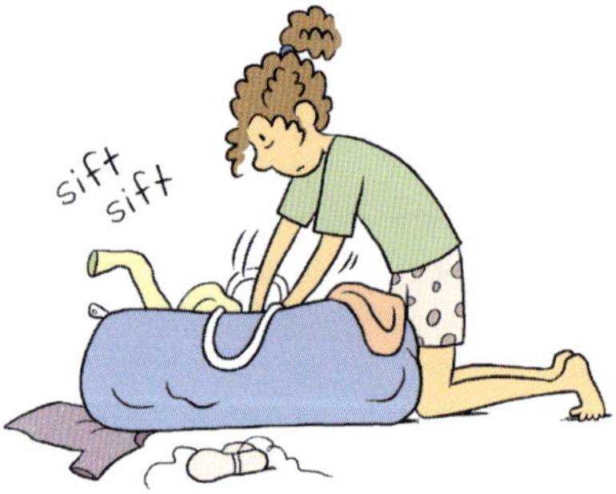
sift
sift

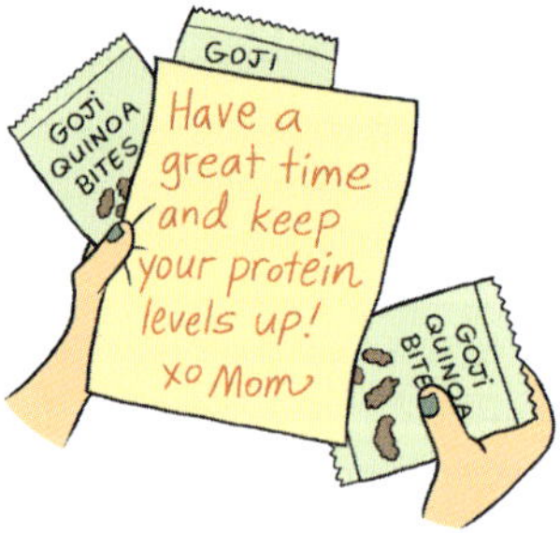
GOJI
GOJI QUINOA BITES
Have a great time and keep your protein levels up!
xo Mom
GOJI QUINOA BITES

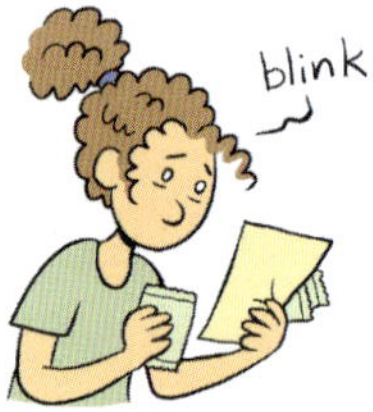
blink

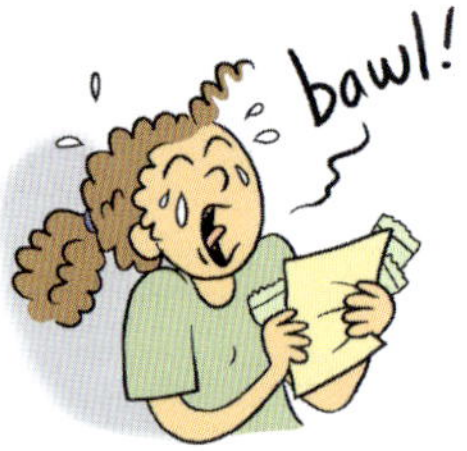
bawl!

Joe

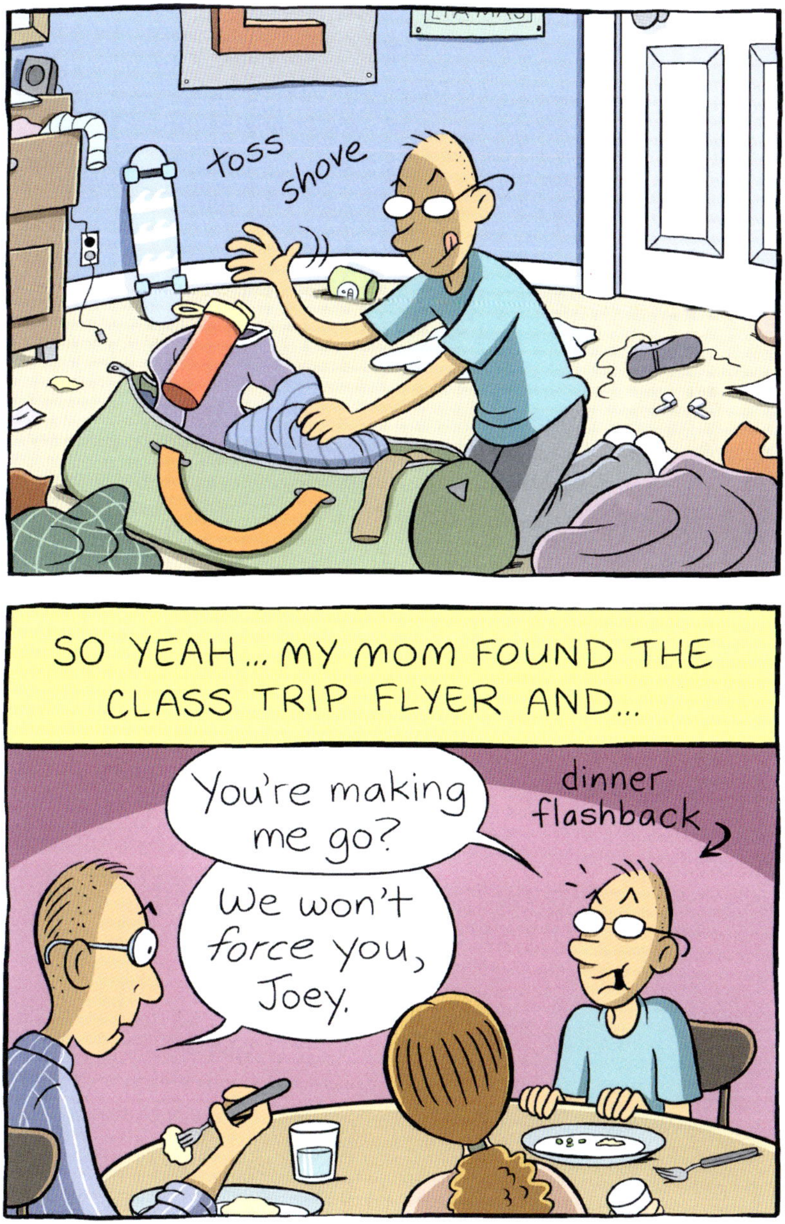
toss
shove
SO YEAH... MY MOM FOUND THE CLASS TRIP FLYER AND...
dinner flashback
You're making me go?
We won't force you, Joey.

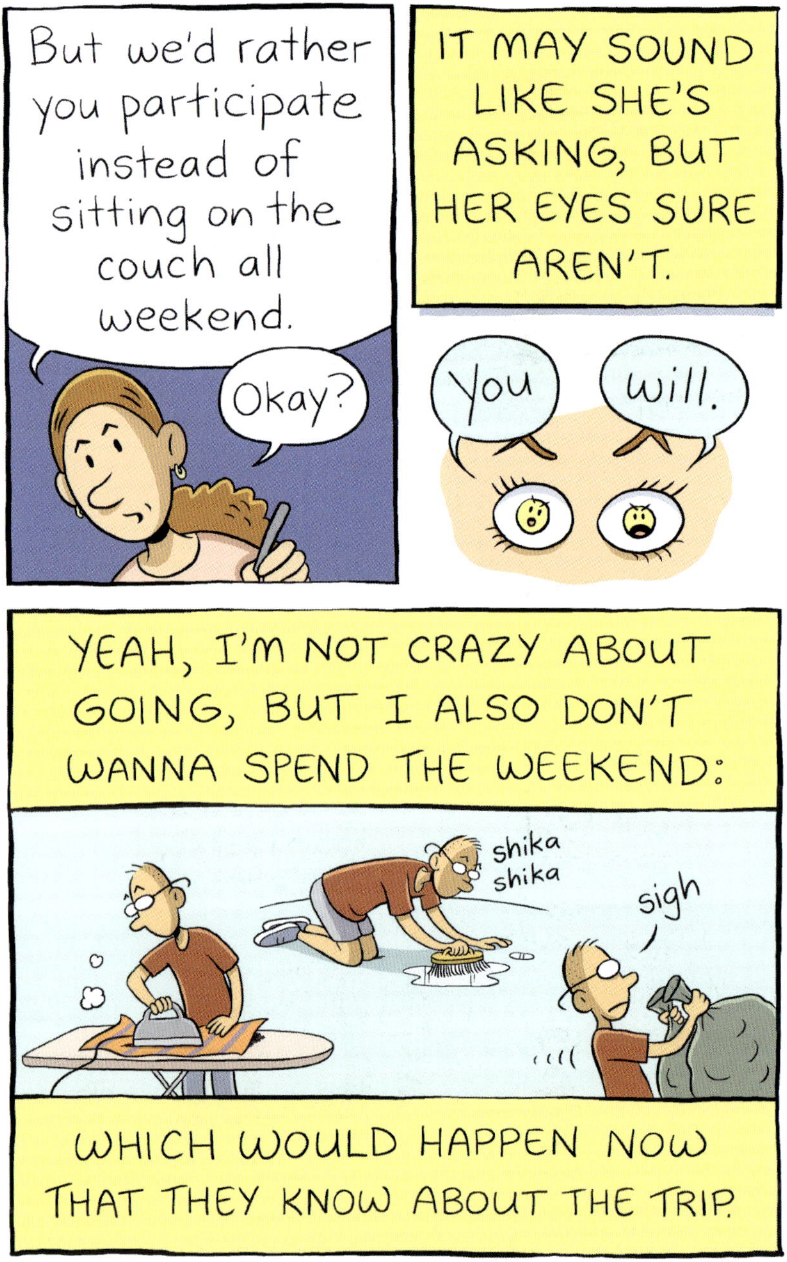
But we'd rather you participate instead of sitting on the couch all weekend.
Okay?
IT MAY SOUND LIKE SHE'S ASKING, BUT HER EYES SURE AREN'T.
You
will.
YEAH, I'M NOT CRAZY ABOUT GOING, BUT I ALSO DON'T WANNA SPEND THE WEEKEND:
shika shika
sigh
WHICH WOULD HAPPEN NOW THAT THEY KNOW ABOUT THE TRIP.

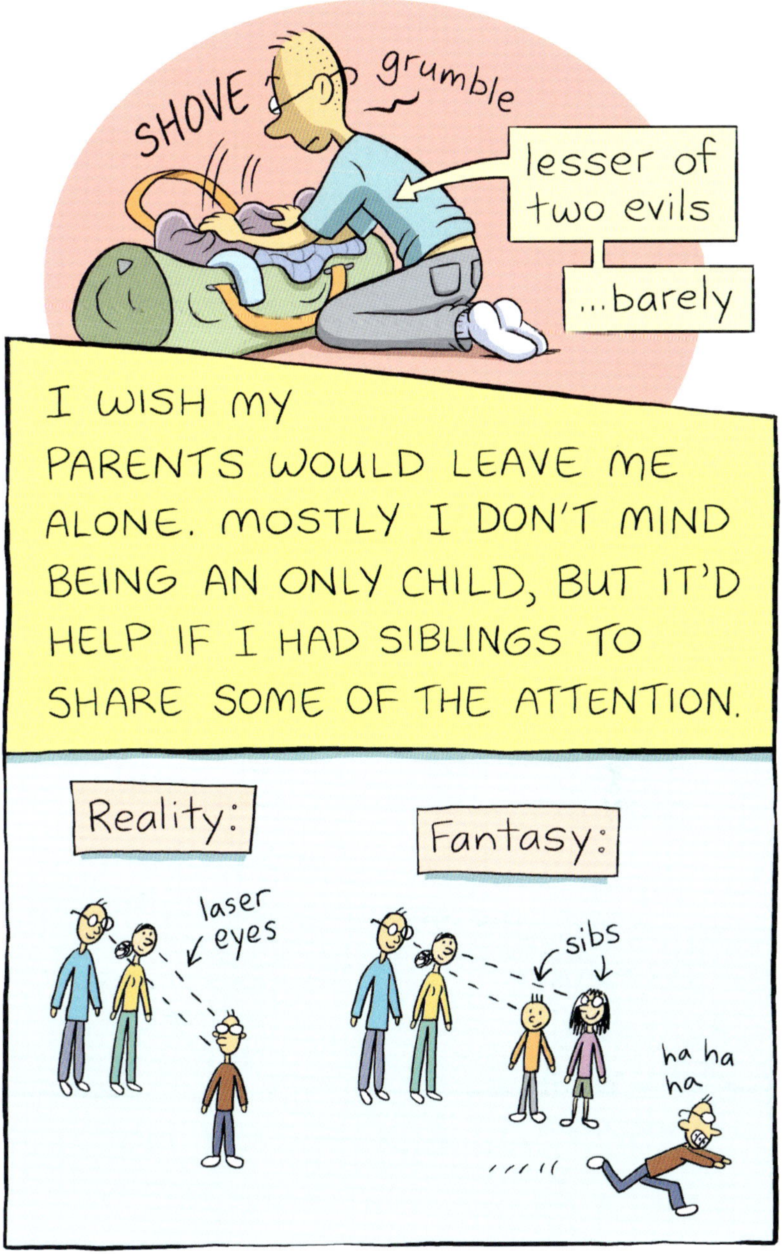
SHOVE
grumble
lesser of two evils
...barely
I WISH MY PARENTS WOULD LEAVE ME ALONE. MOSTLY I DON'T MIND BEING AN ONLY CHILD, BUT IT'D HELP IF I HAD SIBLINGS TO SHARE SOME OF THE ATTENTION.
Reality:
laser eyes
Fantasy:
sibs
ha ha ha

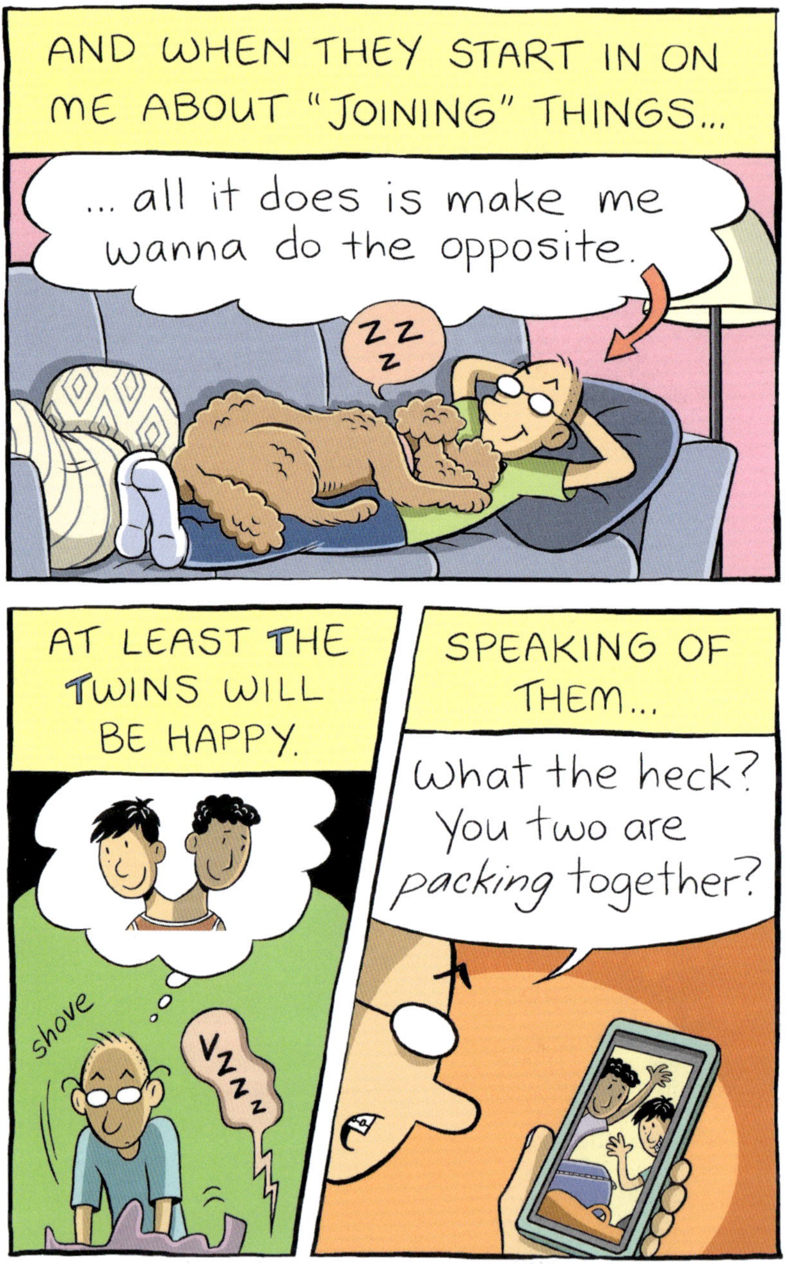
AND WHEN THEY START IN ON ME ABOUT "JOINING" THINGS...
... all it does is make me wanna do the opposite.
ZZZ
AT LEAST THE TWINS WILL BE HAPPY.
shove
VZZZ
SPEAKING OF THEM...
What the heck? You two are packing together?

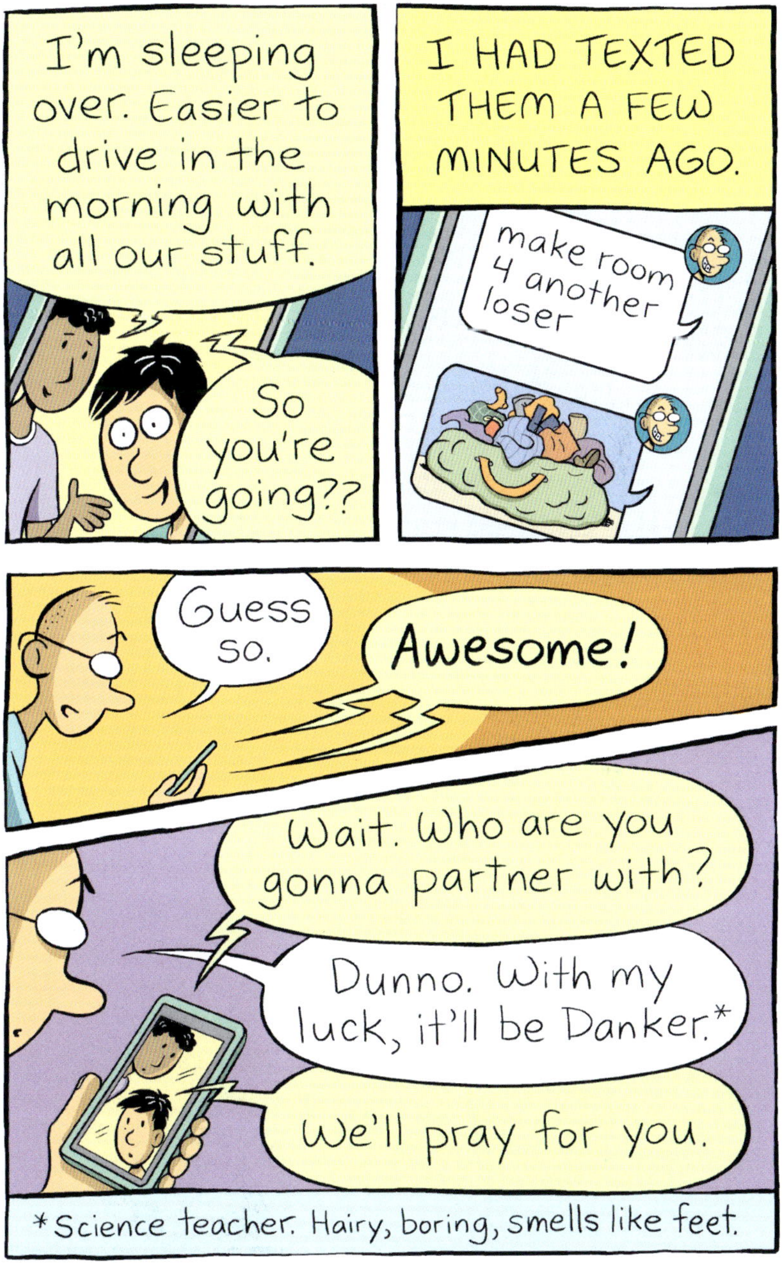
I'm sleeping over. Easier to drive in the morning with all our stuff.
So you're going??
I HAD TEXTED THEM A FEW MINUTES AGO.
make room 4 another loser
Guess so.
Awesome!
Wait. Who are you gonna partner with?
Dunno. With my luck, it'll be Danker.*
We'll pray for you.
*Science teacher. Hairy, boring, smells like feet.

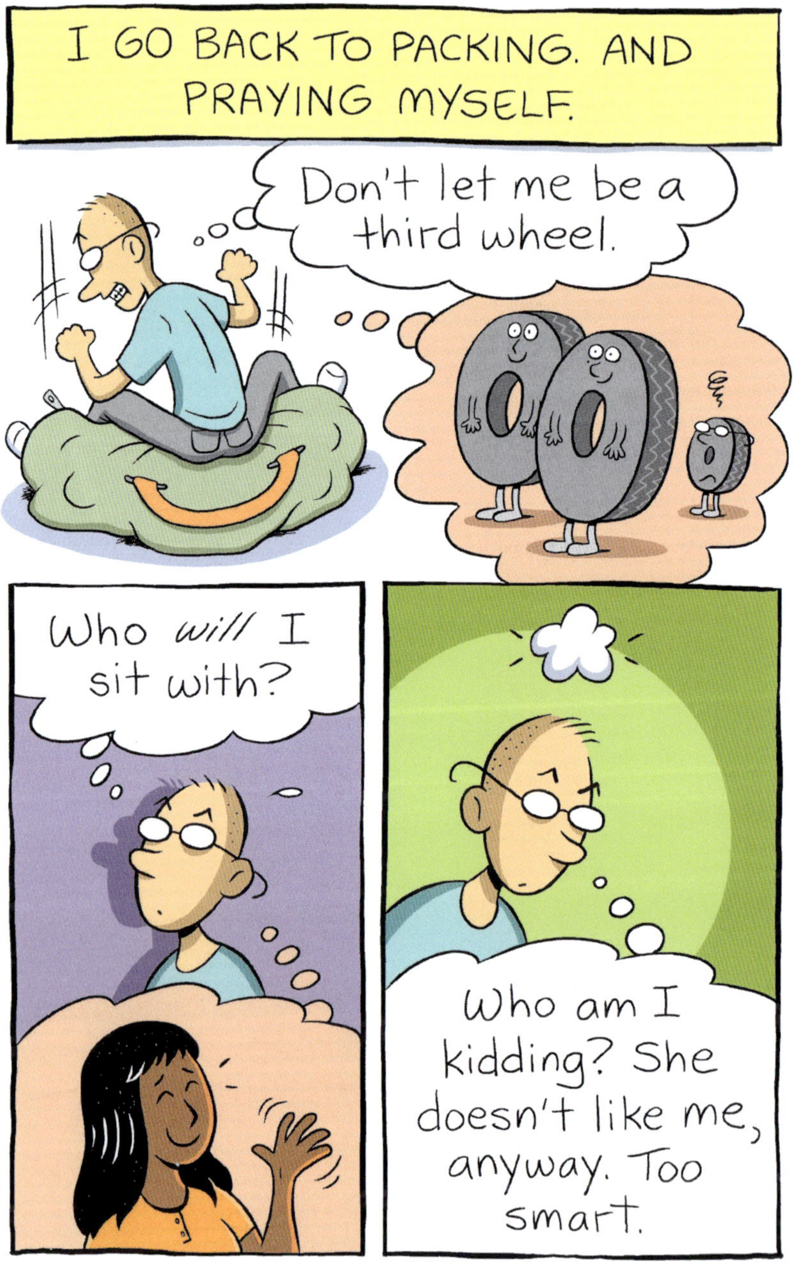

I GO BACK TO PACKING. AND PRAYING MYSELF.
Don't let me be a third wheel.
Who *will* I sit with?
Who am I kidding? She doesn't like me, anyway. Too smart.

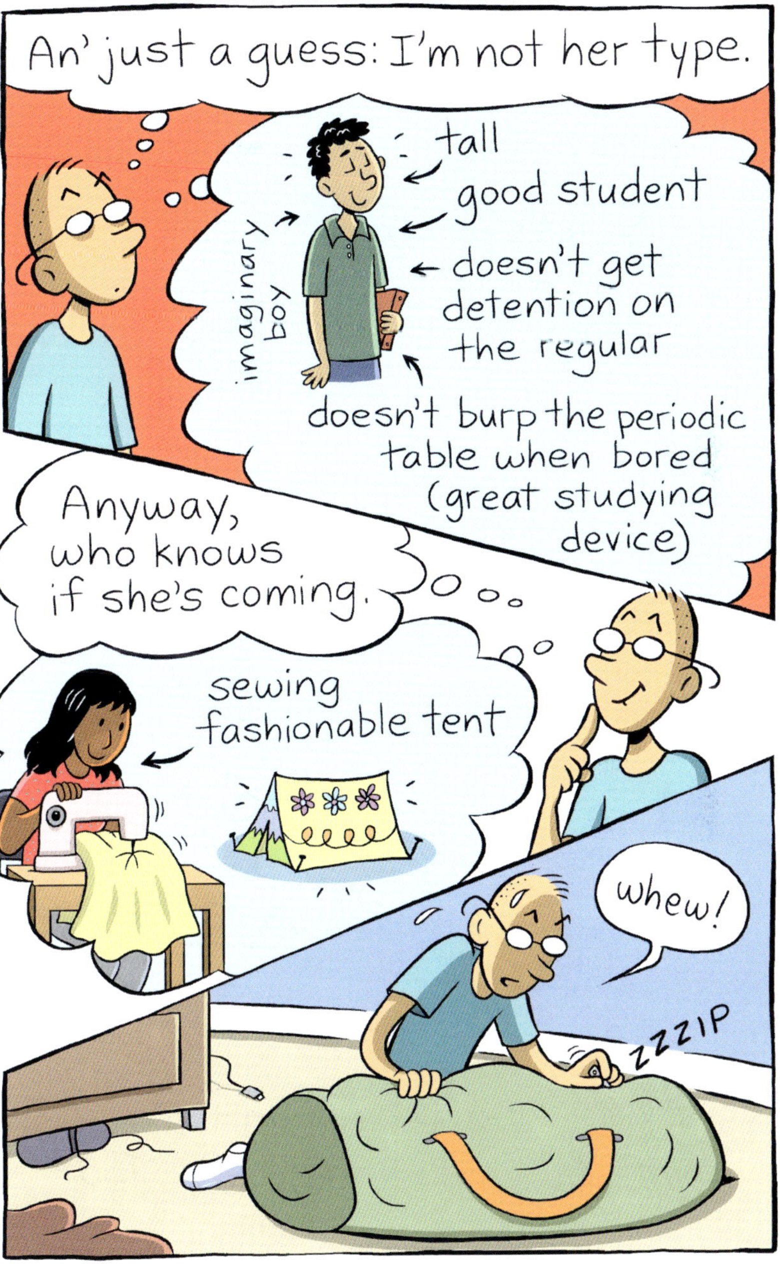
An' just a guess: I'm not her type.
tall
good student
doesn't get detention on the regular
doesn't burp the periodic table when bored (great studying device)
imaginary boy
Anyway, who knows if she's coming.
sewing fashionable tent
whew!
ZZZIP

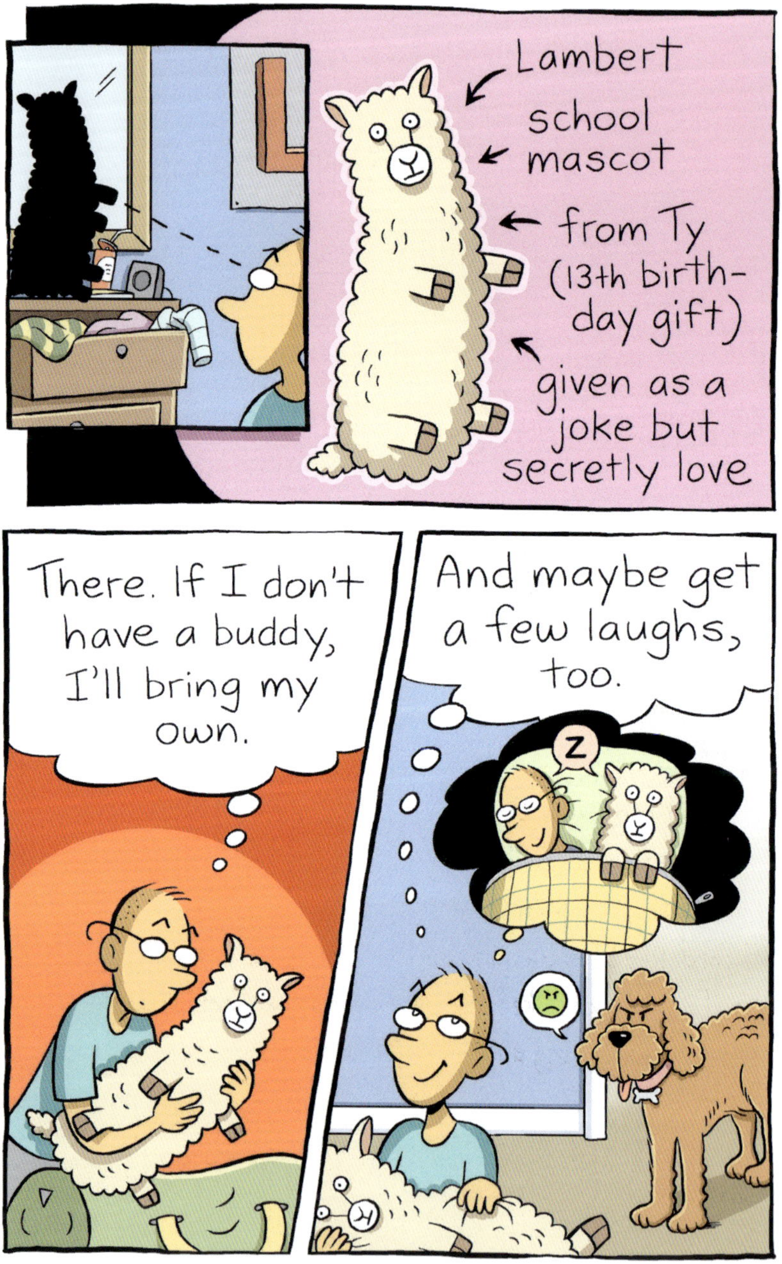

Lambert
school mascot
from Ty (13th birth-day gift)
given as a joke but secretly love
There. If I don't have a buddy, I'll bring my own.
And maybe get a few laughs, too.
Z

EMMIE

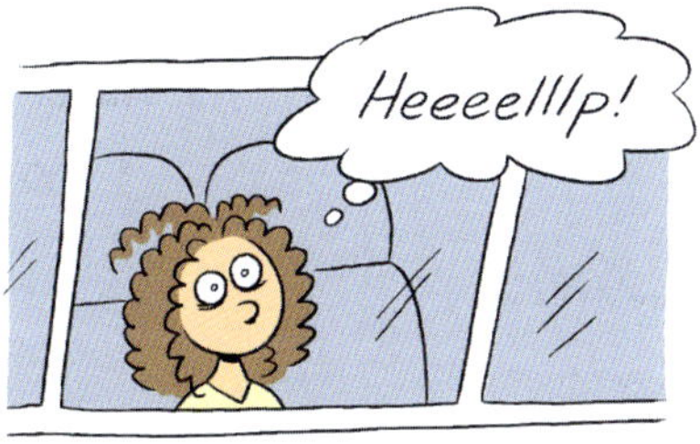
Heeeelllp!

I don't know who I'm pleading to. No one, really. The only ones out there are a few last-minute students being dropped off; the bus driver; Ms. Arnold; and Mr. Bauman, who's holding a clipboard. He's been checking off the students as they get on the bus, and now it looks like he's going over some final details with Ms. Arnold. Or having a little prayer circle.

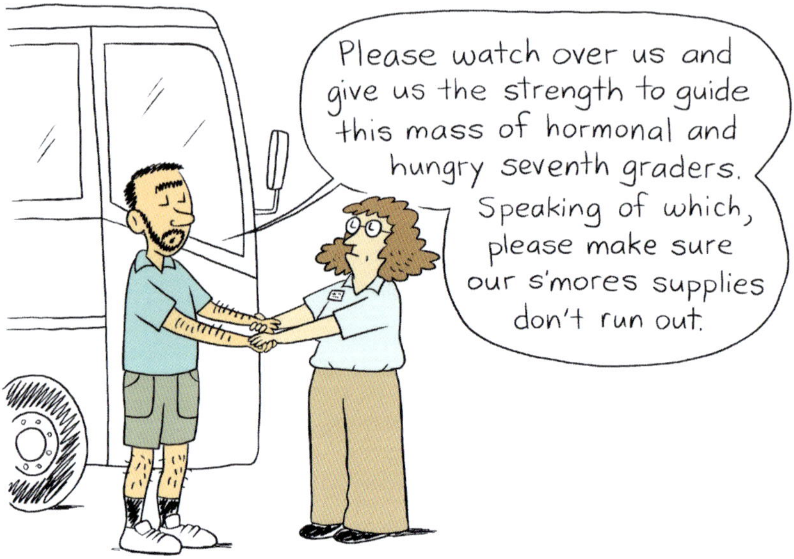
Please watch over us and give us the strength to guide this mass of hormonal and hungry seventh graders. Speaking of which, please make sure our s'mores supplies don't run out.

The bus is huge and almost filled up. There are two buses, actually. These aren't the regular school ones but the dark, comfortable, touristy kind with velvety seats and an actual bathroom in back (although I refuse to use it). To say it's loud in here would be an understatement. The bus isn't even full, and the volume is beyond human level.

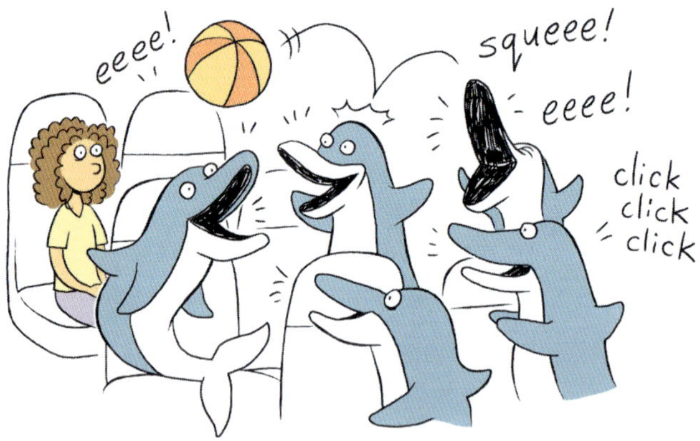
eeee!
squeee!
eeee!
click
click
click

Everyone is amped up. Instead of being infected with excitement, my heart is pounding with anxiety. The worst part is, Trina is helping on the **other** bus.

Instead, we get:

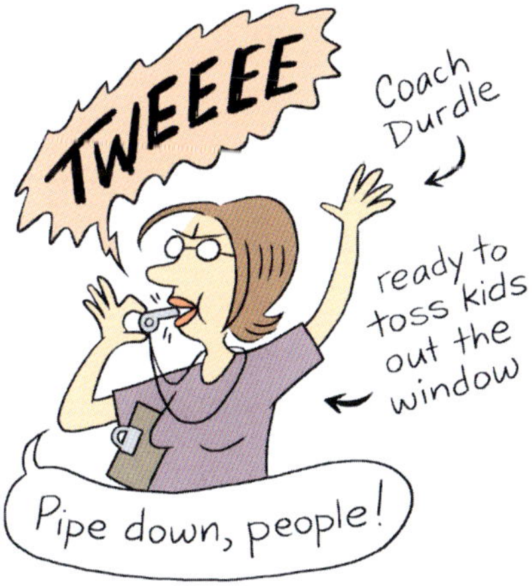
TWEEEE
Coach Durdle
ready to toss kids out the window
Pipe down, people!

There are a bunch of counselors from the high school and one tall girl around Trina's age. Trina said they'd gone to Lakefront High together, and she's also earning college volunteer hours. None of them are doing anything except sitting there and chatting. So much for counseling.

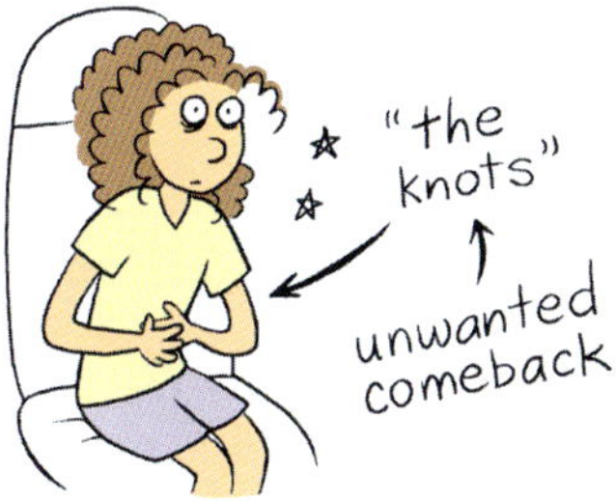
"the knots"
unwanted comeback

I take exactly ten deep breaths and try to "center my spleen" or whatever. It's not working. I'm sitting by myself (so far). No "buddy." Coach said she'd find one. Worst case: I'd partner with a counselor (please let it be Trina!!).

I wonder where Tyler is. Maybe the other bus . . . ?

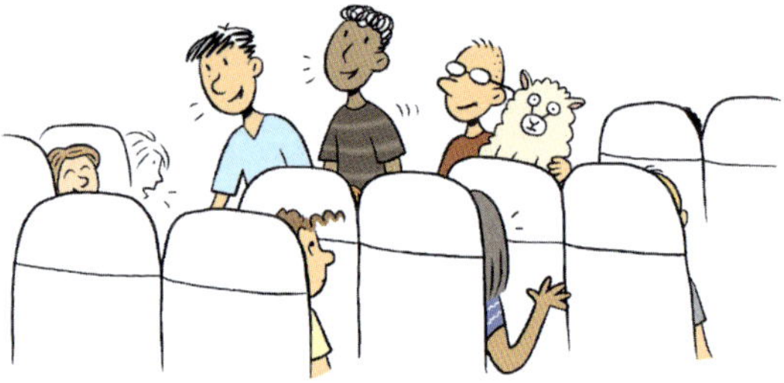

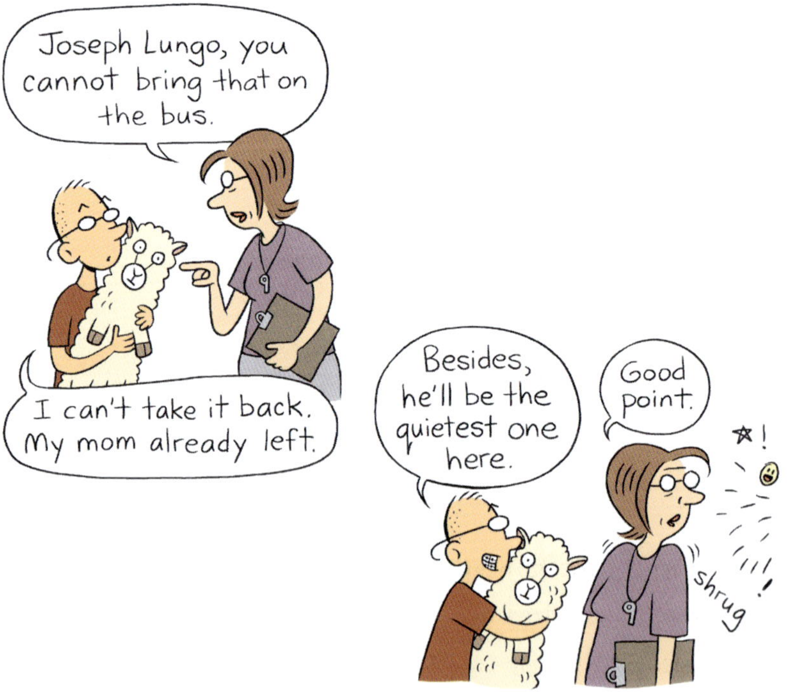

Joseph Lungo, you cannot bring that on the bus.
I can't take it back. My mom already left.
Besides, he'll be the quietest one here.
Good point.
shrug

OMG, they're heading this way! Tyler waves. I nervously wave back. They sit in the empty seats behind me (!!!). Joe, looking a little confused, stands there with that weird stuffed animal—a camel? Oh, a llama, duh. Our mascot.

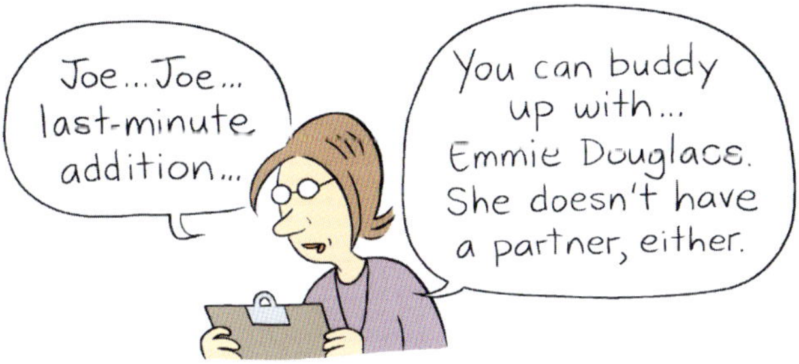
Joe... Joe... last-minute addition...
You can buddy up with... Emmie Douglass. She doesn't have a partner, either.

Could she say that any louder? I see kids staring at us and some of them start to snicker.

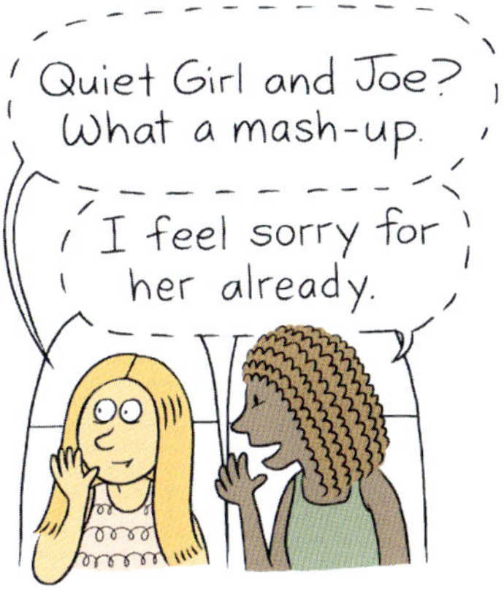
Quiet Girl and Joe? What a mash-up.
I feel sorry for her already.

I feel my cheeks heat up. **Joe?** Really?? The last person I'd ever want to be paired with. He doesn't look exactly thrilled to be partnered with me, either. In fact, I watch his face literally fall.

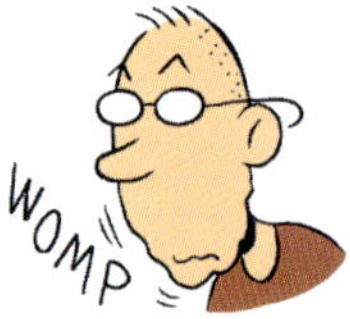
WOMP

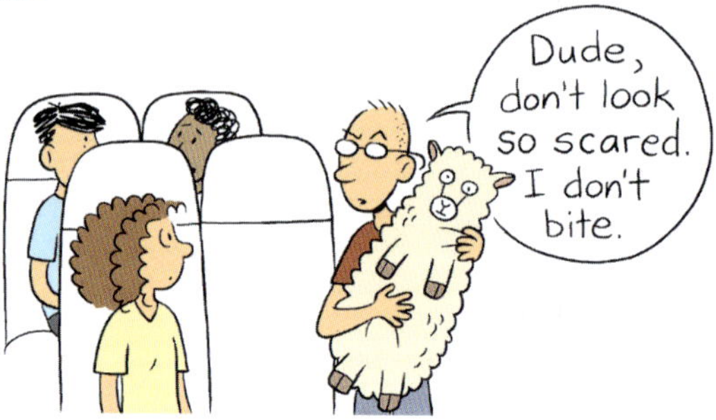
Dude, don't look so scared. I don't bite.

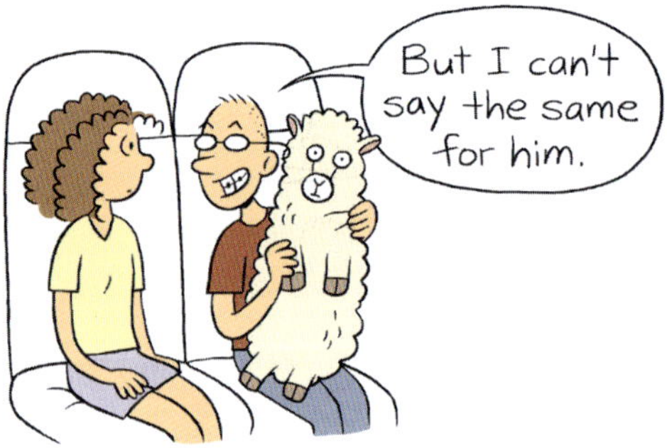
But I can't say the same for him.

He suddenly thrusts the llama in my face, and I jump.

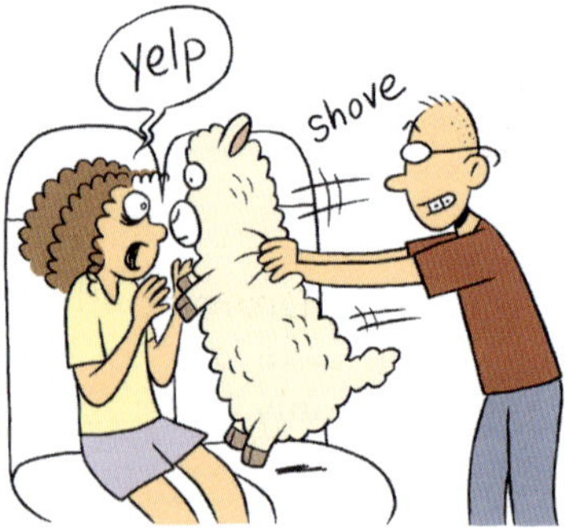
yelp
shove

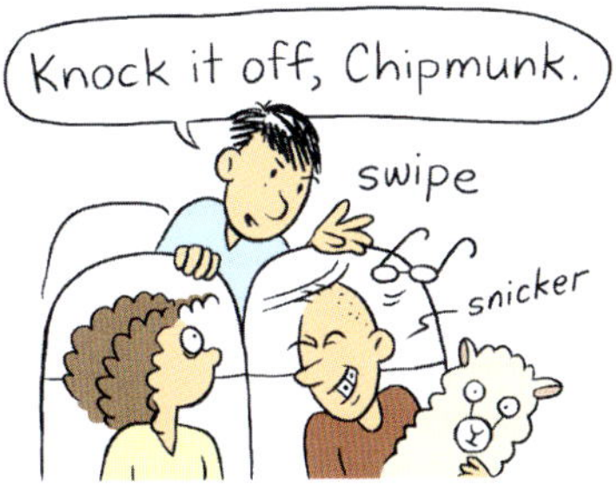
Knock it off, Chipmunk.
swipe
snicker

I'm so grateful, I wanna hug Tyler. But I wouldn't dare.

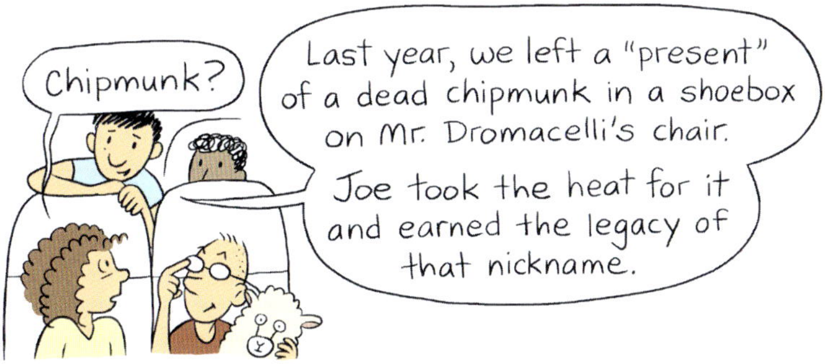
Chipmunk?
Last year, we left a "present" of a dead chipmunk in a shoebox on Mr. Dromacelli's chair.
Joe took the heat for it and earned the legacy of that nickname.

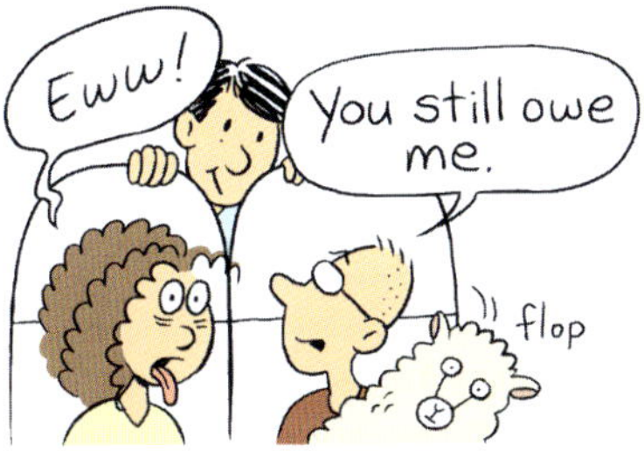
Eww!
You still owe me.
flop

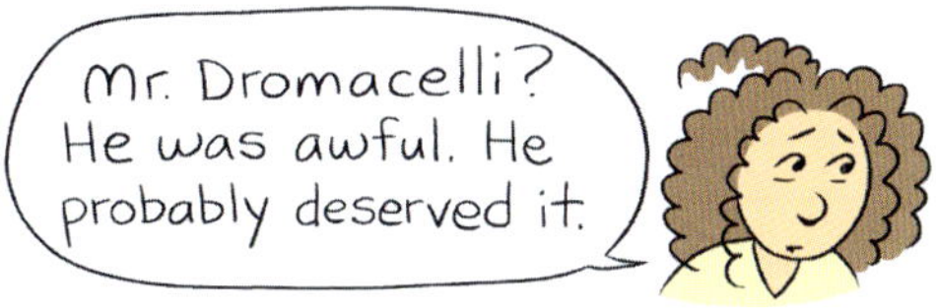
Mr. Dromacelli? He was awful. He probably deserved it.

Joe, looking kinda surprised, grins.

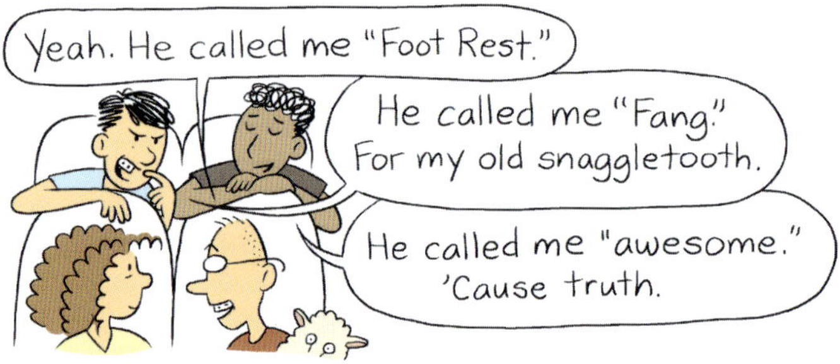
Yeah. He called me "Foot Rest."
He called me "Fang." For my old snaggletooth.
He called me "awesome." 'Cause truth.

Joe clubs Anthony with the llama, Tyler steals it, and we all laugh. Suddenly, I'm feeling a little better . . . even with Joe as my partner.

But then . . .

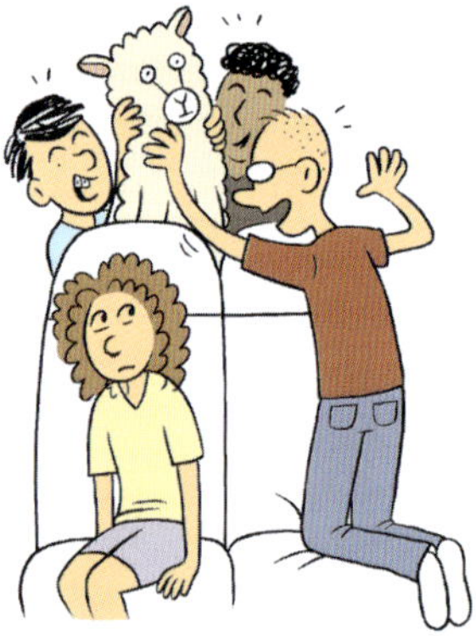

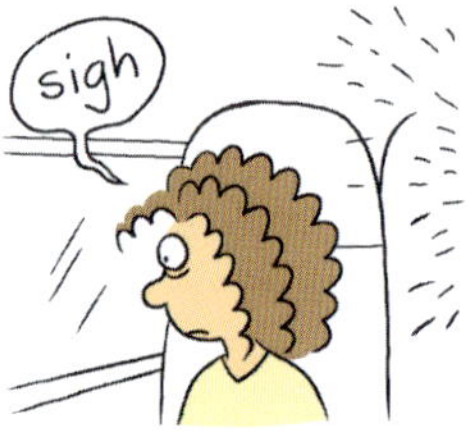
sigh

Back to same old.

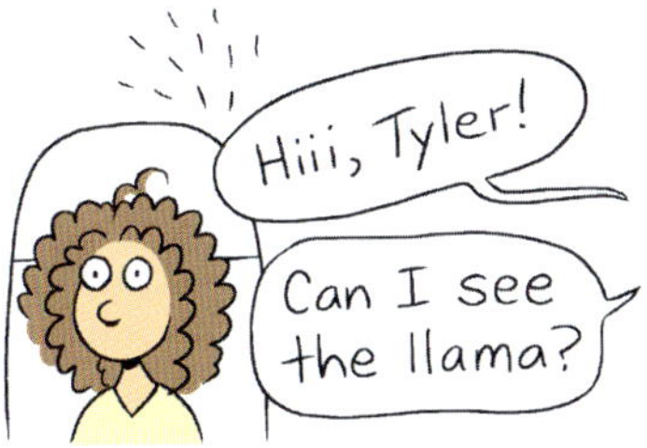
Hiii, Tyler!
Can I see the llama?

I turn around reflexively and catch a cute girl smiling at Tyler. I recognize her as someone on the girls' basketball team, but I can't remember her name. She's not in my classes. I do know she's kind of popular.

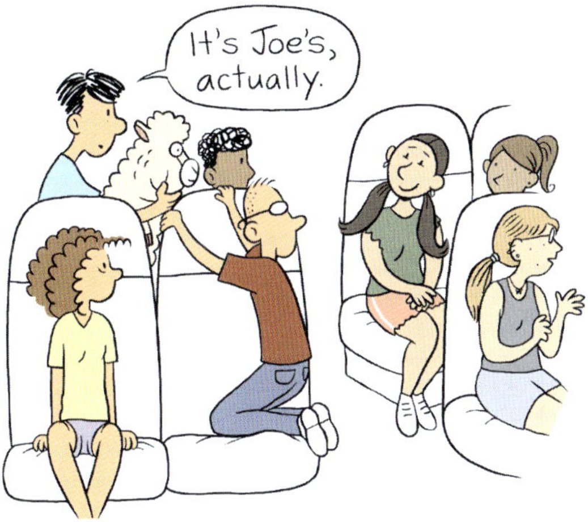
It's Joe's, actually.

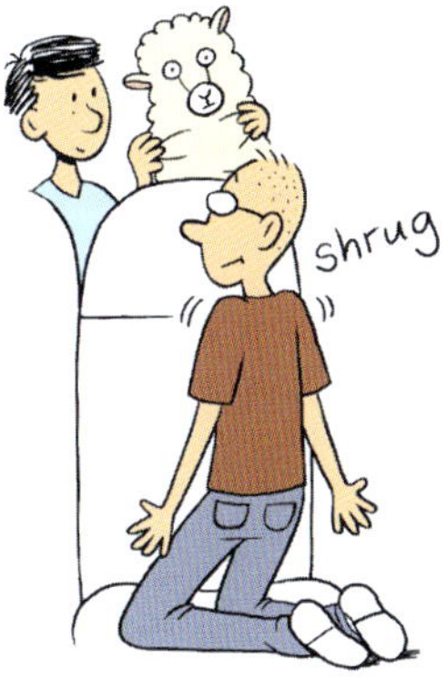
shrug

stomach squeezy again

"shriveled" and "un-juiced"

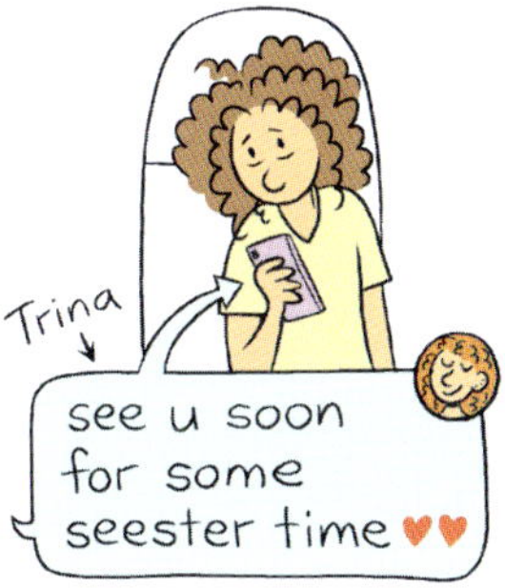
Trina
see u soon for some seester time ♥♥

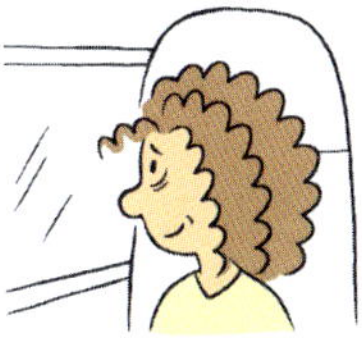

Somehow, Trina always knows when I need her.

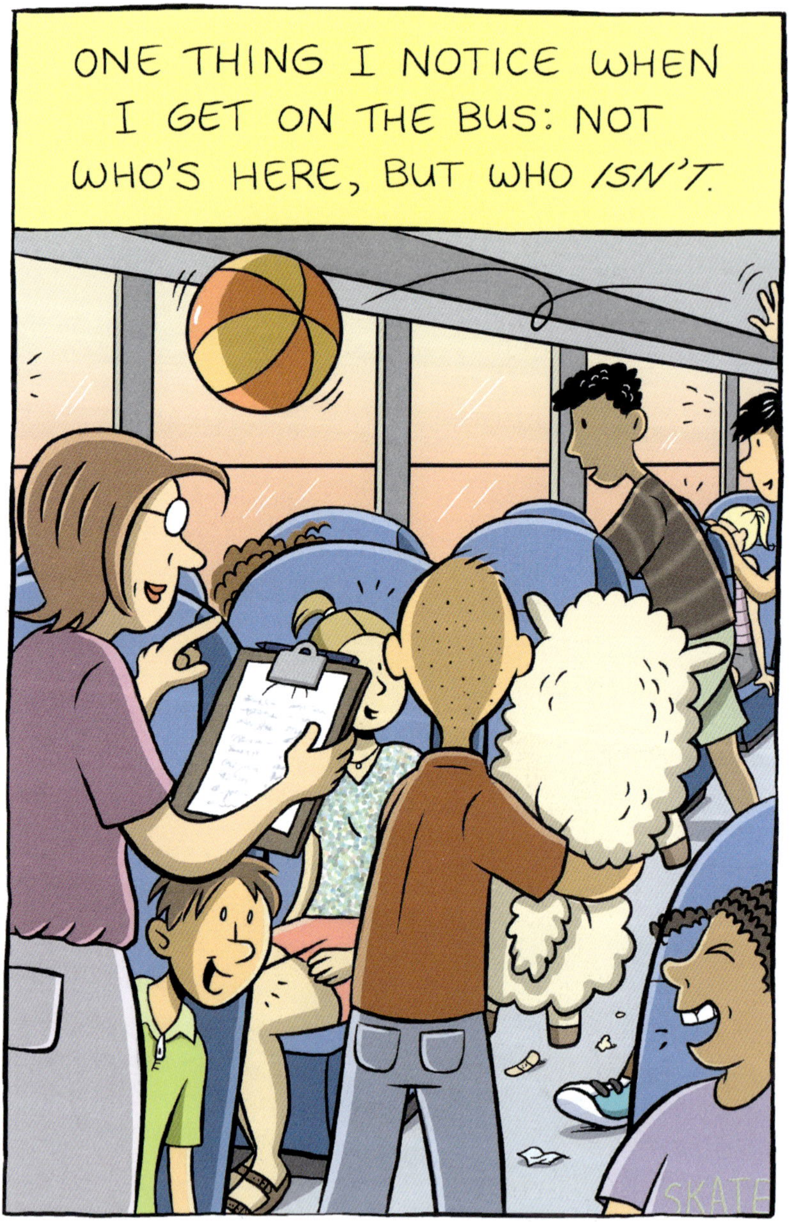
ONE THING I NOTICE WHEN I GET ON THE BUS: NOT WHO'S HERE, BUT WHO *ISN'T.*
SKATE

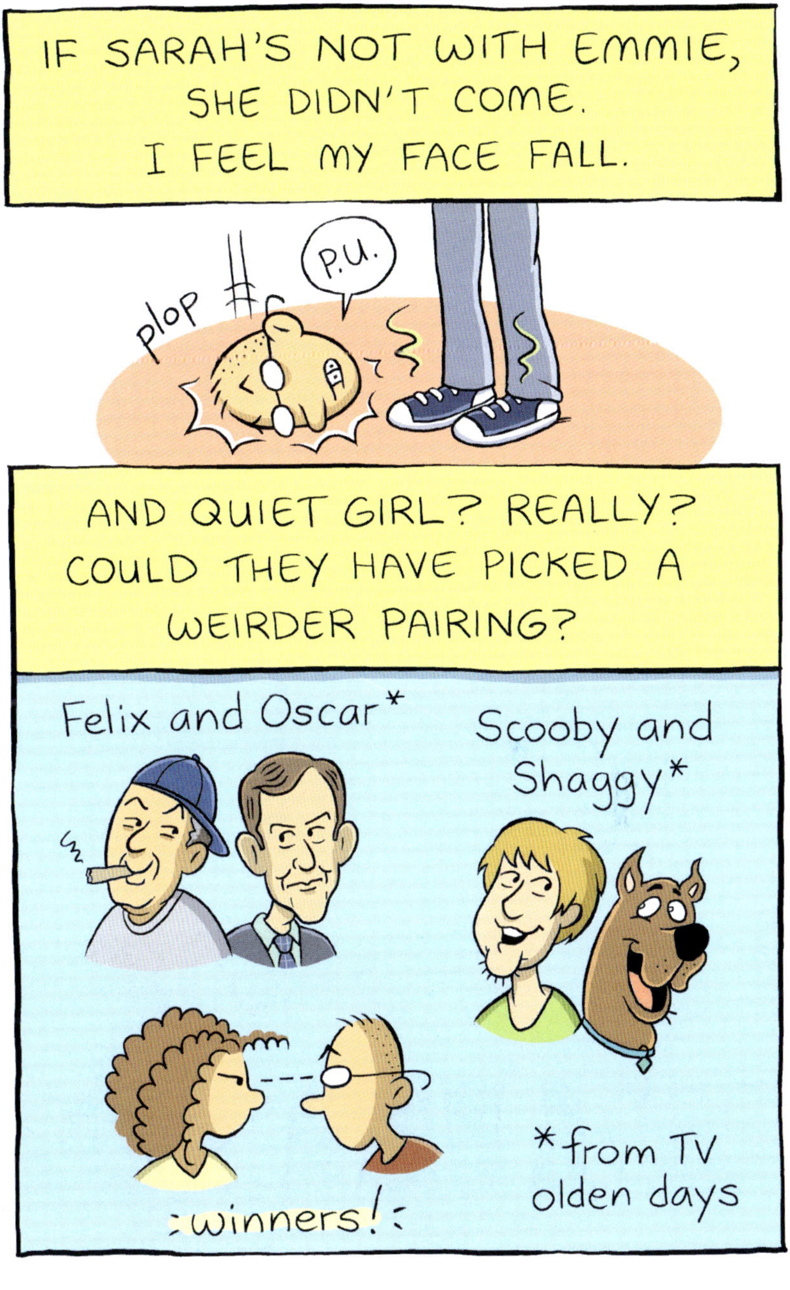
IF SARAH'S NOT WITH EMMIE, SHE DIDN'T COME. I FEEL MY FACE FALL.
plop
P.U.
AND QUIET GIRL? REALLY? COULD THEY HAVE PICKED A WEIRDER PAIRING?
Felix and Oscar*
Scooby and Shaggy*
winners!
*from TV olden days

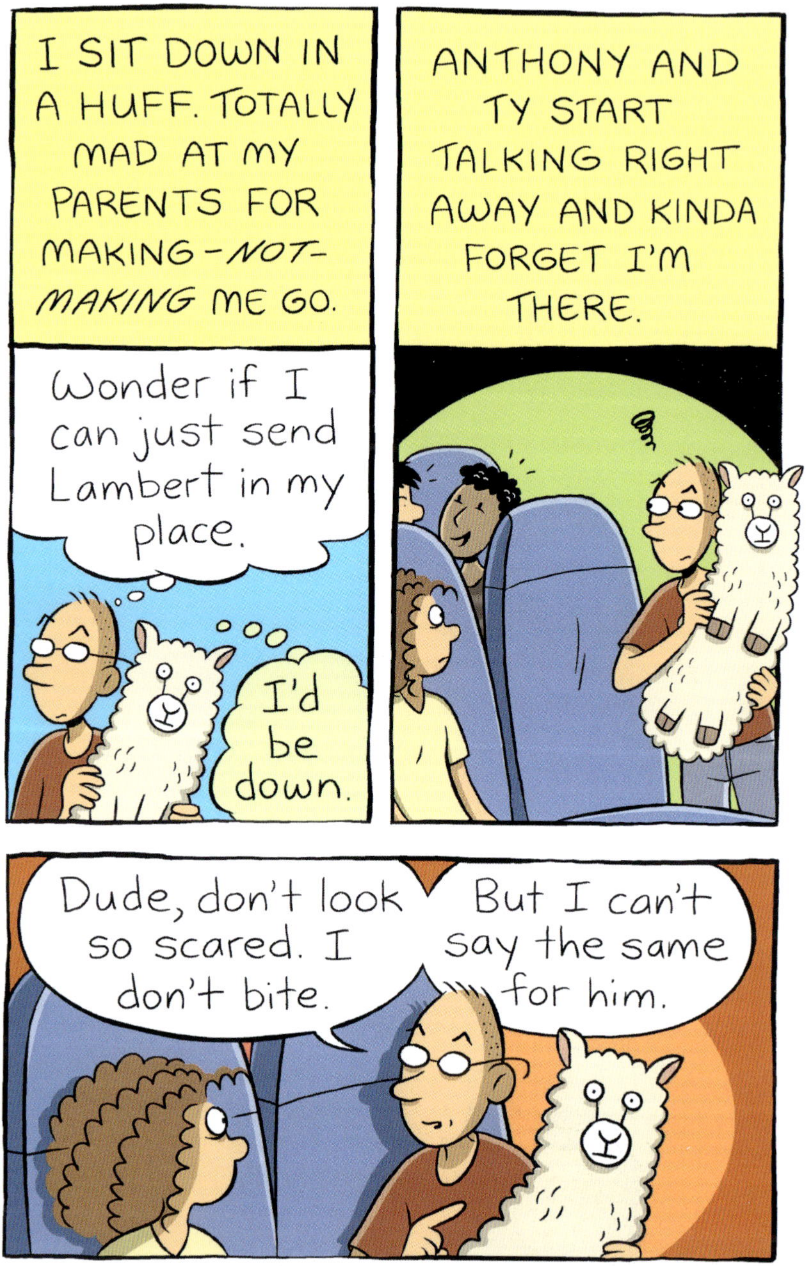
I SIT DOWN IN A HUFF. TOTALLY MAD AT MY PARENTS FOR MAKING—*NOT*-*MAKING* ME GO.
Wonder if I can just send Lambert in my place.
I'd be down.
ANTHONY AND TY START TALKING RIGHT AWAY AND KINDA FORGET I'M THERE.
Dude, don't look so scared. I don't bite.
But I can't say the same for him.

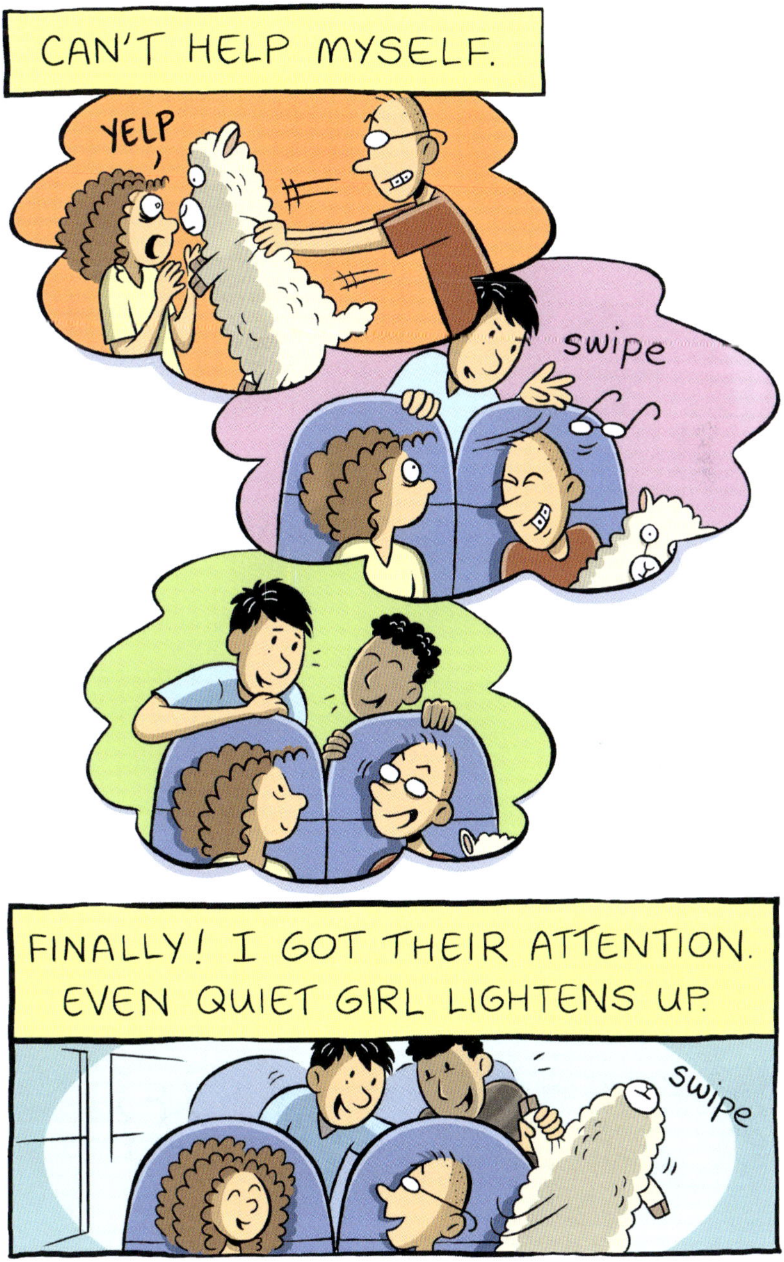
CAN'T HELP MYSELF.
YELP
swipe
FINALLY! I GOT THEIR ATTENTION. EVEN QUIET GIRL LIGHTENS UP.
swipe

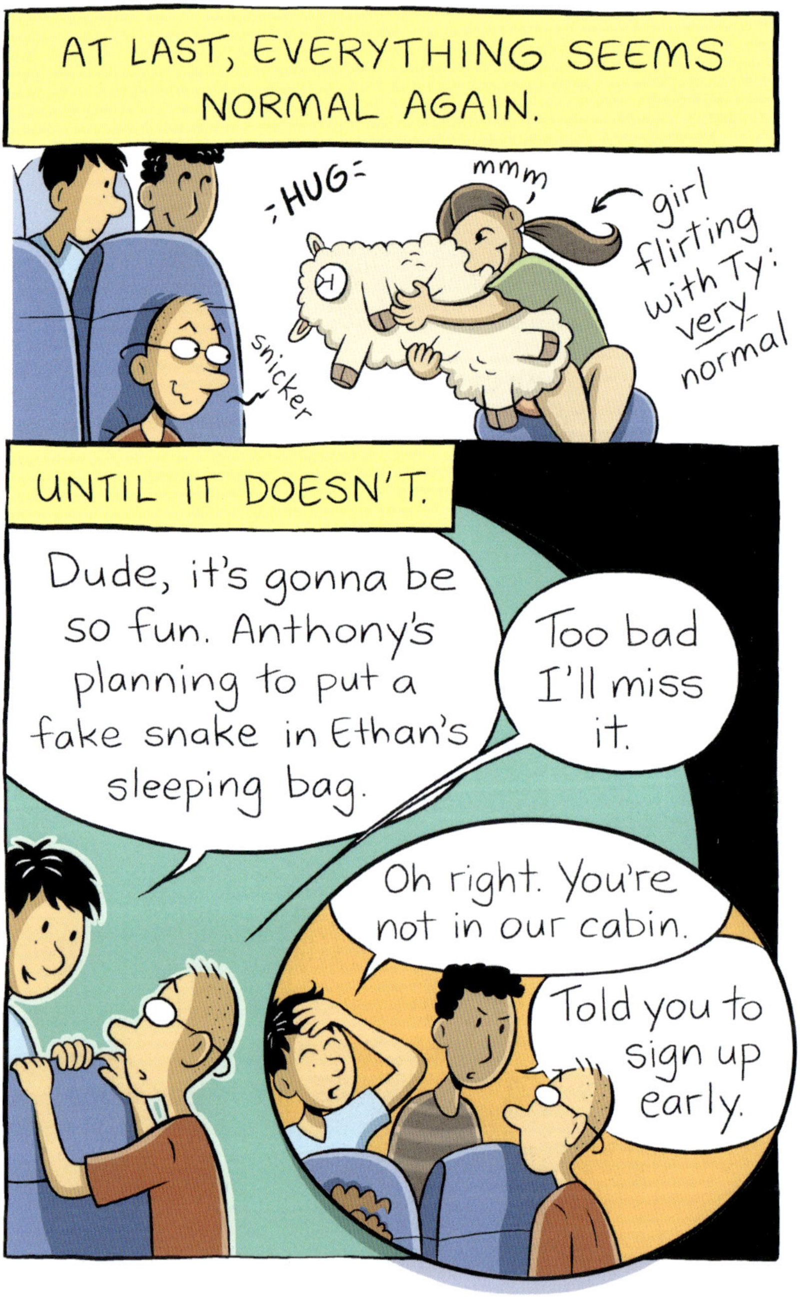
AT LAST, EVERYTHING SEEMS NORMAL AGAIN.
snicker
HUG
mmm
girl flirting with Ty: very normal
UNTIL IT DOESN'T.
Dude, it's gonna be so fun. Anthony's planning to put a fake snake in Ethan's sleeping bag.
Too bad I'll miss it.
Oh right. You're not in our cabin.
Told you to sign up early.

I DON'T POINT OUT THE OBVIOUS:

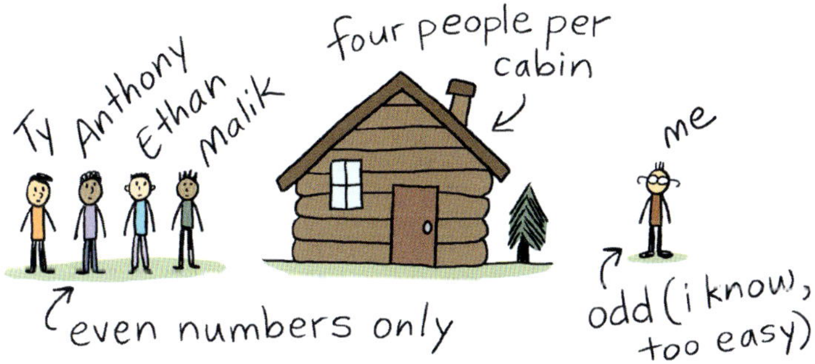
Ty
Anthony
Ethan
Malik
four people per cabin
me
even numbers only
odd (i know, too easy)

IT WOULDN'T HAVE MATTERED WHEN I'D SIGNED UP. IT WOULDN'T HAVE CHANGED ANYTHING.

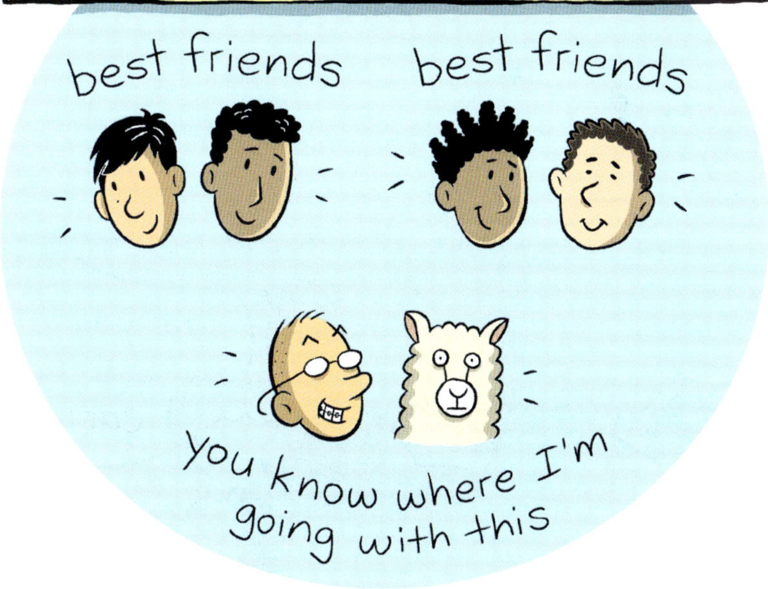
best friends
best friends
you know where I'm going with this

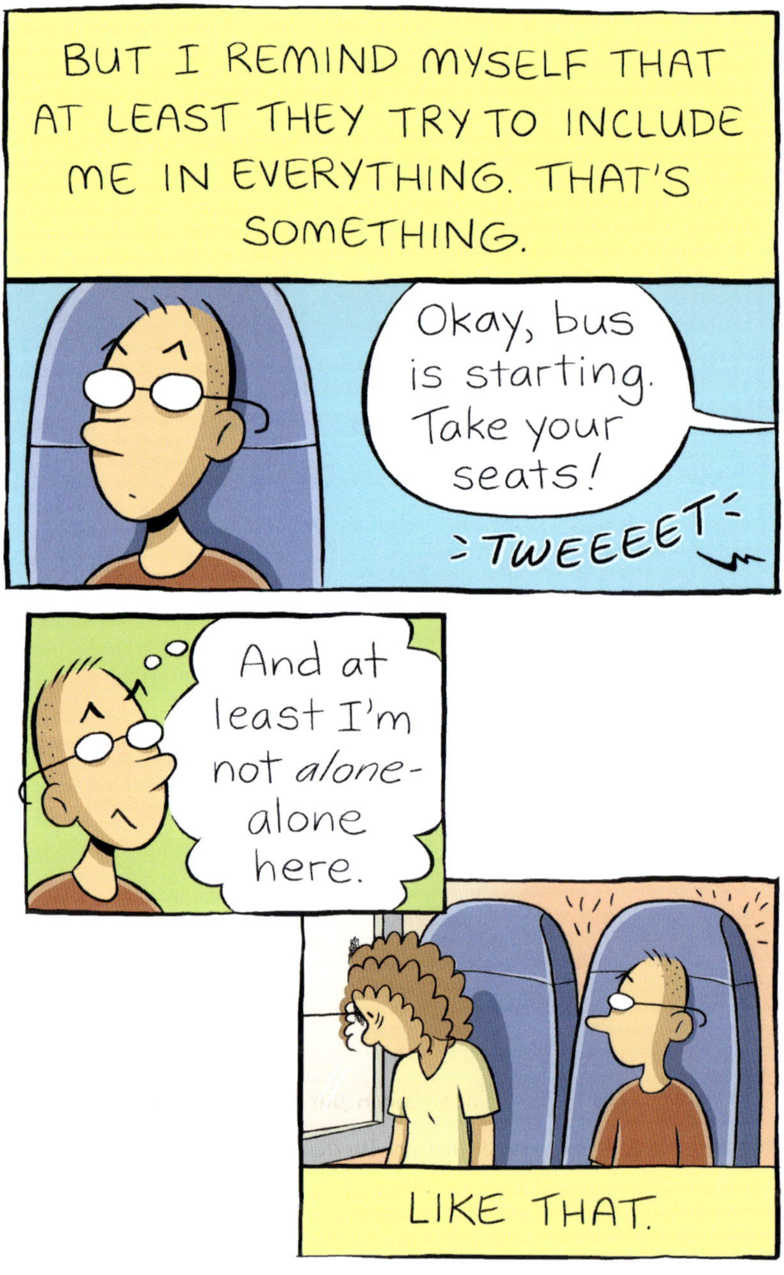
BUT I REMIND MYSELF THAT AT LEAST THEY TRY TO INCLUDE ME IN EVERYTHING. THAT'S SOMETHING.
Okay, bus is starting. Take your seats!
TWEEEEET
And at least I'm not *alone*-alone here.
LIKE THAT.

EMMIE

When we get to the campground (after the longest thirty-minute ride of my life), we pack into the mess hall and sit down at the tables. Mr. Bauman and Coach Durdle go over the rules and orientation. Then they have us take our bags to our assigned cabins.

There are a **lot** of cabins. Coach Durdle said this used to be a woodsy family retreat until they turned it into a camp. Now it's the biggest overnight camp in the region. I'm surprised my parents never sent me here—and also kinda relieved. I feel lost just in our **school**. Anyway, there are only four kids per cabin because—although there are plenty of 'em—they're kinda small.

Trina's in charge of our cabin and the one next to it. Right now, I think she's checking in with the other counselors. I'm the first one here; I don't know who else will show up.

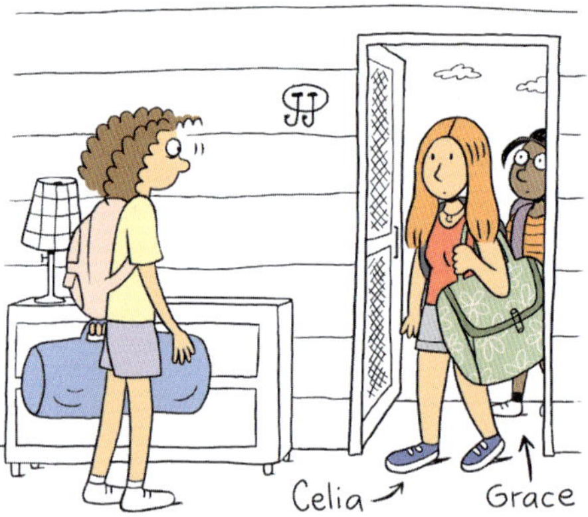
Celia
Grace

Are you kidding me??

They see me and Grace instantly stifles a snort.

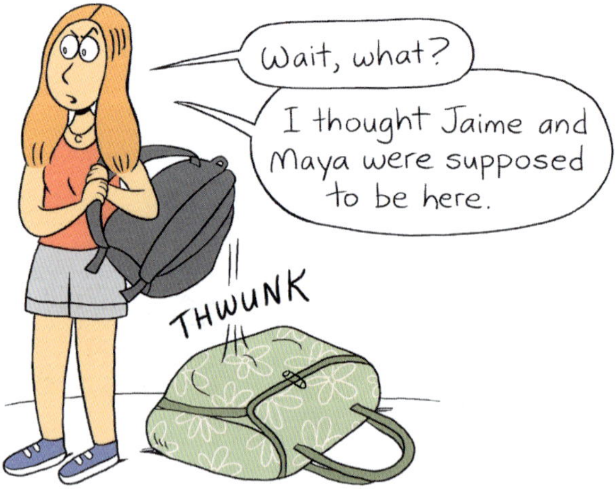
Wait, what?
I thought Jaime and Maya were supposed to be here.
THWUNK

I feel my cheeks get hot. There's no way I can stay with them. They'll eat me alive.

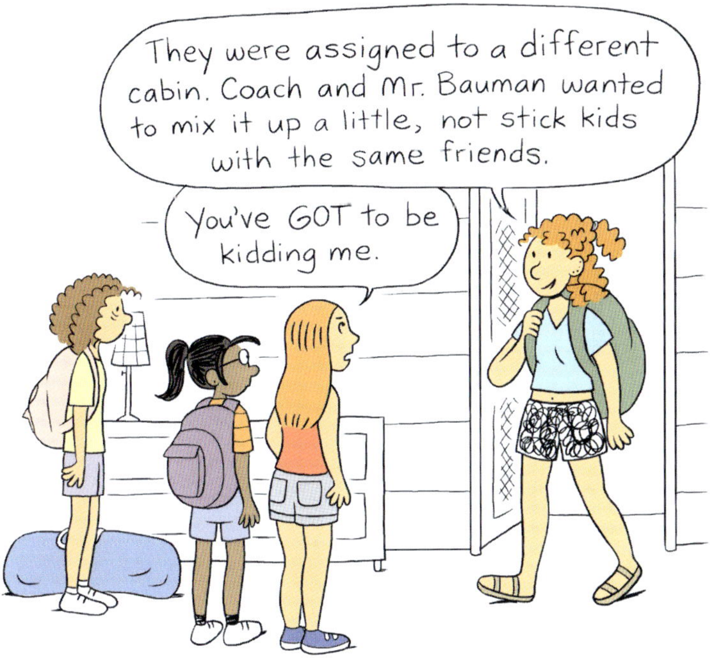
They were assigned to a different cabin. Coach and Mr. Bauman wanted to mix it up a little, not stick kids with the same friends.
You've GOT to be kidding me.

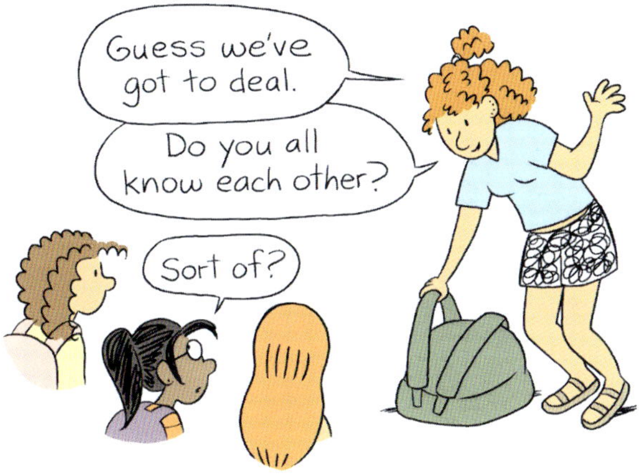
Guess we've got to deal.
Do you all know each other?
Sort of?

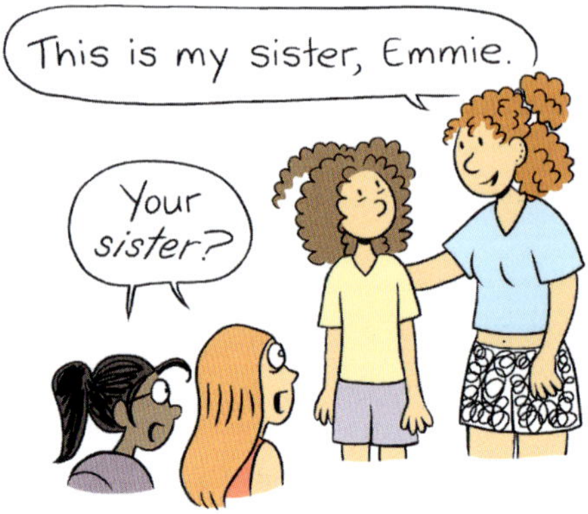
This is my sister, Emmie.
Your sister?

They say it like Trina is related to a three-headed sea slug.

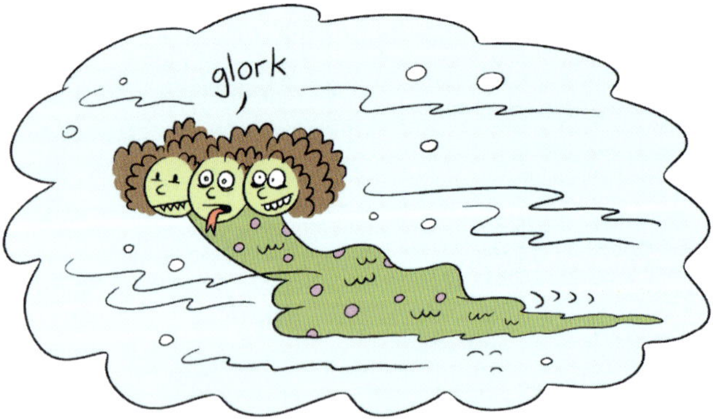
glork

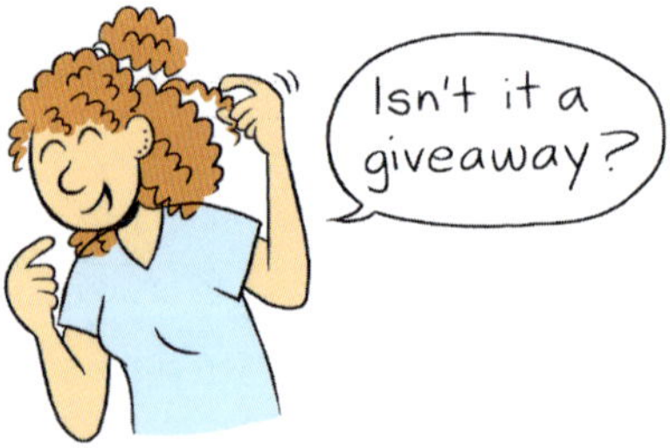
Isn't it a giveaway?

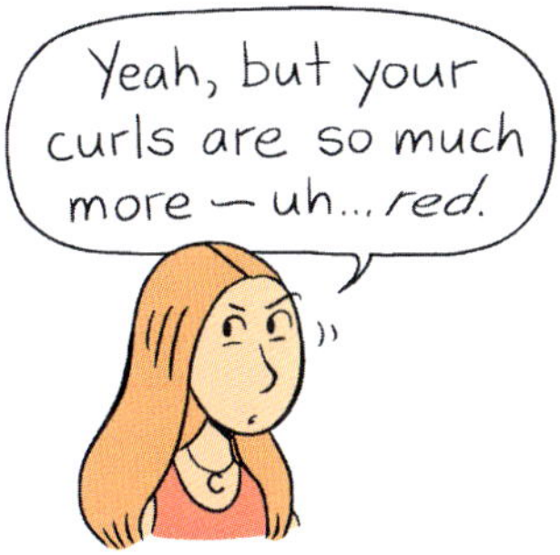
Yeah, but your curls are so much more — uh... *red.*

I know what she was about to say: "combed." Or something like that. As often as my mom and Trina try to pass along their curly hair products, nothing tames my wild mane.

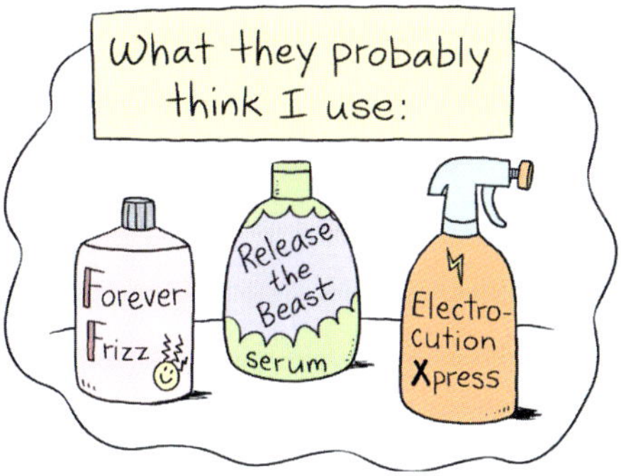
What they probably think I use:
Forever Frizz
Release the Beast Serum
Electro-cution Xpress

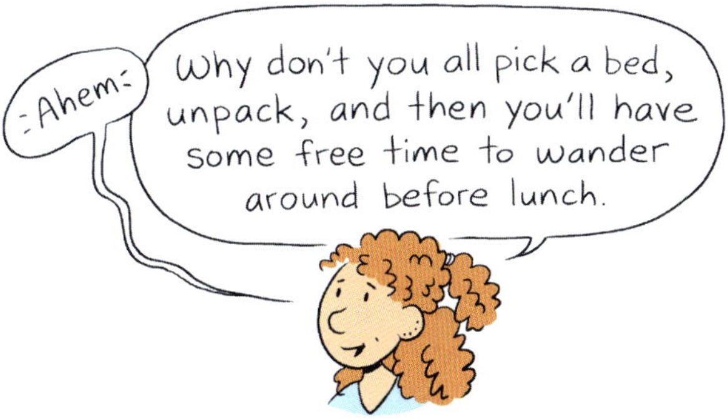
:Ahem:
Why don't you all pick a bed, unpack, and then you'll have some free time to wander around before lunch.

Before I can move, Celia grabs the top bunk near a window. Grace, who clearly has no choice, takes the bottom bunk. I'm left with the bunk next to the bathroom (I take the top). Trina's "official" bed is a cot in the sunroom, but since I'm partnerless, she takes the bottom bunk beneath me. Now I feel bad, 'cause she's closest to the stink zone.

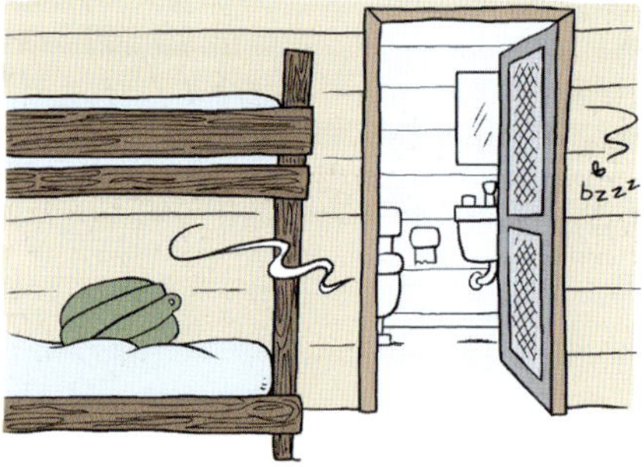
bzzz

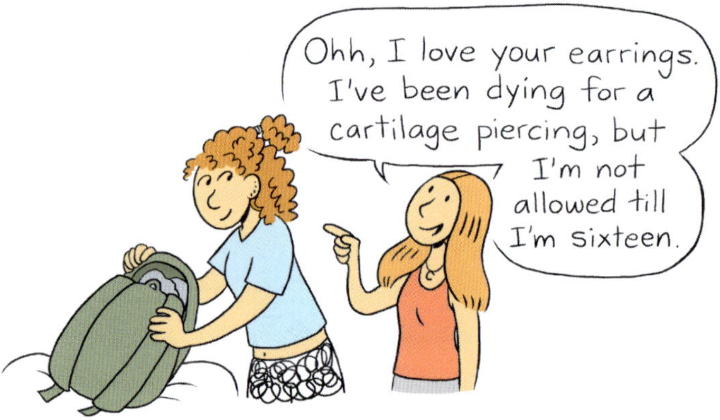
Ohh, I love your earrings. I've been dying for a cartilage piercing, but I'm not allowed till I'm sixteen.

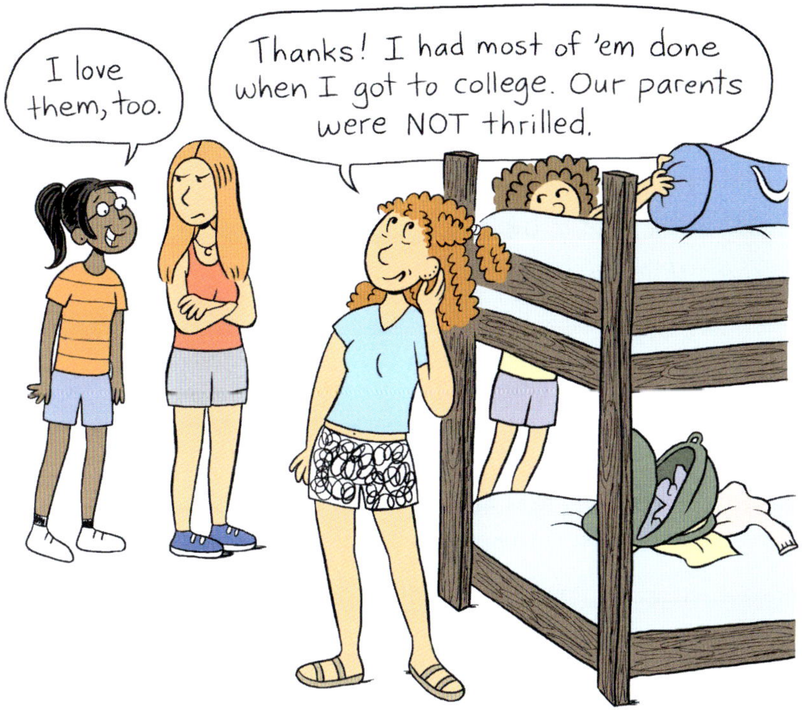
I love them, too.
Thanks! I had most of 'em done when I got to college. Our parents were NOT thrilled.

Celia throws me a surprised glance that says she's already forgotten we're sisters. I mean, I don't blame her. Trina and I are so different. She was always popular, even in middle school and high school. She is also kind and friendly, which is why she's well-liked. Tyler reminds me of her. I wonder what he's doing now . . . ?

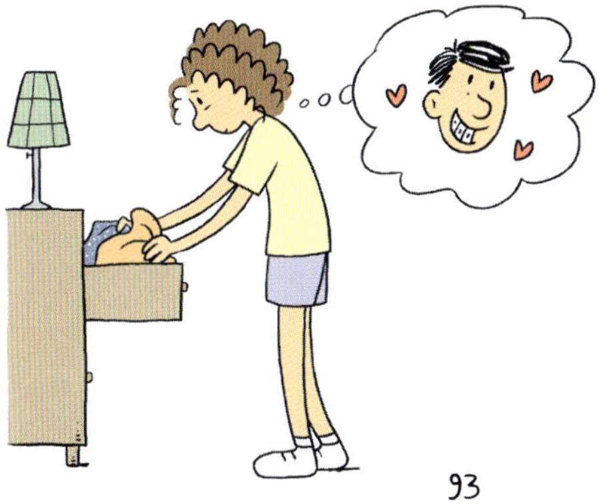

Celia and Grace pretty much ignore me and chat with Trina, who's clearly flattered to be the center of their attention. They gush all over her, going on about her makeup (which I'm pretty sure she's not wearing), her awesome hair, her cool clothes.

I am invisible once again.

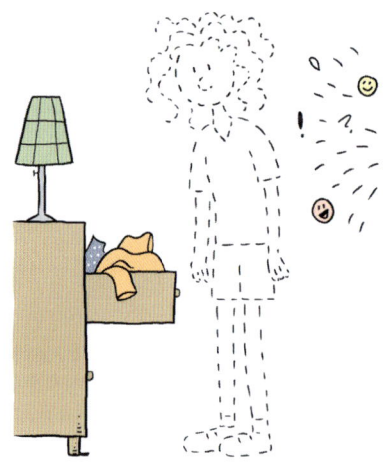

Maybe it's better this way. I just don't fit in. I decide to escape and explore a little.

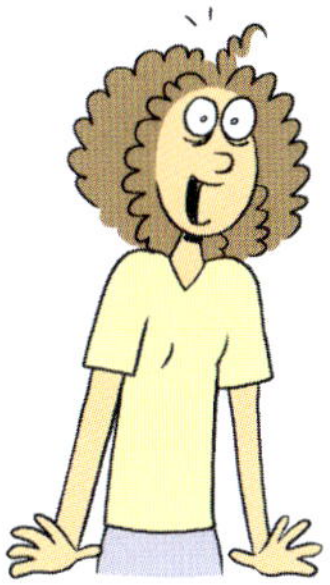

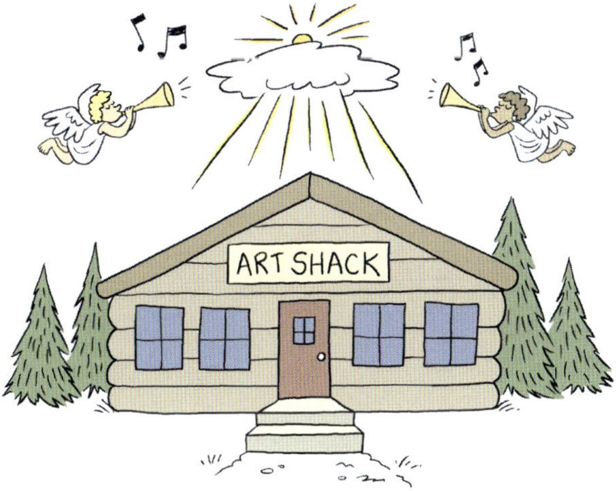
ART SHACK

Excited, I make a beeline.

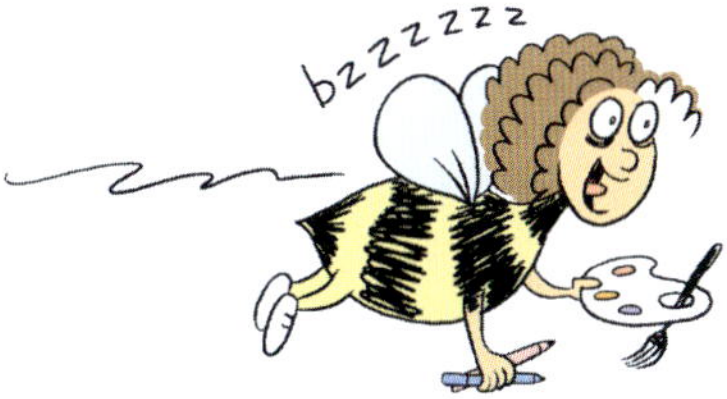
bzzzzzzz

As I practically hurl myself toward the shack, I catch a glimpse of (**gasp!**) Tyler heading there from an opposite path. He spots me, smiles, and trots in my direction. He actually looks excited to see me. I light up from inside.

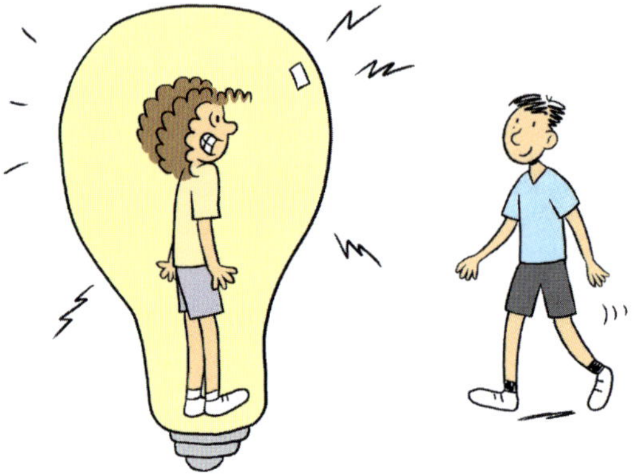

But then . . .

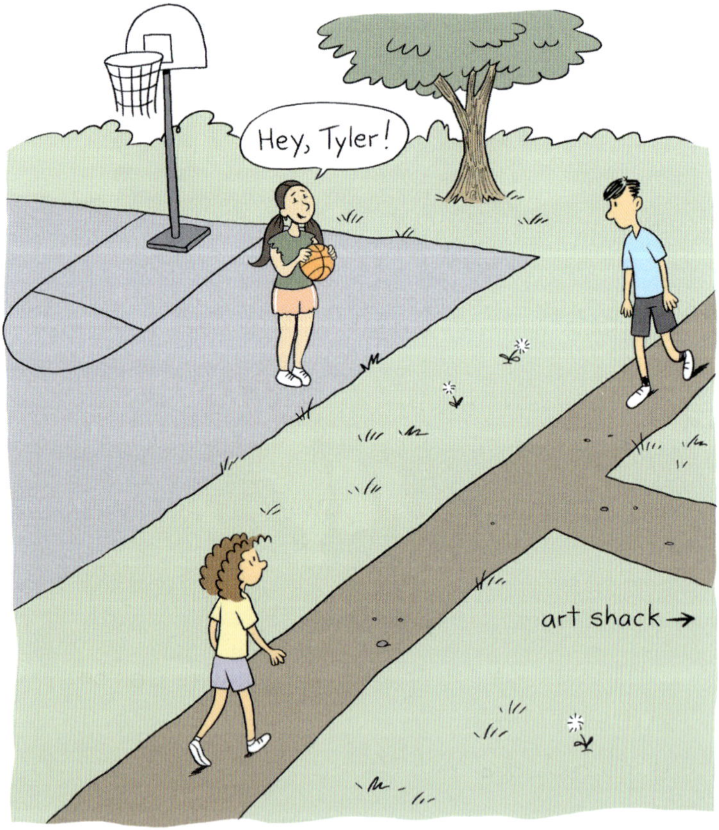
Hey, Tyler!
art shack →

Wanna shoot some hoops?

hair blowing (in no breeze)
braces sparkling
eyes batting (well, they may as well be)

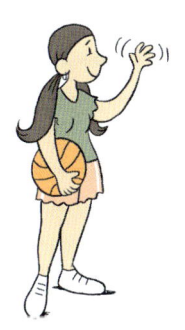

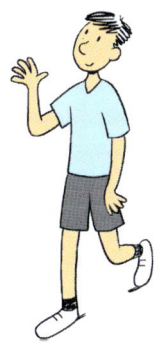

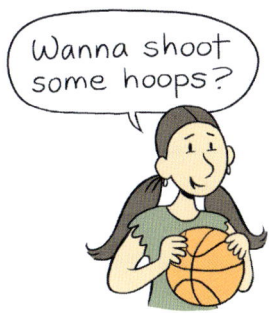

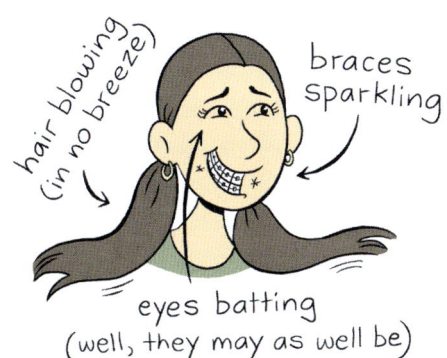

Tyler glances back at me and then at her.

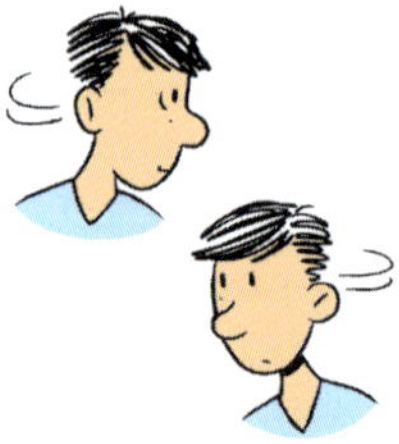

The girl dribbles the ball a few times and smiles again.

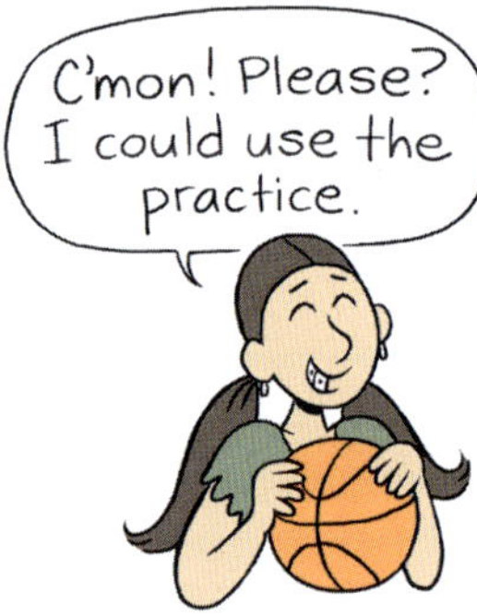
C'mon! Please? I could use the practice.

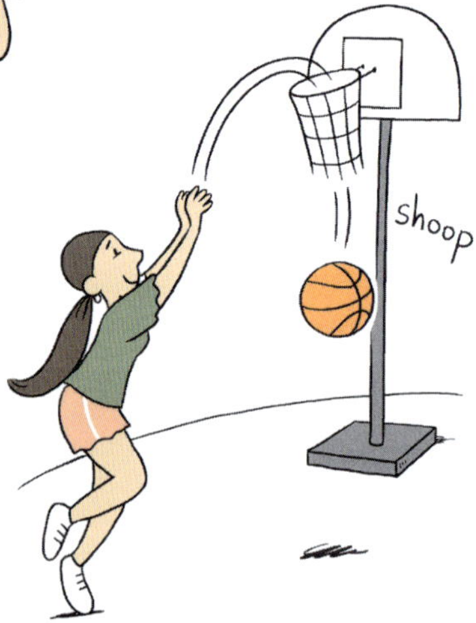
shoop

Right. She clearly needs help.

Tyler doesn't move. The girl dribbles louder, like she's beckoning him with the basketball.

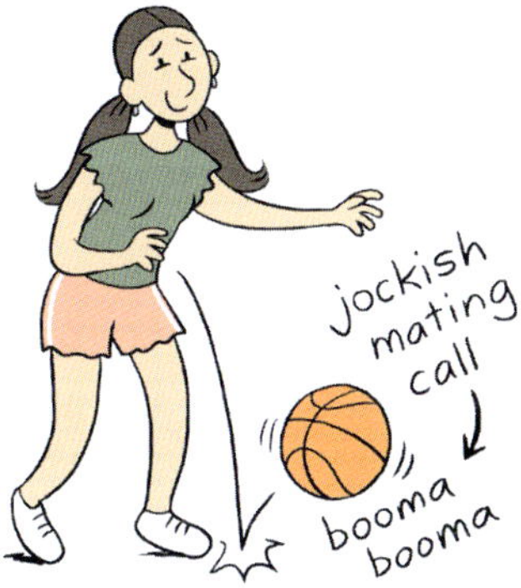
jockish mating call
booma booma

After some final hesitation, Tyler shrugs at me, like, "What can I do?" and takes off in her direction.

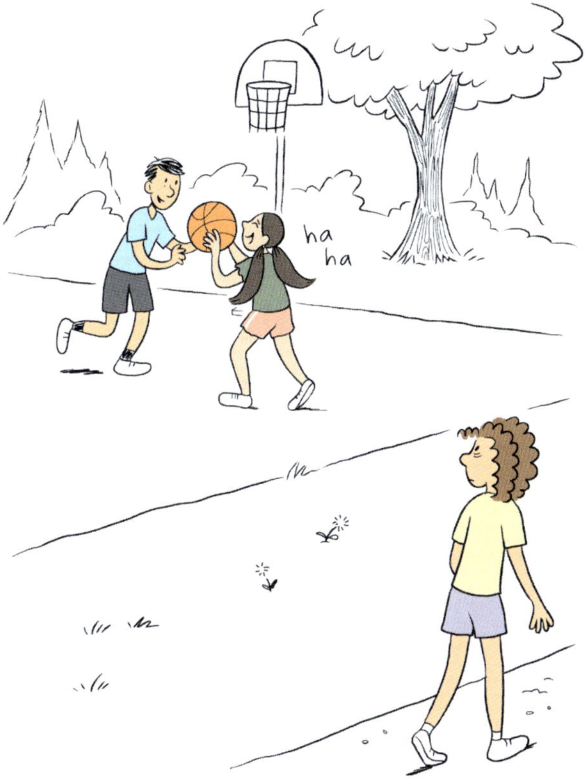
ha ha

Why don't I ever learn? This school is too cliquey. Even if—by some miracle—Tyler liked me, everything would get in our way.

Like **cute basketball girls.**

Inside, the building is larger than it looks. There are low shelves everywhere and lots of wooden tables. Art supplies are stacked in neat bins on the shelves. Screened windows line the walls above. Some ceiling fans swish overhead.

I find a pair of scissors and construction paper in different colors. Maybe I'll make a cut paper design, kind of like Matisse. He's one of my very favorite artists besides Paul Klee* and Yayoi Kusama.*

*Look 'em up. It's worth it.

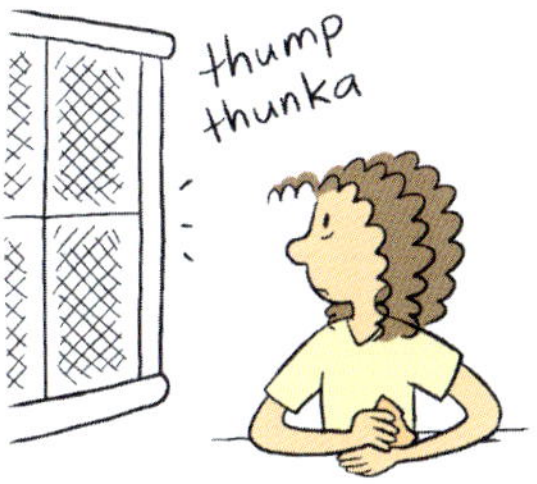
thump
thunka

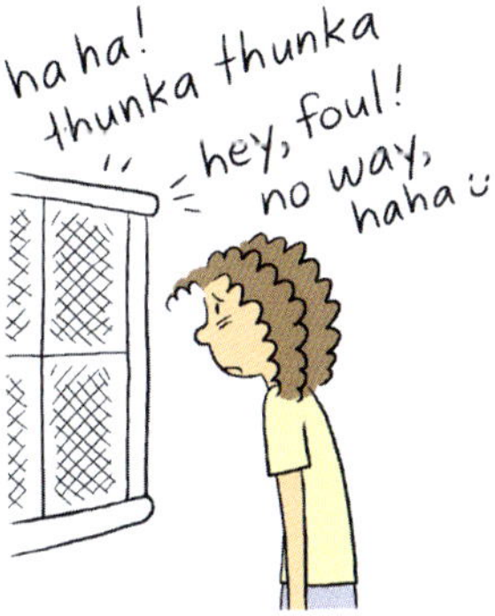
haha!
thunka thunka
hey, foul!
no way,
haha

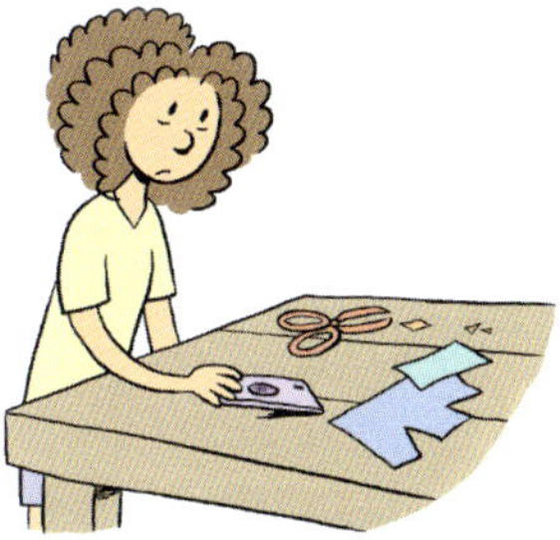

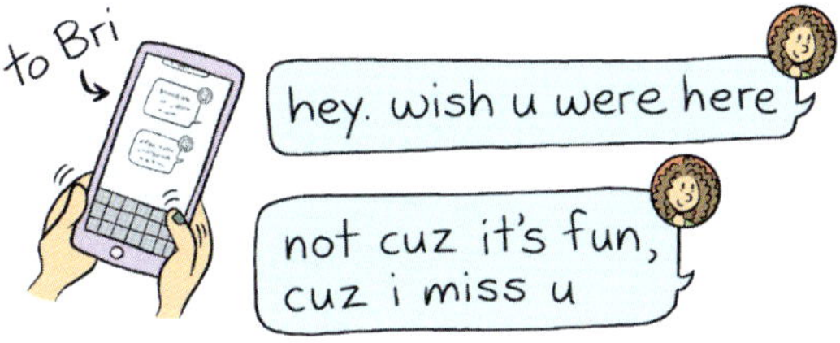
to Bri
hey. wish u were here
not cuz it's fun,
cuz i miss u

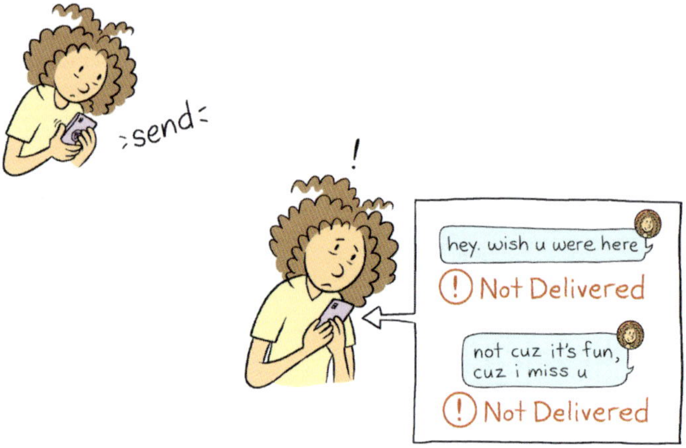
send
!
hey. wish u were here
Not Delivered
not cuz it's fun, cuz i miss u
Not Delivered

The Wi-Fi! I forgot it barely exists here in no-(wo)-man's-land.

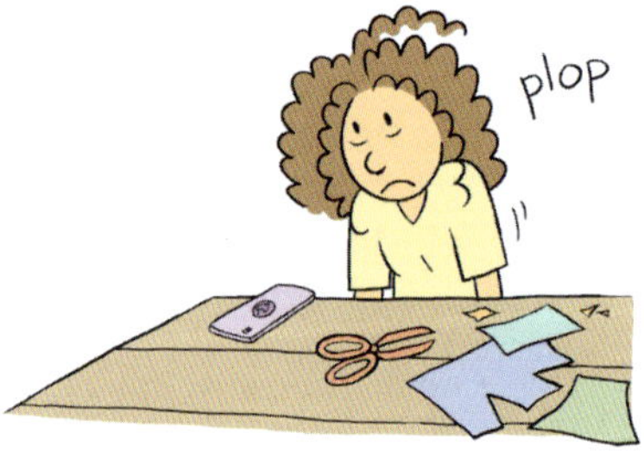
plop

Why did I come?

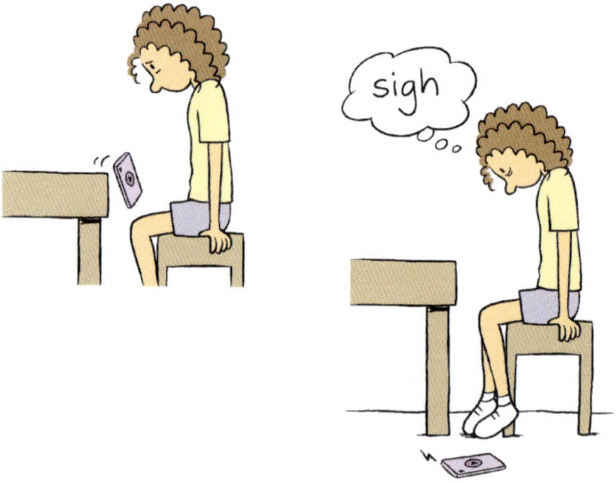
sigh

Joe

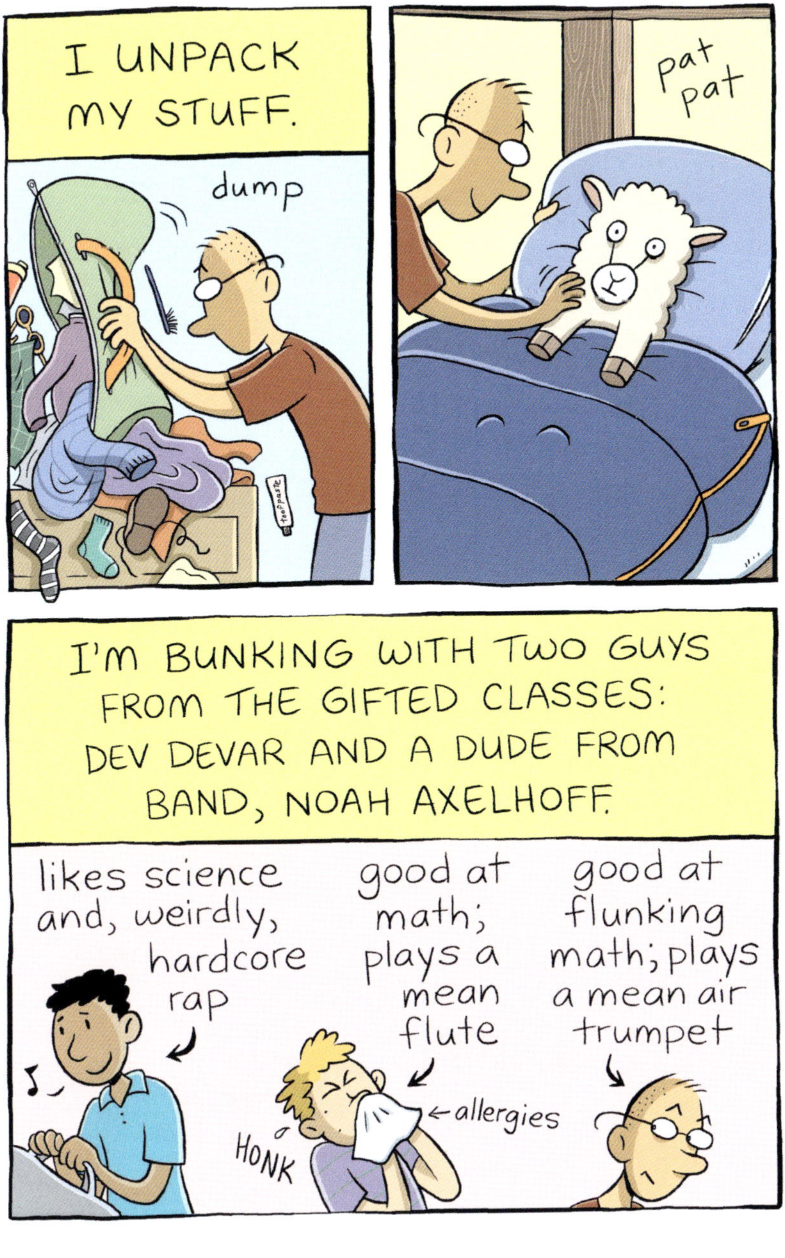
I UNPACK MY STUFF.
dump
toothpaste
pat pat
I'M BUNKING WITH TWO GUYS FROM THE GIFTED CLASSES: DEV DEVAR AND A DUDE FROM BAND, NOAH AXELHOFF.
likes science and, weirdly, hardcore rap
good at math; plays a mean flute
good at flunking math; plays a mean air trumpet
allergies
HONK

NERDS FOR SURE, BUT IT'S NOT LIKE I'M GONNA SPEND ANY TIME HERE EXCEPT TO SLEEP.

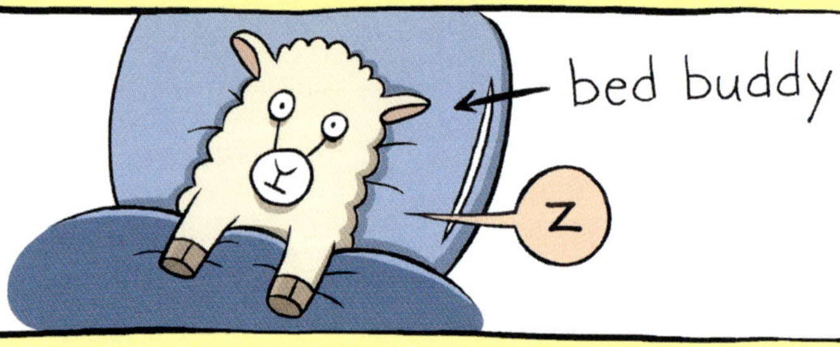

bed buddy
Z

TURNS OUT, TY AND ANTHONY AREN'T BUNKING WITH MALIK AND ETHAN AFTER ALL. THE POWERS THAT BE ARE MIXIN' IT UP, LIKE A BIG SCIENCE EXPERIMENT.

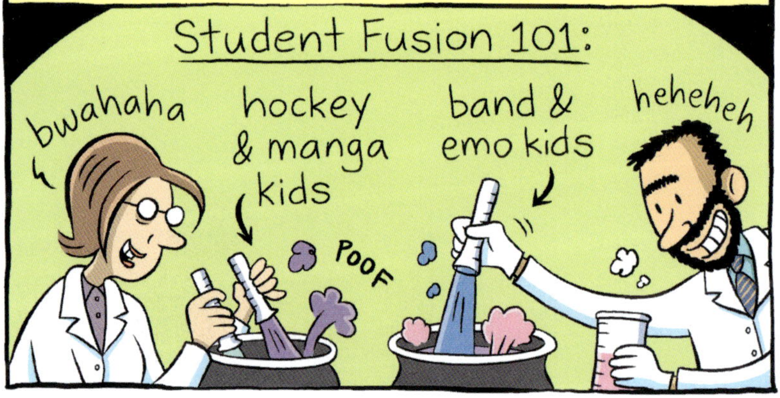

Student Fusion 101:
bwahaha
hockey & manga kids
band & emo kids
heheheh
POOF

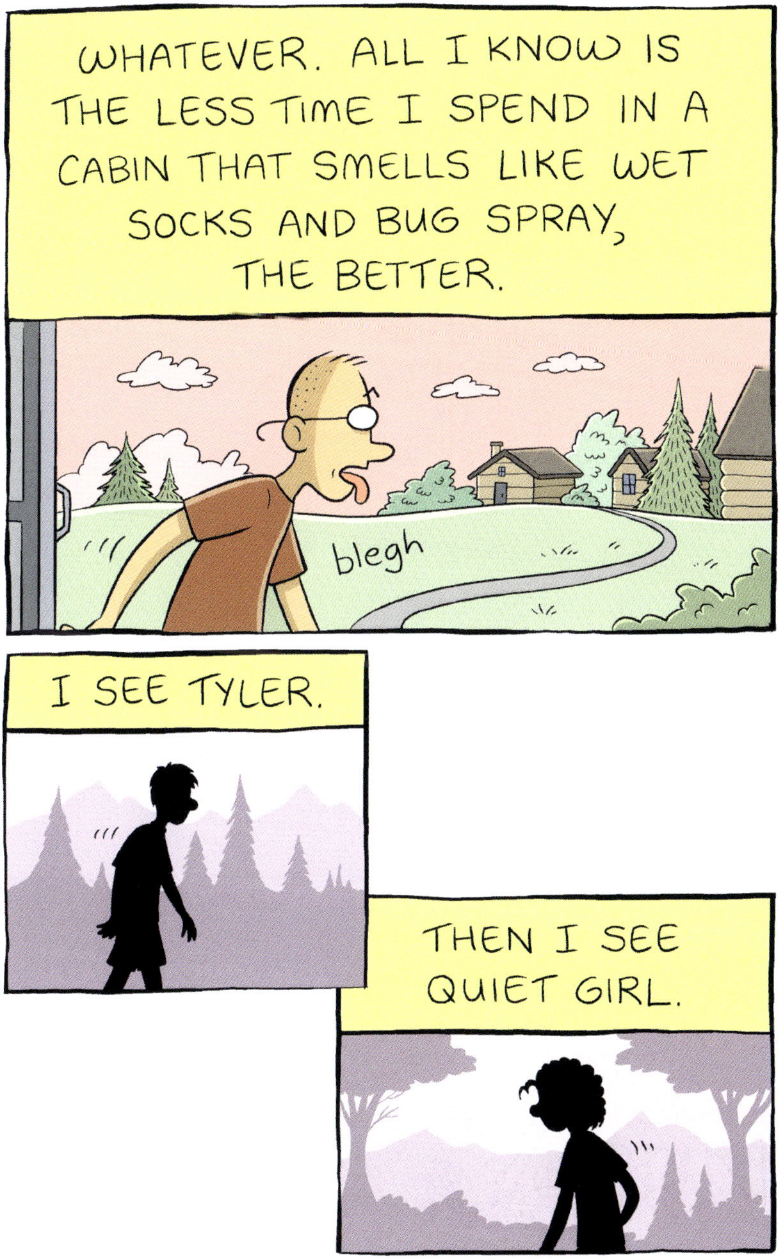
WHATEVER. ALL I KNOW IS THE LESS TIME I SPEND IN A CABIN THAT SMELLS LIKE WET SOCKS AND BUG SPRAY, THE BETTER.
blegh
I SEE TYLER.
THEN I SEE QUIET GIRL.

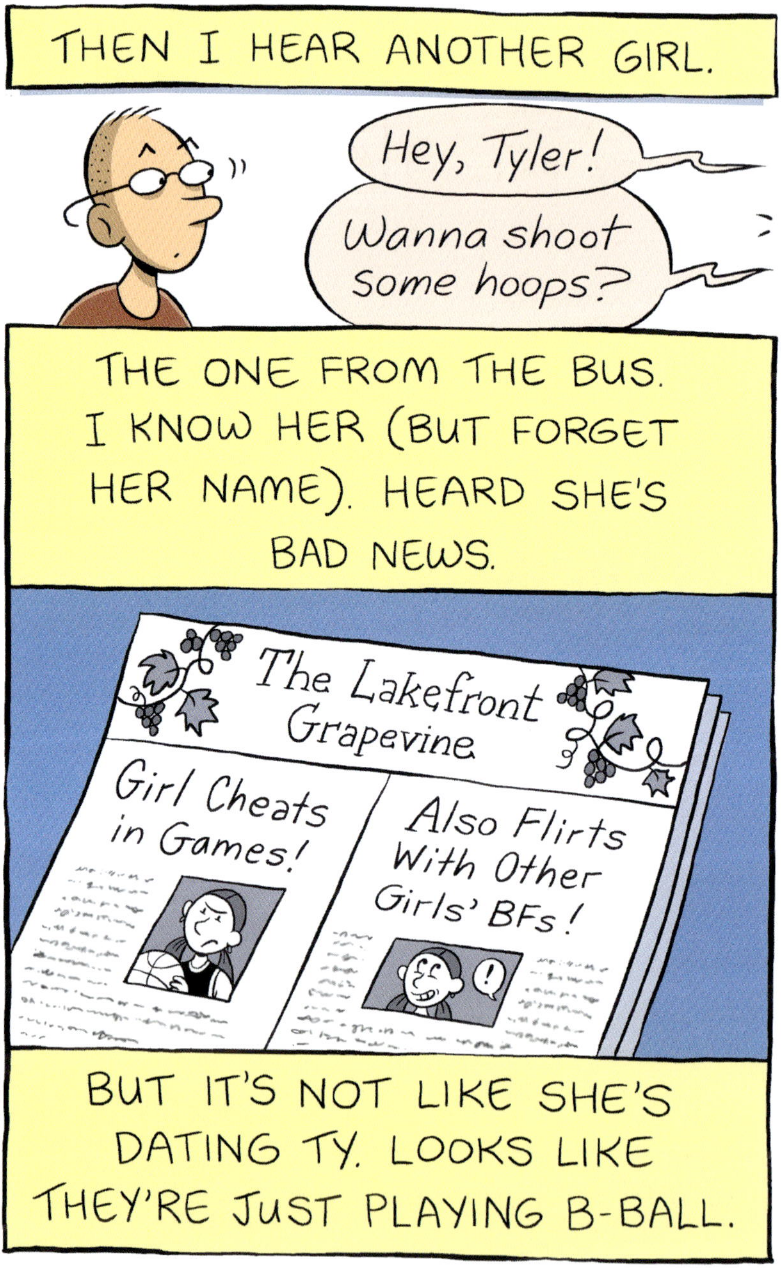

THEN I HEAR ANOTHER GIRL.
Hey, Tyler!
Wanna shoot some hoops?
THE ONE FROM THE BUS. I KNOW HER (BUT FORGET HER NAME). HEARD SHE'S BAD NEWS.
The Lakefront Grapevine
Girl Cheats in Games!
Also Flirts With Other Girls' BFs!
!
BUT IT'S NOT LIKE SHE'S DATING TY. LOOKS LIKE THEY'RE JUST PLAYING B-BALL.

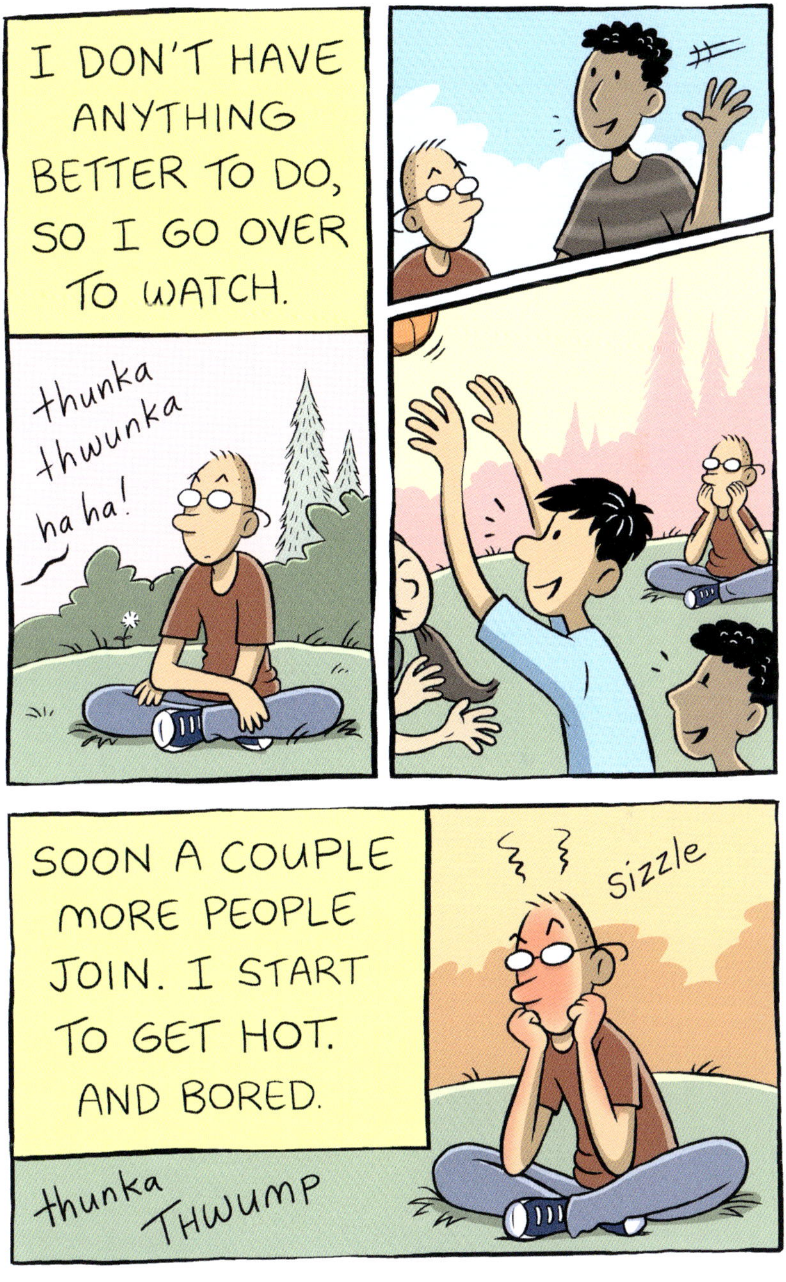
I DON'T HAVE ANYTHING BETTER TO DO, SO I GO OVER TO WATCH.
thunka thwunka
ha ha!
SOON A COUPLE MORE PEOPLE JOIN. I START TO GET HOT. AND BORED.
sizzle
thunka THWUMP

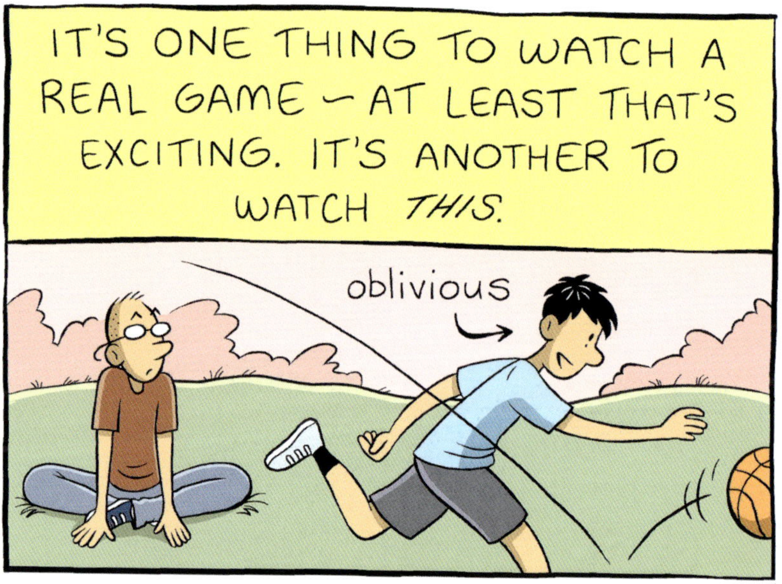
IT'S ONE THING TO WATCH A REAL GAME — AT LEAST THAT'S EXCITING. IT'S ANOTHER TO WATCH *THIS*.
oblivious

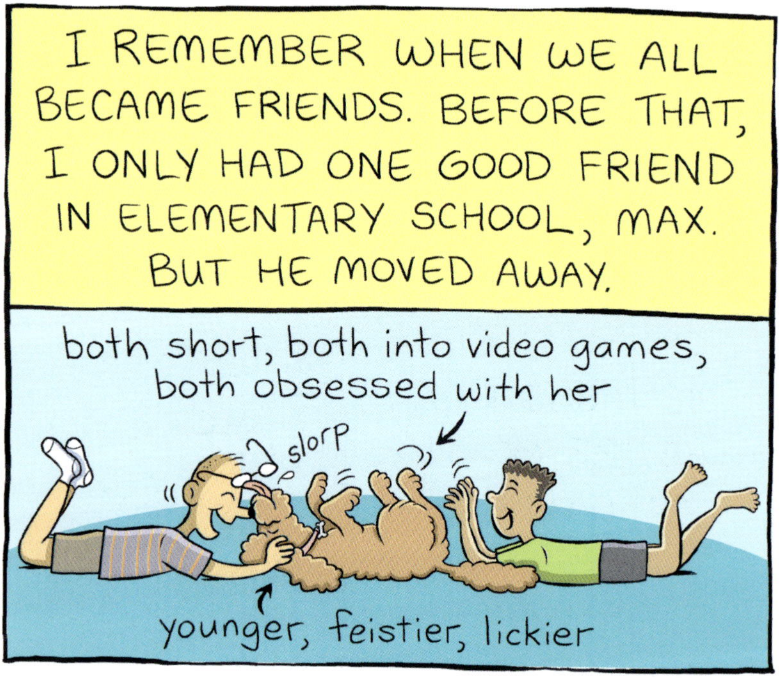
I REMEMBER WHEN WE ALL BECAME FRIENDS. BEFORE THAT, I ONLY HAD ONE GOOD FRIEND IN ELEMENTARY SCHOOL, MAX. BUT HE MOVED AWAY.
both short, both into video games, both obsessed with her
slorp
younger, feistier, lickier

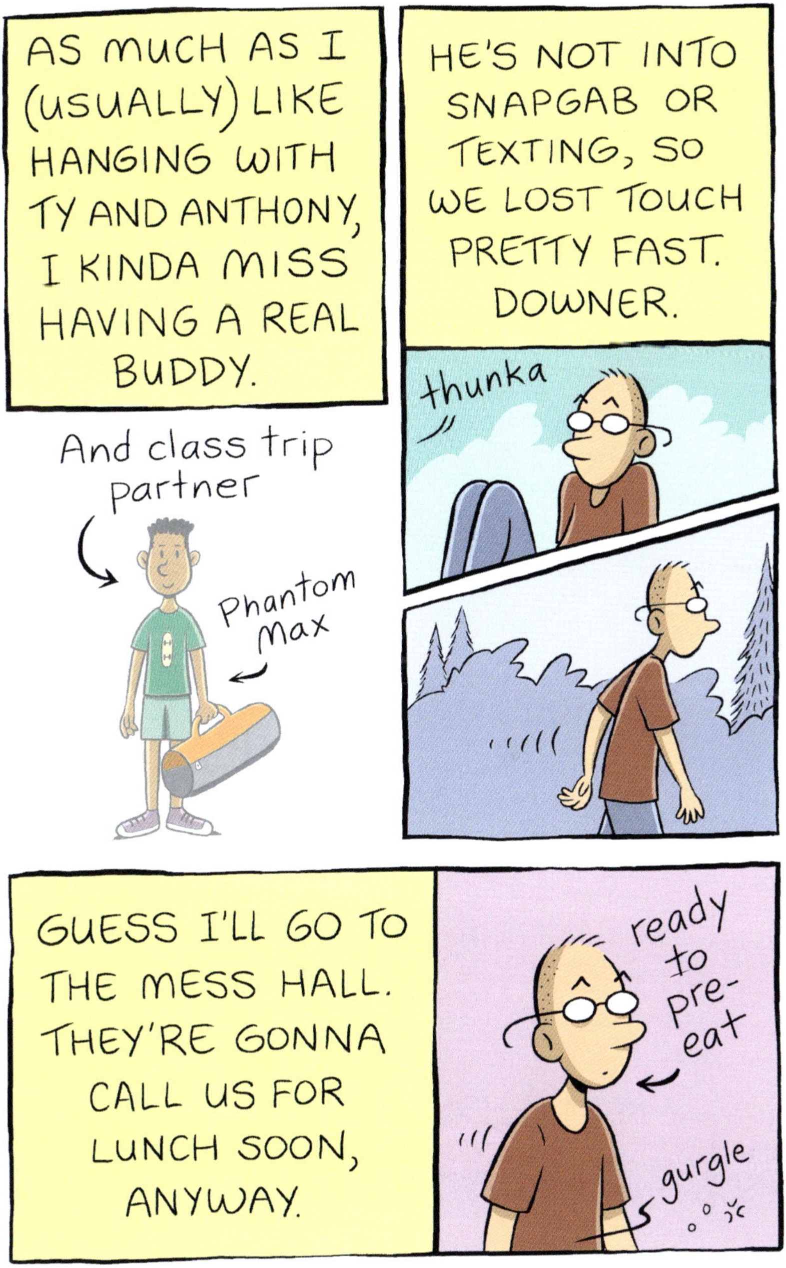
AS MUCH AS I (USUALLY) LIKE HANGING WITH TY AND ANTHONY, I KINDA MISS HAVING A REAL BUDDY.
HE'S NOT INTO SNAPGAB OR TEXTING, SO WE LOST TOUCH PRETTY FAST. DOWNER.
And class trip partner
Phantom Max
thunka
GUESS I'LL GO TO THE MESS HALL. THEY'RE GONNA CALL US FOR LUNCH SOON, ANYWAY.
ready to pre-eat
gurgle

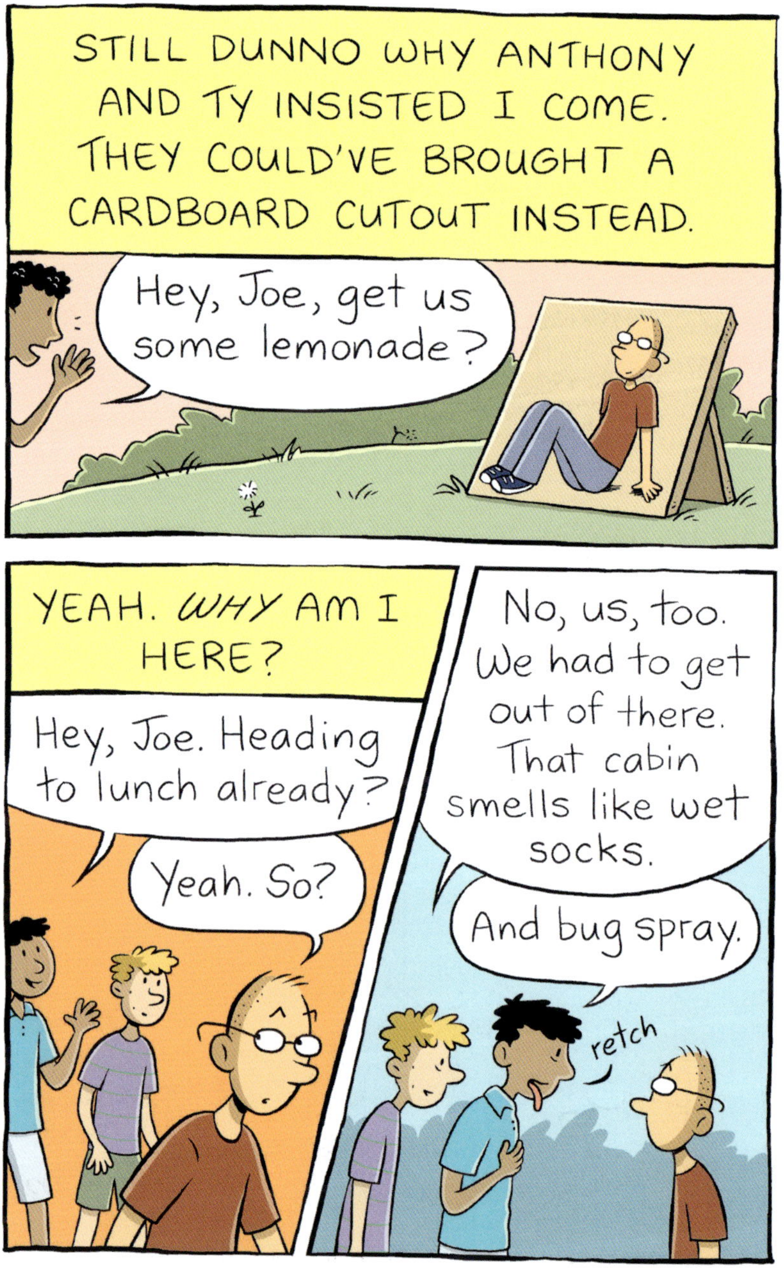
STILL DUNNO WHY ANTHONY AND TY INSISTED I COME. THEY COULD'VE BROUGHT A CARDBOARD CUTOUT INSTEAD.
Hey, Joe, get us some lemonade?
YEAH. *WHY* AM I HERE?
Hey, Joe. Heading to lunch already?
Yeah. So?
No, us, too. We had to get out of there. That cabin smells like wet socks.
And bug spray.
retch

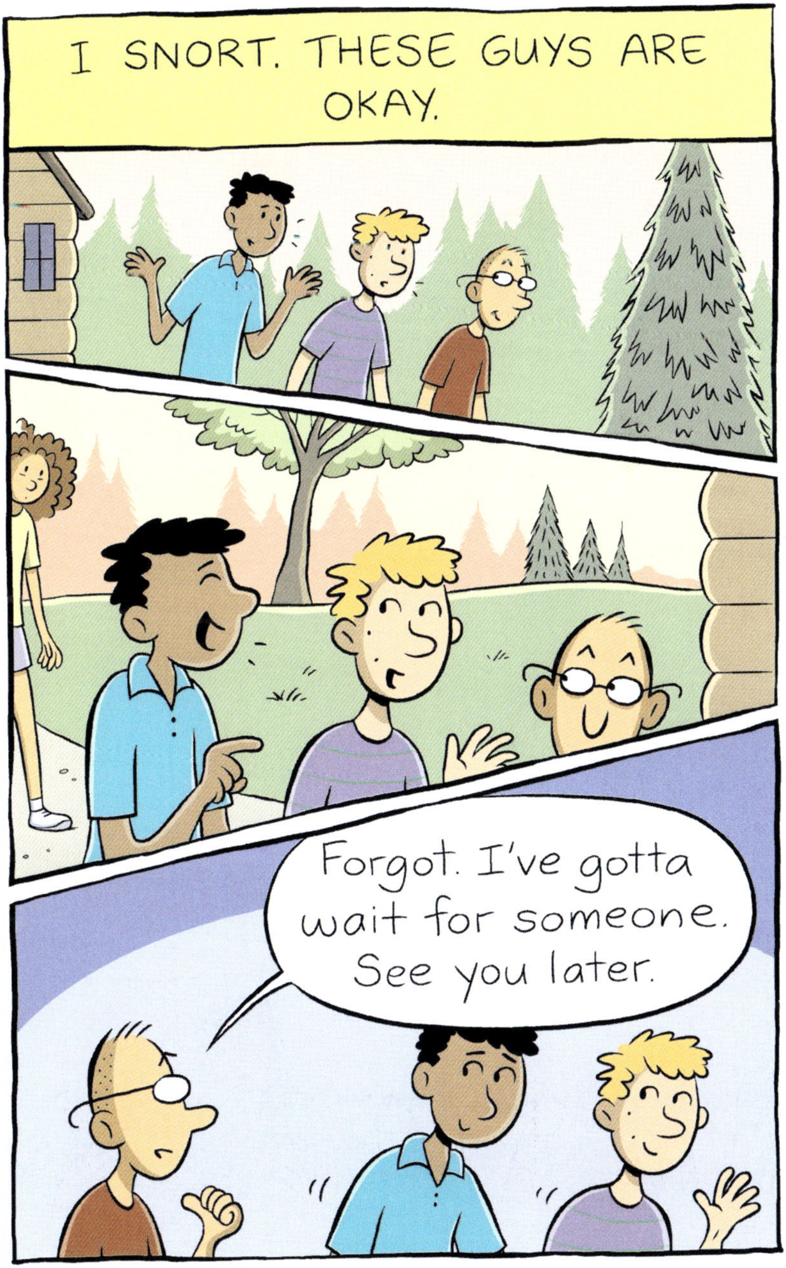
I SNORT. THESE GUYS ARE OKAY.
Forgot. I've gotta wait for someone. See you later.

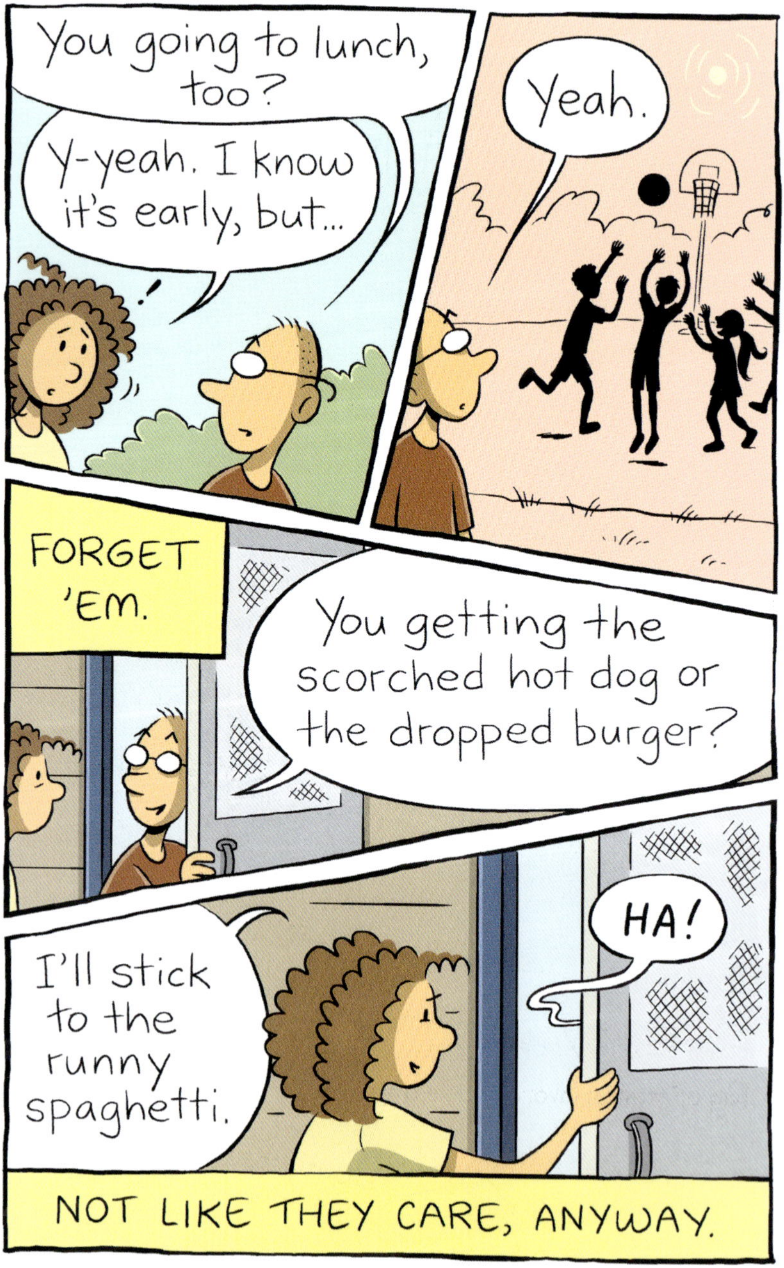
You going to lunch, too?
Y-yeah. I know it's early, but...
Yeah.
FORGET 'EM.
You getting the scorched hot dog or the dropped burger?
I'll stick to the runny spaghetti.
HA!
NOT LIKE THEY CARE, ANYWAY.

EMMIE

I eat lunch alone. Well, not alone-alone, 'cause the place is packed. I just don't really know the kids sitting near me. I'm trying to make an effort, though, I really am. I purposely chose a table with some of the art kids, but they're clingy even with each other.

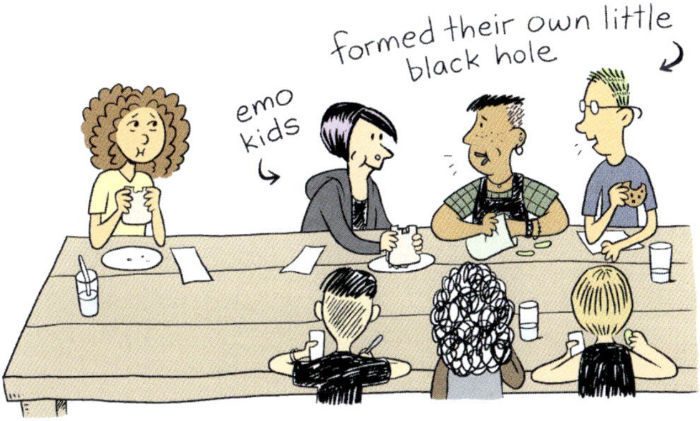

formed their own little black hole
emo kids

At least they're polite. One of 'em offers me their unwanted bag of pickle-flavored kettle chips.

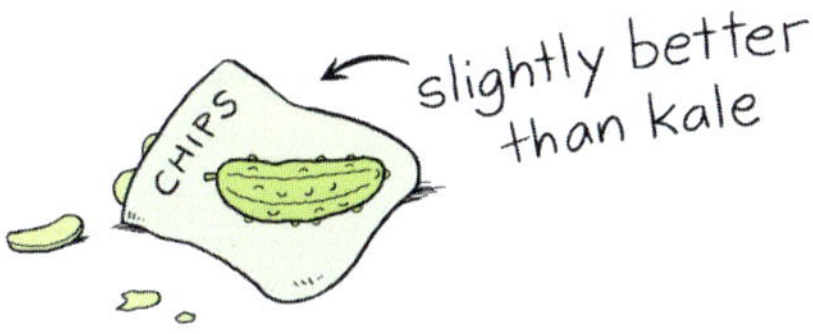

CHIPS
slightly better than kale

Tyler sits with Anthony. I see them beckon to Joe, who joins them (although he looks kinda unthrilled). I don't want to bother Tyler and, anyway, I'm not cool enough for that crowd. Trina is nowhere to be seen. I'm disappointed, but she's probably needed for an activity. Toward the end of lunch, Coach Durdle announces that we'll be changing into swimsuits and heading to the lake. I guess we're going swimming.

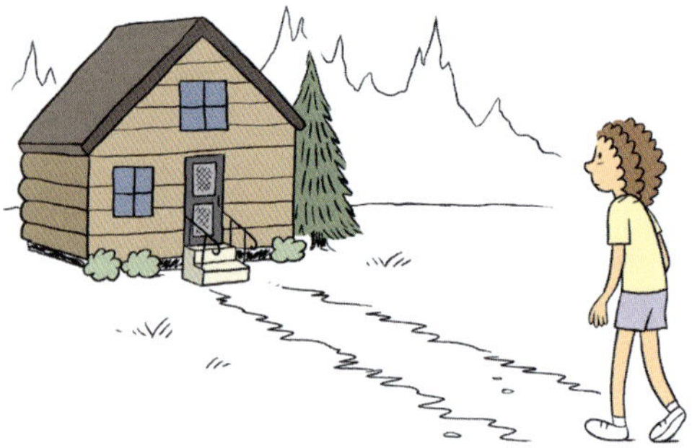

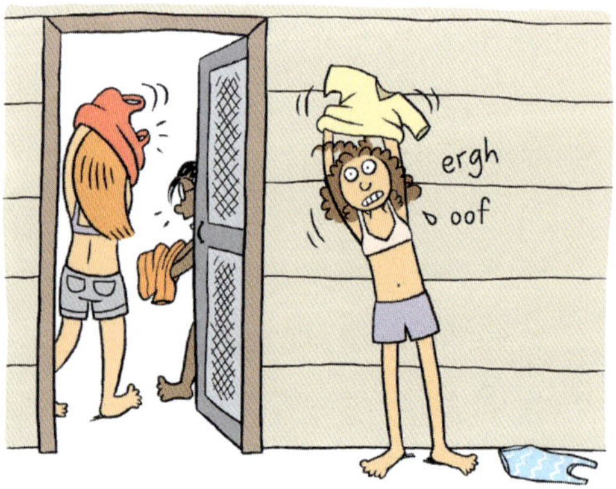
ergh
oof

I've never changed so fast in my life. **No way** I want those two to see my body (or lack of one). I wish I'd hurry up and develop already. My one hope: Trina went from "flat to filled" in eighth grade.

before:
after:
bust
hips
(also acne, backne, and feetne*)
*according to Trina

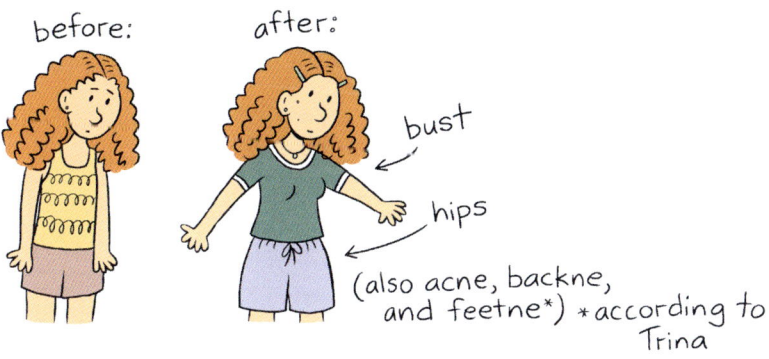

I slather on SPF and head out with my towel and swim shoes. I make my way down an unmarked path, following a bunch of other kids and hoping **they** at least have a sense of direction.

They do. We end up in a small clearing near the water. The lake isn't big, but it's really pretty and clear. It even has a little beach. I spy Trina near a bunch of boards and paddles that are lying on the sand. There are two other counselors talking to Trina, including the older girl who had gone to her high school.

When everyone arrives, Trina announces that we're going to do a paddleboard activity (yes!). All the kids cheer. We divide into three different groups. I stay near Trina, along with Tyler (yay!), Anthony, and Joe. Celia and Grace break away from another group and join ours, motioning for Jaime and Maya (Gossip Girls) to follow. Celia waves at Trina, who smiles and waves back.

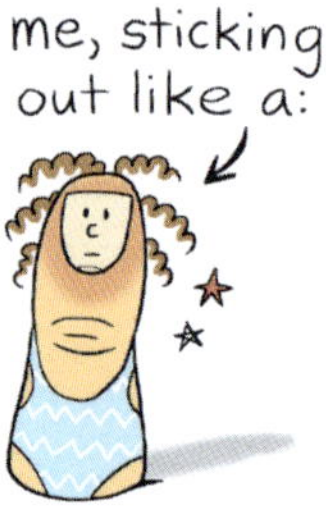
me, sticking out like a:

Trina gets started. She goes over every step in full detail. We listen, although I'm distracted by the basketball girl (in a nearby group), who's aiming her big, silvery, megawatt smile at Tyler. She sure doesn't have a flat chest and skinny baby chicken legs. I feel a pang of jealousy.

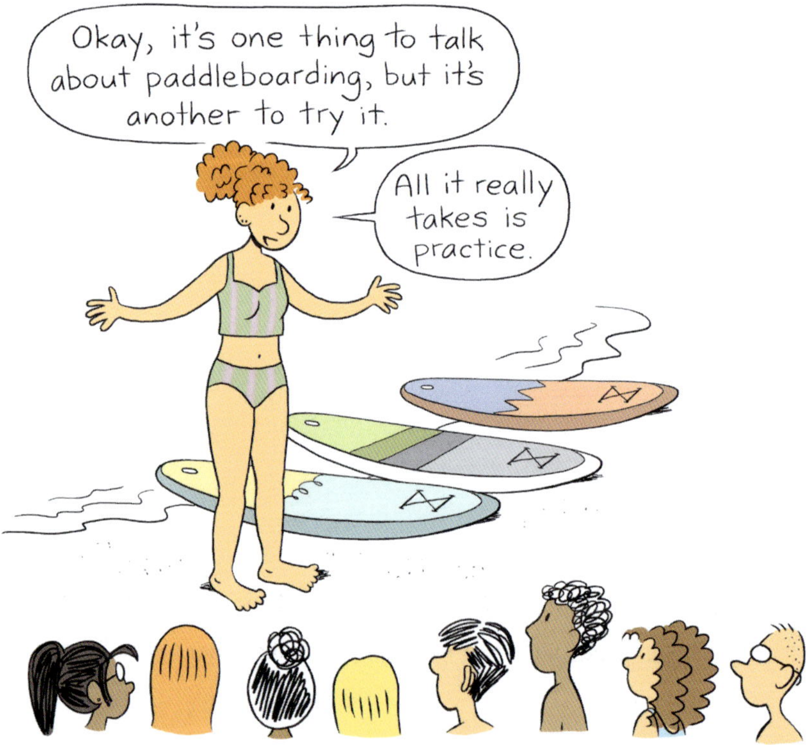
Okay, it's one thing to talk about paddleboarding, but it's another to try it.
All it really takes is practice.

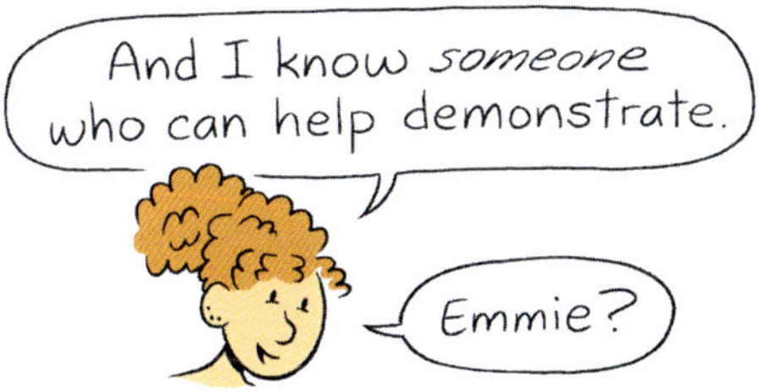
And I know *someone* who can help demonstrate.
Emmie?

Wait, what?

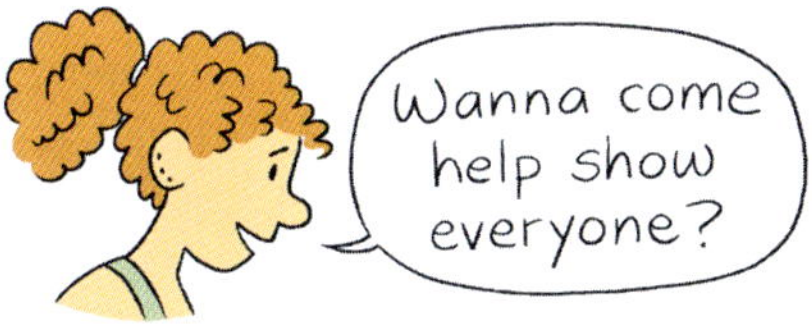
Wanna come help show everyone?

I shake my head.

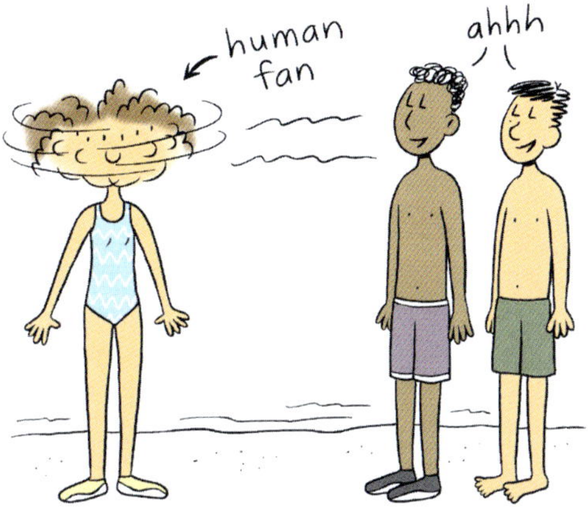
human fan
ahhh

But then I glance at Tyler, who looks at me kinda encouragingly. Trina pleads with her eyes. So, I swallow hard and trudge over to the edge of the lake, feeling every eye on me.

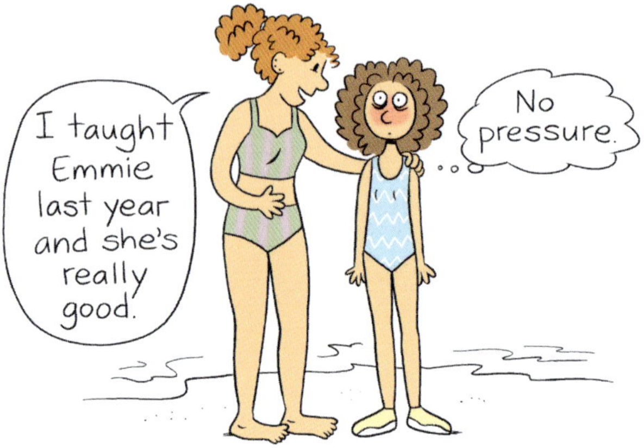
I taught Emmie last year and she's really good.
No pressure.

I wade into the (surprisingly warmish) water and climb onto a paddleboard. I kneel, and Trina "leashes" my ankle, tethering it to the board. Then she hands me a paddle and gives me a little shove away from the shore. When we're in deep enough water, I shakily get to my feet—one leg at a time—while she holds the board steady. I'm doing it! Except I'm doing it in front of, like, thirty classmates. Yeek!

Now that I feel everyone's eyes on me, I wanna close mine. It's like I'm on display. **Why** didn't I get the swimsuit with the padding?

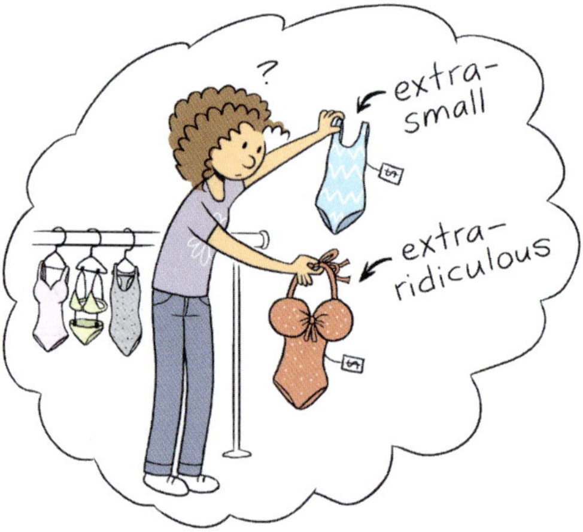
?
extra-small
extra-ridiculous

Trina squints up at me, and with an encouraging nod, asks:

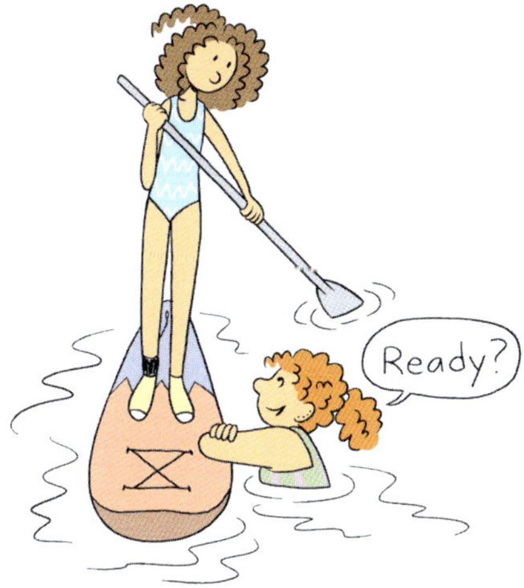
Ready?

Do I have a choice? I nod back and start paddling the way I remember, four strokes at a time on each side.

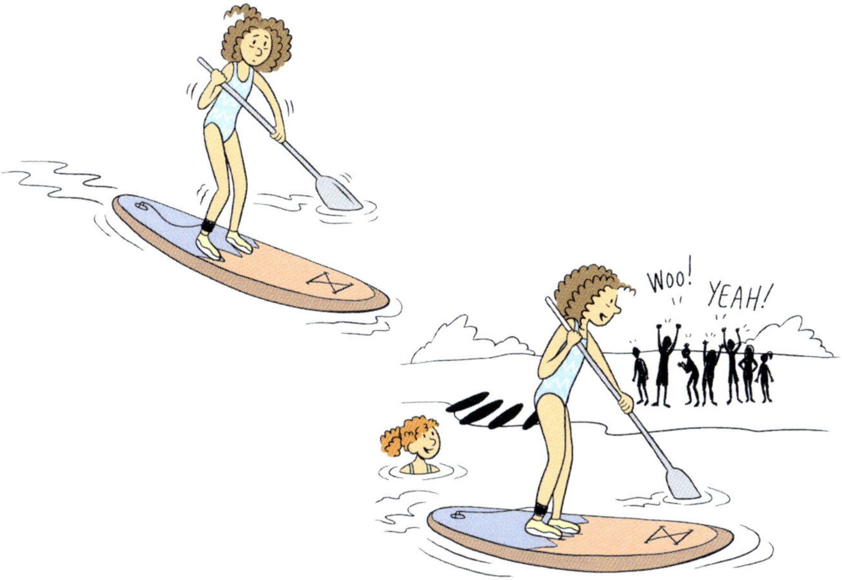
WOO!
YEAH!

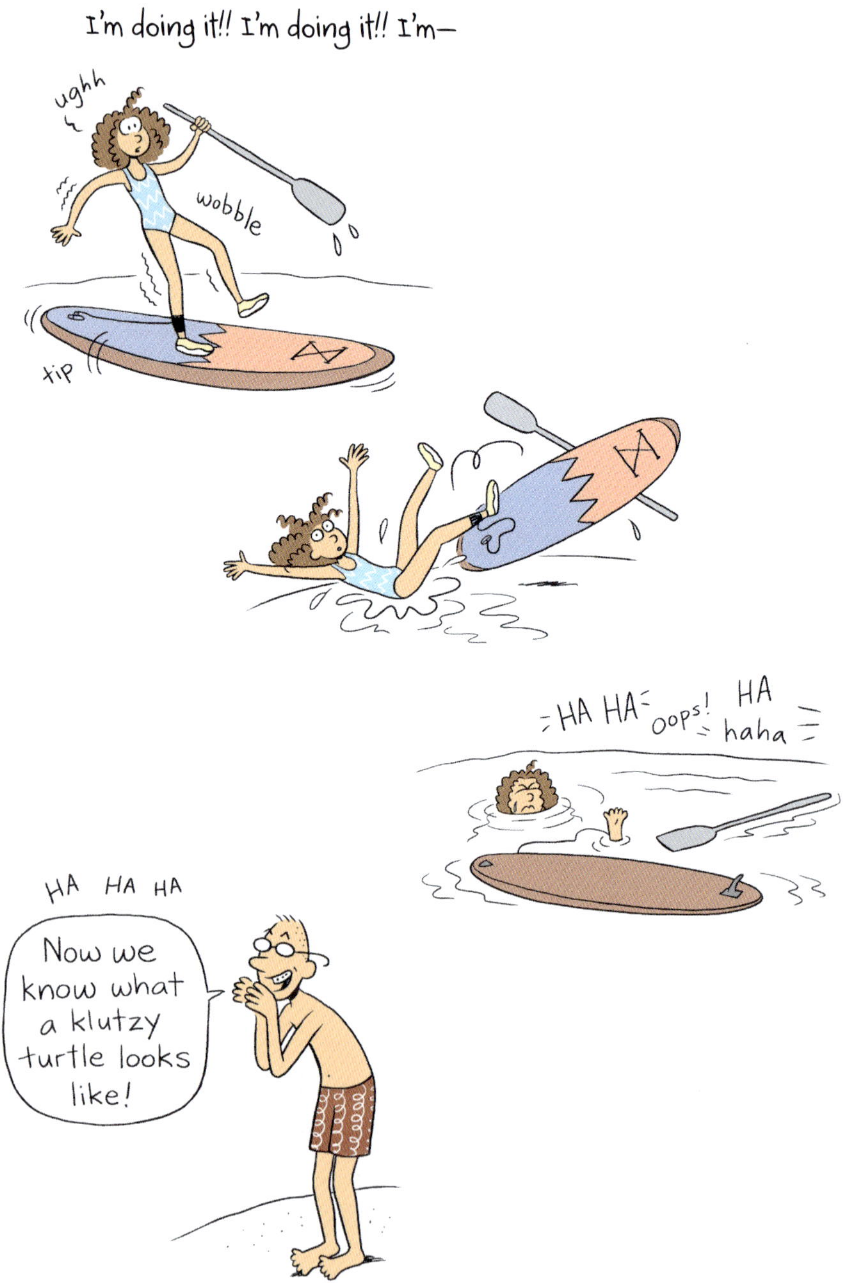
I'm doing it!! I'm doing it!! I'm—
ughh
wobble
tip
HA HA
oops!
HA
haha
HA HA HA
Now we know what a klutzy turtle looks like!

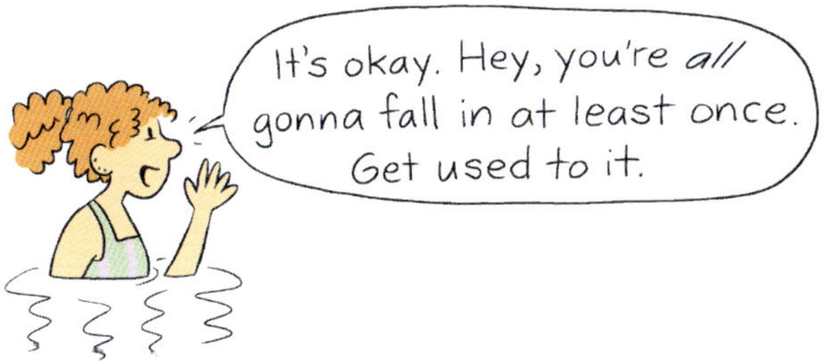
It's okay. Hey, you're *all* gonna fall in at least once. Get used to it.

But I'm mortified. And humiliated. I'm **mortiliated.**

Trina whispers:

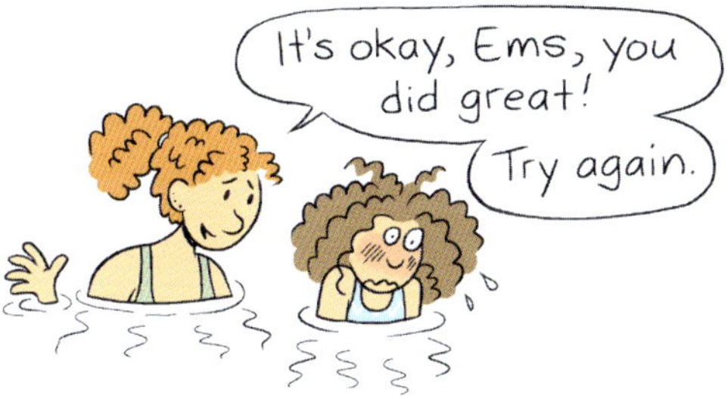
It's okay, Ems, you did great!
Try again.

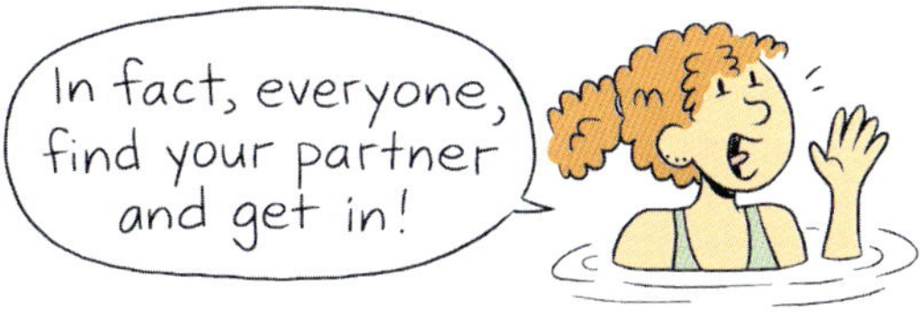
In fact, everyone, find your partner and get in!

Joe grabs a board and paddle and wades toward me. I want to punch him, but I swallow my pride and help him get situated. He does surprisingly well getting himself up from a kneeling position; maybe 'cause he's closer to the board than most.

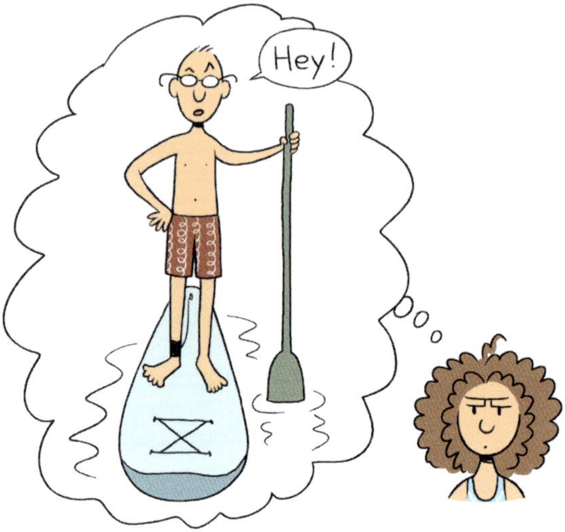
Hey!

I'm back on my feet, too. I'm much steadier this time (my muscle memory returns from last summer), but now no one notices 'cause they're too busy having fun.

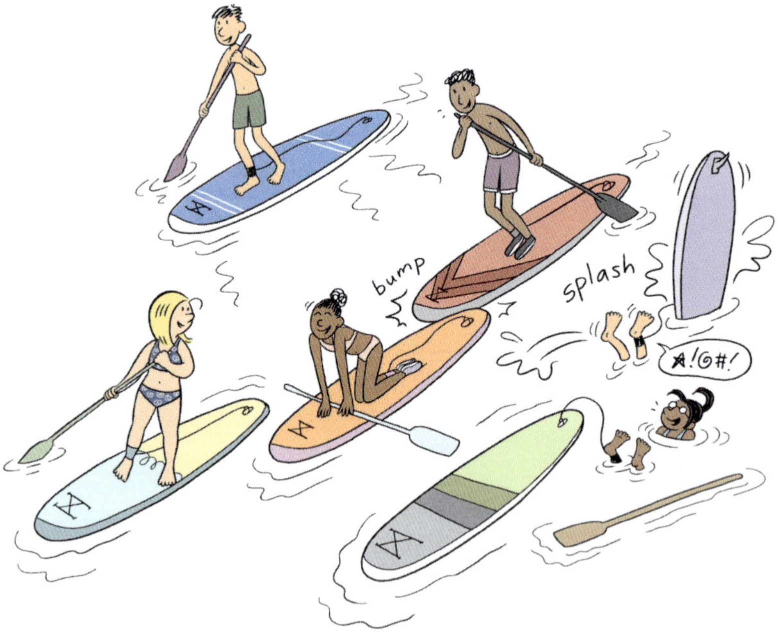
bump
splash

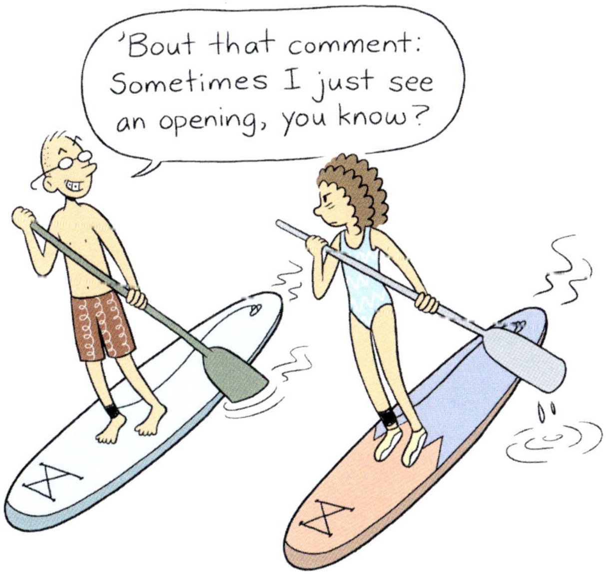
'Bout that comment: Sometimes I just see an opening, you know?

I don't respond. I paddle faster and faster, away from Joe. We're not really supposed to leave our potentially drowning partners, but I think the world would understand in this case.

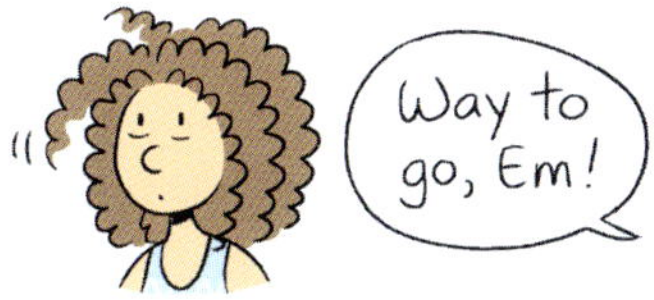
Way to go, Em!

I stop paddling and look to my left (a little wobbly). I see Tyler grinning at me. He's such a natural. I mean, of course he is. He's a total athlete. I suddenly forget about my falling-in incident and light up inside (again).

But then:

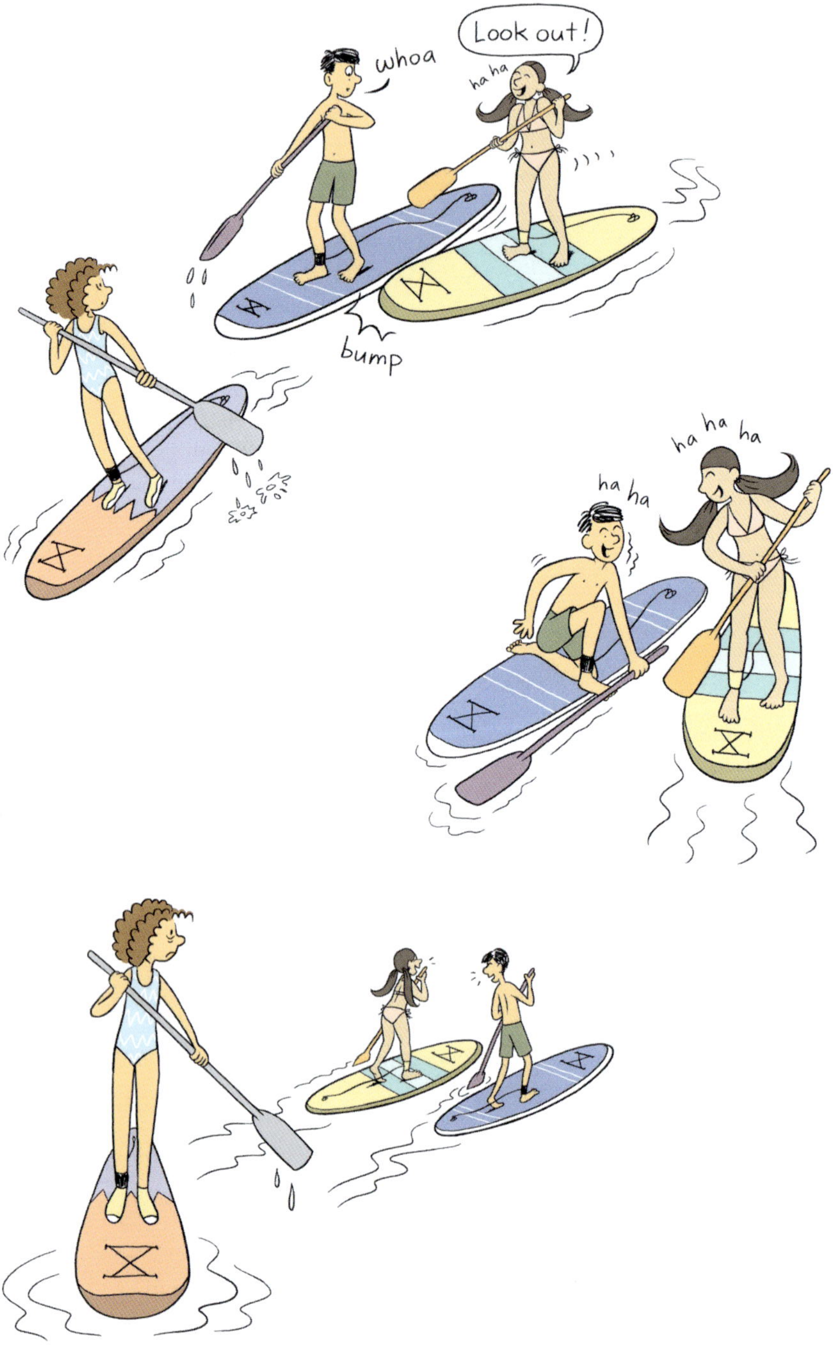

whoa
Look out!
ha ha
bump
ha ha ha
ha ha

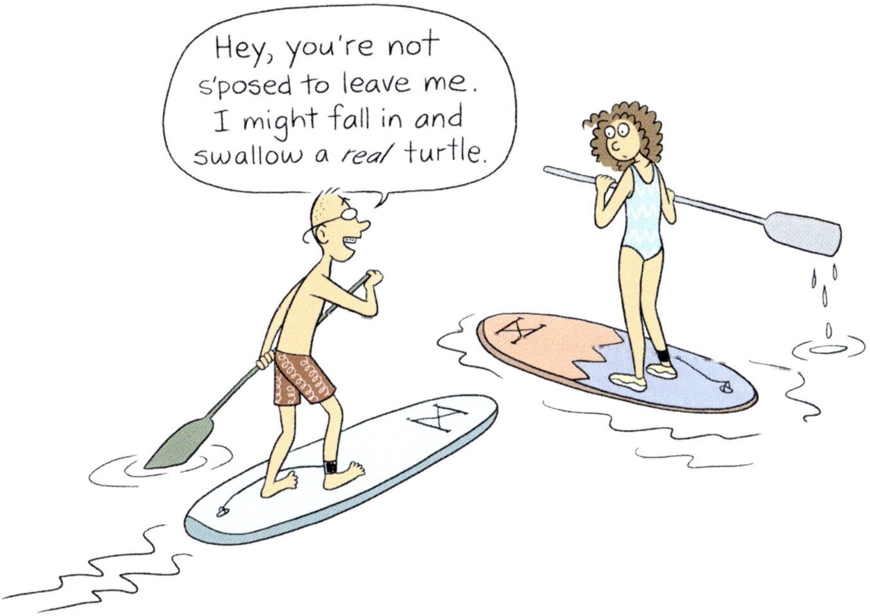
Hey, you're not s'posed to leave me. I might fall in and swallow a *real* turtle.

Ughhh. I wish he **would** go and swallow a turtle. Ten of them. Both him **and** Trina!

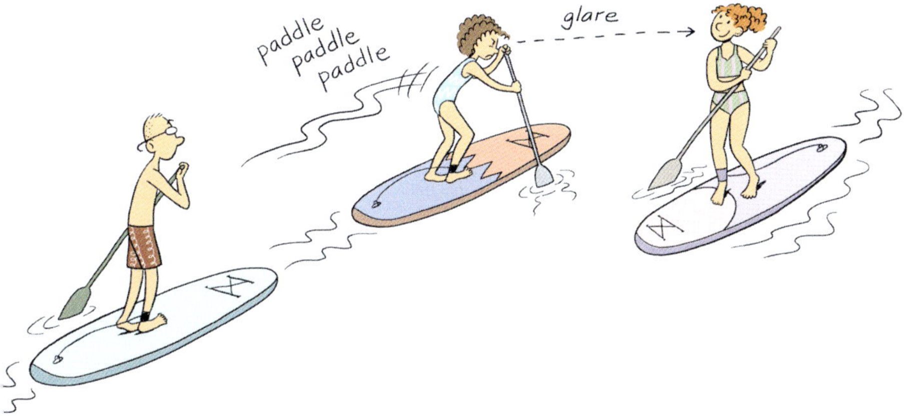
paddle
paddle
paddle
glare

How could she single me out, anyway? She knows I hate that.

We stay out there for a while. Joe, sensing my hostility, keeps away. But (like me) I notice him watching Tyler with BG (Basketball

Girl) as well as Anthony branching off with the Gossip Girls. Joe doesn't look too happy. Good.

Eventually, everyone gets tired, and we start paddling back to shore. I avoid meeting eyes with Trina; instead, I dry off and head straight to the cabin, latch the bathroom door closed, and shower quickly before anyone else arrives. I hear Celia and Grace walk in as I change.

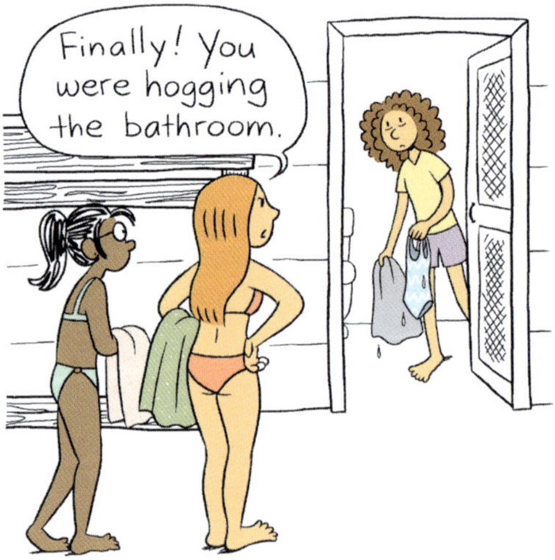
Finally! You were hogging the bathroom.

Seriously? They just got here!

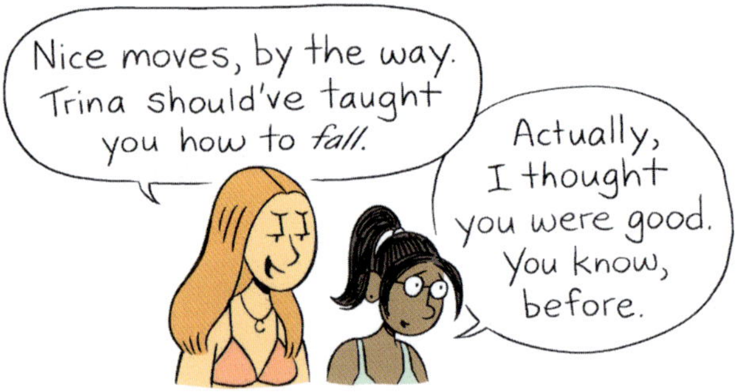
Nice moves, by the way. Trina should've taught you how to *fall.*
Actually, I thought you were good. You know, before.

I give her a small, grateful smile, but Celia rolls her eyes.

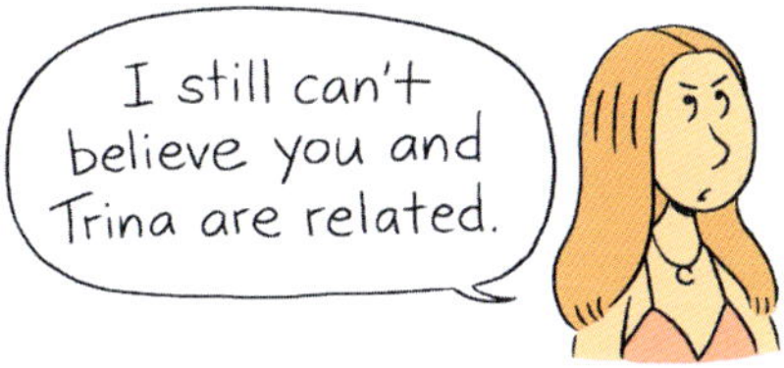
I still can't believe you and Trina are related.

I don't say anything, I just blush furiously. Why is she so mean?

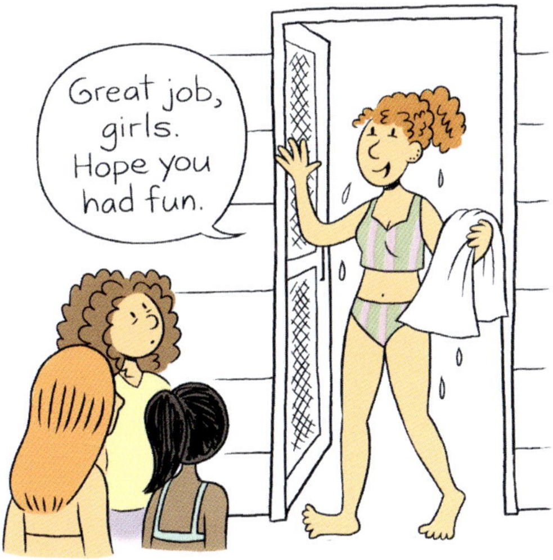
Great job, girls. Hope you had fun.

She, Celia, and Grace high-five. Now it's my turn to roll my eyes when they aren't looking.

Celia gives Trina the detailed rundown of her paddleboarding moves. Since there's time before dinner, I decide to go to the art shack to escape.

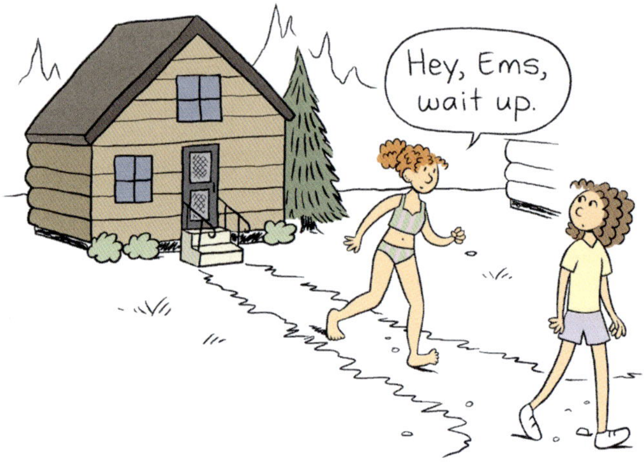
Hey, Ems, wait up.

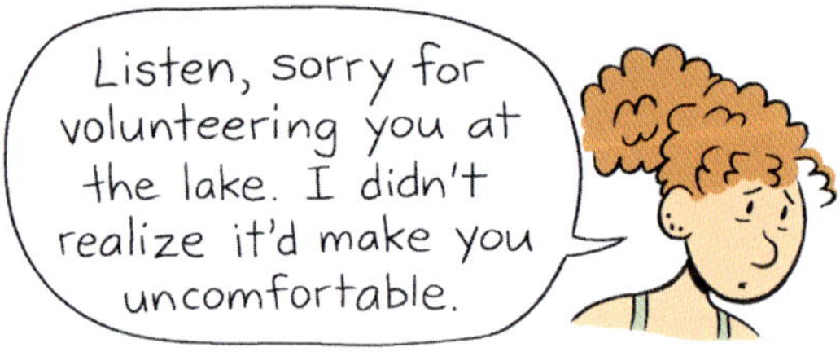
Listen, sorry for volunteering you at the lake. I didn't realize it'd make you uncomfortable.

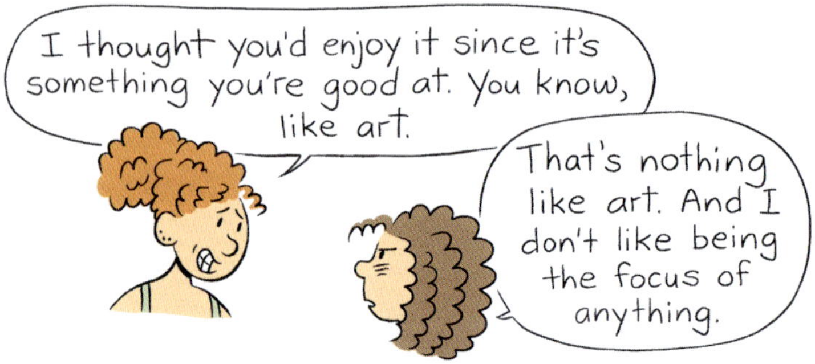
I thought you'd enjoy it since it's something you're good at. You know, like art.
That's nothing like art. And I don't like being the focus of anything.

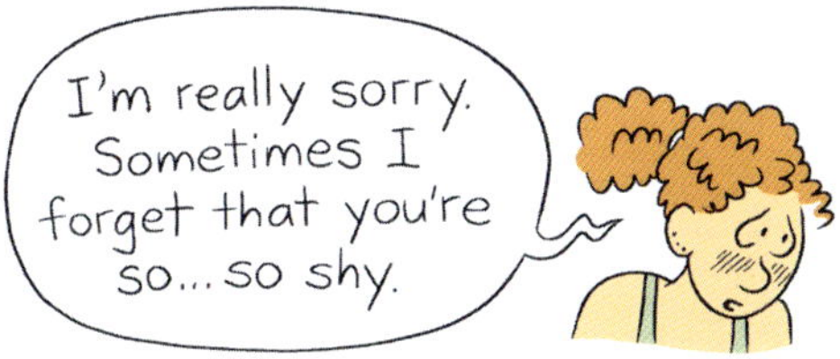
I'm really sorry. Sometimes I forget that you're so... so shy.

My cheeks heat up and I stare at the ground. I always forget that Trina only knows the "home" me, who is much more at ease. Even then, Trina's barely around. So how can I blame her?

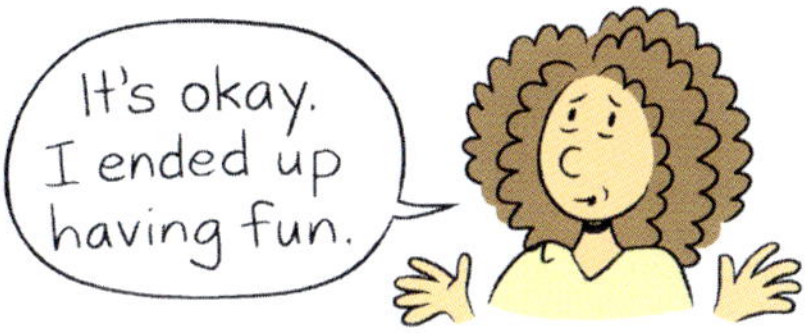
It's okay. I ended up having fun.

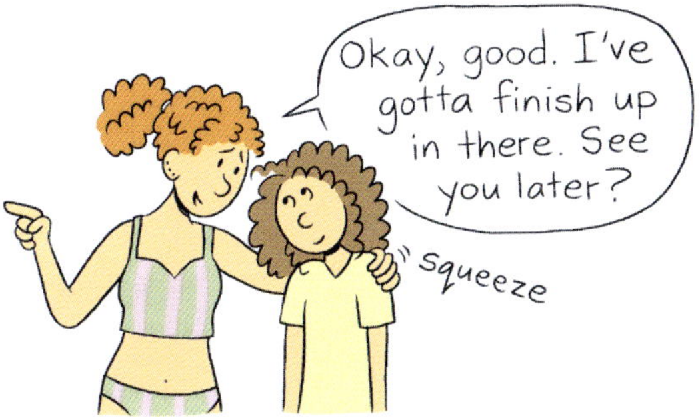
Okay, good. I've gotta finish up in there. See you later?
squeeze

I nod.

"Fun" is a strong word, but I don't wanna make Trina feel worse. So, I try to shake it all off as I head toward the art shack.

And . . .

. . . I try not to think about Tyler.

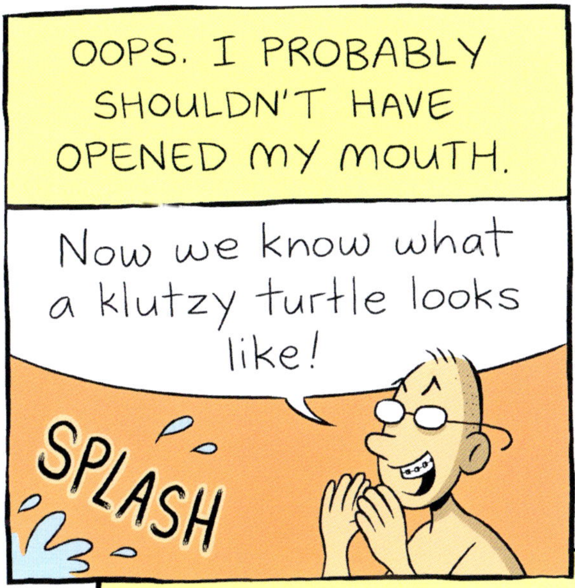
OOPS. I PROBABLY SHOULDN'T HAVE OPENED MY MOUTH.
Now we know what a klutzy turtle looks like!
SPLASH

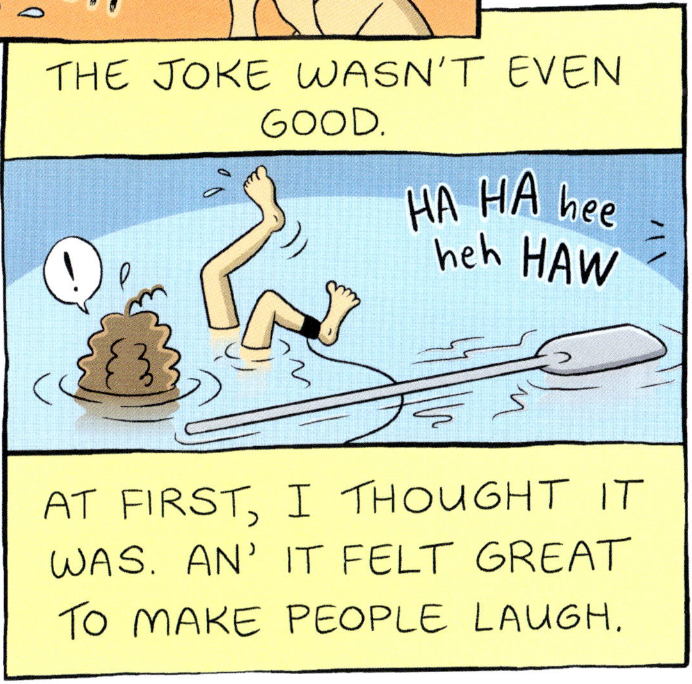
THE JOKE WASN'T EVEN GOOD.
!
HA HA hee heh HAW
AT FIRST, I THOUGHT IT WAS. AN' IT FELT GREAT TO MAKE PEOPLE LAUGH.

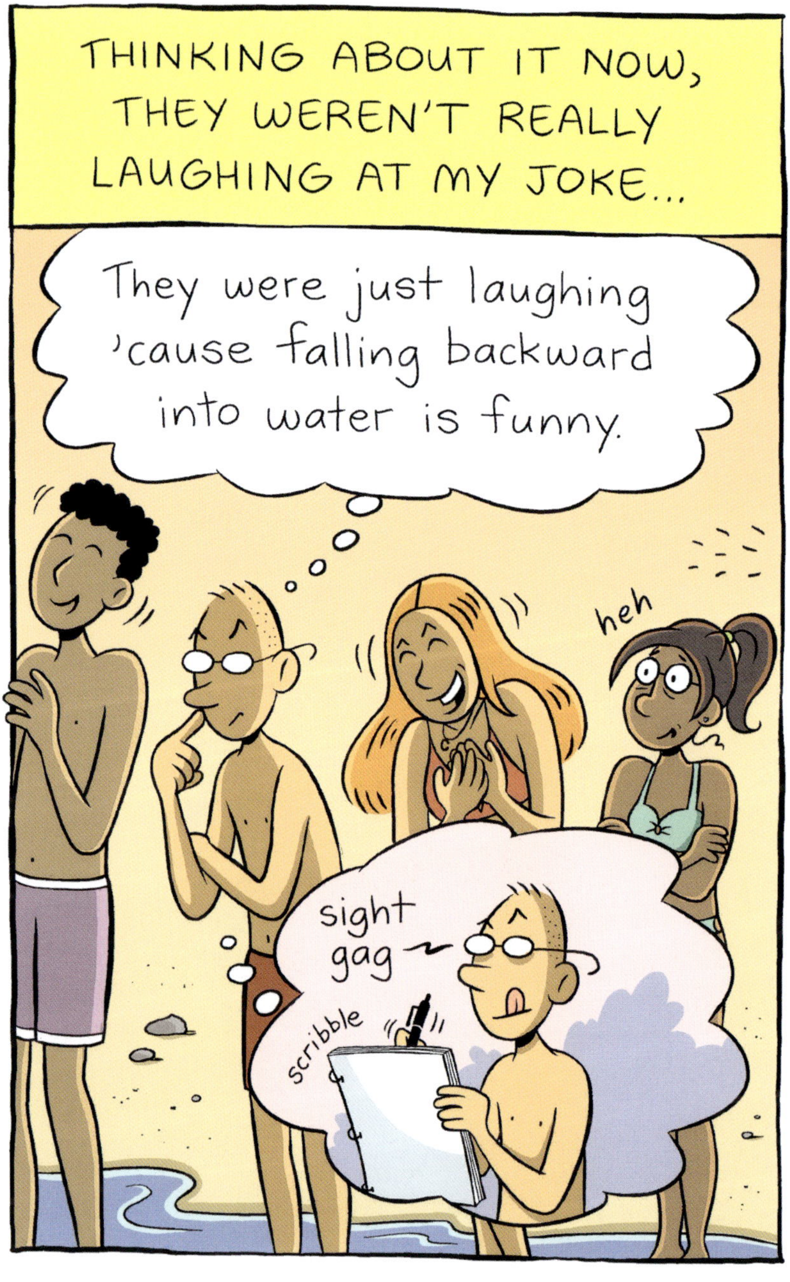
THINKING ABOUT IT NOW, THEY WEREN'T REALLY LAUGHING AT MY JOKE...
They were just laughing 'cause falling backward into water is funny.
heh
sight gag
scribble

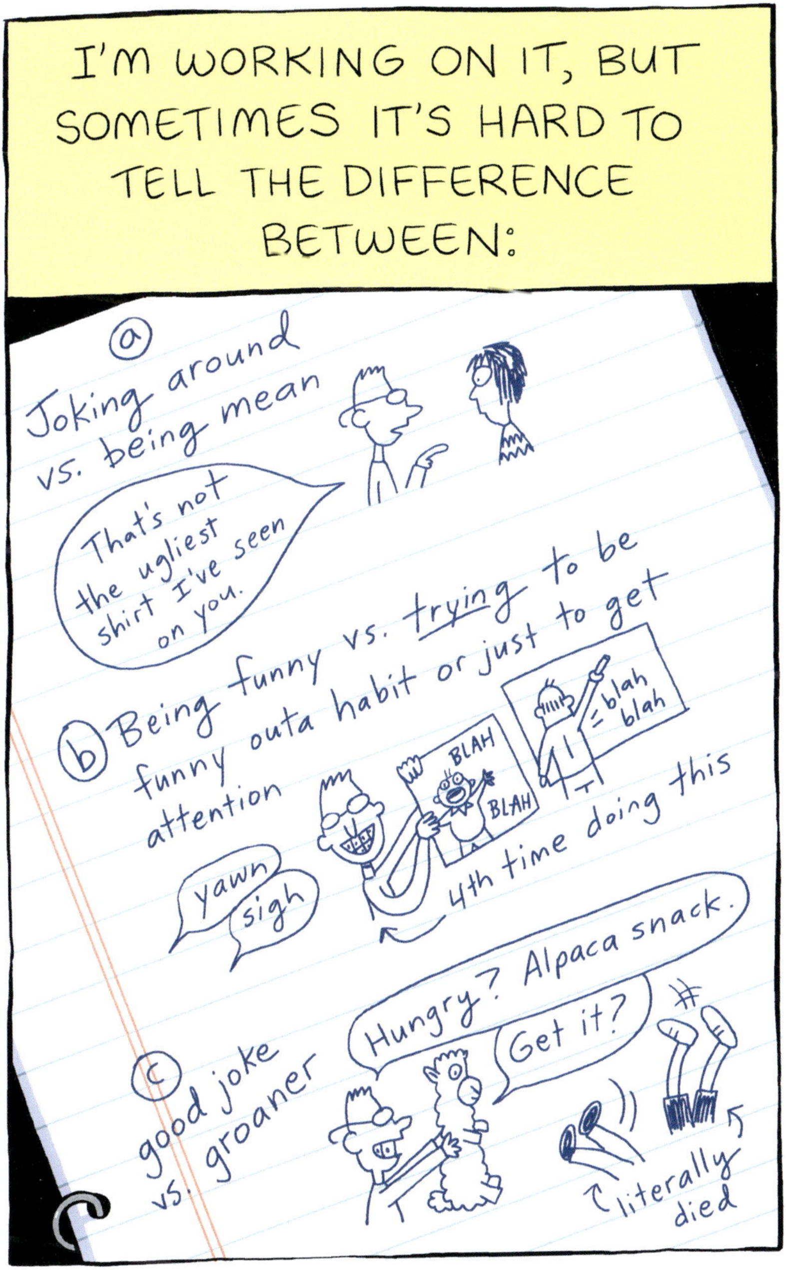
I'M WORKING ON IT, BUT SOMETIMES IT'S HARD TO TELL THE DIFFERENCE BETWEEN:
(a) Joking around vs. being mean
That's not the ugliest shirt I've seen on you.
(b) Being funny vs. trying to be funny outa habit or just to get attention
blah blah
BLAH
BLAH
yawn
sigh
4th time doing this
(c) good joke vs. groaner
Hungry? Alpaca snack.
Get it?
literally died

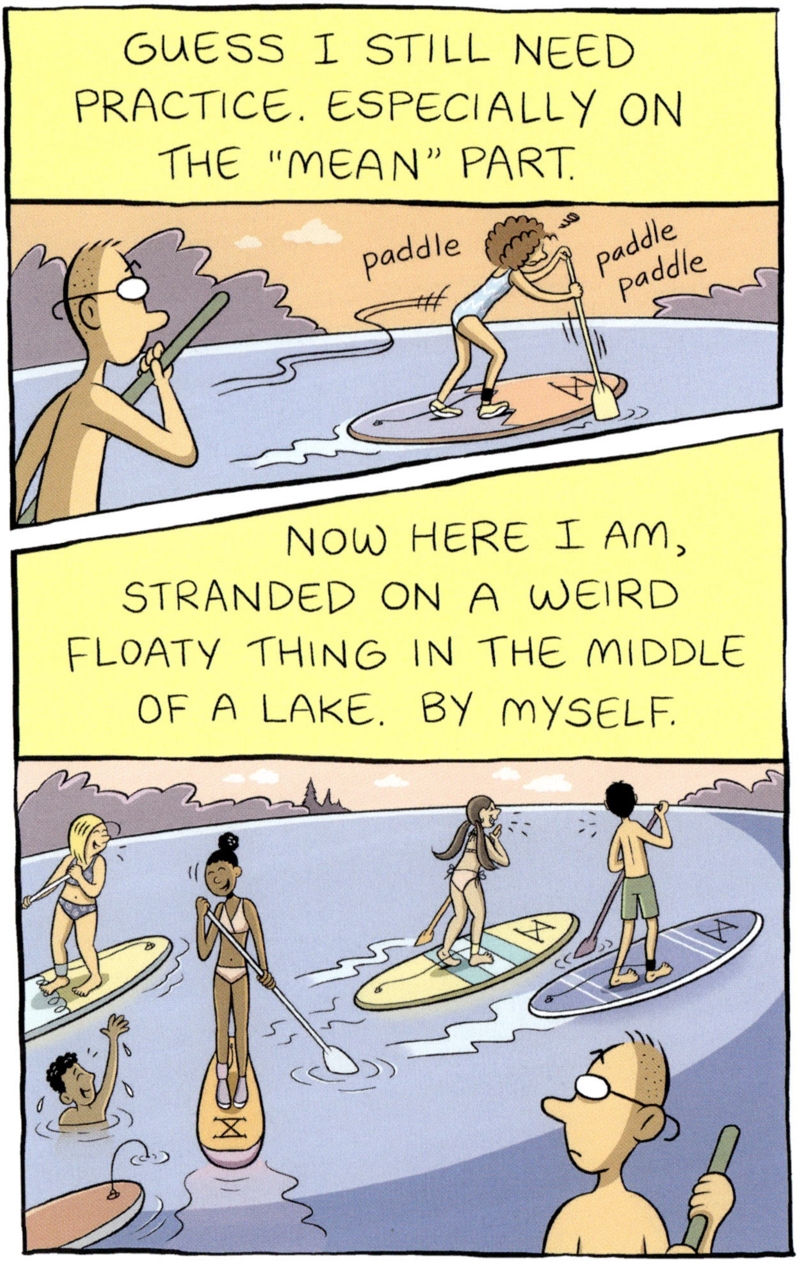
GUESS I STILL NEED PRACTICE. ESPECIALLY ON THE "MEAN" PART.
paddle
paddle
paddle
NOW HERE I AM, STRANDED ON A WEIRD FLOATY THING IN THE MIDDLE OF A LAKE. BY MYSELF.

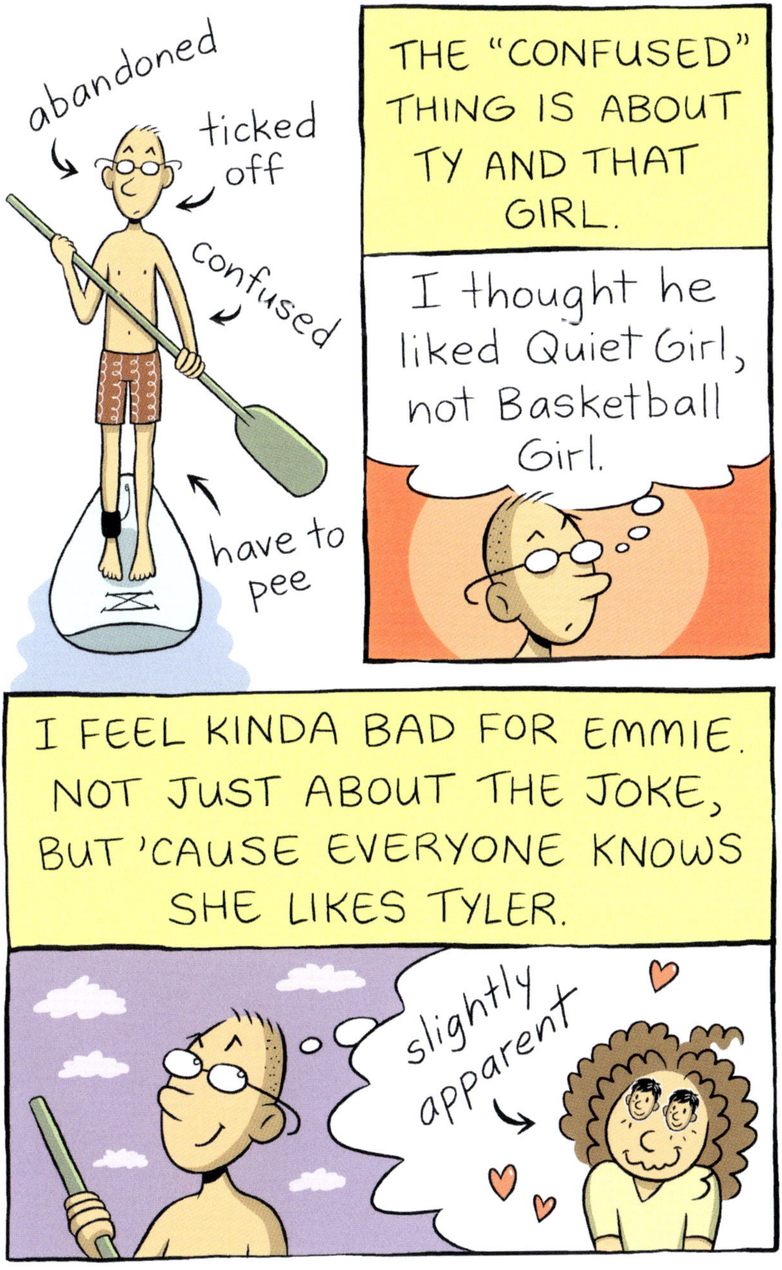
abandoned
ticked off
confused
have to pee
THE "CONFUSED" THING IS ABOUT TY AND THAT GIRL.
I thought he liked Quiet Girl, not Basketball Girl.
I FEEL KINDA BAD FOR EMMIE. NOT JUST ABOUT THE JOKE, BUT 'CAUSE EVERYONE KNOWS SHE LIKES TYLER.
slightly apparent

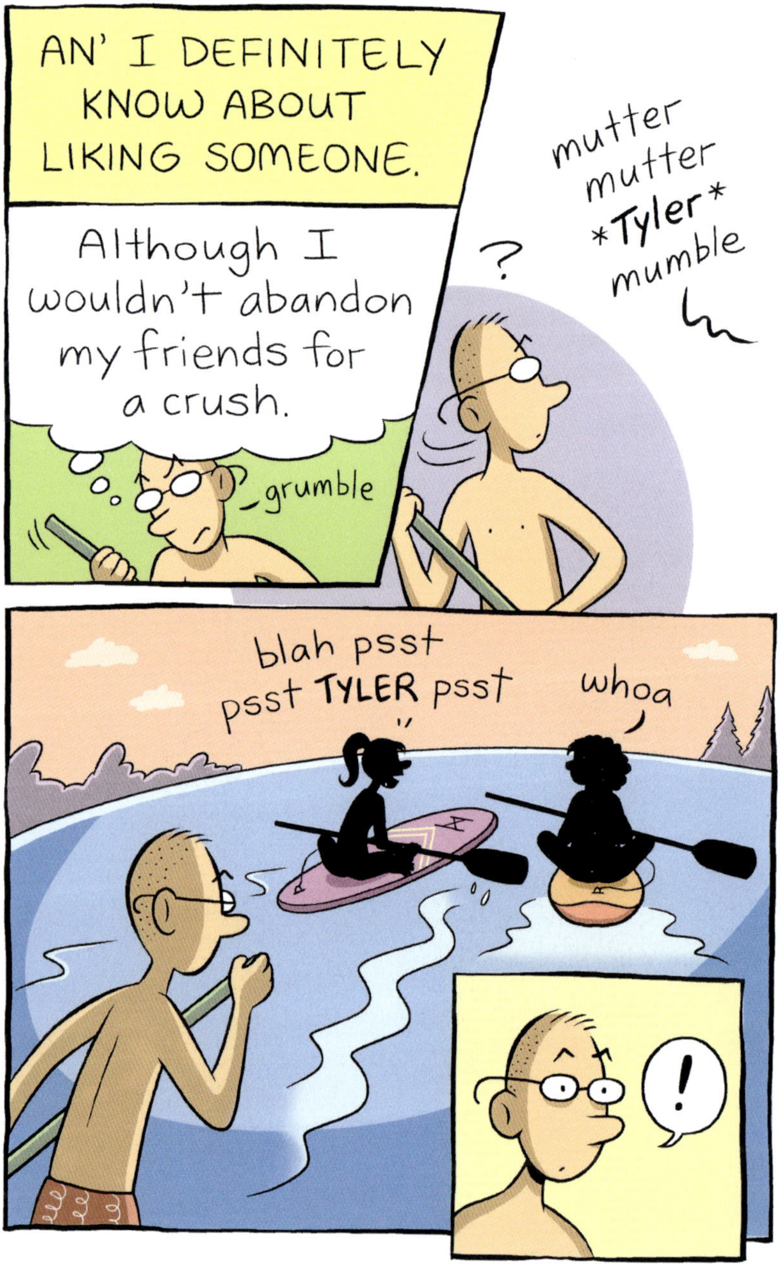
AN' I DEFINITELY KNOW ABOUT LIKING SOMEONE.
Although I wouldn't abandon my friends for a crush.
grumble
?
mutter mutter *Tyler* mumble
blah psst psst TYLER psst
whoa
!

EMMIE

Nighttime.

I'm trying to be a good sport, but honestly . . .

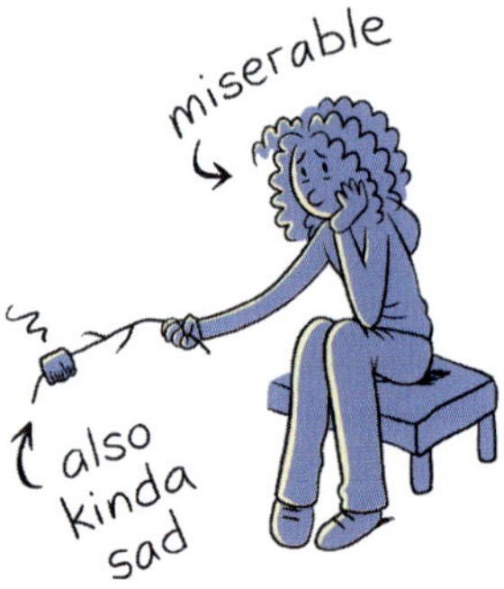
miserable
also kinda sad

I miss Bri and Sarah so much. Even with the whole Tyler-BG thing, and my embarrassing paddleboard incident, they would've made this bearable. Probably helped joke everything off or distract me or something.

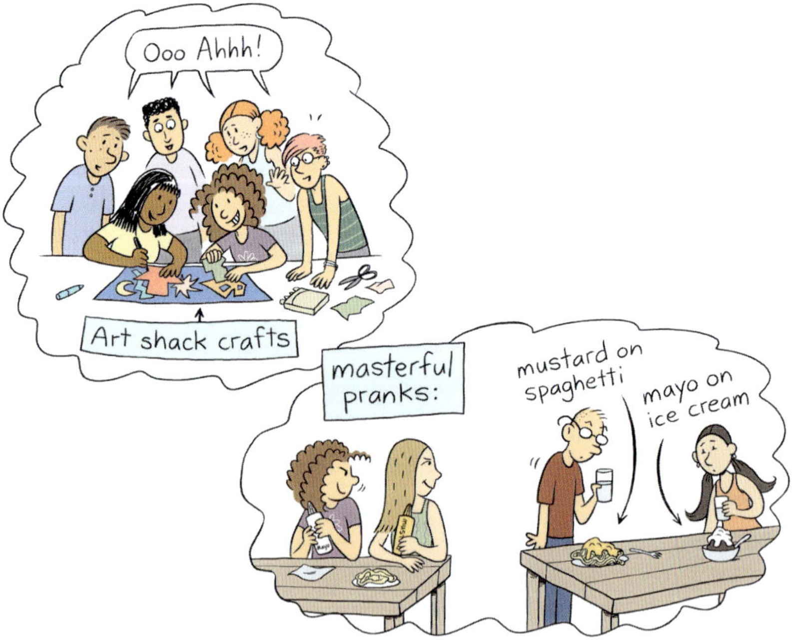
Ooo Ahhh!
Art shack crafts
masterful pranks:
mustard on spaghetti
mayo on ice cream

I've never felt more alone. And that's saying something.

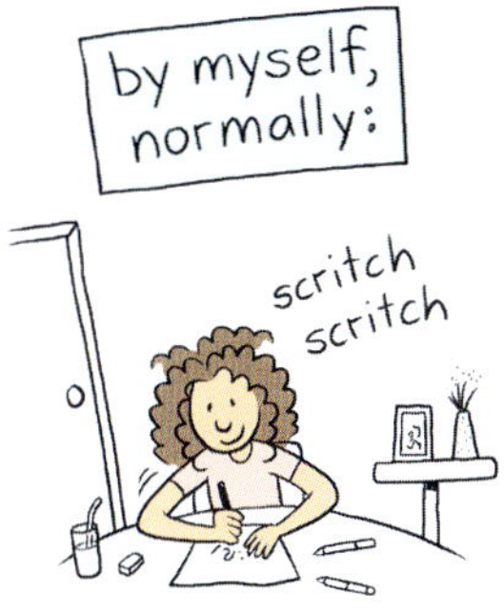
by myself, normally:
scritch scritch

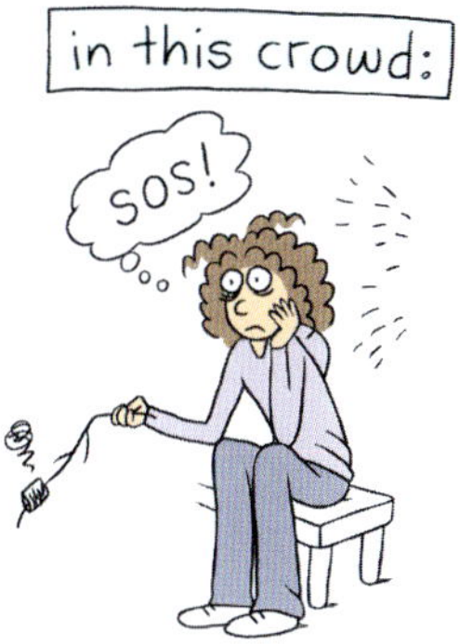
in this crowd:
SOS!

Really . . . I just wanna go home.

They're gonna start ghost stories soon. Right now, I'm watching my **own** horror show.

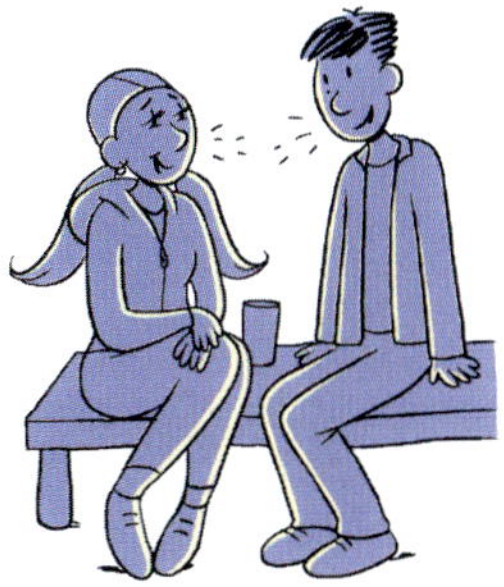

I don't know whether I want to cry or throw up.

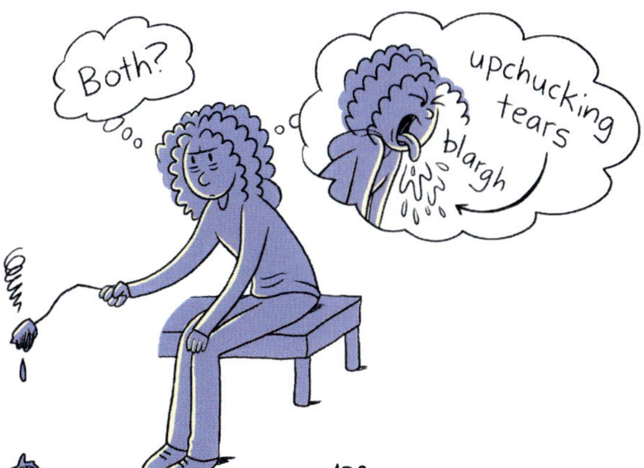
Both?
upchucking tears
blargh

On top of everything, I've got Mr. Stand-up next to me.

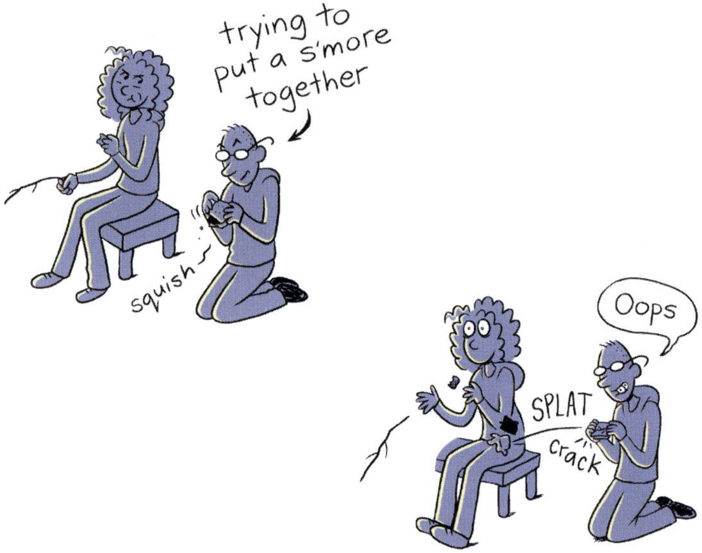
trying to put a s'more together
squish
Oops
SPLAT
crack

I sigh and wipe marshmallow goo off my leg. I don't even care. That's how checked out I am.

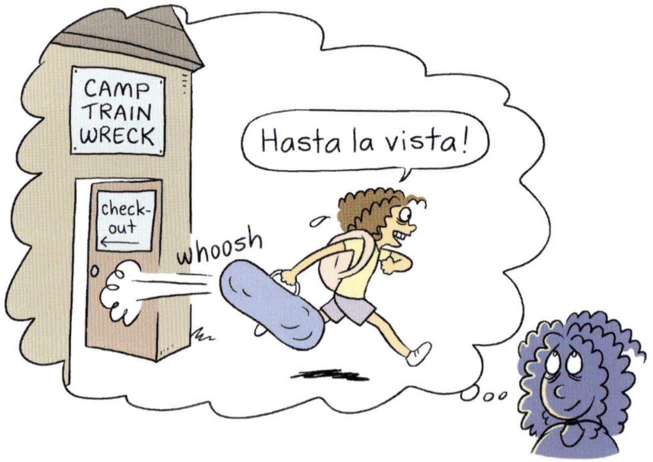
CAMP TRAIN WRECK
check-out
Hasta la vista!
whoosh

I spy Trina and that other counselor her age eating marshmallows straight out of a bag (against the rules!) and talking closely. Trina seems happy. That's good, I guess. But that's another thing: I thought we were gonna have more sister time together. Instead . . .

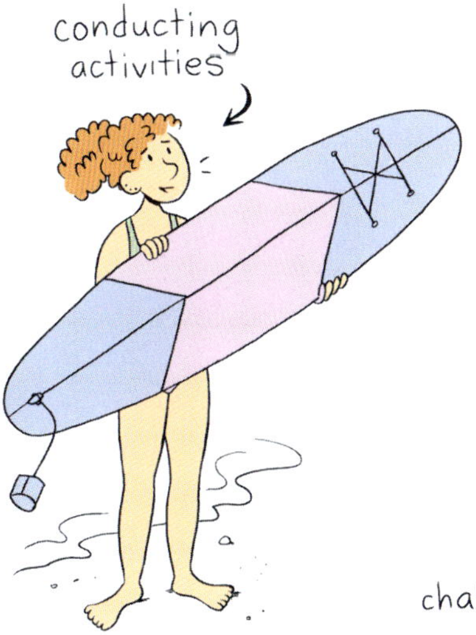
conducting activities

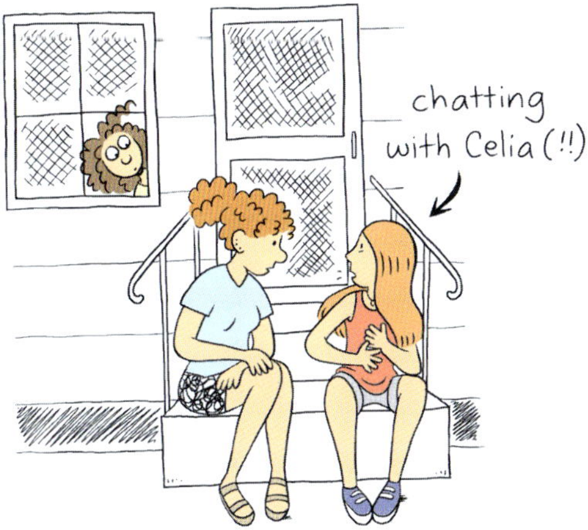
chatting with Celia (!!)

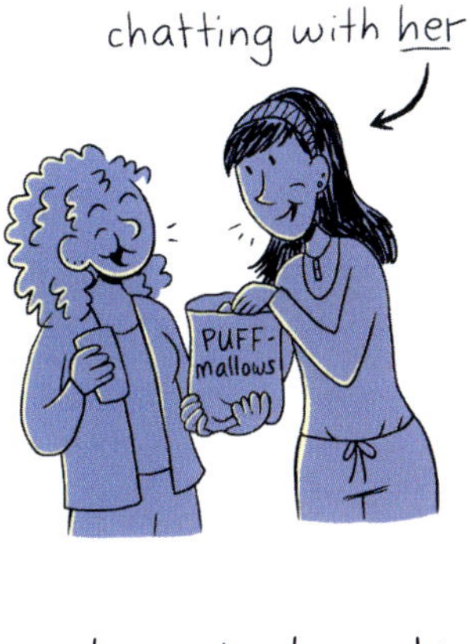
chatting with her
PUFF-mallows

A counselor named Jon stands up, shines a flashlight under his chin, and announces in a spooky voice:

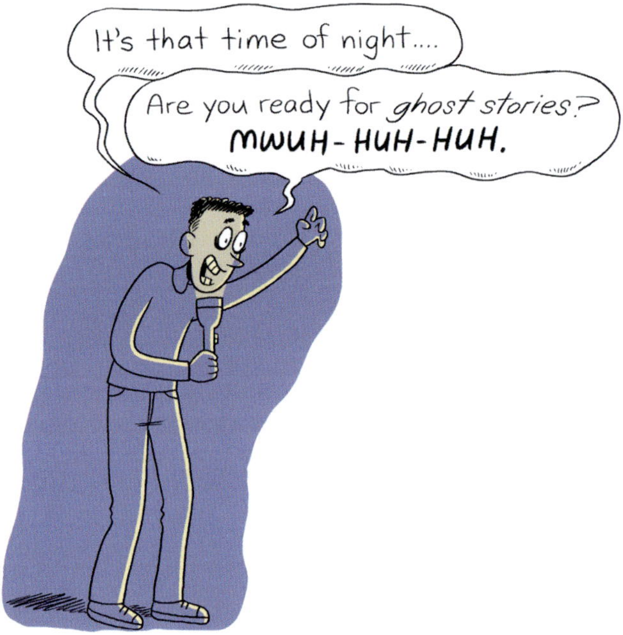
It's that time of night....
Are you ready for *ghost stories?*
MWUH-HUH-HUH.

I can practically hear the collective eye roll. But there's mass giggling, anyway.

Jon starts in. He tells a story about a group of kids who go into the woods at night with a Ouija board to try to make contact with a young girl who died there decades ago. No one knows if she was eaten by wolves, fell down a ravine and got stuck, or what. They want to find out.

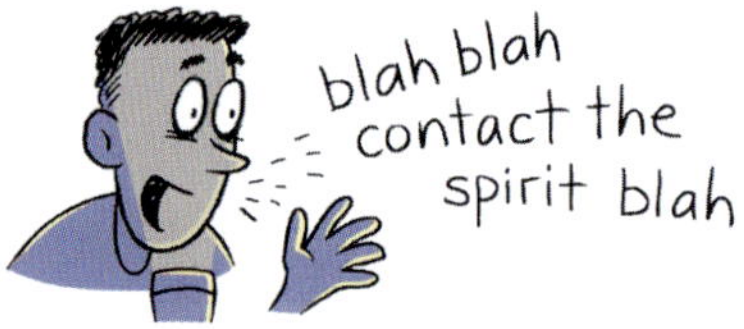
blah blah
contact the
spirit blah

I can't help it, I'm captivated.

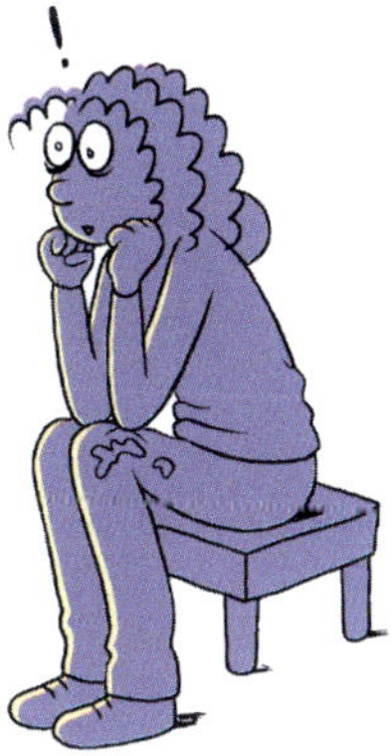
!

He goes on. The kids start "talking" to the dead girl. They ask her questions, and she answers through the board. They are just getting to the part where they ask how she died, and they're completely absorbed in the "answer" when suddenly one of the kids hears a twig snap, feels a ghostly tap on her shoulder, and . . .

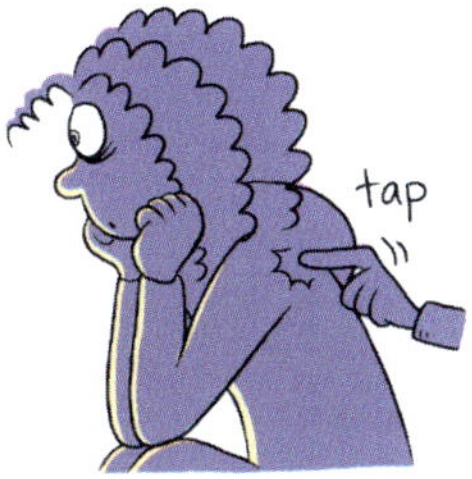
tap

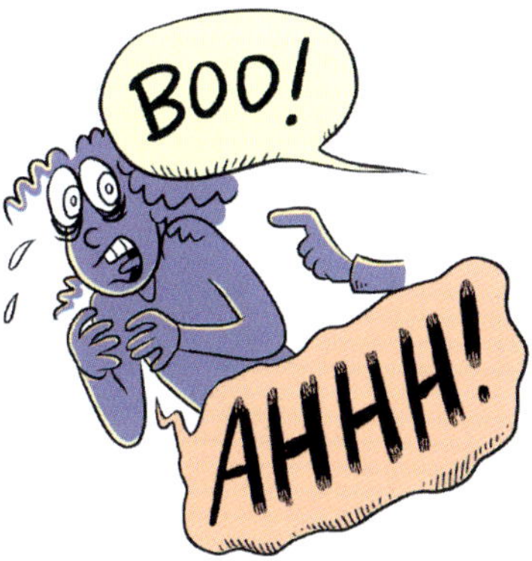
BOO!
AHHH!

Everyone looks confused for a second, and then:

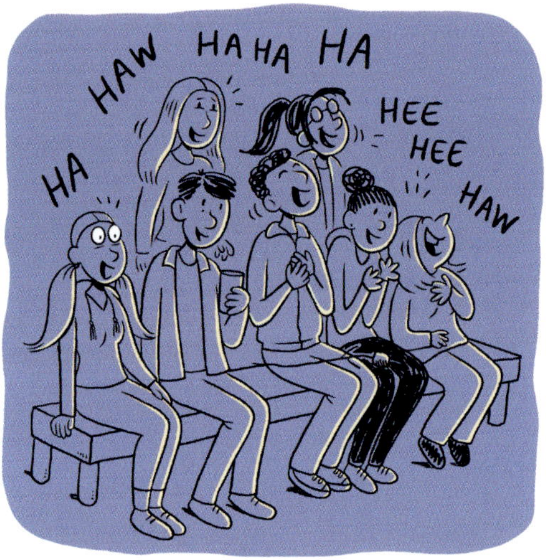
HA
HAW
HA HA
HA
HEE
HEE
HAW

JOE!!

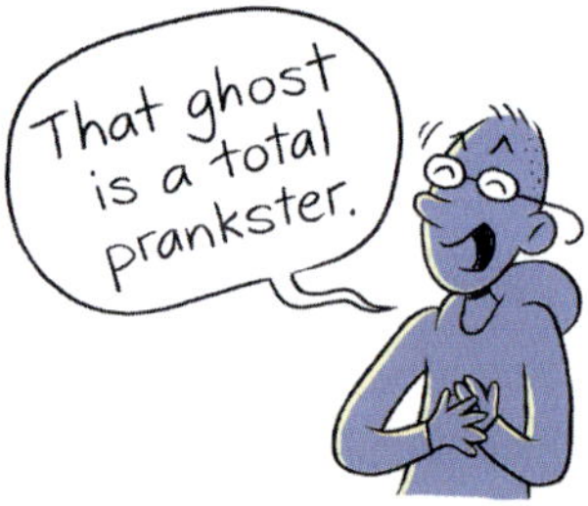
That ghost is a total prankster.

I squeeze my eyes shut. I can't cry. I won't! It takes all my willpower not to.

Somehow, I force myself to join in the laughter. Even as the butt of a joke (again), I don't want anyone to feel sorry for me.

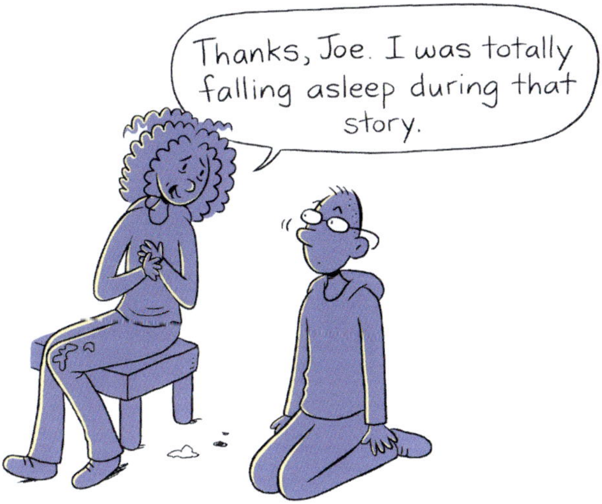
Thanks, Joe. I was totally falling asleep during that story.

Joe looks amazed by my comeback. I even surprised myself. I hear a couple of kids giggle. Eventually, the laughter dies down, and Jon goes back to finishing the ghost story. I don't listen anymore, though. Instead, I get up to use the bathroom in the mess hall nearby.

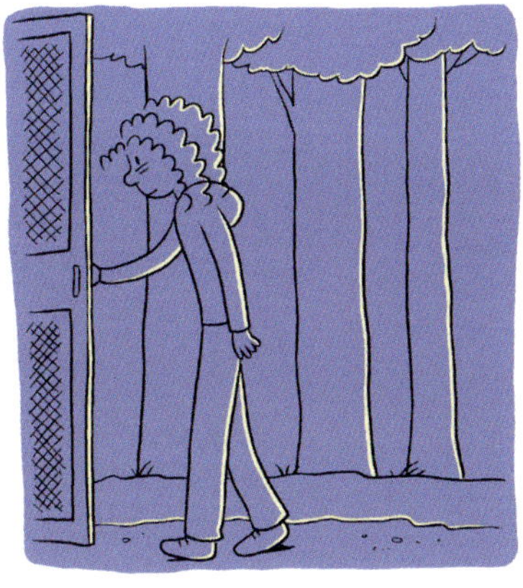

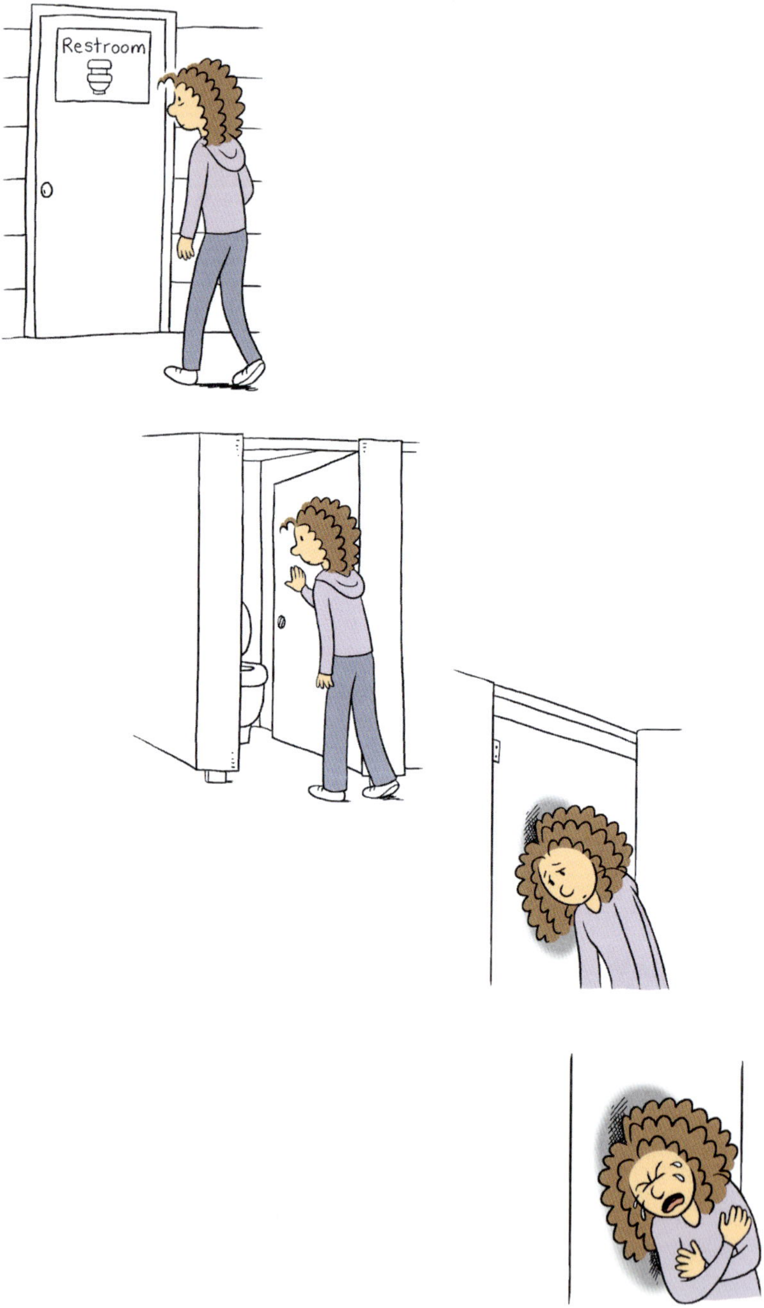
Restroom

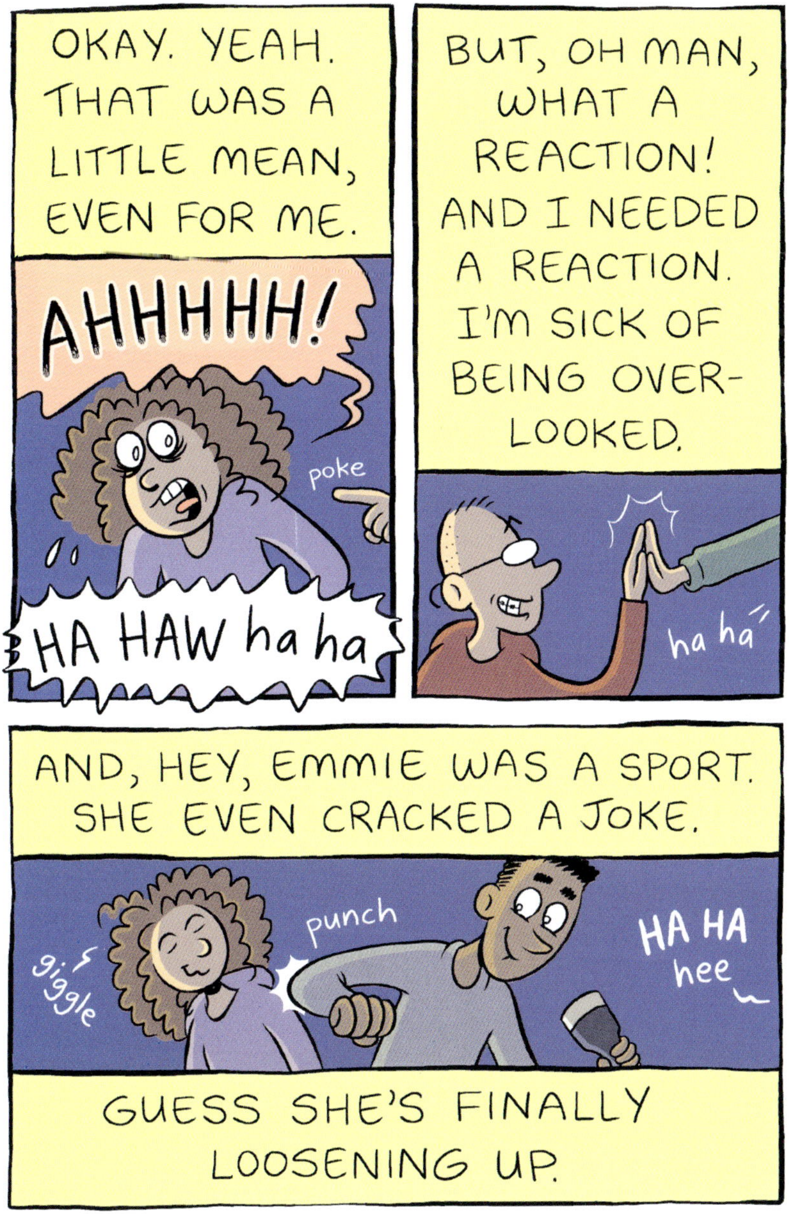
OKAY. YEAH. THAT WAS A LITTLE MEAN, EVEN FOR ME.
AHHHHH!
poke
HA HAW ha ha
BUT, OH MAN, WHAT A REACTION! AND I NEEDED A REACTION. I'M SICK OF BEING OVER-LOOKED.
ha ha
AND, HEY, EMMIE WAS A SPORT. SHE EVEN CRACKED A JOKE.
giggle
punch
HA HA hee
GUESS SHE'S FINALLY LOOSENING UP.

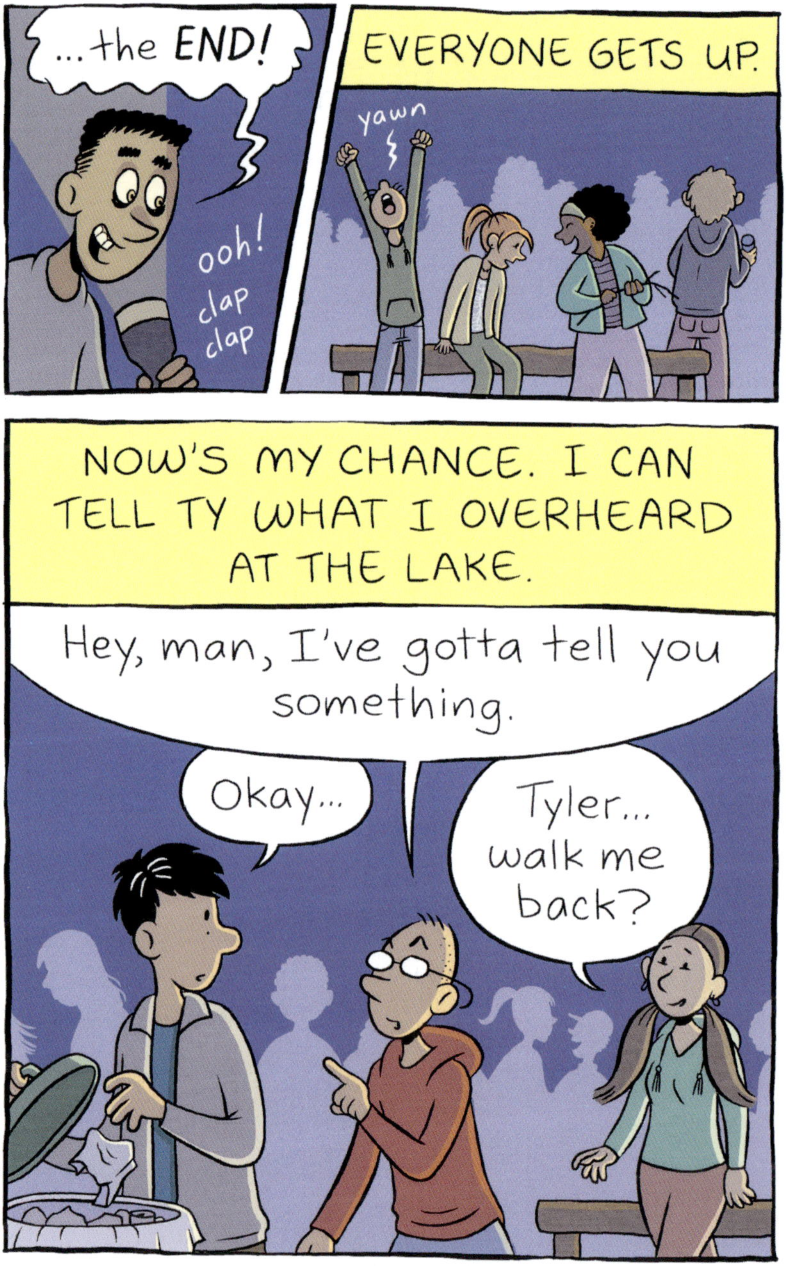
...the END!
ooh!
clap
clap
EVERYONE GETS UP.
yawn
NOW'S MY CHANCE. I CAN TELL TY WHAT I OVERHEARD AT THE LAKE.
Hey, man, I've gotta tell you something.
Okay...
Tyler... walk me back?

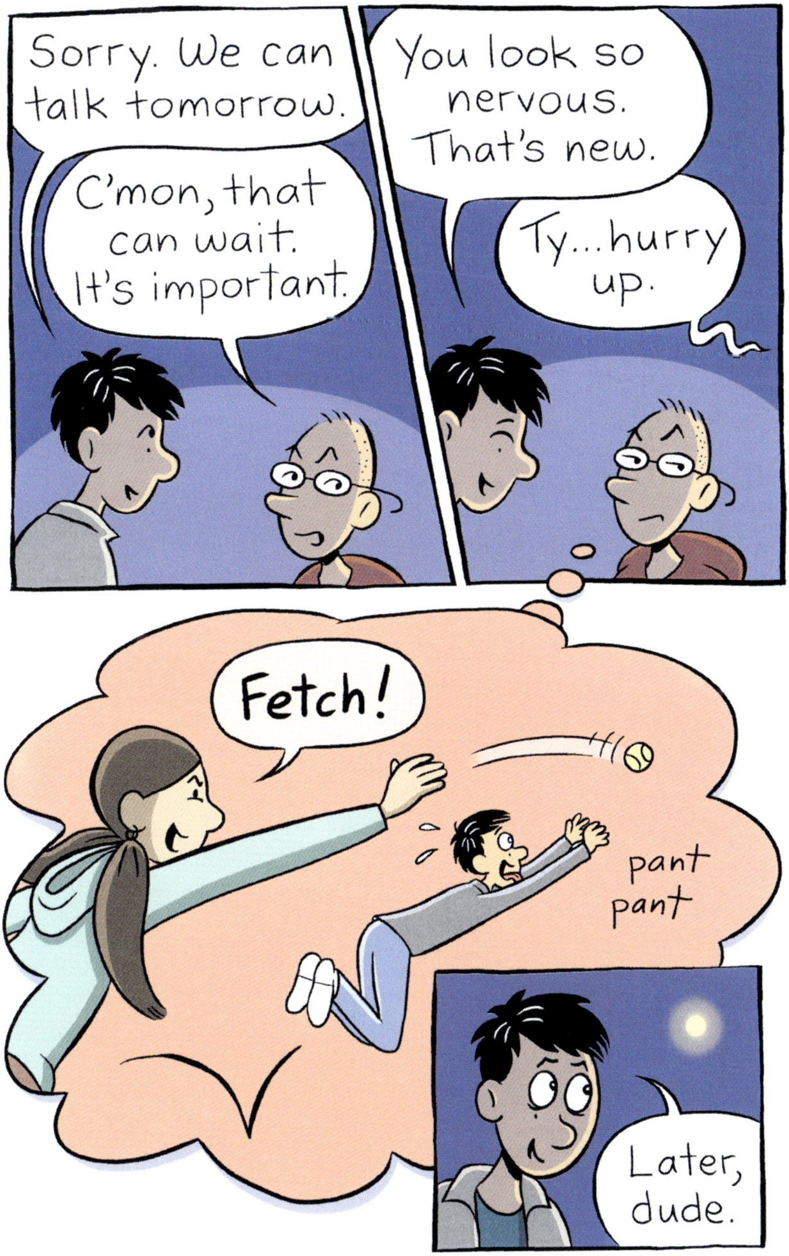
Sorry. We can talk tomorrow.
C'mon, that can wait. It's important.
You look so nervous. That's new.
Ty...hurry up.
Fetch!
pant pant
Later, dude.

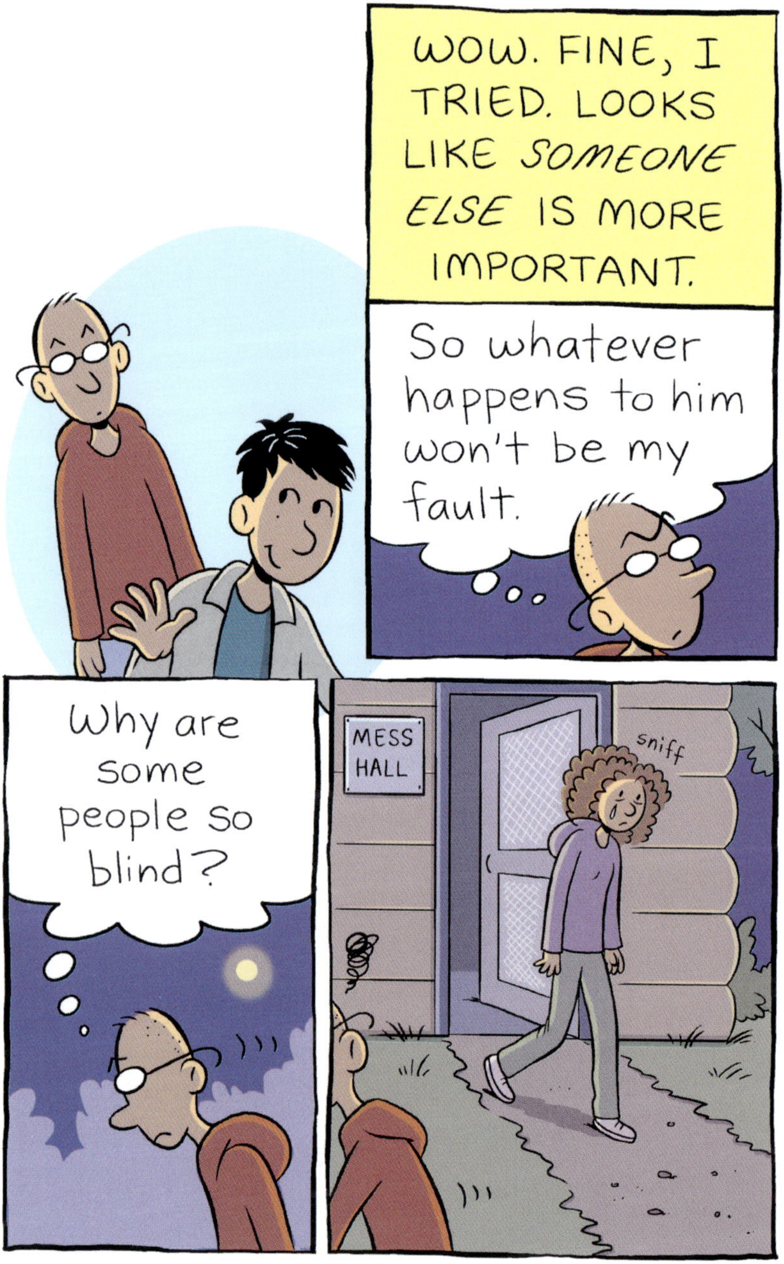
WOW. FINE, I TRIED. LOOKS LIKE *SOMEONE ELSE* IS MORE IMPORTANT.
So whatever happens to him won't be my fault.
Why are some people so blind?
MESS HALL
sniff

EMMIE

OMG!!

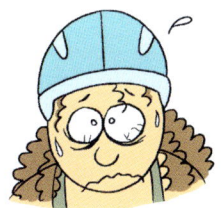

What am I doing here?! I wanna be mad at someone, but I did this to myself.

Okay, lemme back up.

my life
old-timey TV
old-timey VCR thingy
rewinding
click

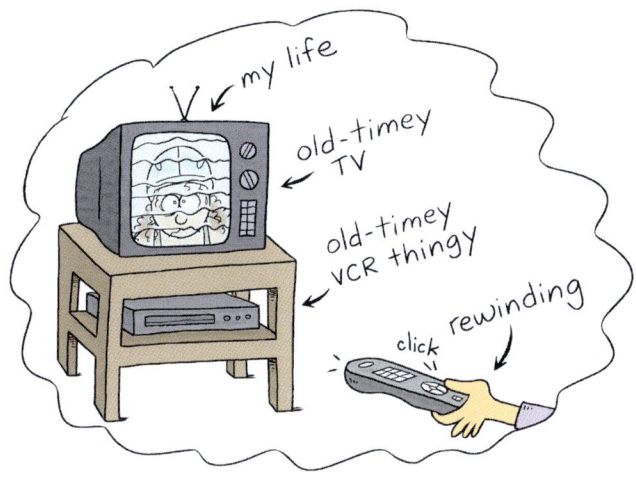

Things started off okay this morning. I wasn't in the best mood (who would be after being laughed at twice in one day), but once I slept and had breakfast, I felt better.

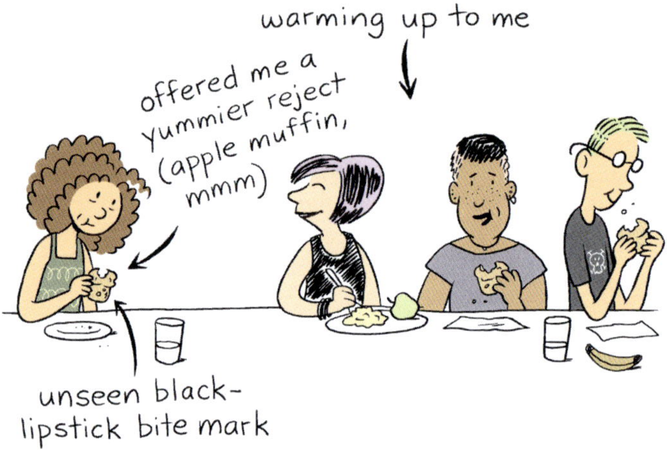
warming up to me
offered me a yummier reject (apple muffin, mmm)
unseen black-lipstick bite mark

At the end of breakfast, Coach Durdle announced that we'd be doing some fun activities.

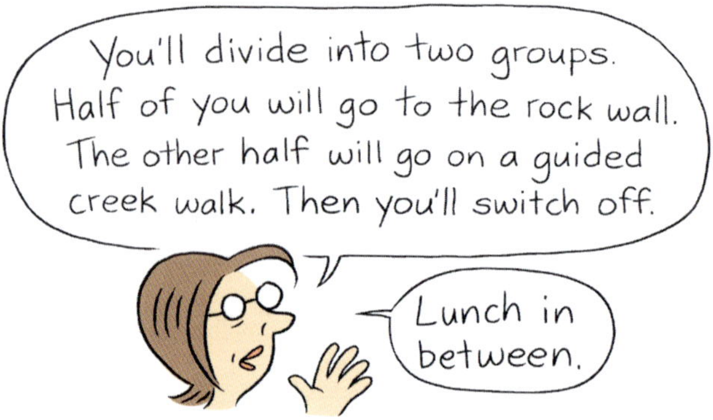
You'll divide into two groups. Half of you will go to the rock wall. The other half will go on a guided creek walk. Then you'll switch off.
Lunch in between.

She and Mr. Bauman called off each group. I was in the rock wall one. I tried not to think about all the mortifying things that could happen.

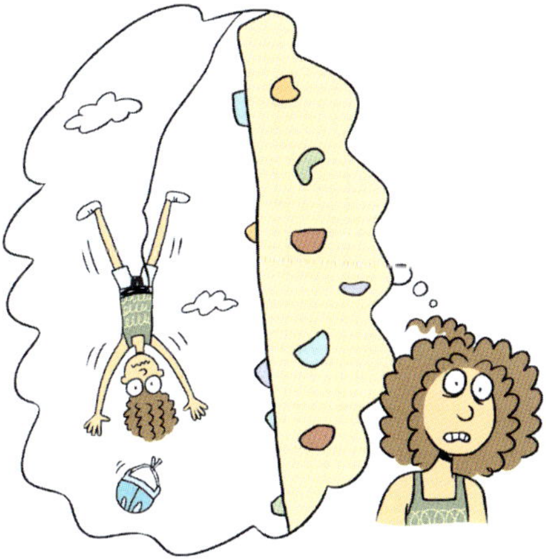

We still had to stick with our buddies, so Joe was in my group.

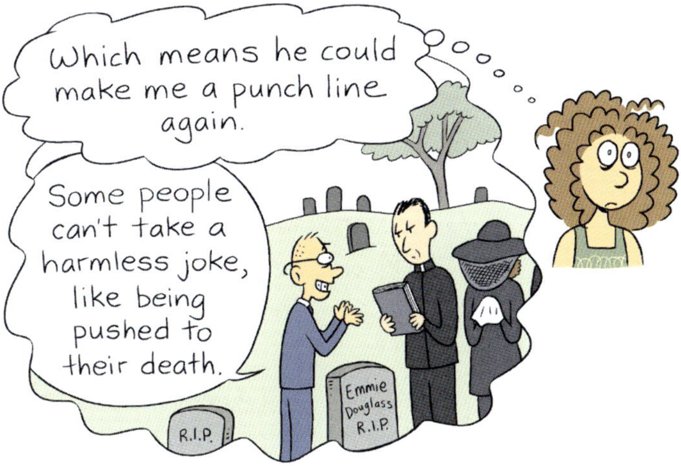
Which means he could make me a punch line again.
Some people can't take a harmless joke, like being pushed to their death.
Emmie Douglass R.I.P.
R.I.P.

We headed over. The rock-climbing wall was **huge**.

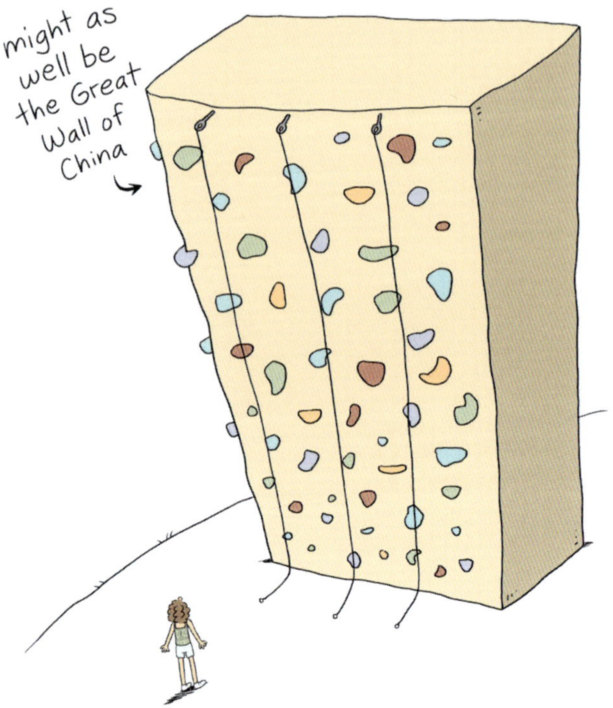
might as well be the Great Wall of China

That tall counselor—the girl Trina knows—announced:

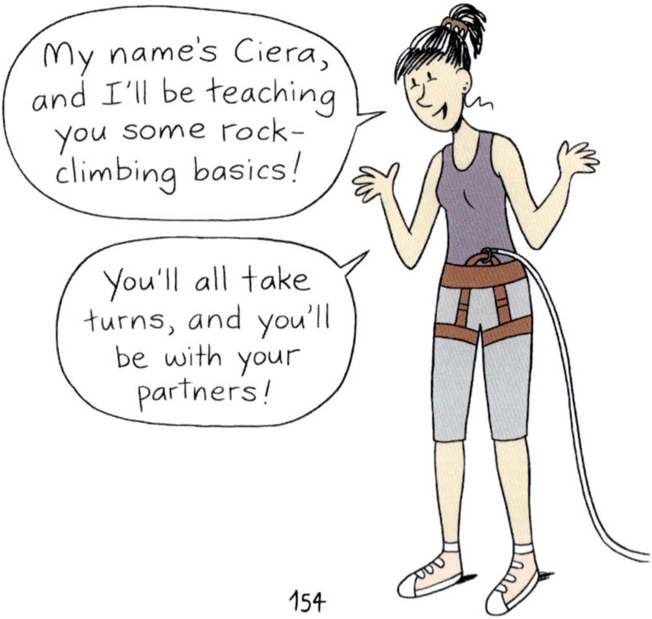
My name's Ciera, and I'll be teaching you some rock-climbing basics!
You'll all take turns, and you'll be with your partners!

Perfect.

Ciera took us through the rules and safety tips and then talked about climbing tricks. It was almost hard to pay attention—she's one of those people who speaks entirely in exclamation points.

You don't want to stick your butt out! You want to keep your center of gravity close to the wall!!

She demonstrated how we should focus on using the tips of our feet and straight arms.

Like a monkey!

That, of course, ignited this:

ooo! eee! eee! ooo!

After each rule, she and Jon did a demo of the techniques.

overly ripped calves (was not expecting those)

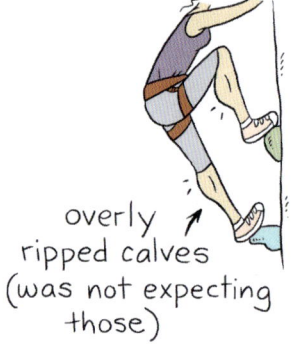

Afterward, a few kids volunteered. Eventually, it was our turn.

calm on the outside
pile of nerves inside

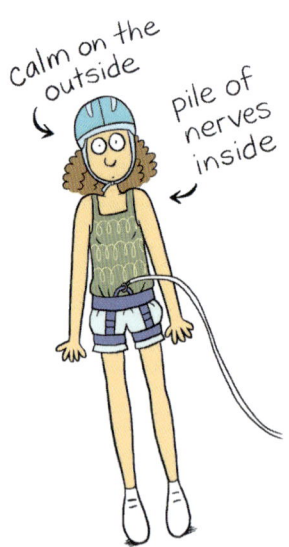

Ciera and Jon harnessed us up and we got started. I wanted to bite my nails, but my fingers weren't available. They were grasping the nearest (fake) rock.

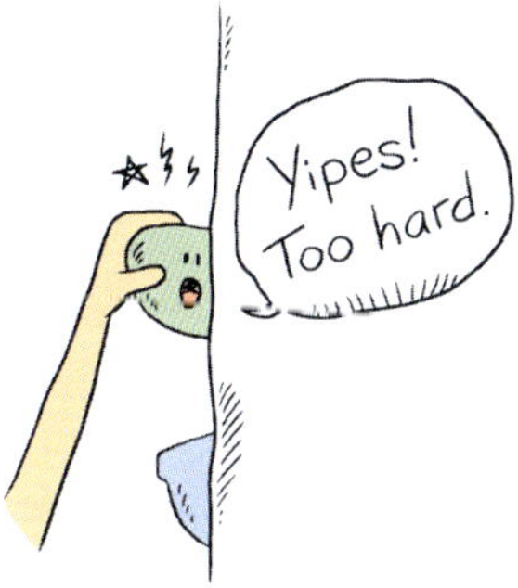
Yipes! Too hard.

I tried not to look at Joe, who was next to me. I didn't want to be distracted. I started out cautiously, focusing on the wall, my feet, and my pounding heart.

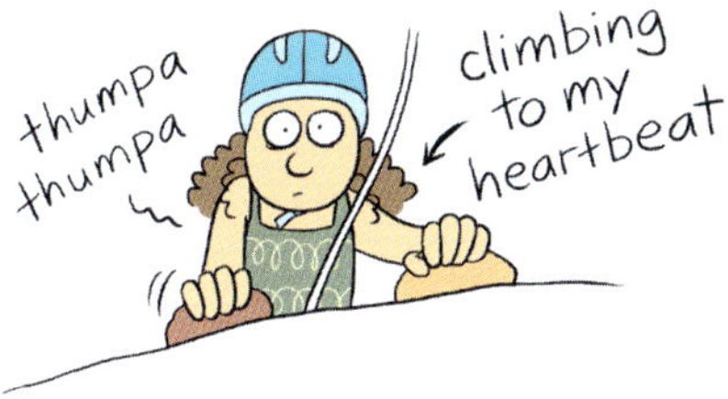
thumpa thumpa
climbing to my heartbeat

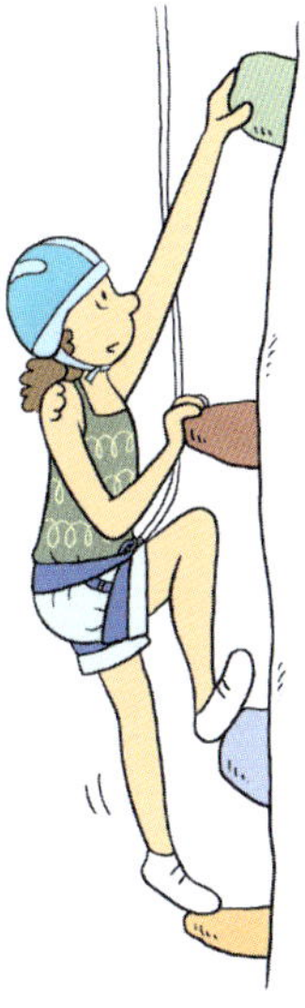

And . . .

I was doing it! For real!

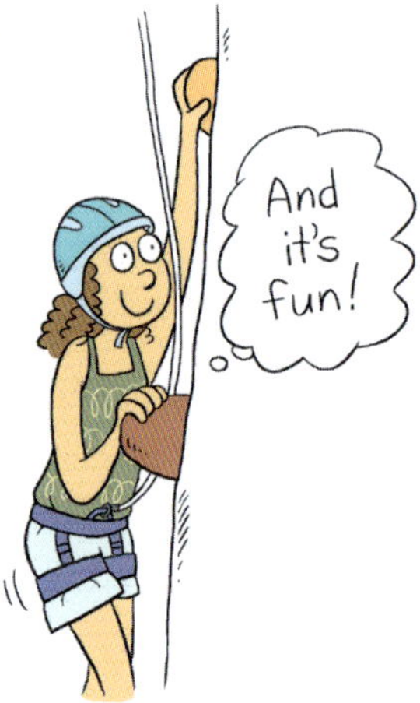
And it's fun!

I remembered Ciera's techniques, and I tried to climb "like a monkey."

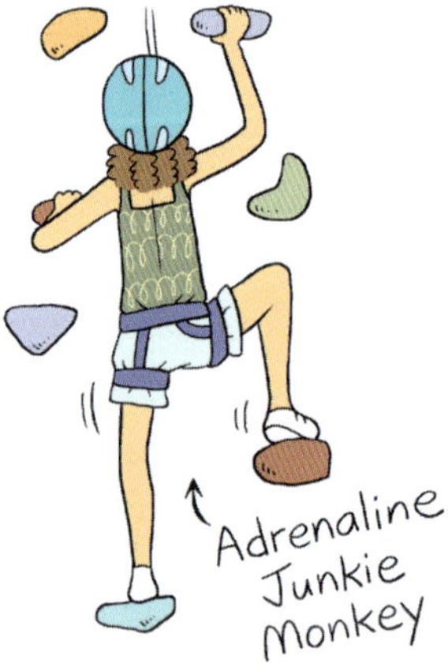
Adrenaline Junkie Monkey

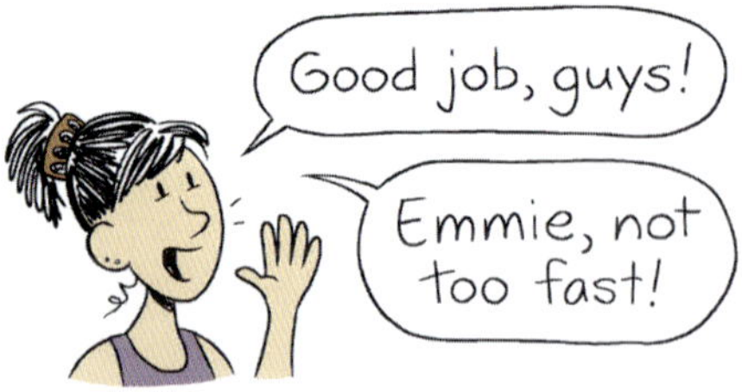
Good job, guys!
Emmie, not too fast!

Her words stopped me.
Suddenly, I looked down (I know, the one thing I shouldn't do).

ant people

And now . . .

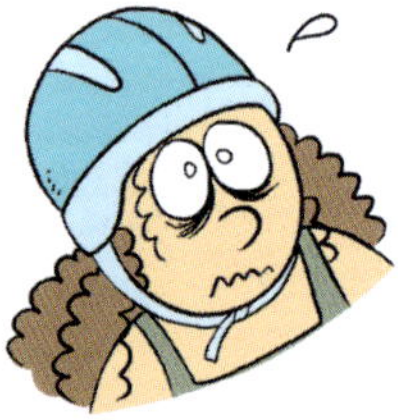

I'm frozen.

I start to shake. My arms and legs feel like skinny rattlesnakes. Why do things like this keep happening? Now Ciera and her pumped-up calves have to come save me.

I want to call out, but it feels like any little movement might make me stumble. True, I'm all harnessed up, but what if the rope breaks? There's no net below. I'd probably fall on a bunch of angry kids. And die.

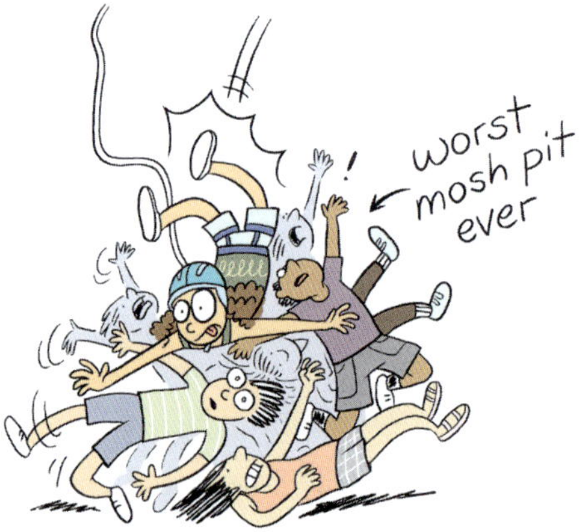
worst mosh pit ever

Panicky, I try to figure out what to do next when I hear a quiet voice nearby.

Bend your knees, keep your left arm straight, and grab the rock below. Lower your foot directly down at the same time.
Also, don't wet your pants. I'm right below you.
Joe?

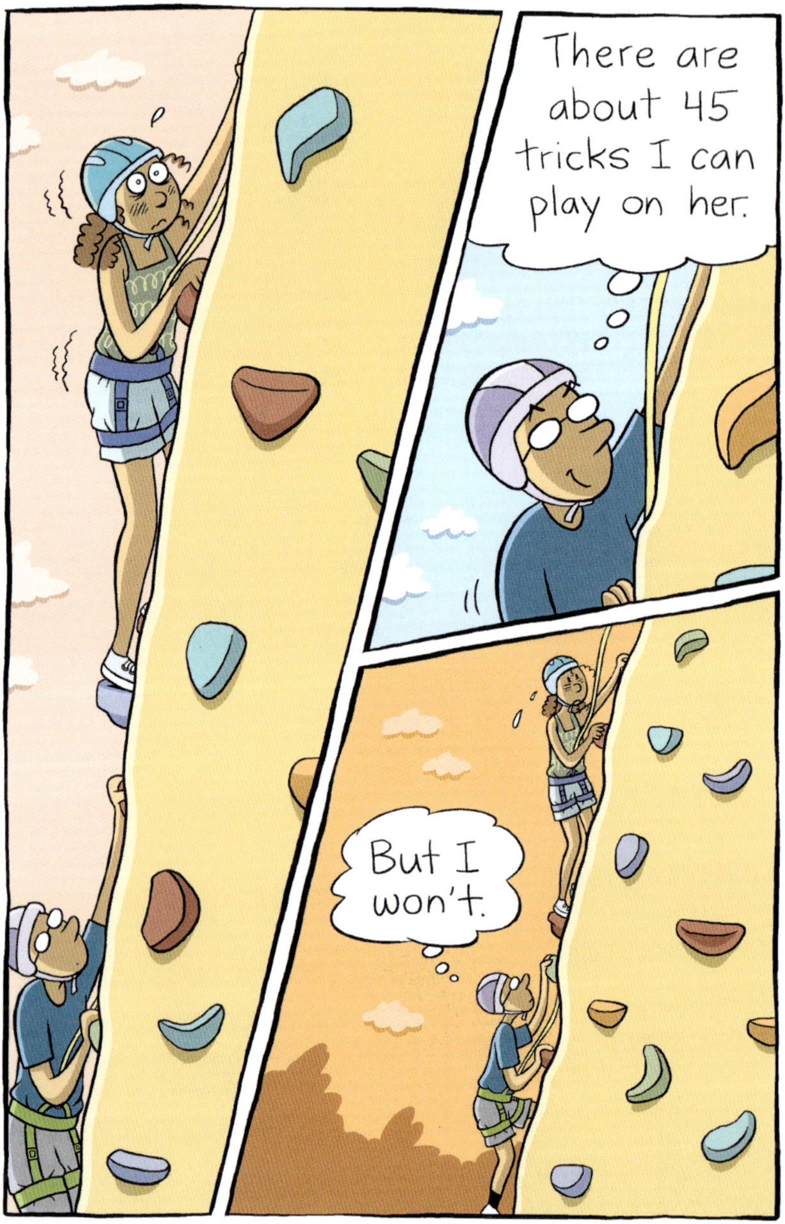
There are about 45 tricks I can play on her.
But I won't.

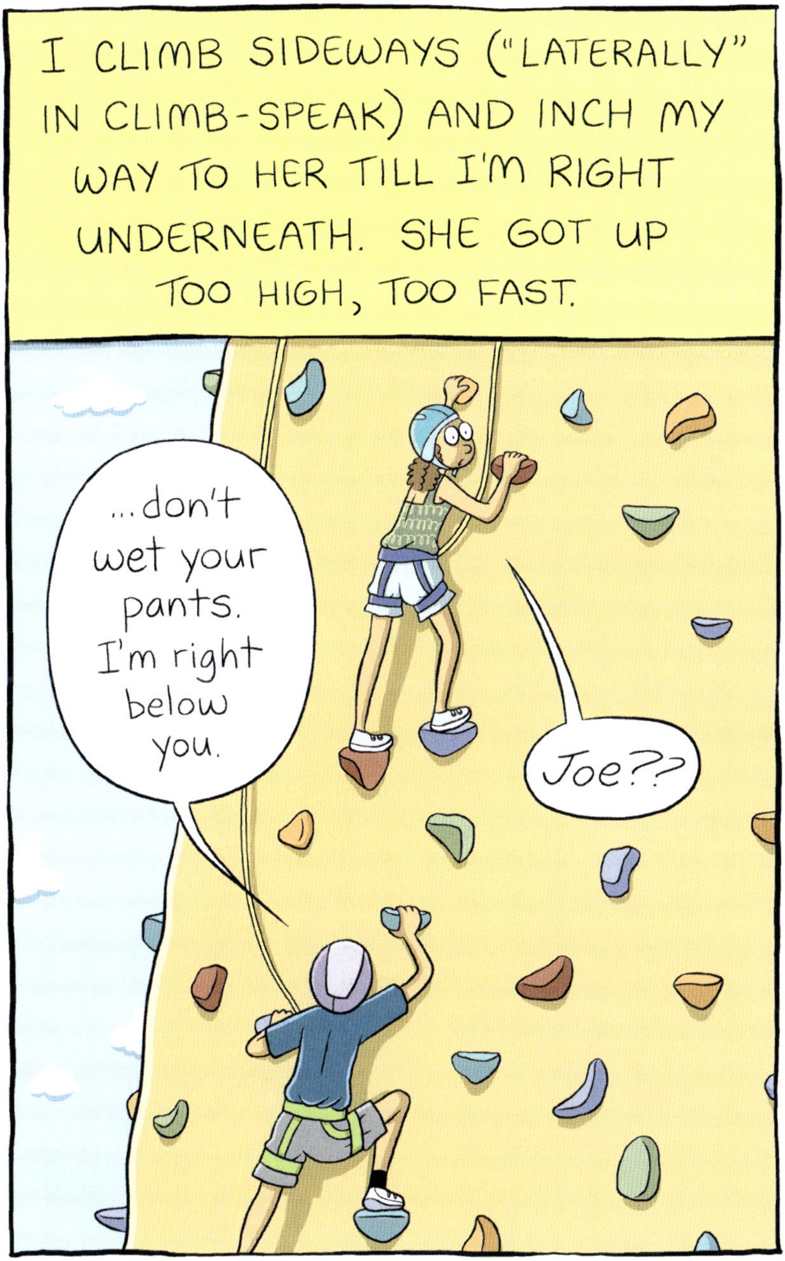
I CLIMB SIDEWAYS ("LATERALLY" IN CLIMB-SPEAK) AND INCH MY WAY TO HER TILL I'M RIGHT UNDERNEATH. SHE GOT UP TOO HIGH, TOO FAST.
Joe??
...don't wet your pants. I'm right below you.

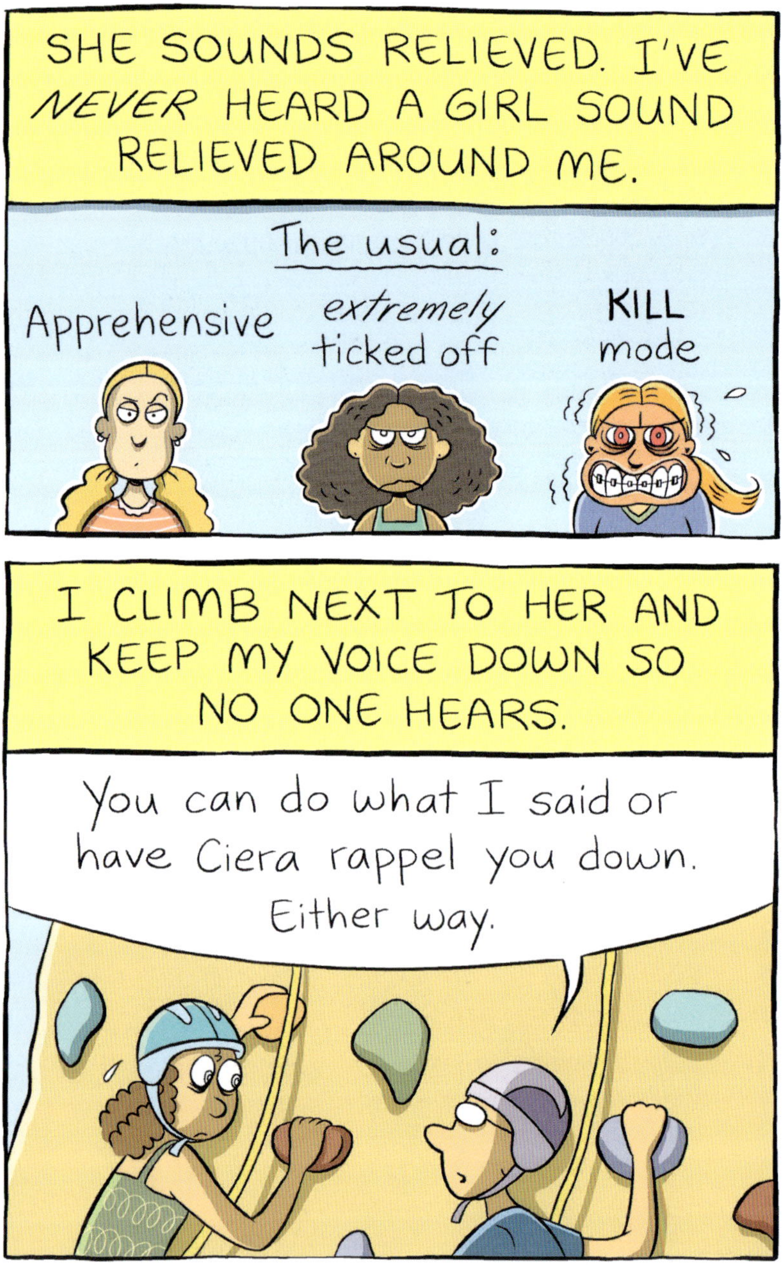
SHE SOUNDS RELIEVED. I'VE *NEVER* HEARD A GIRL SOUND RELIEVED AROUND ME.
The usual:
Apprehensive
extremely ticked off
KILL mode
I CLIMB NEXT TO HER AND KEEP MY VOICE DOWN SO NO ONE HEARS.
You can do what I said or have Ciera rappel you down. Either way.

SHE LOOKS BELOW.

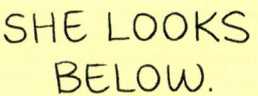

I THINK SHE'S SCARED THE ROPE'LL BREAK OR SOMETHING.

Okay, look, grab that lower rock, arm straight. You can turn sideways, too. It'll be easier.

SHE DOES IT. IT WORKS.

I KEEP GUIDING HER DOWN SLOWLY. CIERA AND JON HOLD ON TO OUR ROPES.

First time I climbed, I put the harness on backward *and* took the advanced route. They practically called in a helicopter.

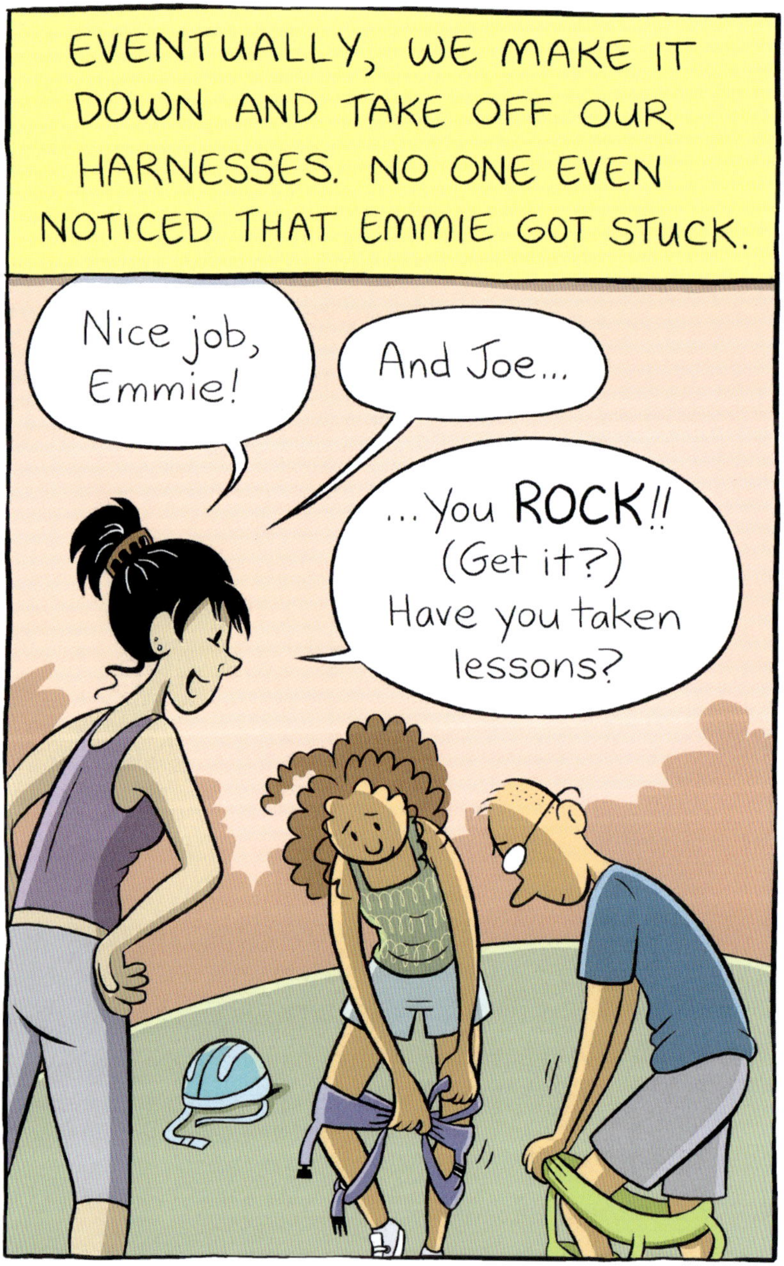
EVENTUALLY, WE MAKE IT DOWN AND TAKE OFF OUR HARNESSES. NO ONE EVEN NOTICED THAT EMMIE GOT STUCK.
Nice job, Emmie!
And Joe...
...You **ROCK**!! (Get it?) Have you taken lessons?

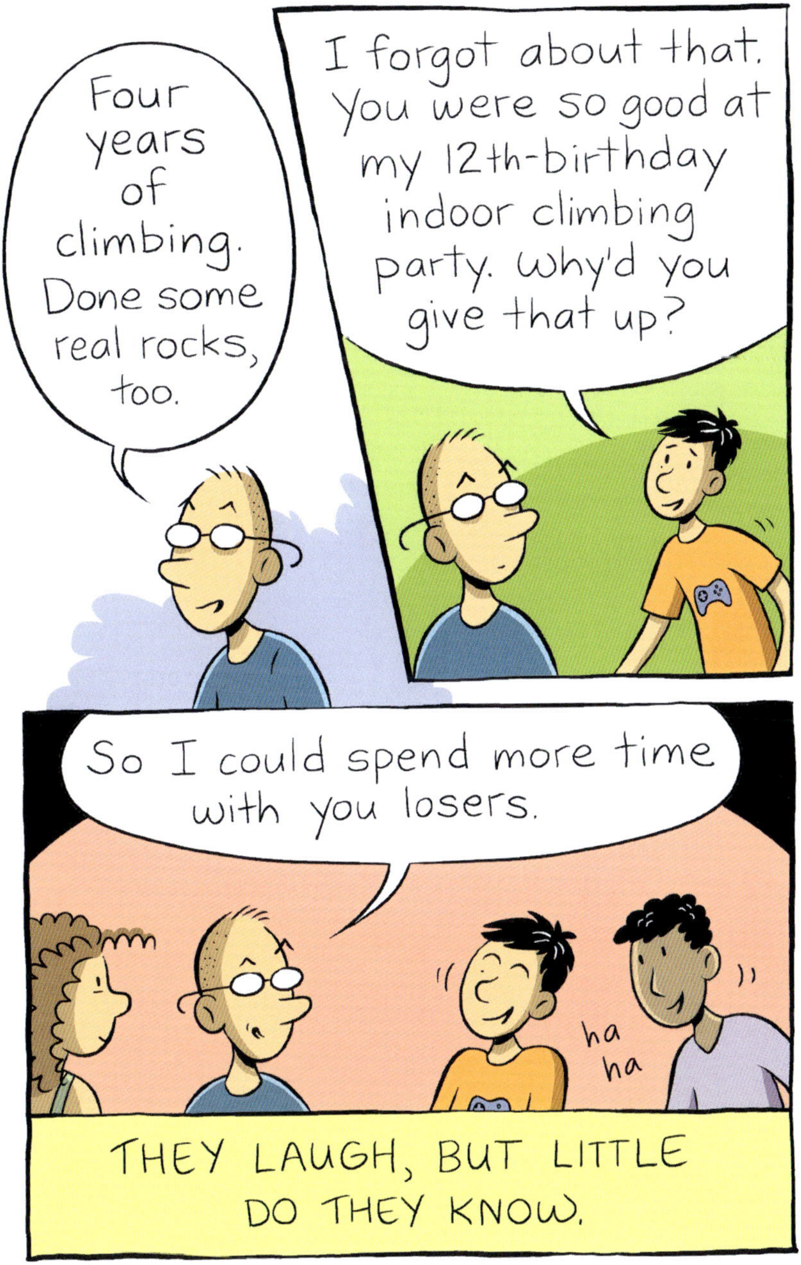
Four years of climbing. Done some real rocks, too.
I forgot about that. You were so good at my 12th-birthday indoor climbing party. Why'd you give that up?
So I could spend more time with you losers.
ha ha
THEY LAUGH, BUT LITTLE DO THEY KNOW.

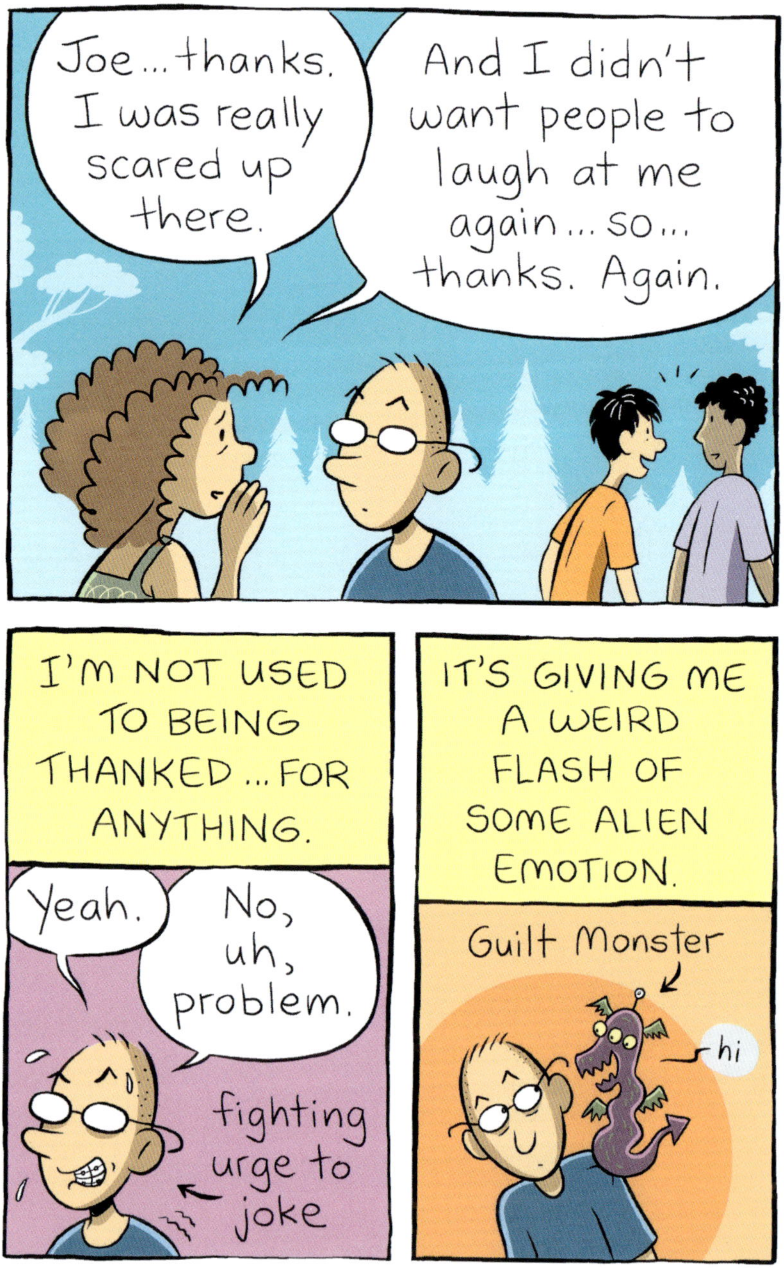
Joe... thanks. I was really scared up there.
And I didn't want people to laugh at me again... so... thanks. Again.
I'M NOT USED TO BEING THANKED... FOR ANYTHING.
IT'S GIVING ME A WEIRD FLASH OF SOME ALIEN EMOTION.
Yeah.
No, uh, problem.
fighting urge to joke
Guilt Monster
hi

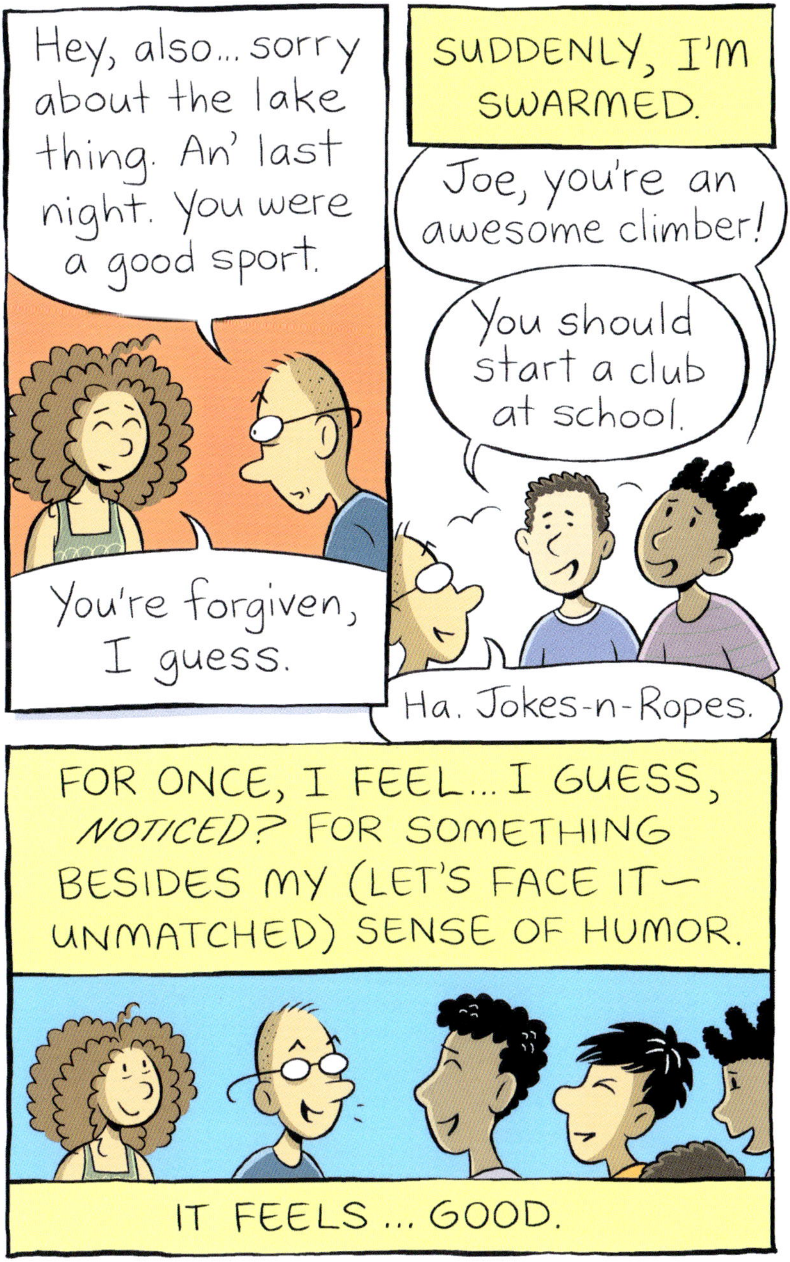
Hey, also... sorry about the lake thing. An' last night. You were a good sport.
You're forgiven, I guess.
SUDDENLY, I'M SWARMED.
Joe, you're an awesome climber!
You should start a club at school.
Ha. Jokes-n-Ropes.
FOR ONCE, I FEEL... I GUESS, *NOTICED?* FOR SOMETHING BESIDES MY (LET'S FACE IT— UNMATCHED) SENSE OF HUMOR.
IT FEELS ... GOOD.

EMMIE

We have a quick lunch in the mess hall (runny spaghetti for real!). I see Trina grabbing some food, but before I can get near her, that other counselor Ciera steals her away.

I watch as they sit together, eyes only on each other.

!
SPLAT
Huh.

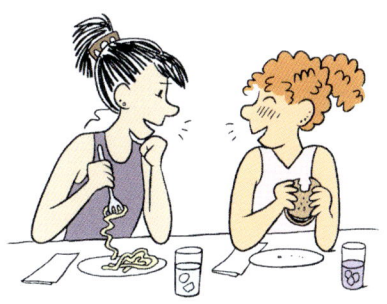

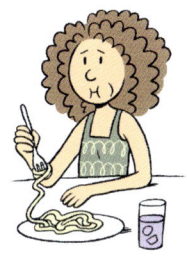

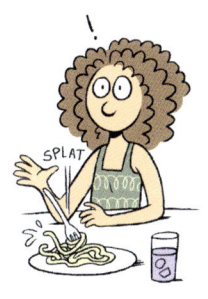

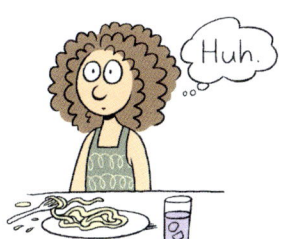

Before I can dwell on **that**, Coach Durdle rounds up our group for a creek walk.

Don't forget your swim shoes.
And grab your partners.

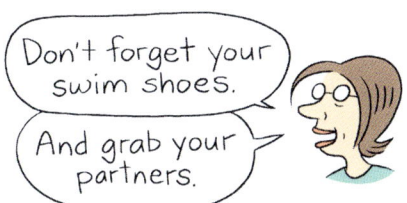

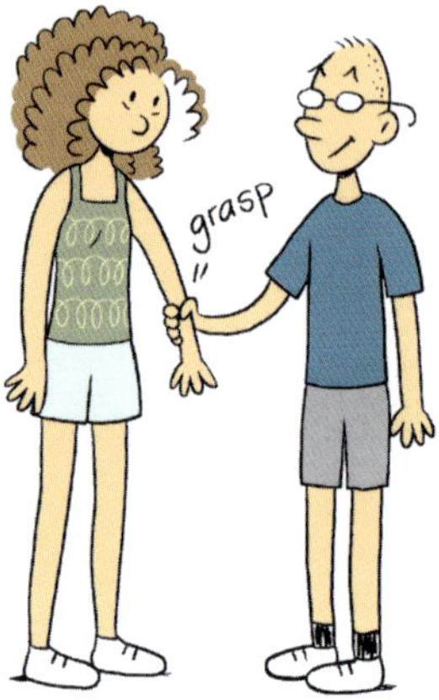
grasp

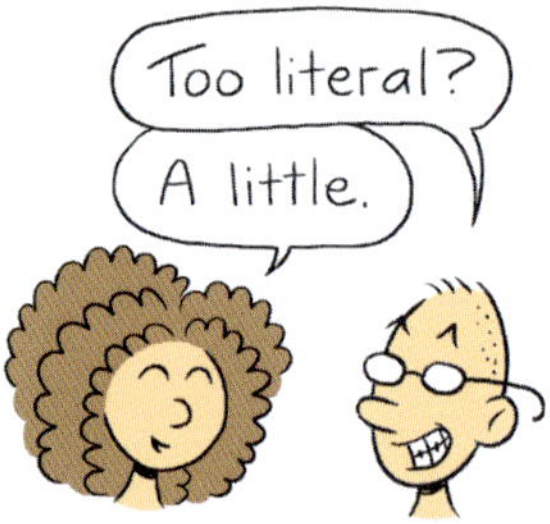
Too literal?
A little.

We follow Coach down a stony dirt path for a while until we reach the creek. I can hear it before I see it. It sounds bubbly and welcoming.

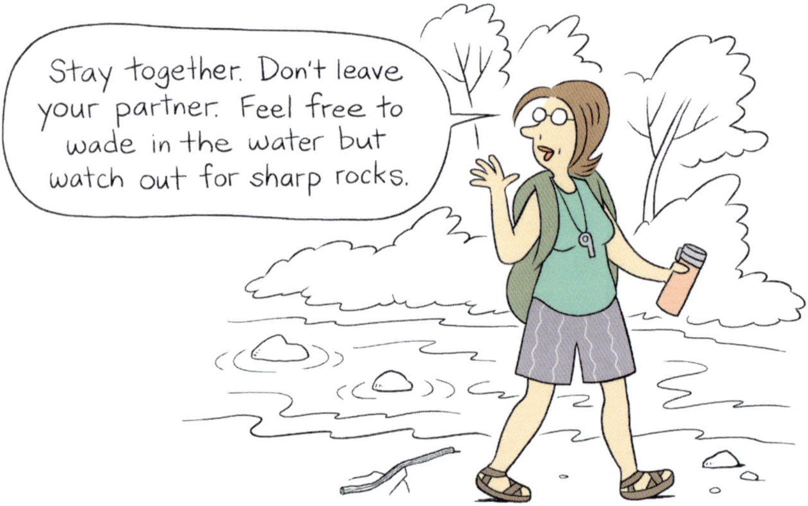
Stay together. Don't leave your partner. Feel free to wade in the water but watch out for sharp rocks.

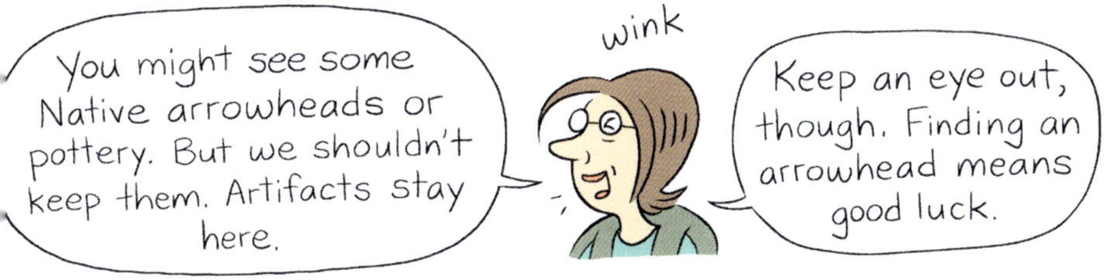
You might see some Native arrowheads or pottery. But we shouldn't keep them. Artifacts stay here.
wink
Keep an eye out, though. Finding an arrowhead means good luck.

We start. The creek looks inviting, so Joe and I wade in. The water goes up to my ankles and reaches Joe's mid-calves.

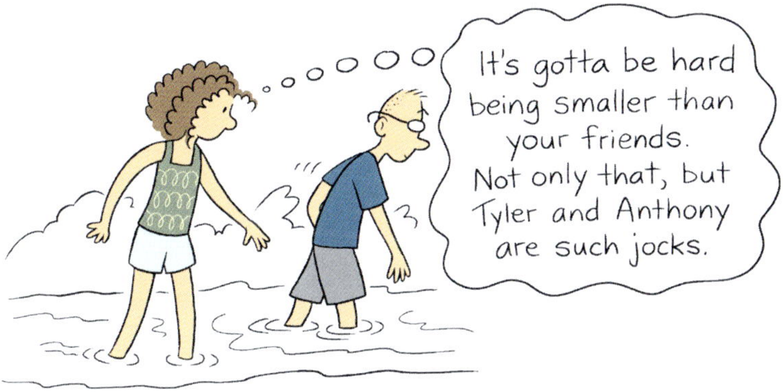
It's gotta be hard being smaller than your friends. Not only that, but Tyler and Anthony are such jocks.

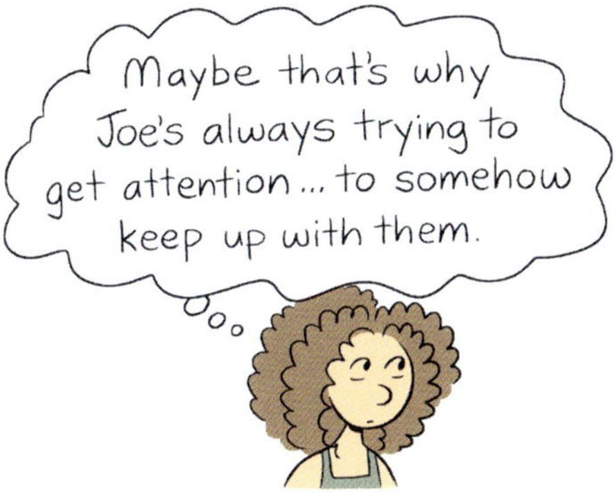
Maybe that's why Joe's always trying to get attention ... to somehow keep up with them.

In case you haven't noticed, I'm softening a little toward Joe. When I was stuck on the climbing wall, he totally could've done the "Joe" thing and made it worse.

But, by some miracle, he grew a heart.

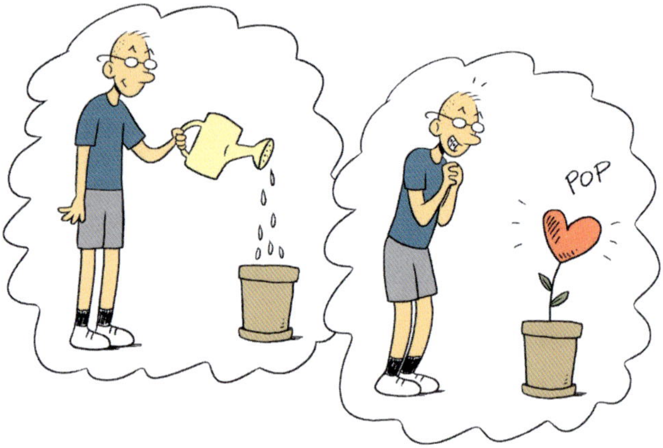
POP

Anyway, I'm thankful.

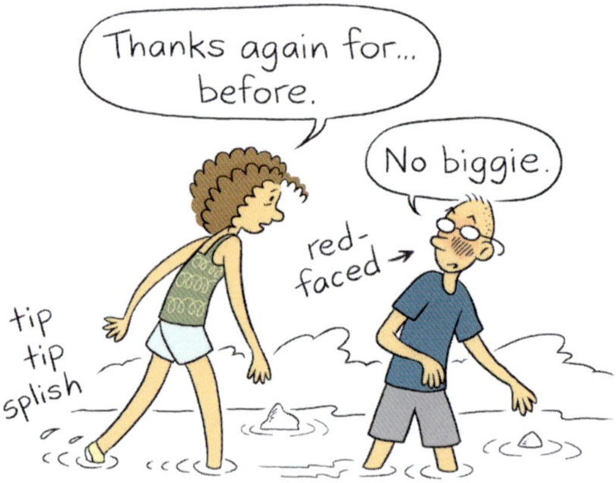
Thanks again for... before.
No biggie.
red-faced
tip
tip
splish

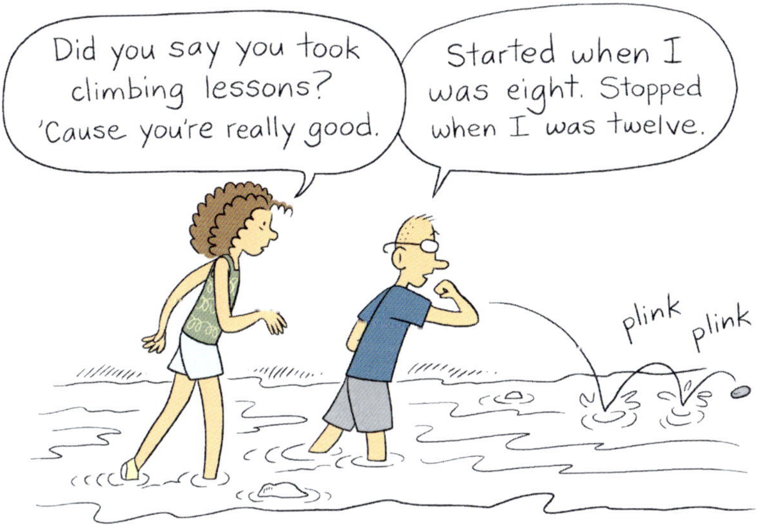
Did you say you took climbing lessons? 'Cause you're really good.
Started when I was eight. Stopped when I was twelve.
plink
plink

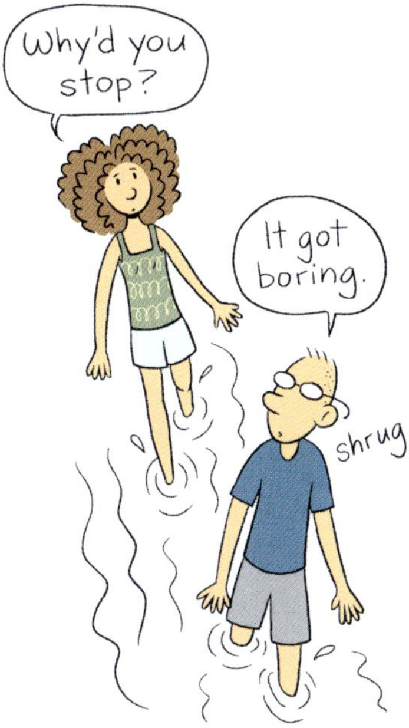
Why'd you stop?
It got boring.
shrug

He kinda hesitated there. But I don't say anything.

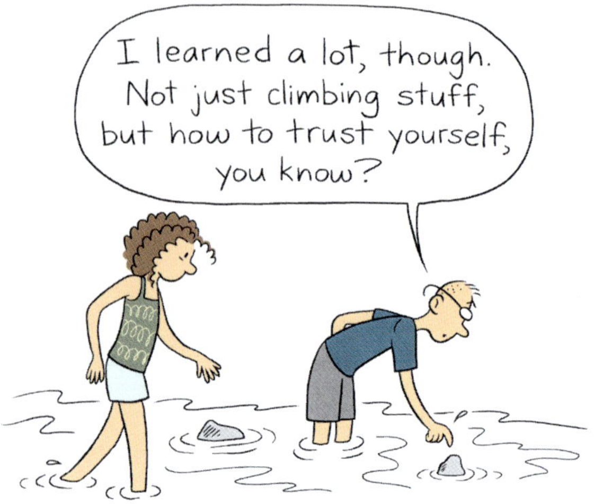
I learned a lot, though. Not just climbing stuff, but how to trust yourself, you know?

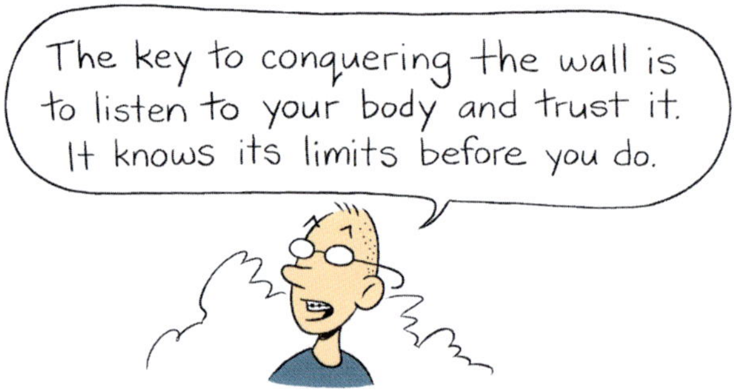
The key to conquering the wall is to listen to your body and trust it. It knows its limits before you do.

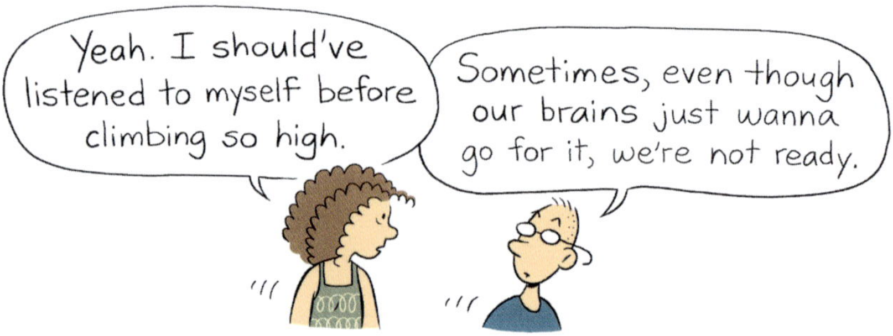
Yeah. I should've listened to myself before climbing so high.
Sometimes, even though our brains just wanna go for it, we're not ready.

Every once in a while, our group stops to look for pottery and arrowheads. So far, no one's found any. I dip my hands in the water and feel it rush over my fingers.

I take a chance and ask Joe about Tyler, who I haven't stopped thinking about since the Campfire Fiasco. BG must be with him. I try not to think about **that**.

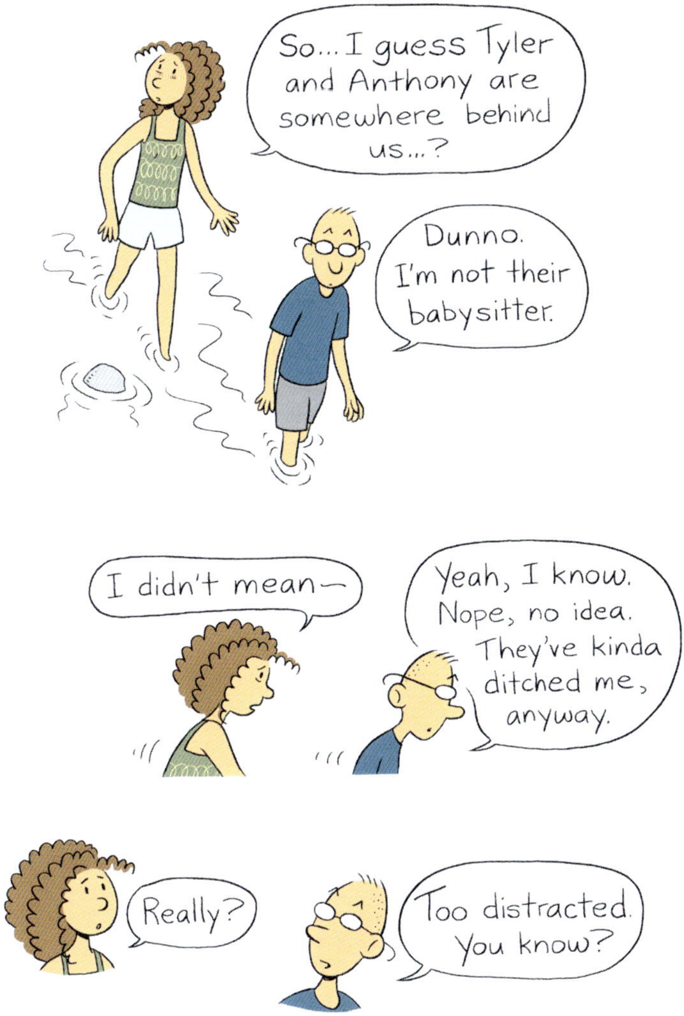
So... I guess Tyler and Anthony are somewhere behind us...?
Dunno. I'm not their babysitter.
I didn't mean—
Yeah, I know. Nope, no idea. They've kinda ditched me, anyway.
Really?
Too distracted. You know?

I do know. And it's depressing.

But . . .

. . . I'm not sure if it's the calmness of the creek walk, or the sunny afternoon, or the fact that Joe is being human, but I don't feel as upset as I did yesterday.

I **do** start to feel bad for Joe (I can't believe I'm saying that). To be ditched by your best friends? That's low. I mean, yeah, I have a crush on Tyler, but I'm not his **girlfriend**. As bad as I feel, he has every right to be with someone else. But poor Joe. Never thought I'd say this, but Tyler and Anthony are being . . .

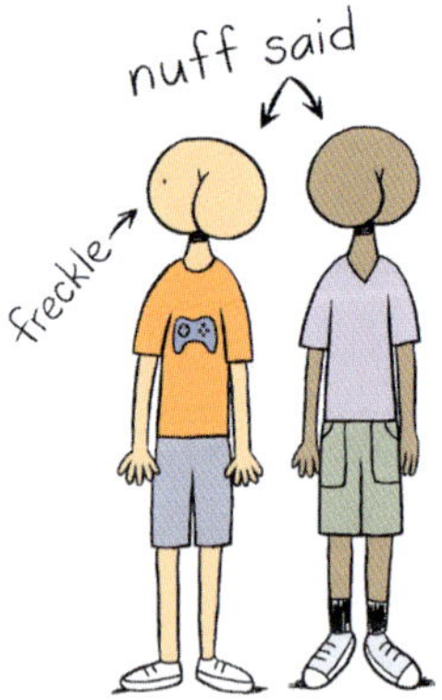
nuff said
freckle

Something reddish glints in the water. Joe and I see it at once. He bends down and scoops it up.

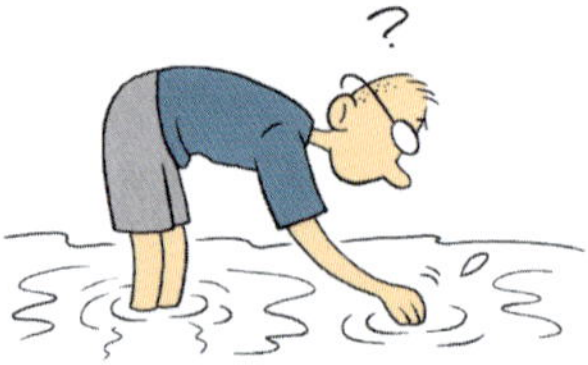
?

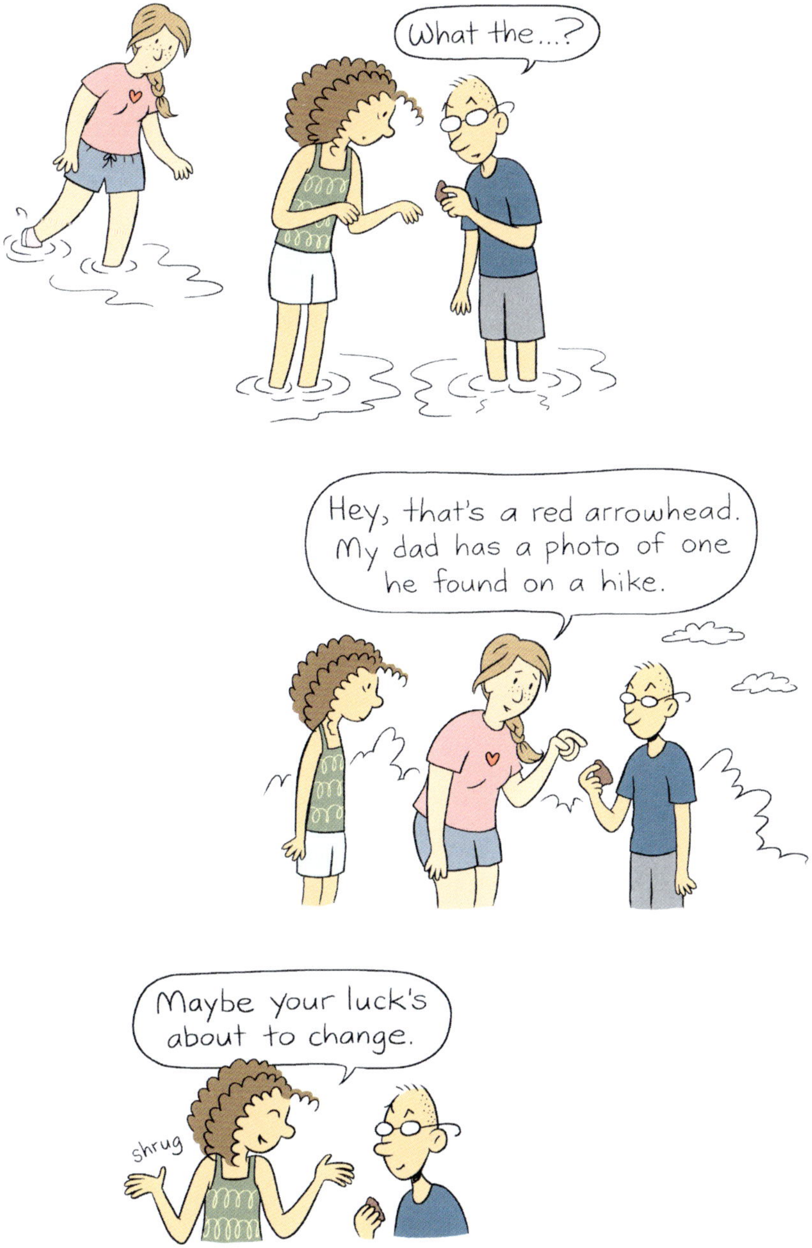
What the...?
Hey, that's a red arrowhead. My dad has a photo of one he found on a hike.
Maybe your luck's about to change.
shrug

Joe

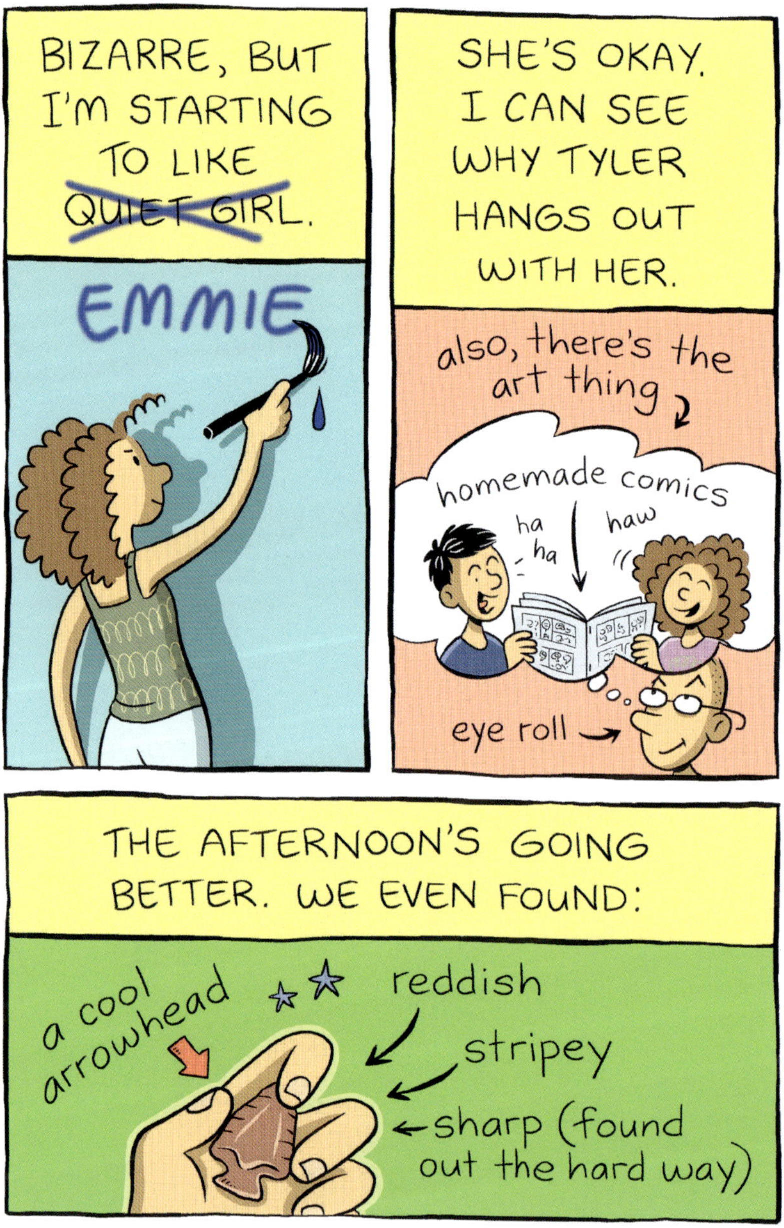
BIZARRE, BUT I'M STARTING TO LIKE QUIET GIRL.
EMMIE
SHE'S OKAY. I CAN SEE WHY TYLER HANGS OUT WITH HER.
also, there's the art thing
homemade comics
ha ha
haw
eye roll
THE AFTERNOON'S GOING BETTER. WE EVEN FOUND:
a cool arrowhead
reddish
stripey
sharp (found out the hard way)

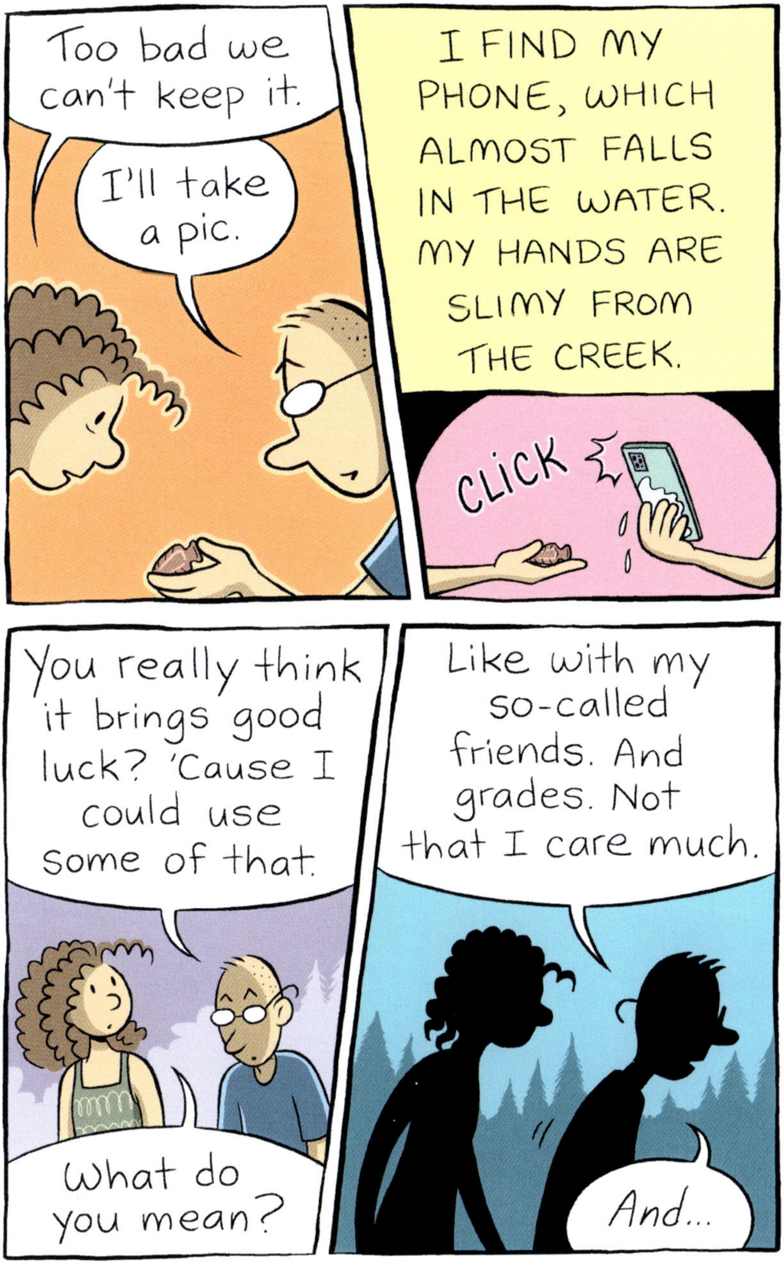
Too bad we can't keep it.
I'll take a pic.
I FIND MY PHONE, WHICH ALMOST FALLS IN THE WATER. MY HANDS ARE SLIMY FROM THE CREEK.
CLICK
You really think it brings good luck? 'Cause I could use some of that.
What do you mean?
Like with my so-called friends. And grades. Not that I care much.
And...

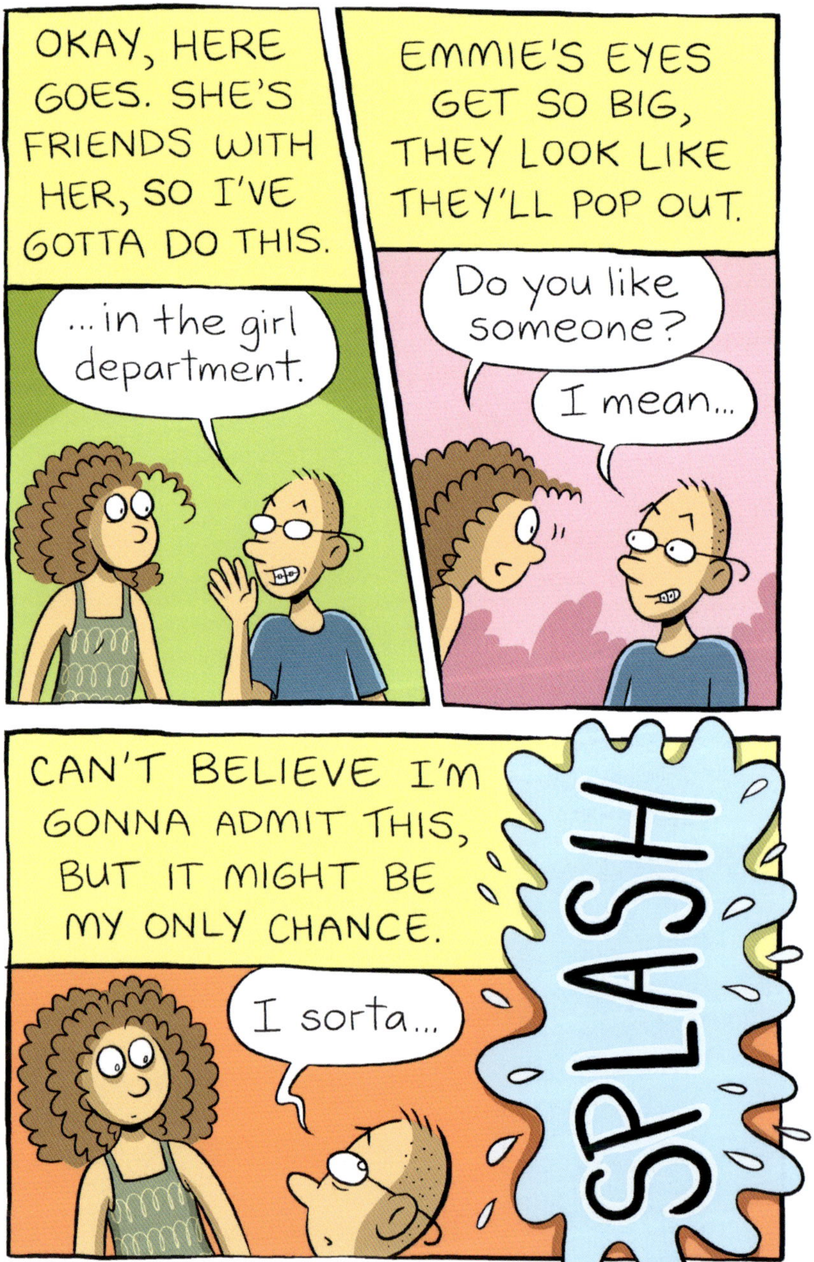
OKAY, HERE GOES. SHE'S FRIENDS WITH HER, SO I'VE GOTTA DO THIS.
...in the girl department.
EMMIE'S EYES GET SO BIG, THEY LOOK LIKE THEY'LL POP OUT.
Do you like someone?
I mean...
CAN'T BELIEVE I'M GONNA ADMIT THIS, BUT IT MIGHT BE MY ONLY CHANCE.
I sorta...
SPLASH

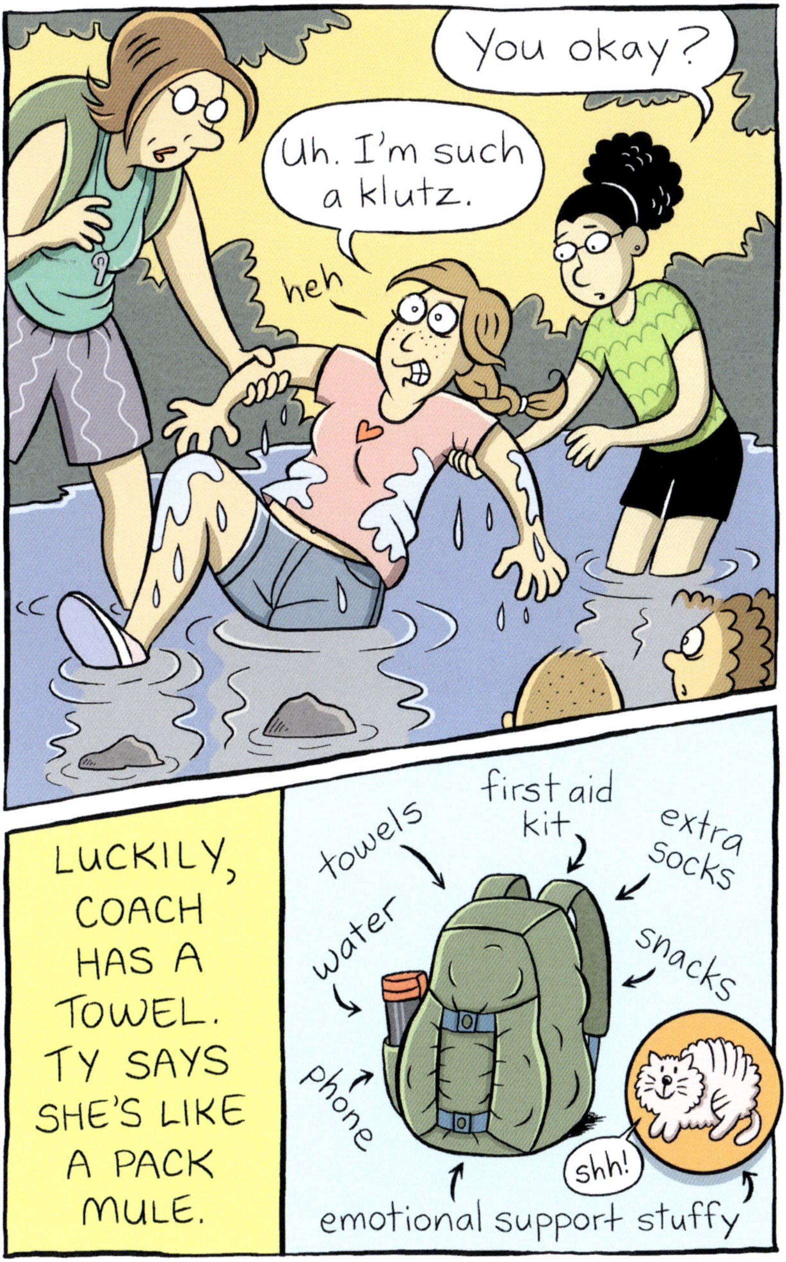
You okay?
Uh. I'm such a klutz.
heh
LUCKILY, COACH HAS A TOWEL. TY SAYS SHE'S LIKE A PACK MULE.
first aid kit
towels
extra socks
water
snacks
phone
shh!
emotional support stuffy

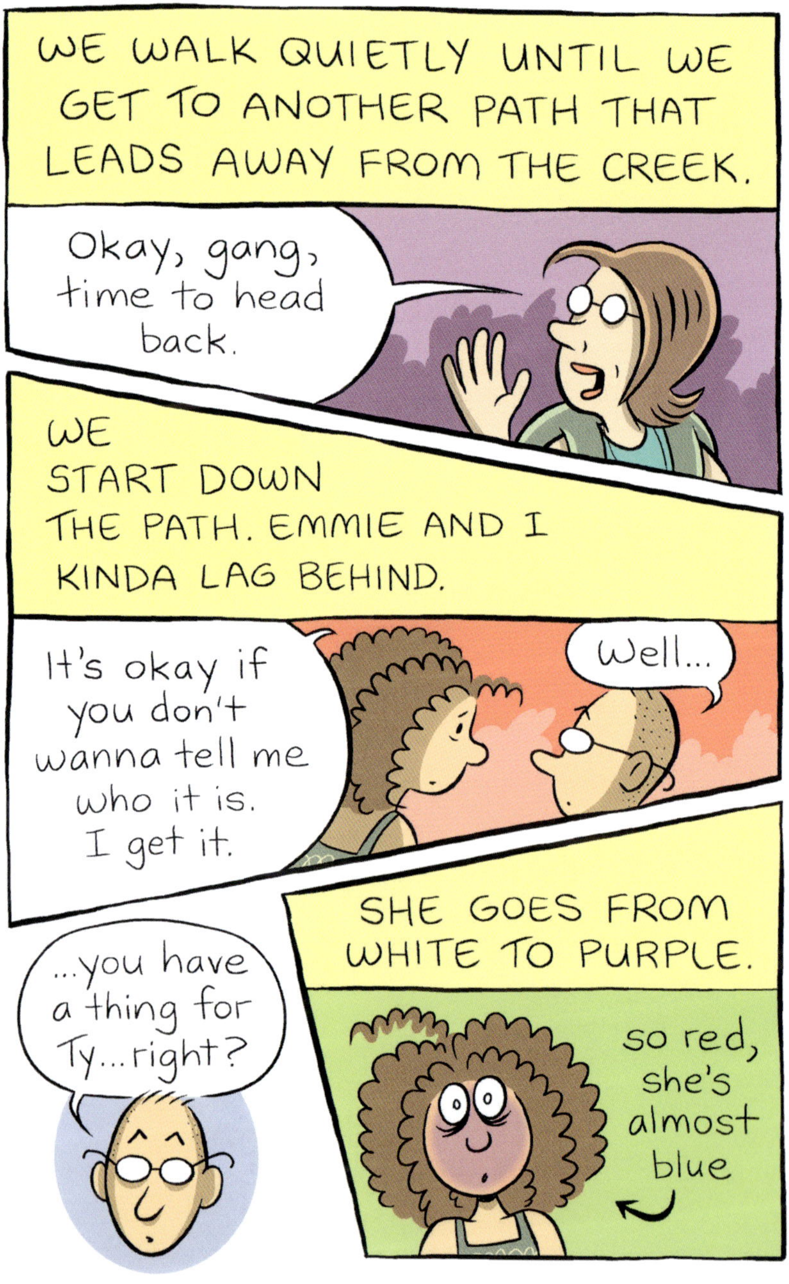
WE WALK QUIETLY UNTIL WE GET TO ANOTHER PATH THAT LEADS AWAY FROM THE CREEK.
Okay, gang, time to head back.
WE START DOWN THE PATH. EMMIE AND I KINDA LAG BEHIND.
It's okay if you don't wanna tell me who it is. I get it.
Well...
...you have a thing for Ty...right?
SHE GOES FROM WHITE TO PURPLE.
so red, she's almost blue

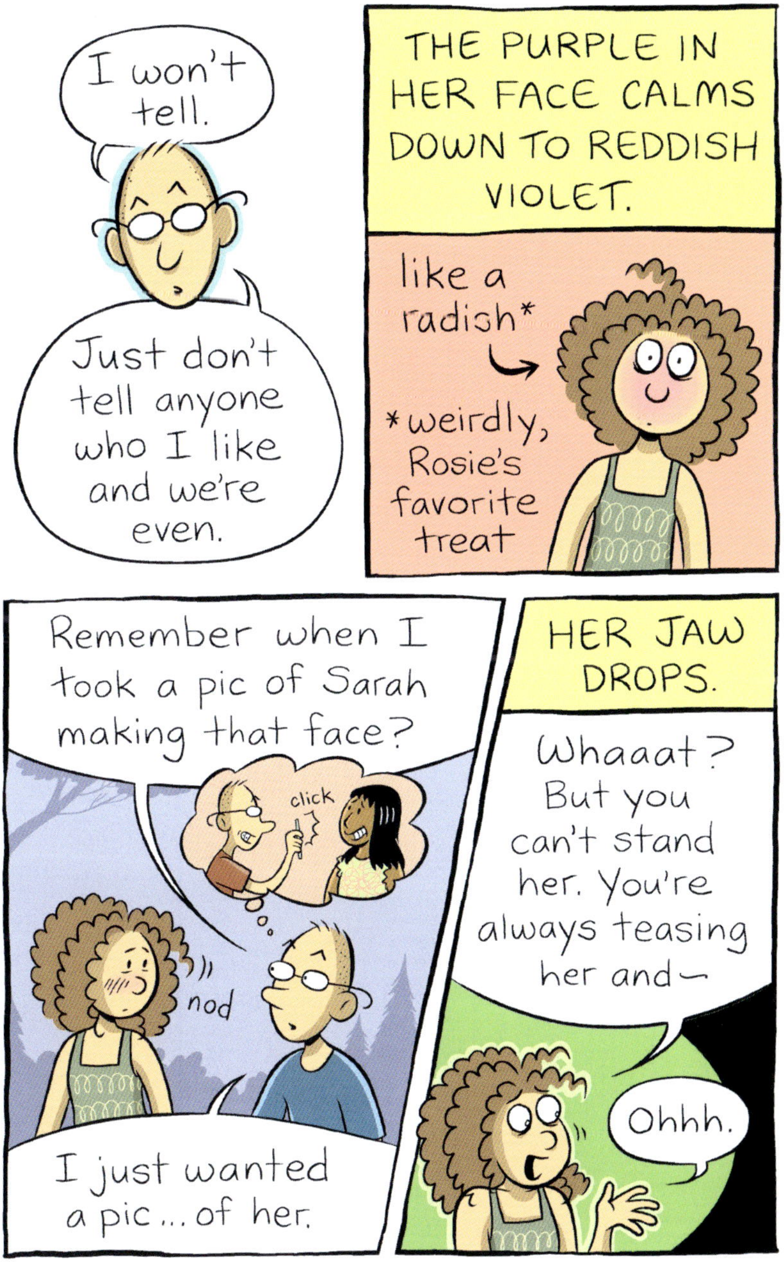
I won't tell.
Just don't tell anyone who I like and we're even.
THE PURPLE IN HER FACE CALMS DOWN TO REDDISH VIOLET.
like a radish*
*weirdly, Rosie's favorite treat
Remember when I took a pic of Sarah making that face?
click
nod
I just wanted a pic... of her.
HER JAW DROPS.
Whaaat? But you can't stand her. You're always teasing her and–
Ohhh.

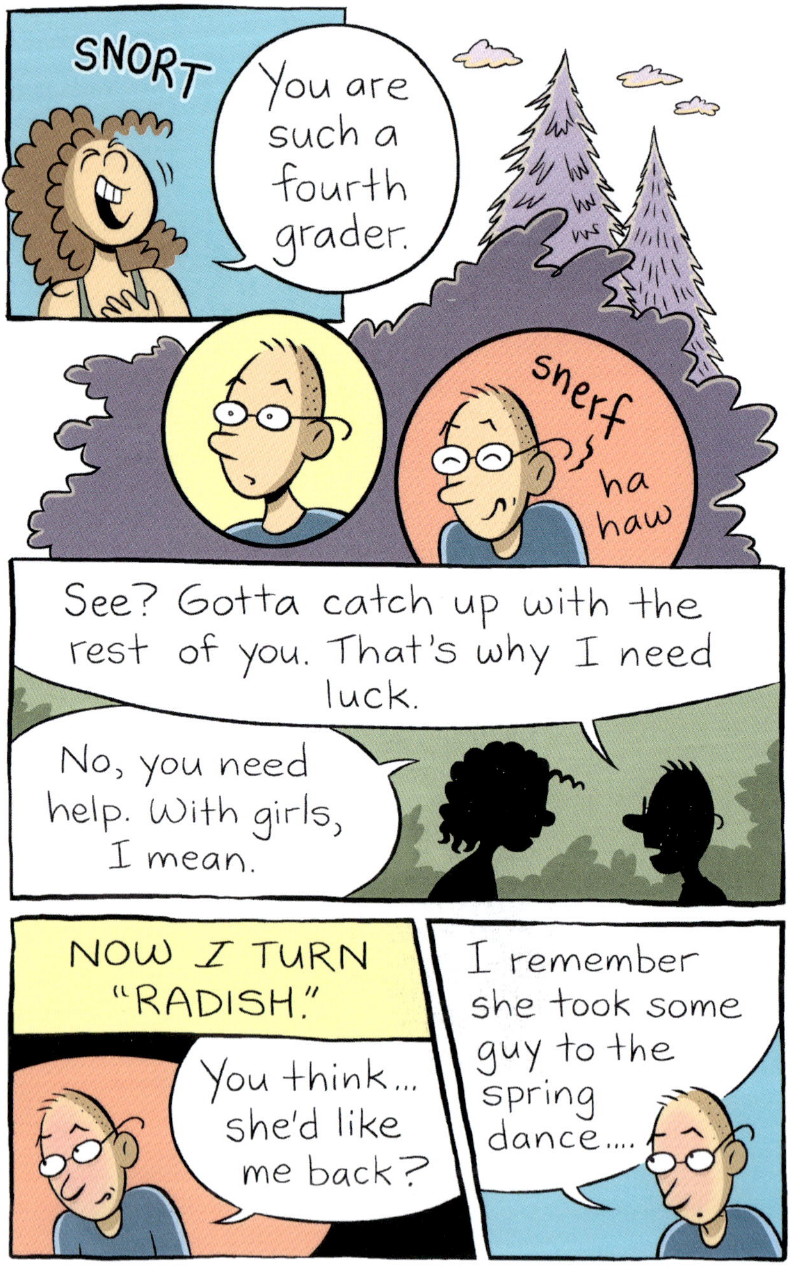
SNORT
You are such a fourth grader.
snerf
ha haw
See? Gotta catch up with the rest of you. That's why I need luck.
No, you need help. With girls, I mean.
NOW I TURN "RADISH."
You think... she'd like me back?
I remember she took some guy to the spring dance....

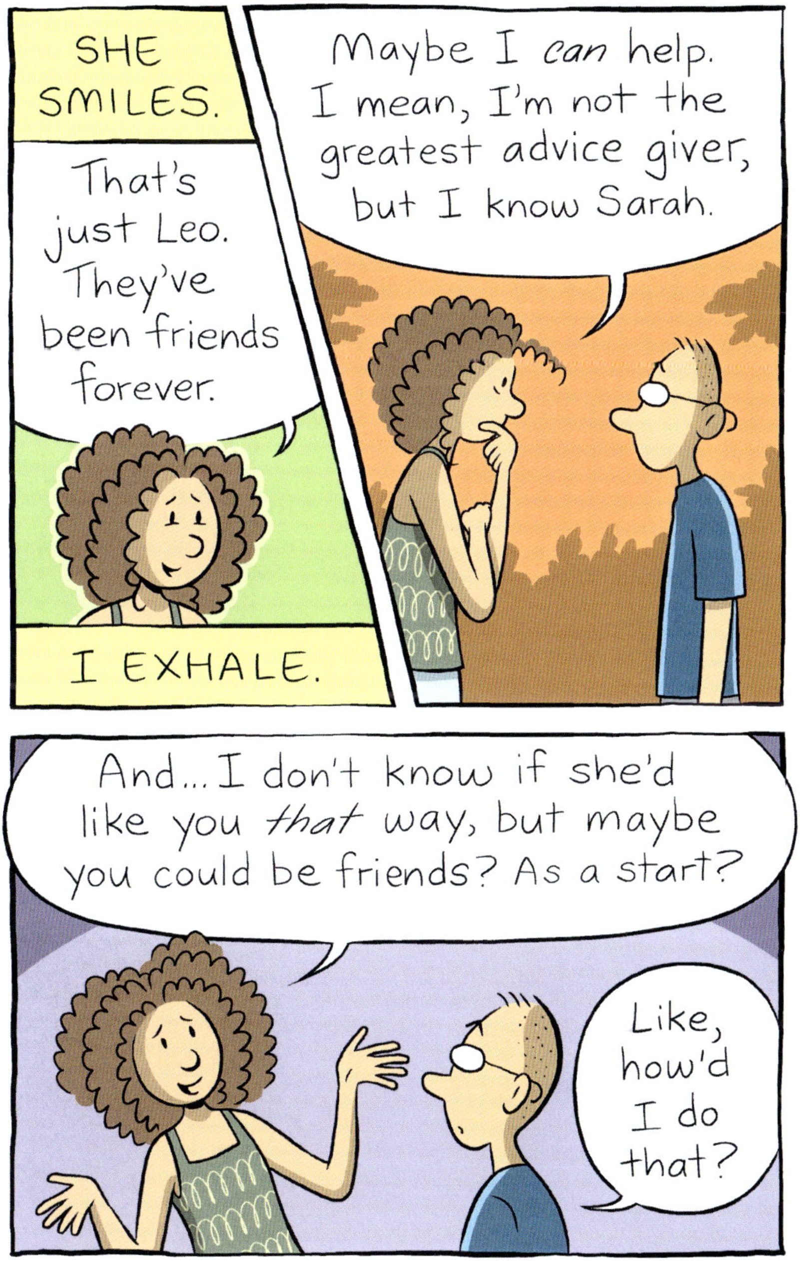
SHE SMILES.
That's just Leo. They've been friends forever.
I EXHALE.
Maybe I *can* help. I mean, I'm not the greatest advice giver, but I know Sarah.
And... I don't know if she'd like you *that* way, but maybe you could be friends? As a start?
Like, how'd I do that?

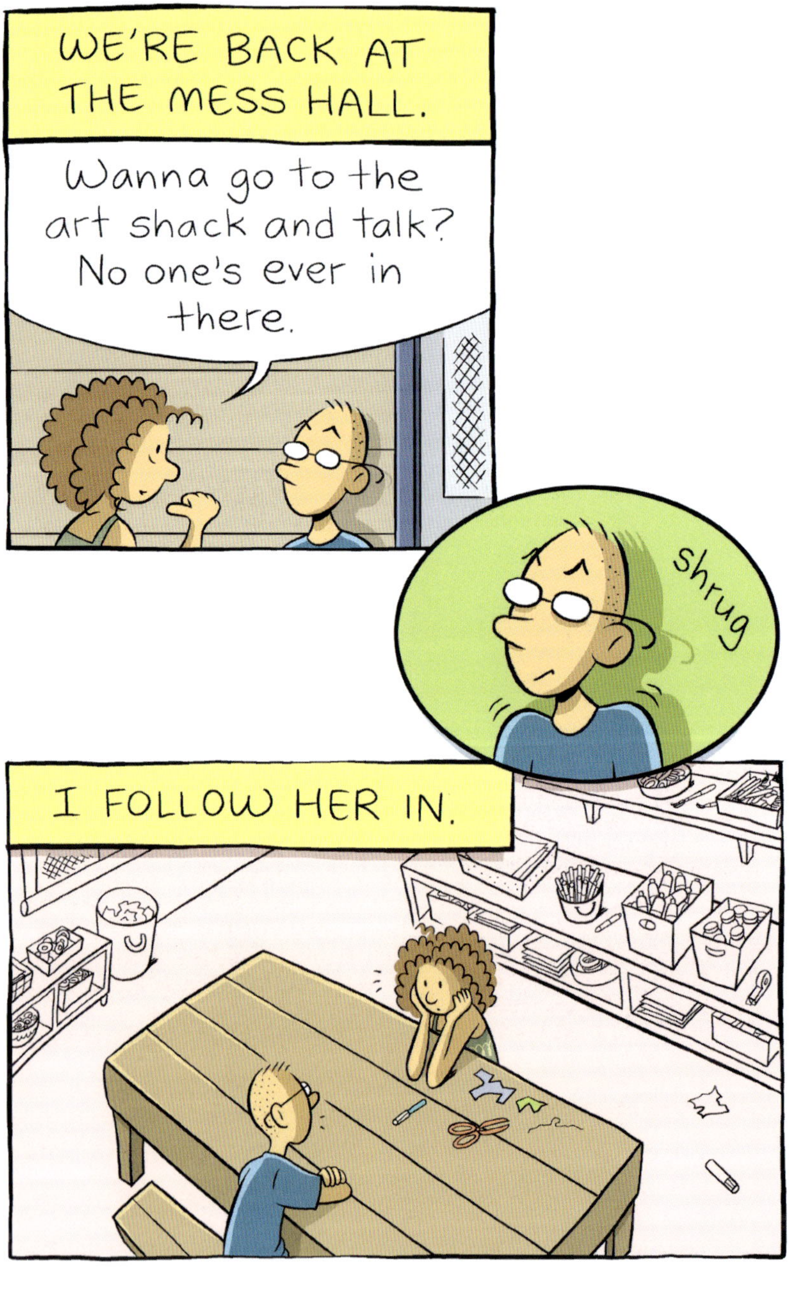
WE'RE BACK AT THE MESS HALL.
Wanna go to the art shack and talk? No one's ever in there.
shrug
I FOLLOW HER IN.

EMMIE

Back at the campfire.

I can't believe I'm saying this, but I'm actually having fun.
We've already played a few games, like Would you Rather and Heads Up, Seven Up. Now we're doing Prop-a-Skit. That's where we divide into groups and create funny little skits using a bunch

of props that the counselors give us. Joe, Tyler, and I are in the same group, and we've been totally hamming it up with:

Hula-Hoop
lobster claw mittens
fake beard
large inflatable retro car phone
Joe's stuffed llama

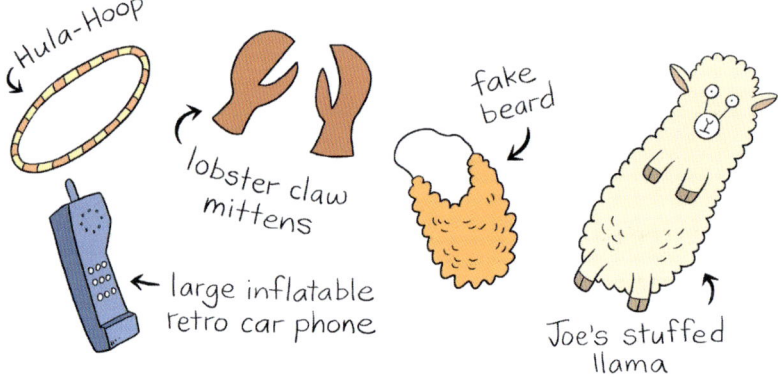

Doing an impromptu skit would normally scare me silly, but being with Tyler, who's sweet and fun (and BG's off in a different group), and Joe, who I feel a **lot** more comfortable around now—really made me loosen up.

making it up as we go

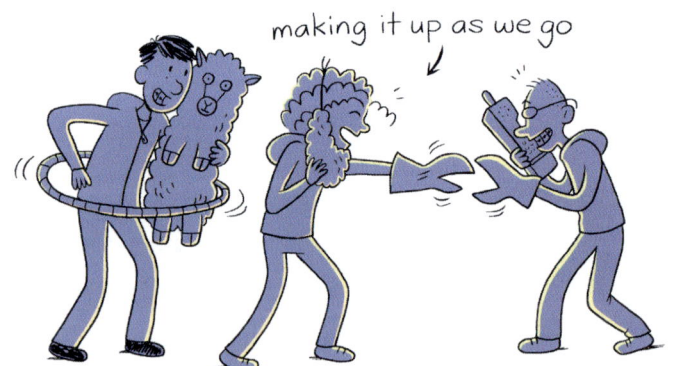

By the time the skits end, I'm laughing so hard, I have to sit on a bench to catch my breath. We wind down with s'mores and hot chocolate.

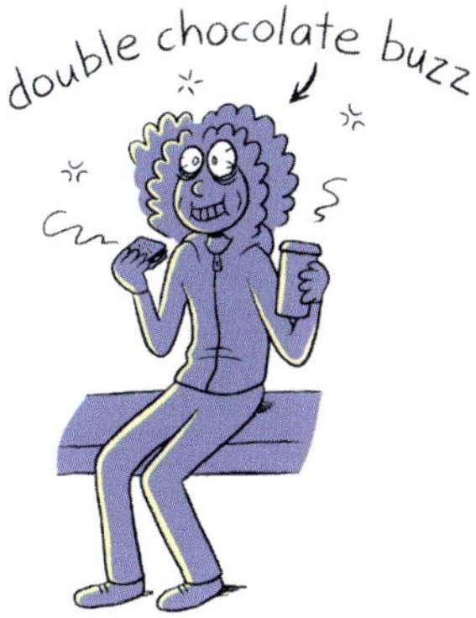
double chocolate buzz

It's gotten really dark. Joe sits next to me and pretends to have Lambert toast marshmallows. I giggle. Tyler gets up to—I assume—go use the bathroom in the mess hall.

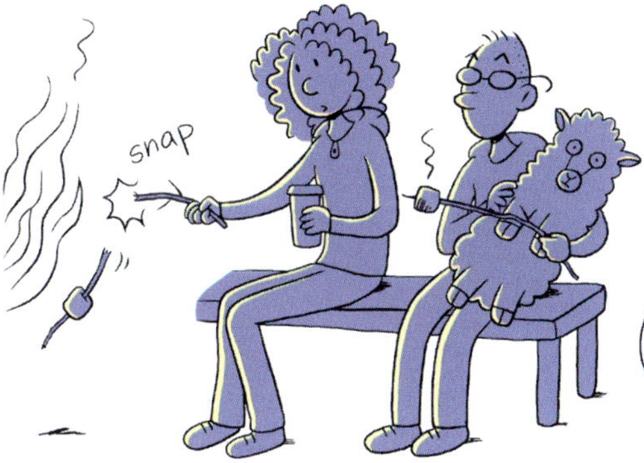
snap

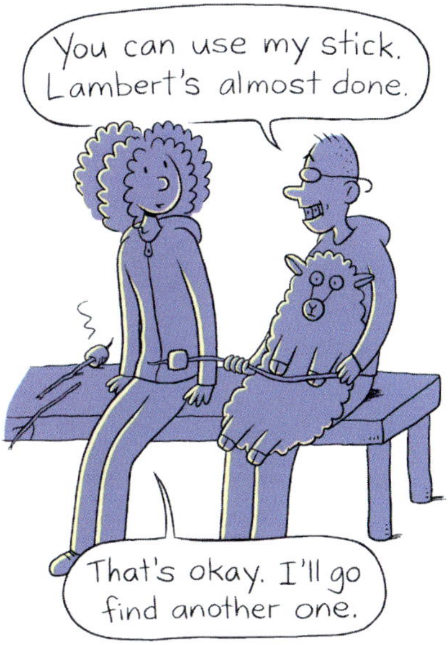
You can use my stick. Lambert's almost done.
That's okay. I'll go find another one.

A lot of people are heading back to the cabins. Everyone is exhausted from the day's activities. I'm still kinda wired (sugar?), so I decide to stay up a little longer. I walk away from the fire and over to the edge of the woods to find a new stick.

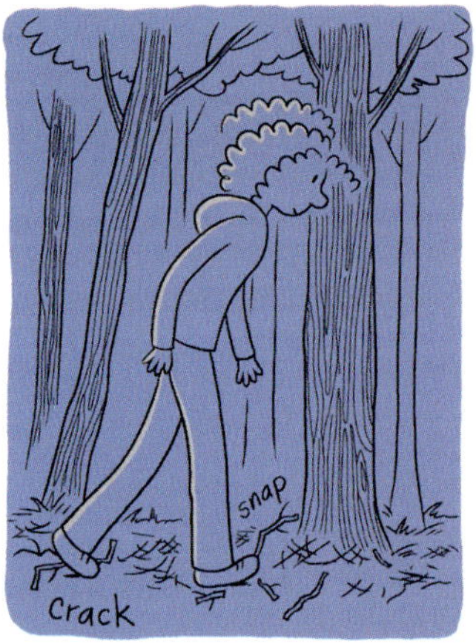
snap
crack

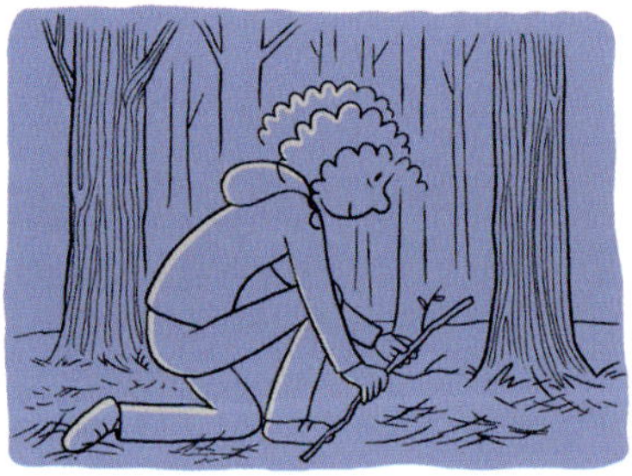

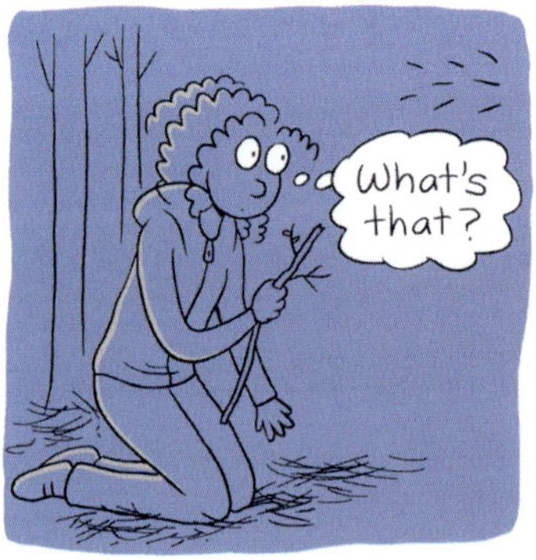
What's that?

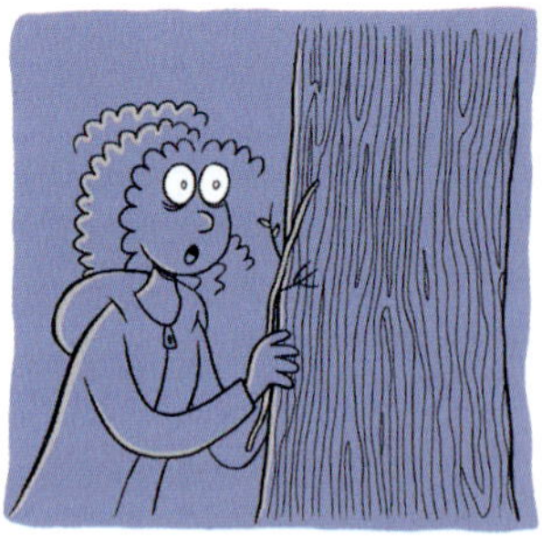

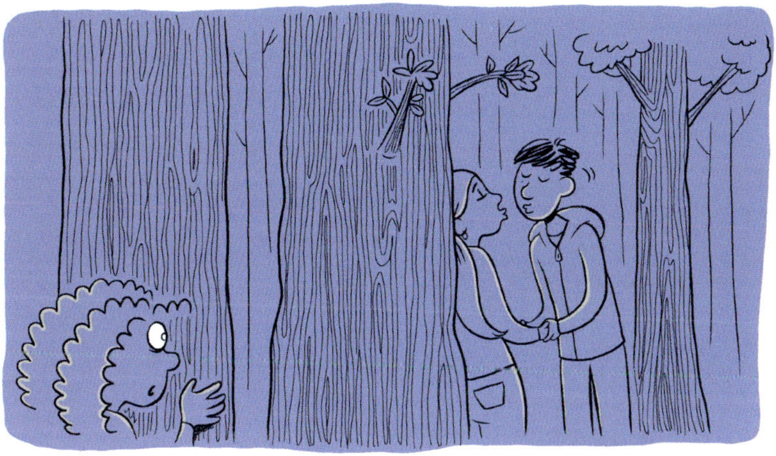

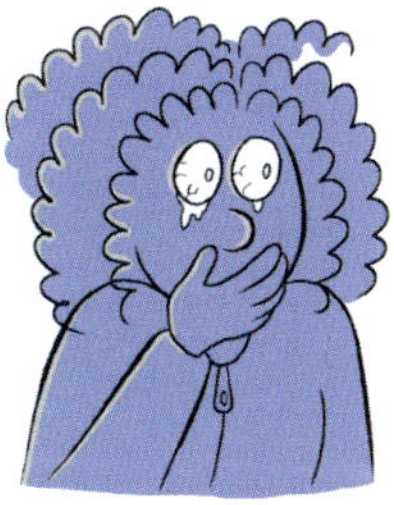

NO!

I can't move. I can't think.

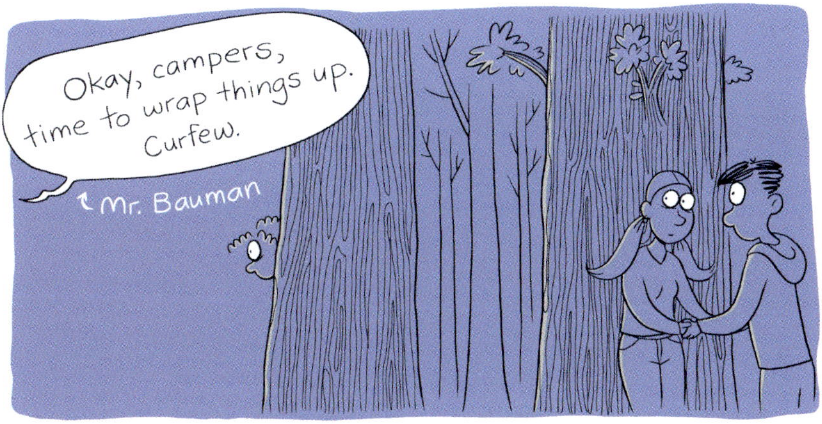
Okay, campers, time to wrap things up. Curfew.
Mr. Bauman

Somehow, I manage to tear myself away before they see me.

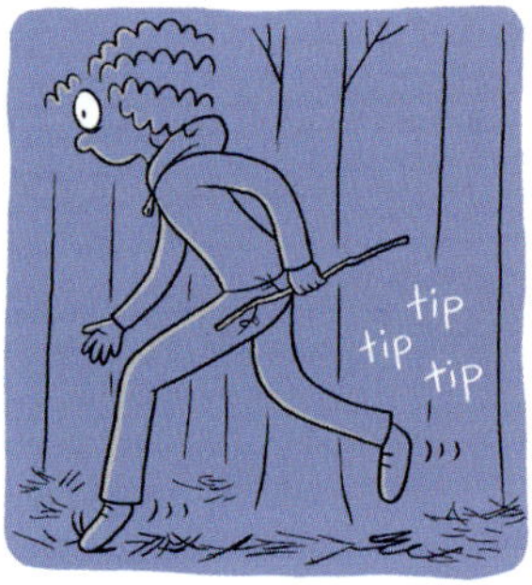
tip
tip
tip

Now it all hits.

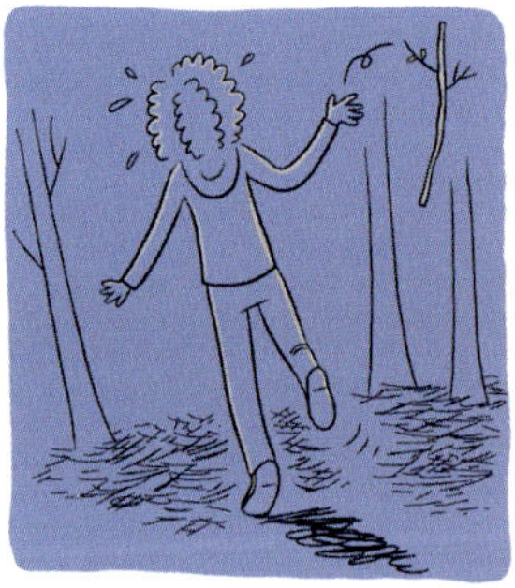

I can't handle this. My best friends aren't here. My heart feels like it's breaking in two (just like that stick). I need to talk to Trina.

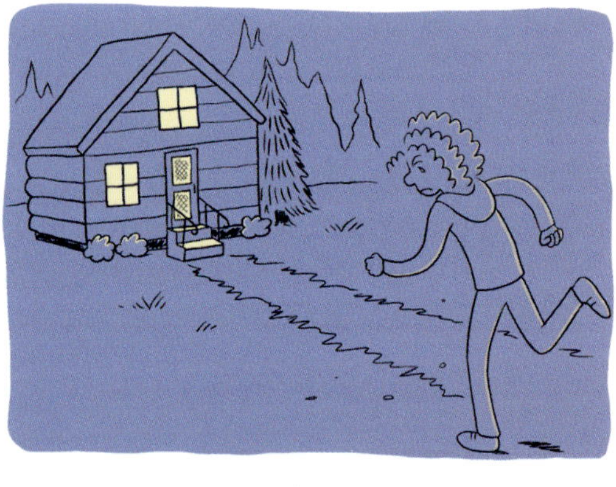

So that's it, then. Tyler **definitely** doesn't like me back. Instead, he's smitten with some girl jock who's about a thousand times cuter and—well, isn't a total dweeb who falls in lakes and gets stuck on walls.

And my own **sister** is paying more attention to Queen Cee than me.

Why do I have to be so . . .

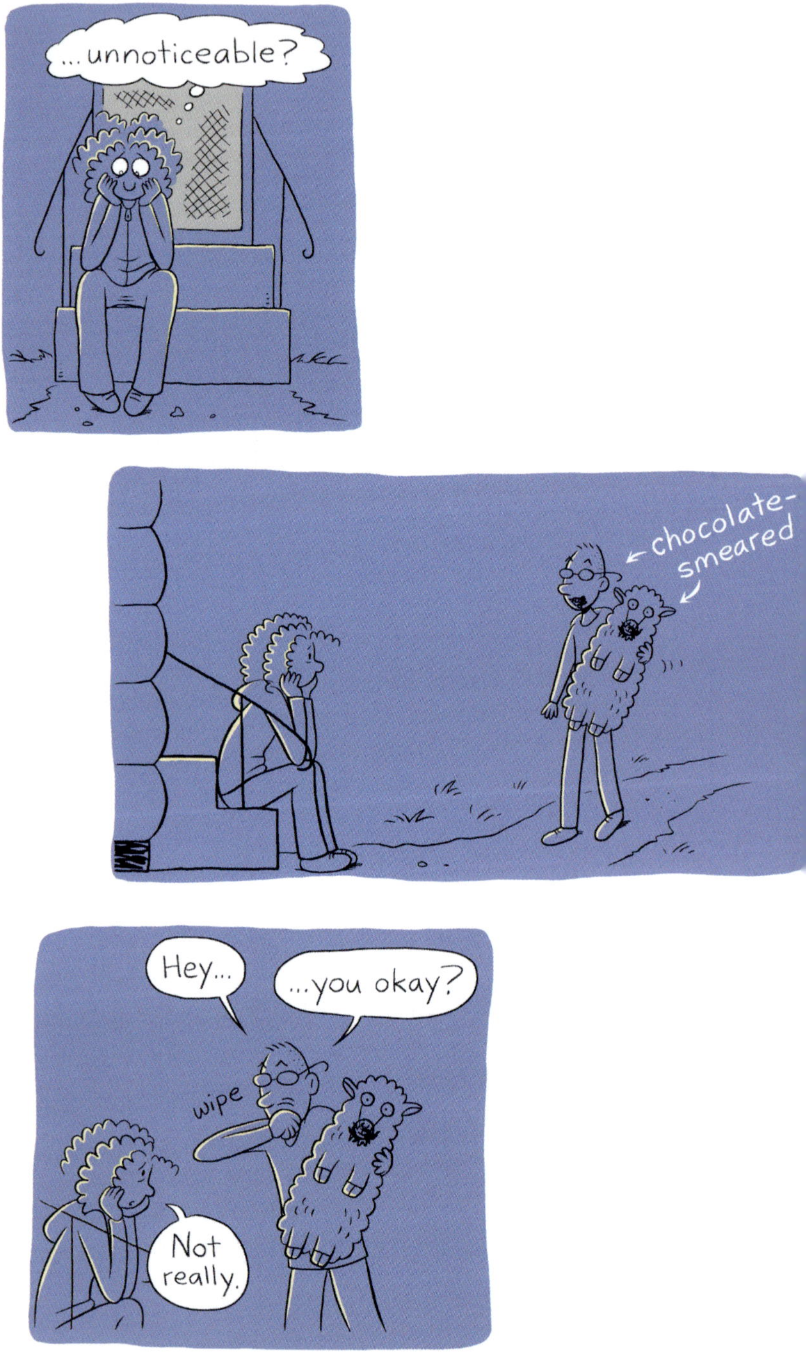
...unnoticeable?
chocolate-smeared
Hey...
...you okay?
wipe
Not really.

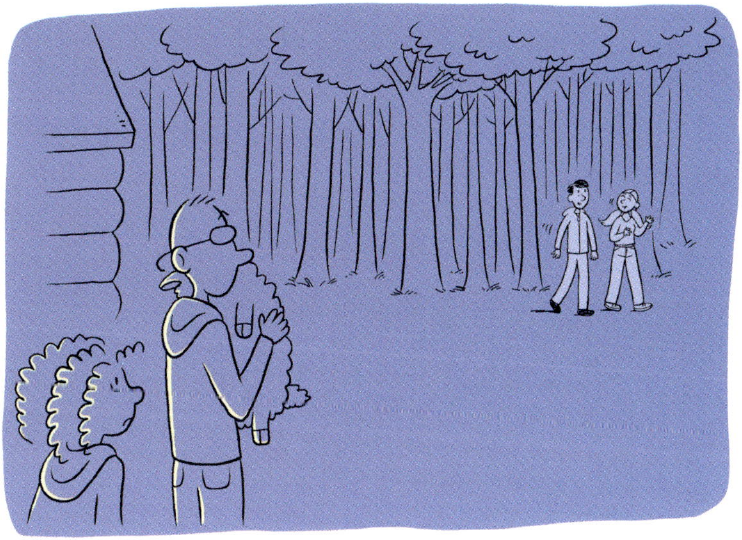

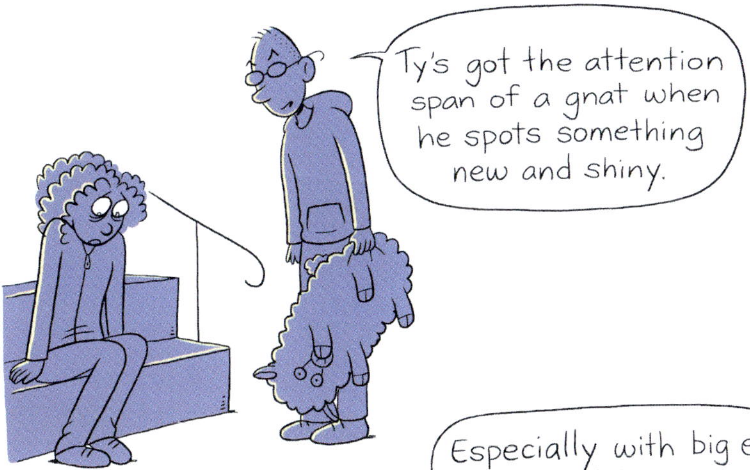
Ty's got the attention span of a gnat when he spots something new and shiny.

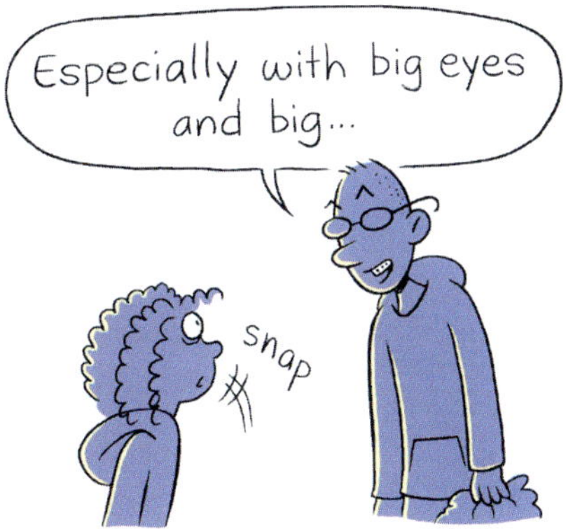
Especially with big eyes and big...
snap

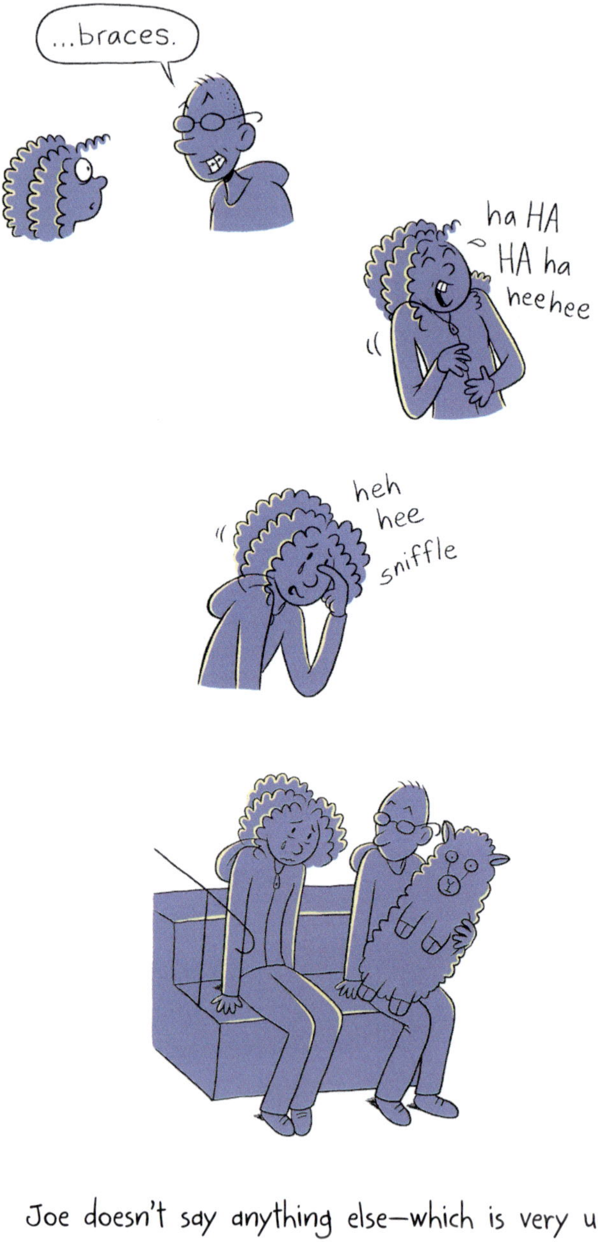
...braces.
ha HA
HA ha
heehee
heh
hee
sniffle

Joe doesn't say anything else—which is very un-Joe-like. Instead, he hands me:

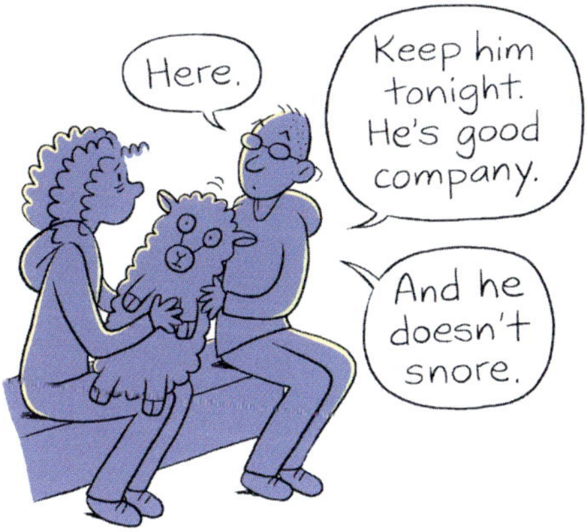
Here.
Keep him tonight. He's good company.
And he doesn't snore.

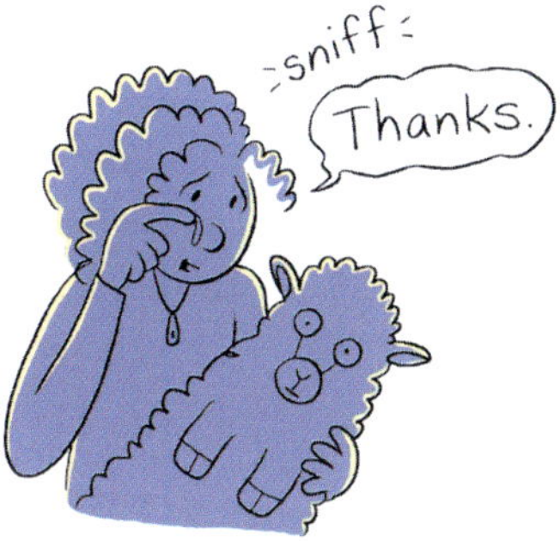
sniff
Thanks.

Again, we don't talk for a bit. But then Joe suddenly turns toward me and says:

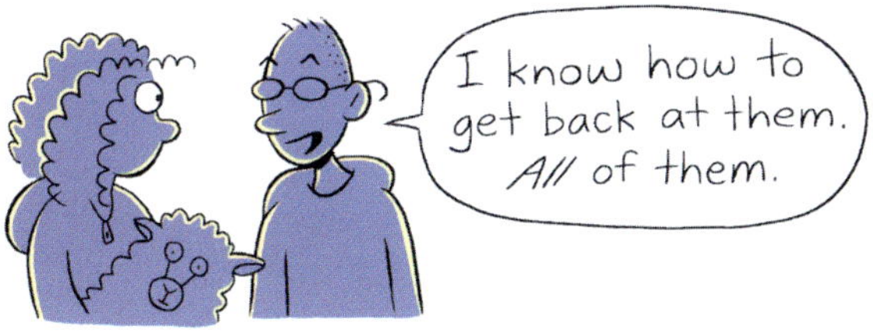
I know how to get back at them. *All* of them.

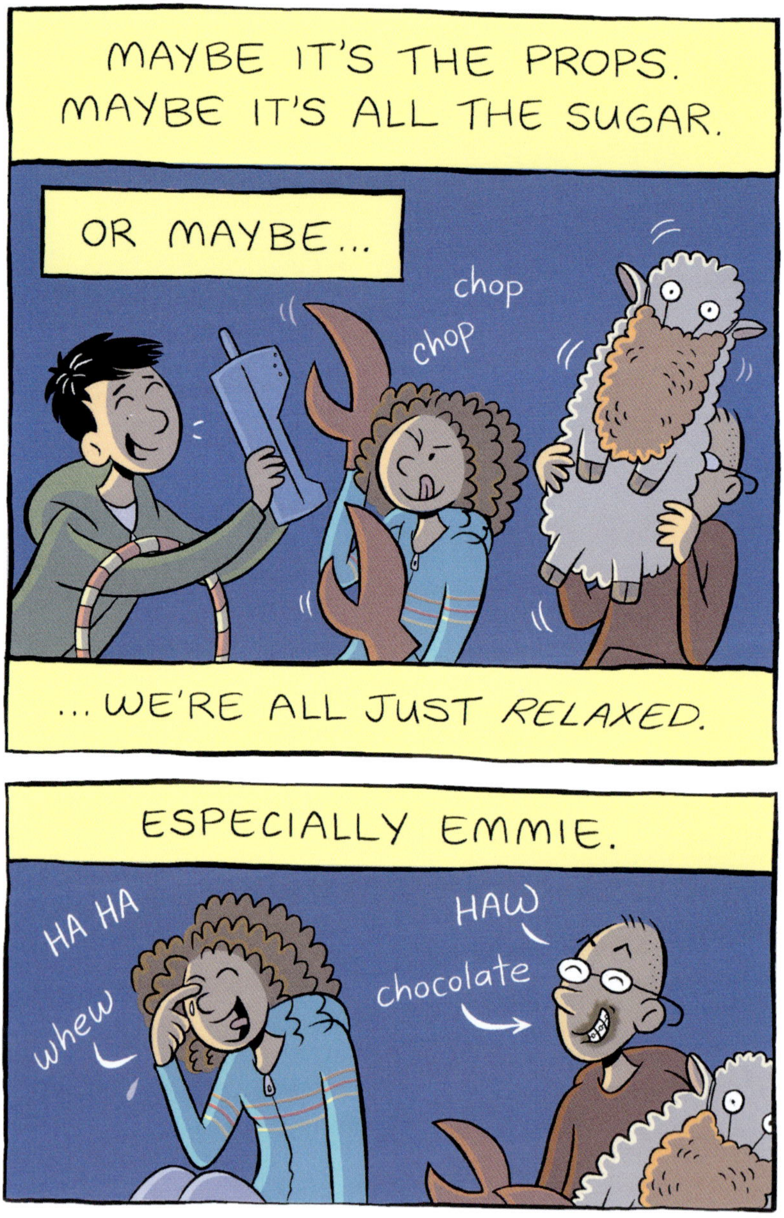
MAYBE IT'S THE PROPS. MAYBE IT'S ALL THE SUGAR.
OR MAYBE...
chop
chop
...WE'RE ALL JUST *RELAXED*.
ESPECIALLY EMMIE.
HA HA
whew
HAW
chocolate

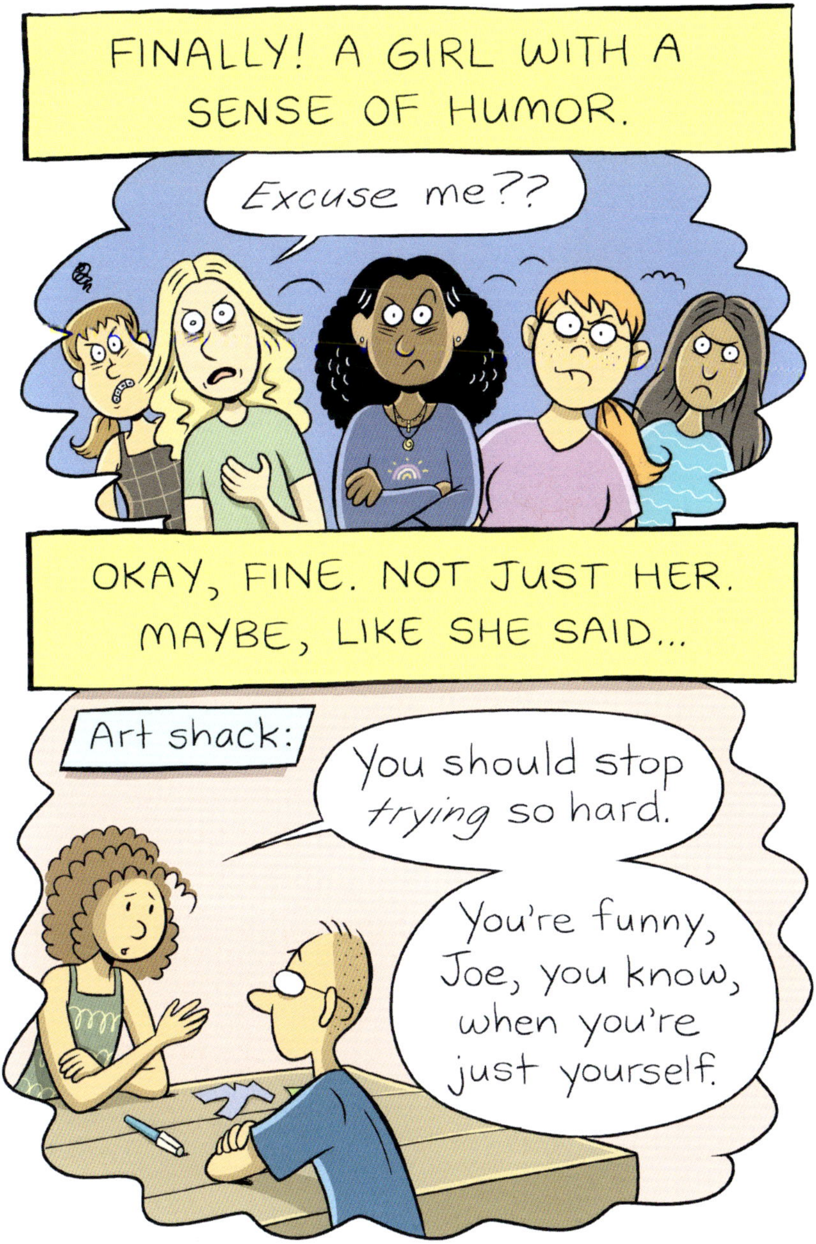
FINALLY! A GIRL WITH A SENSE OF HUMOR.
Excuse me??
OKAY, FINE. NOT JUST HER. MAYBE, LIKE SHE SAID...
Art shack:
You should stop *trying* so hard.
You're funny, Joe, you know, when you're just yourself.

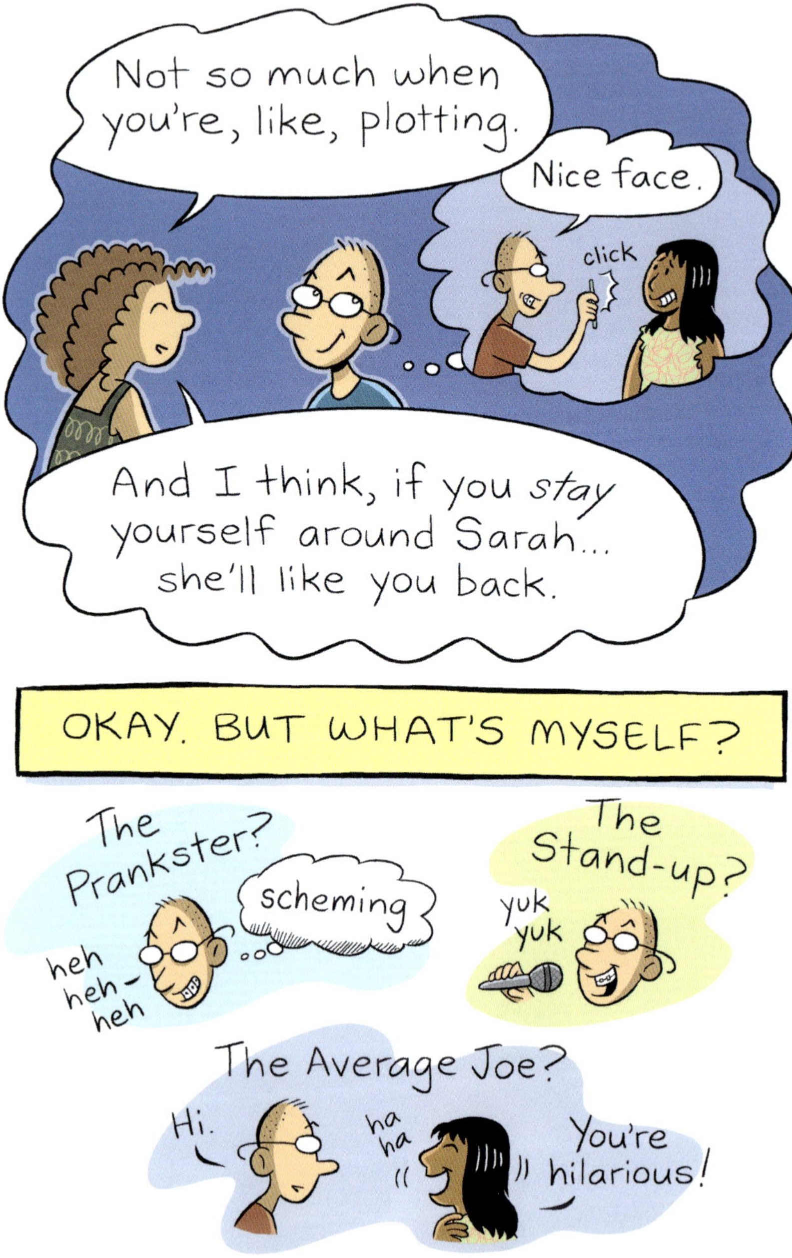

Not so much when you're, like, plotting.
Nice face.
click
And I think, if you *stay* yourself around Sarah... she'll like you back.
OKAY. BUT WHAT'S MYSELF?
The Prankster?
scheming
heh heh-heh
The Stand-up?
yuk yuk
The Average Joe?
Hi.
ha ha
You're hilarious!

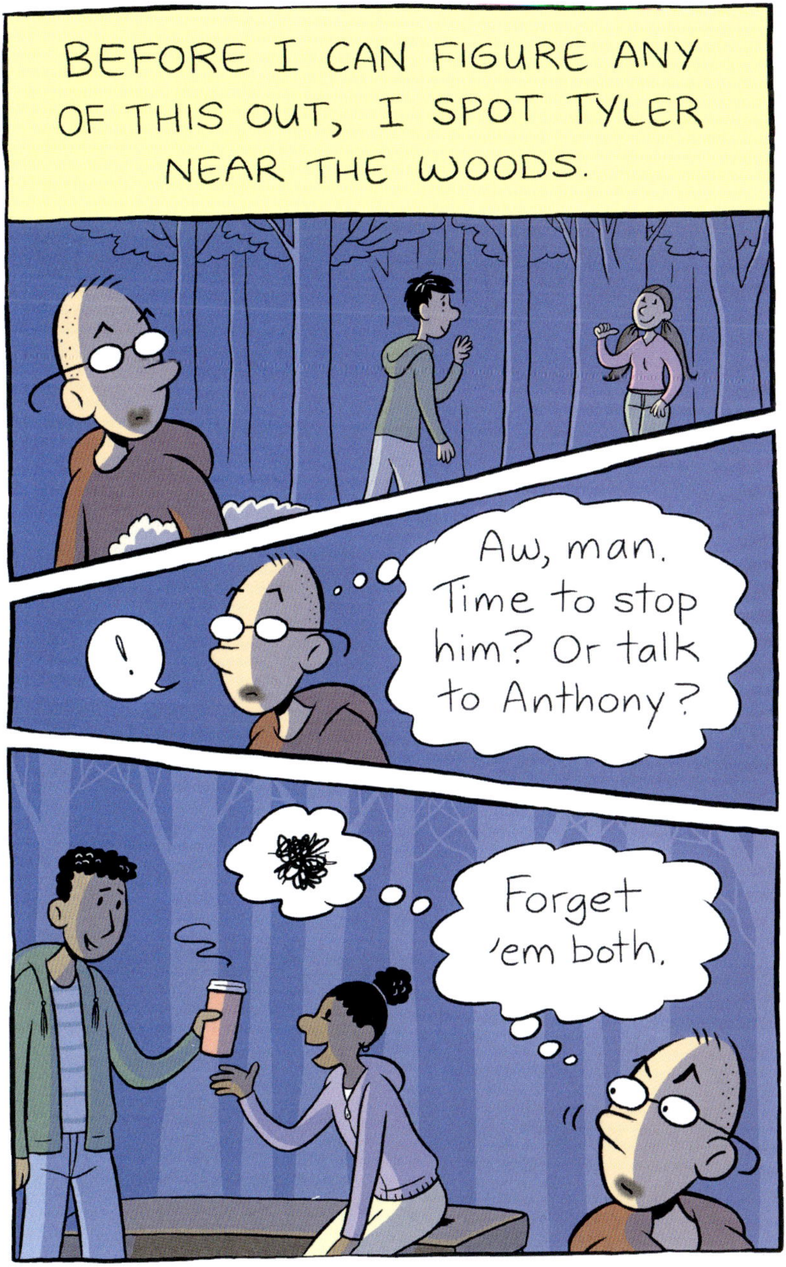
BEFORE I CAN FIGURE ANY OF THIS OUT, I SPOT TYLER NEAR THE WOODS.
!
Aw, man. Time to stop him? Or talk to Anthony?
Forget 'em both.

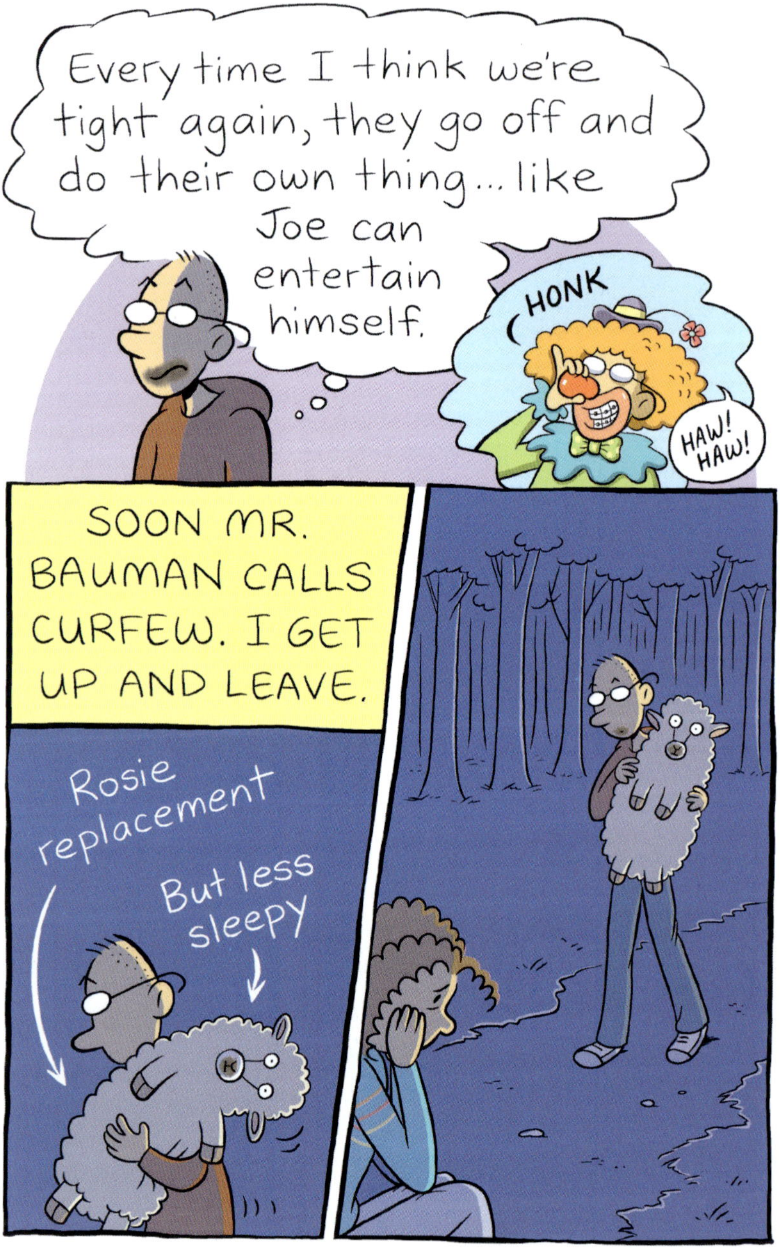
Every time I think we're tight again, they go off and do their own thing... like Joe can entertain himself.
HONK
HAW! HAW!
SOON MR. BAUMAN CALLS CURFEW. I GET UP AND LEAVE.
Rosie replacement
But less sleepy

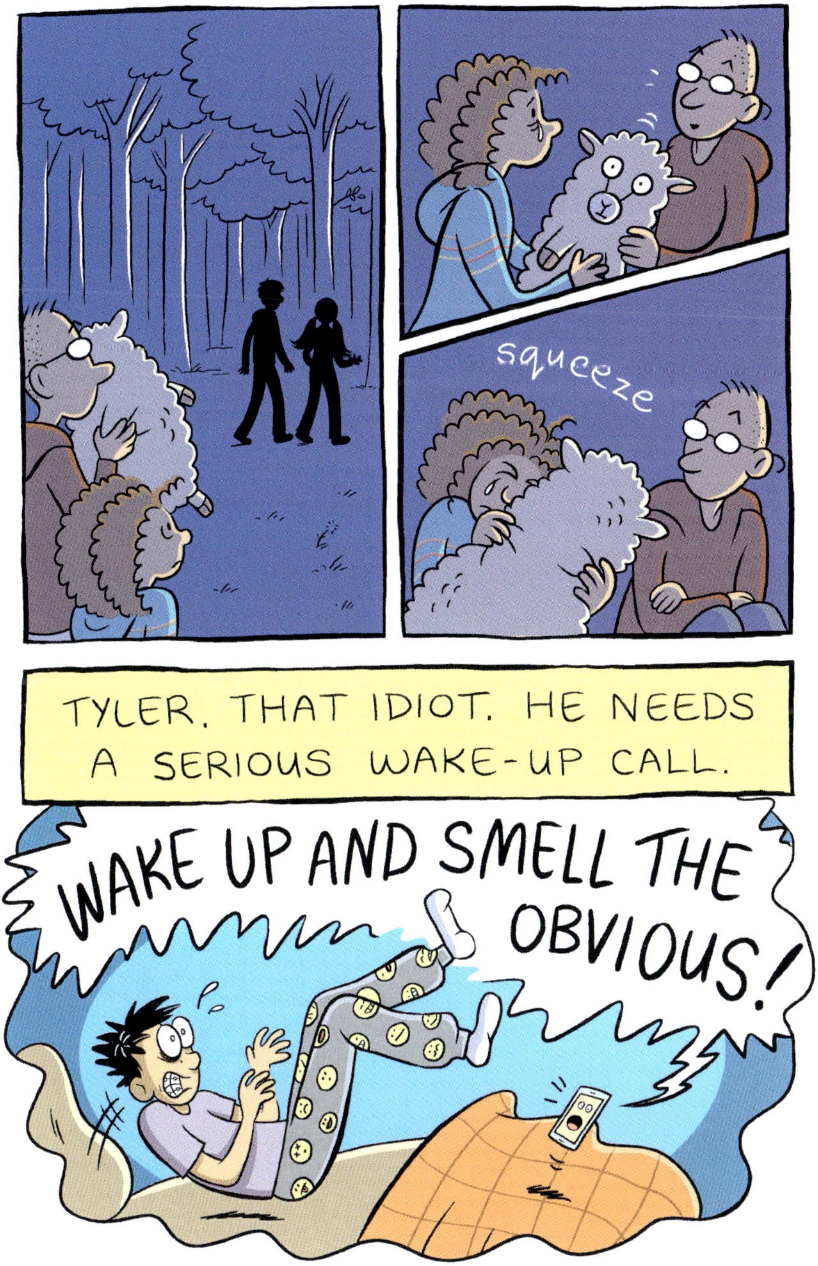
squeeze
TYLER. THAT IDIOT. HE NEEDS A SERIOUS WAKE-UP CALL.
WAKE UP AND SMELL THE OBVIOUS!

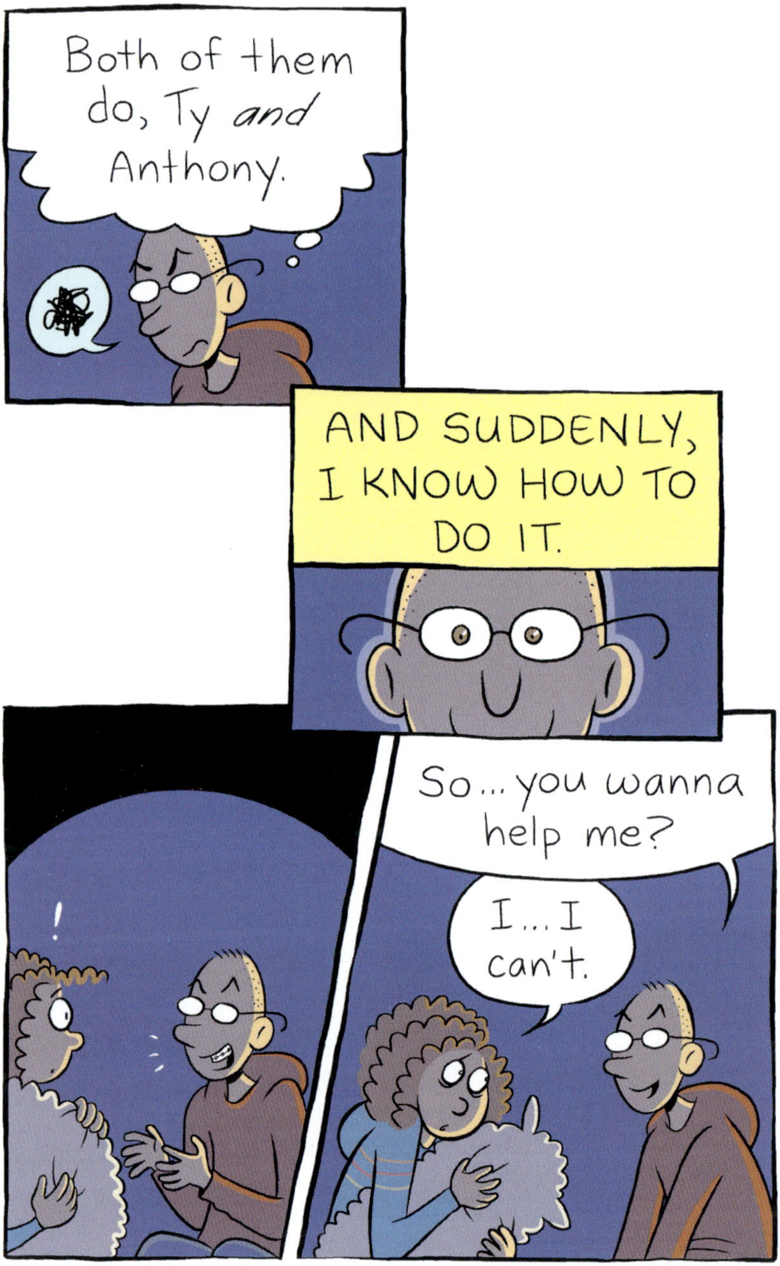
Both of them do, Ty *and* Anthony.
AND SUDDENLY, I KNOW HOW TO DO IT.
!
So... you wanna help me?
I... I can't.

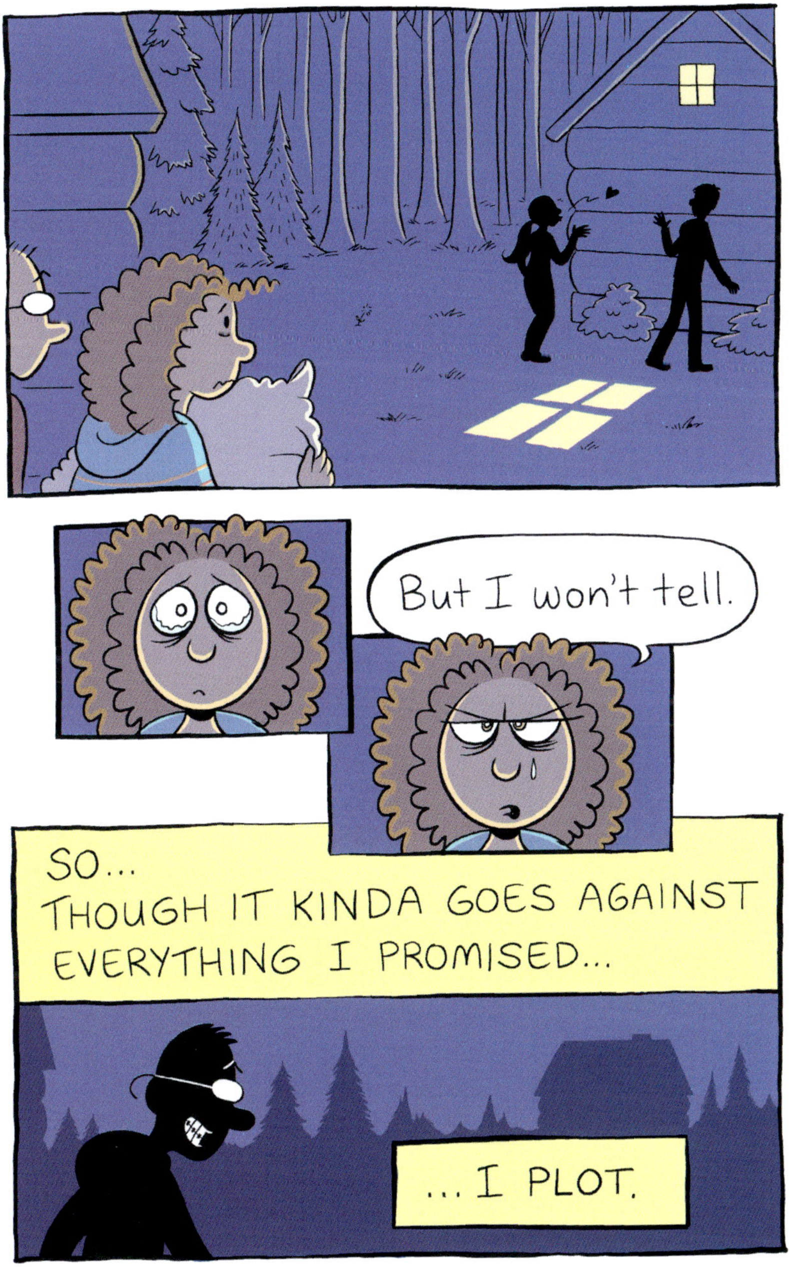
But I won't tell.
SO...
THOUGH IT KINDA GOES AGAINST EVERYTHING I PROMISED...
... I PLOT.

EMMIE

Sunday morning. Trina, Celia, and Grace are at breakfast. I'm skipping. No appetite. Anyway, I have an apple from yesterday and still have my mom's cracker packets in case I get hungry.

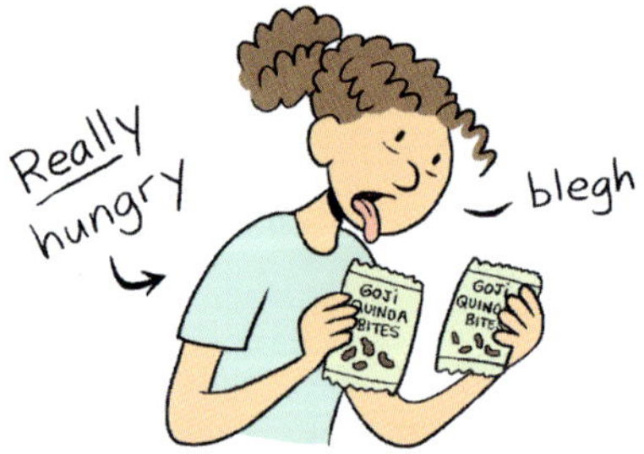
Really hungry
blegh
GOJI QUINOA BITES
GOJI QUINOA BITES

I pretended I was still asleep while everybody else got ready. I didn't feel like talking to anyone. I'm still peeved at Trina, and I didn't want another morning of listening to Celia and Grace laugh at my bed head.

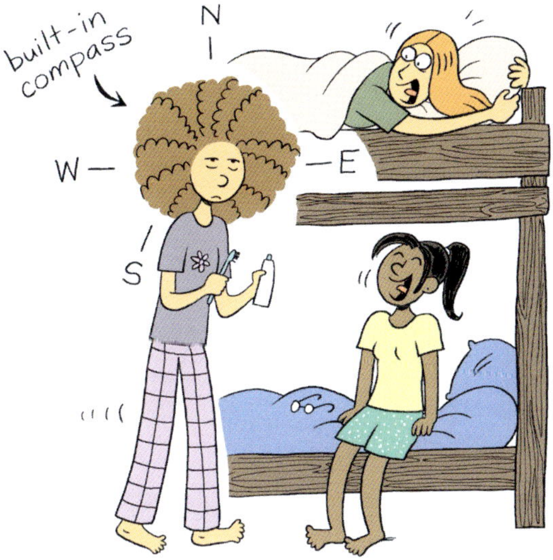
built-in compass
N
W
E
S

Just changed into a T-shirt and shorts. Grabbing a hoodie for later. After breakfast, we're taking the buses to some park to explore a gorge and do some trail hiking. That part I don't really mind.

But the bus ride?

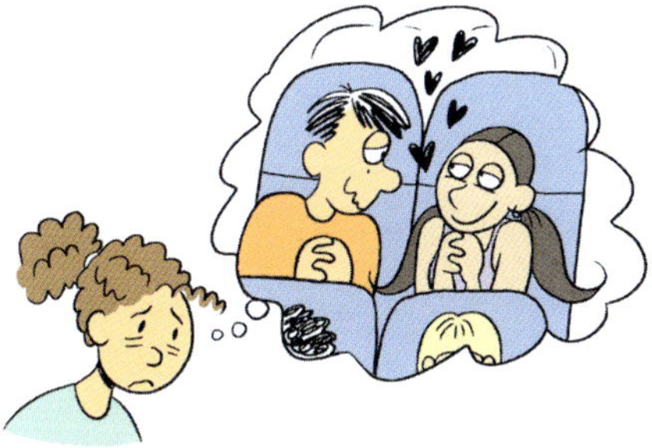

Ughh. I yawn miserably. I didn't get much sleep last night. I kept replaying that whole nightmare in my head.

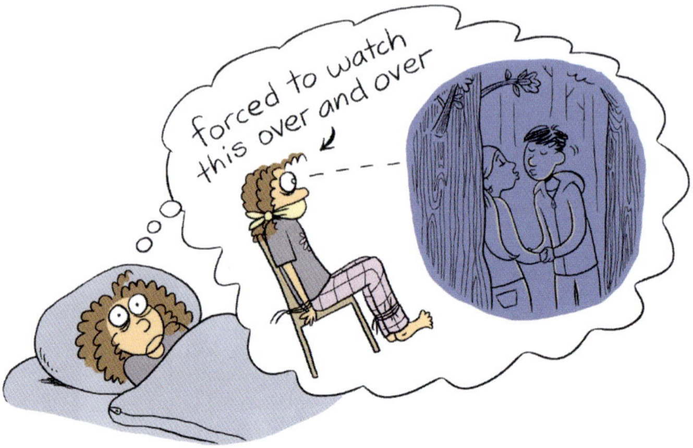
forced to watch this over and over

Also, Celia kept talking into the night and hogging Trina's attention. I felt sorry for Grace, who probably felt like she had dropped off the planet.

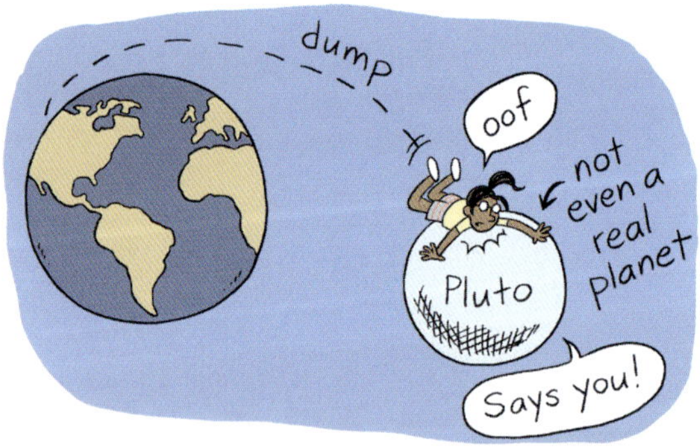
dump
oof
not even a real planet
Pluto
Says you!

To be honest, I'm just done with this trip. I know I've said that before, but this time I really mean it. Like, **triple mean** it. I just want to be back in my own room with my pencil collection and sketchbook, my bed with the big fuzzy pillows (even the one with the giant foot-shaped juice stain), and my colorful art posters.

Also, I miss my best friends. But I **won't** miss boys. I don't wanna be around them anymore. Well, just one in particular. One too-cute-for-his-own-good, fickle-faced boy with the freckle (which, by the way, I no longer think is adorable).

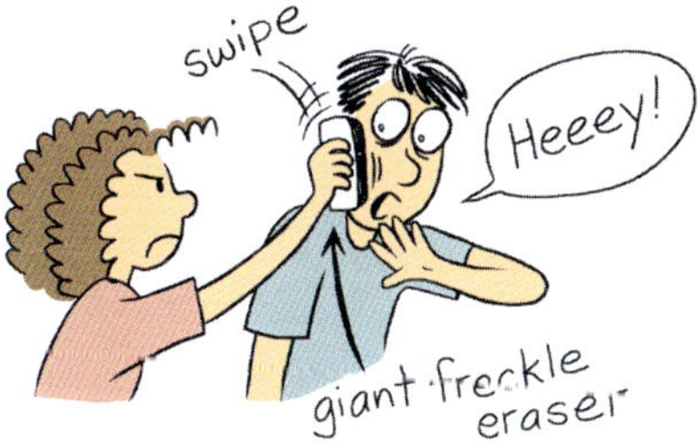
swipe
Heeey!
giant freckle eraser

As I search for my missing water bottle (why do I always lose it?), I hear some commotion outside.

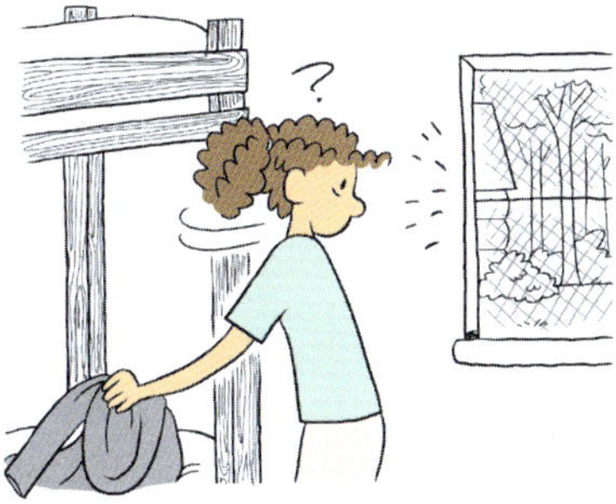
?

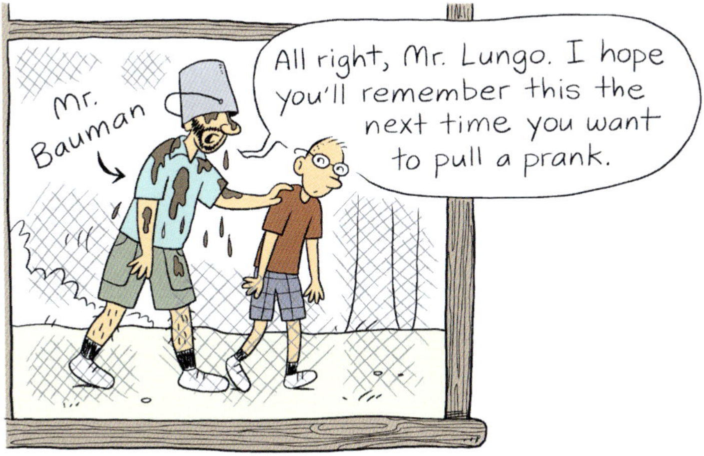
Mr. Bauman
All right, Mr. Lungo. I hope you'll remember this the next time you want to pull a prank.

Prank? Why did Joe pull a—

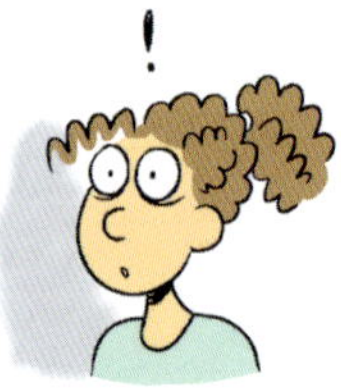
!

Ohhhh no . . .

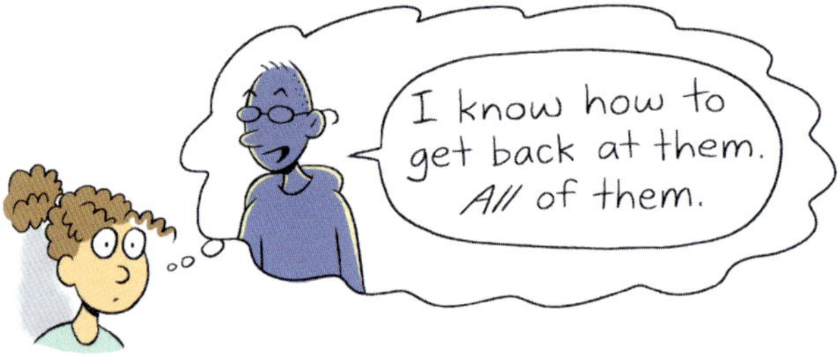
I know how to get back at them. *All* of them.

I totally forgot Joe was plotting something. He didn't tell me what it was, just that it would be "epic." But I didn't want to get involved (or in trouble). Also, I assumed he'd change his mind this morning. I mean, he told me how much he wanted to see the gorge, so why would he risk it?

Strength:

zeroing in on someone's insecurity and making fun of it.

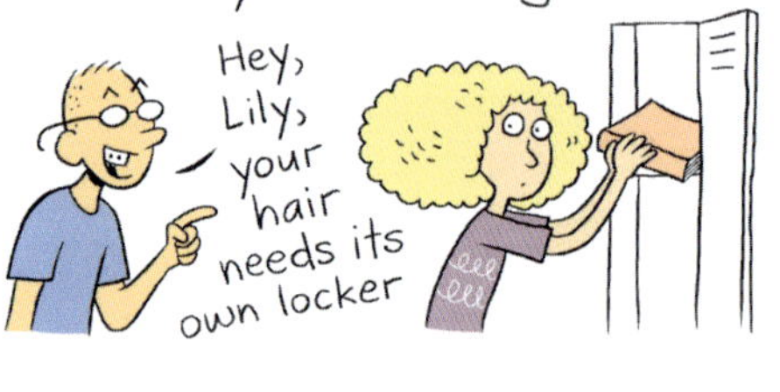
Hey, Lily, your hair needs its own locker

Weakness:

thinking things through.

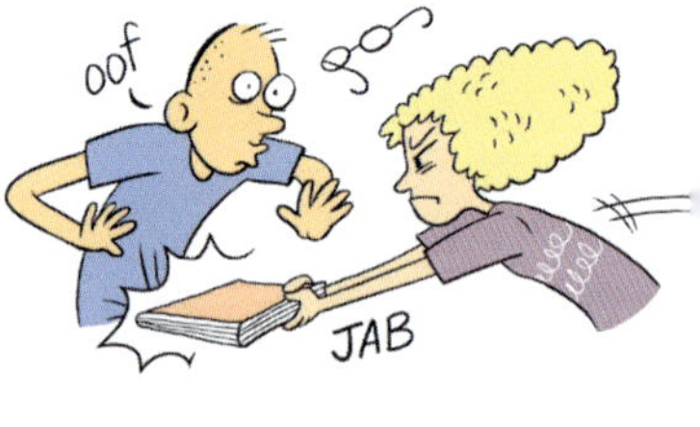
oof
JAB

Sometimes Joe can be so dumb. Not that he **is** dumb . . . he's actually kinda smart. But he still does such dumb things. It's so frustrating, and . . .

. . . why do I even care?

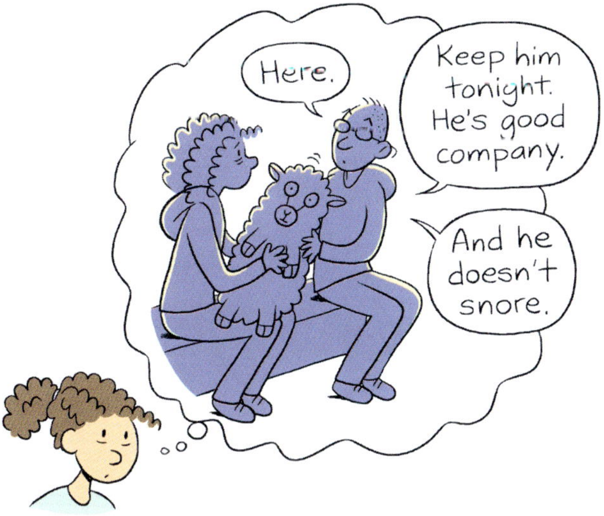
Here.
Keep him tonight. He's good company.
And he doesn't snore.

I sigh.

I head out to see what's going on.

And maybe . . .

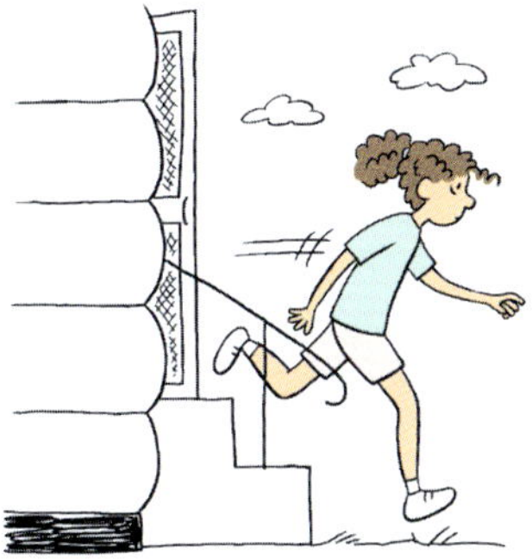

. . . to help.

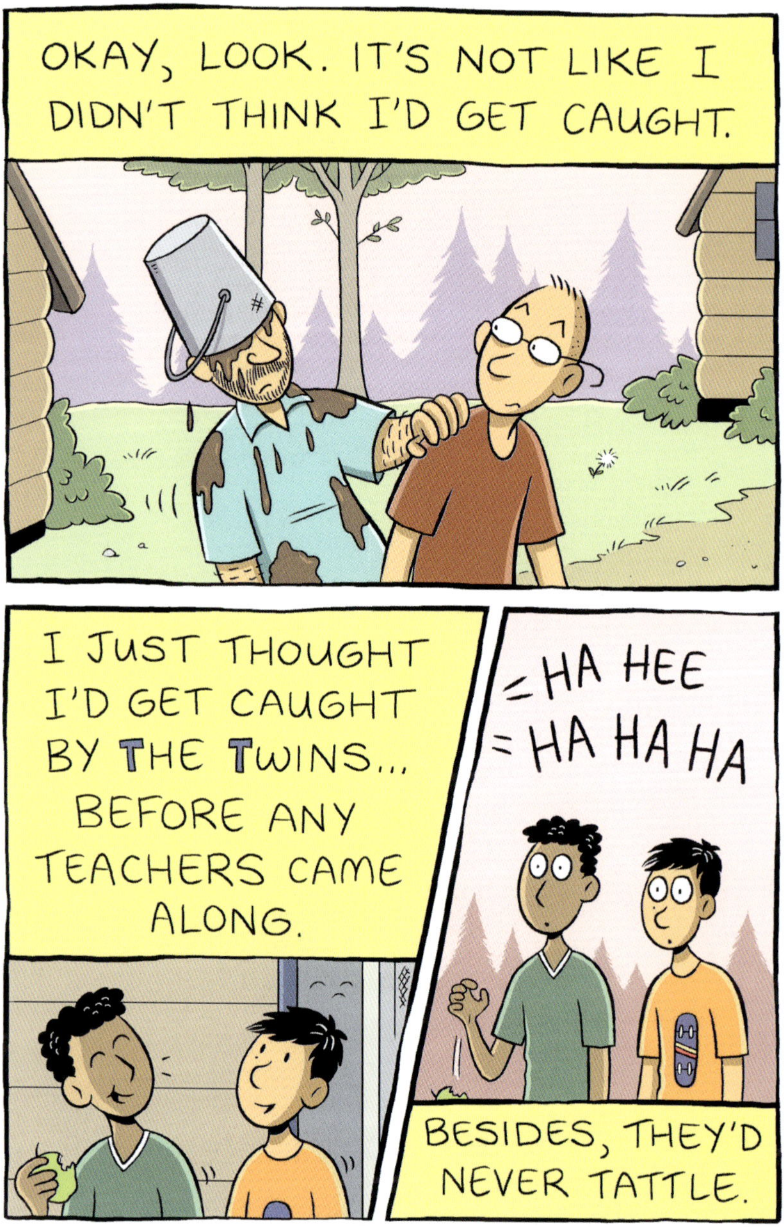
OKAY, LOOK. IT'S NOT LIKE I DIDN'T THINK I'D GET CAUGHT.
I JUST THOUGHT I'D GET CAUGHT BY THE TWINS... BEFORE ANY TEACHERS CAME ALONG.
HA HEE
HA HA HA HA
BESIDES, THEY'D NEVER TATTLE.

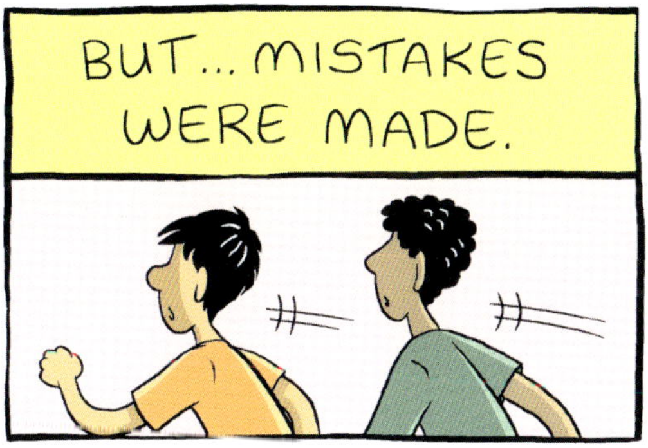
BUT... MISTAKES WERE MADE.

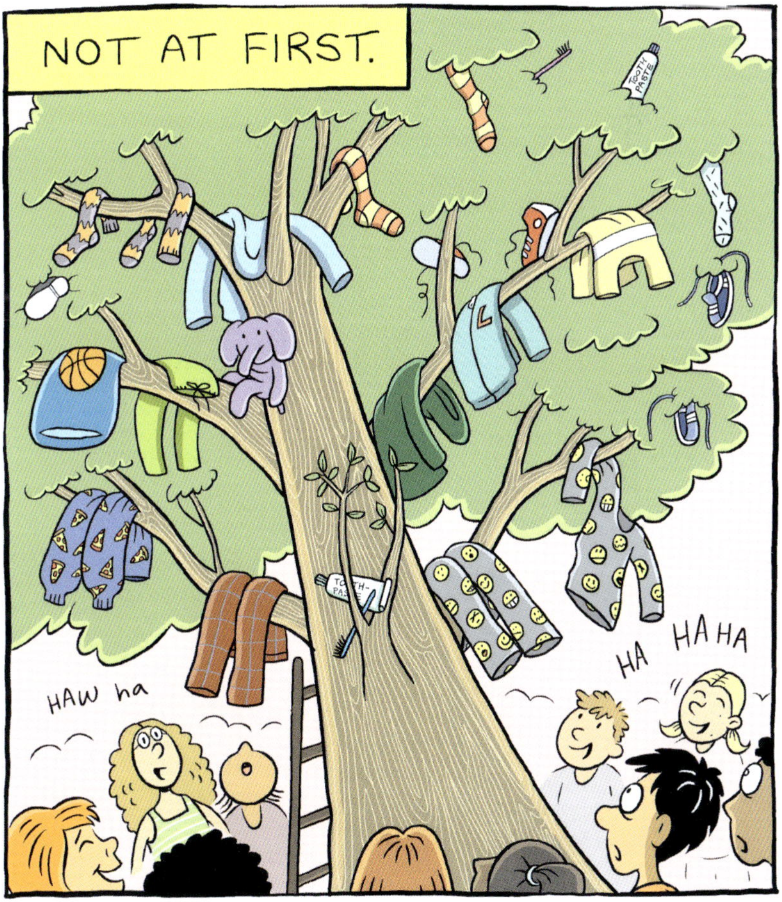
NOT AT FIRST.
TOOTH PASTE
TOOTH-PASTE
HAW ha
HA HA HA

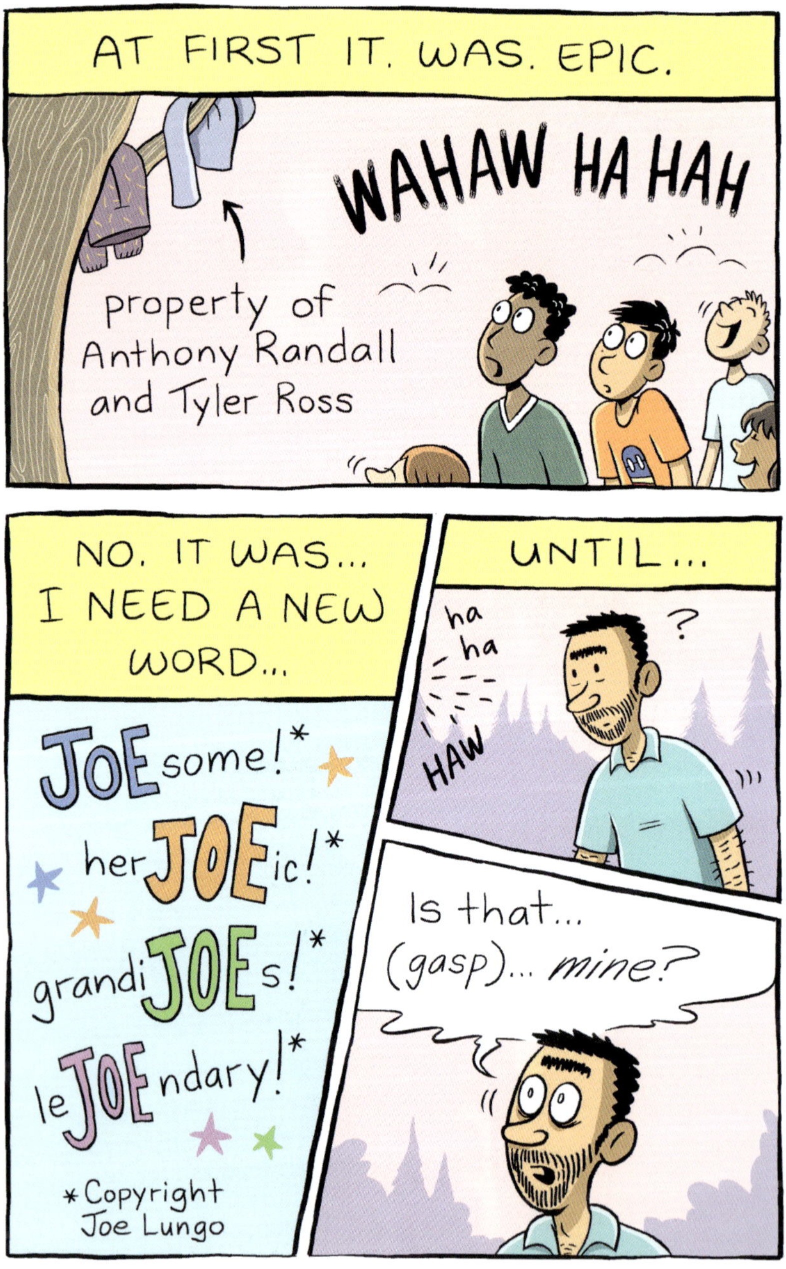
AT FIRST IT. WAS. EPIC.
WAHAW HA HAH
property of Anthony Randall and Tyler Ross
NO. IT WAS... I NEED A NEW WORD...
JOEsome!*
herJOEic!*
grandiJOEs!*
leJOEndary!*
*Copyright Joe Lungo
UNTIL...
ha ha
HAW
?
Is that... (gasp)... *mine?*

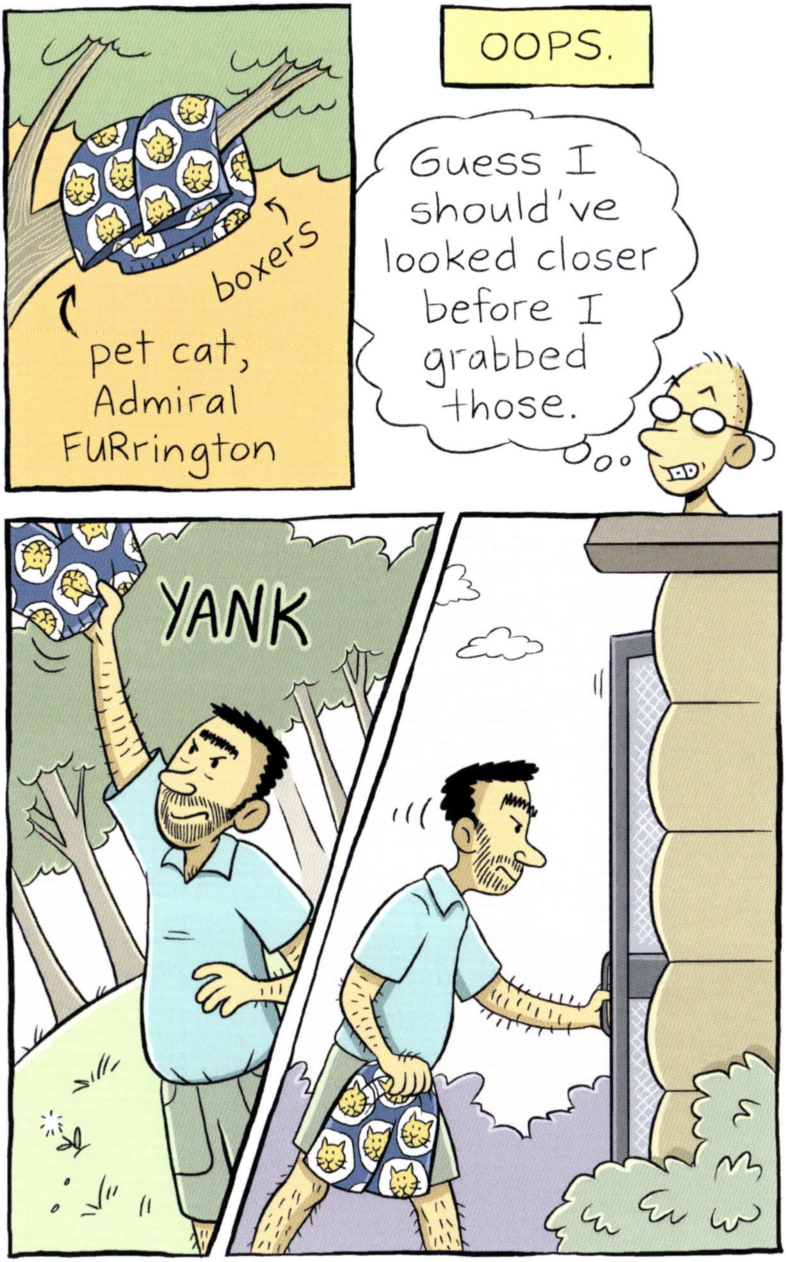
boxers
pet cat, Admiral FURrington
OOPS.
Guess I should've looked closer before I grabbed those.
YANK

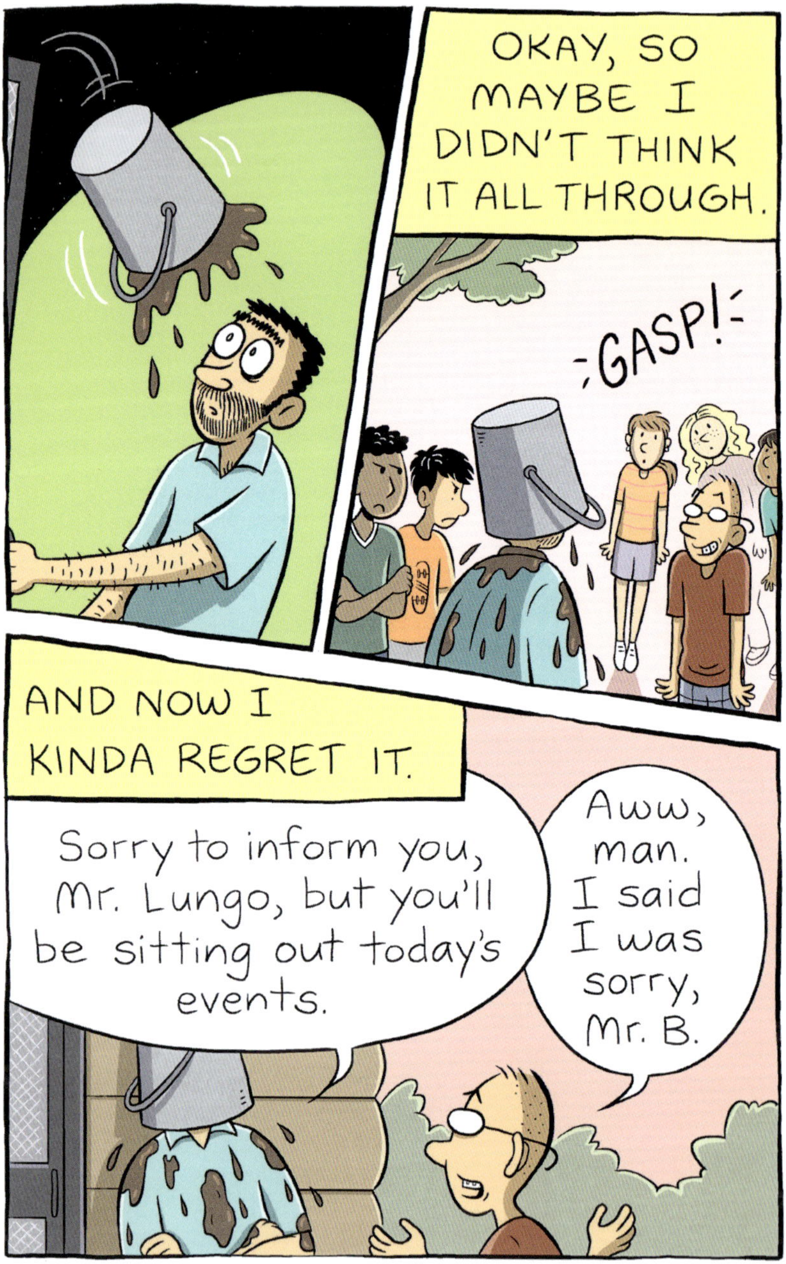

OKAY, SO MAYBE I DIDN'T THINK IT ALL THROUGH.
GASP!
AND NOW I KINDA REGRET IT.
Sorry to inform you, Mr. Lungo, but you'll be sitting out today's events.
Aww, man. I said I was sorry, Mr. B.

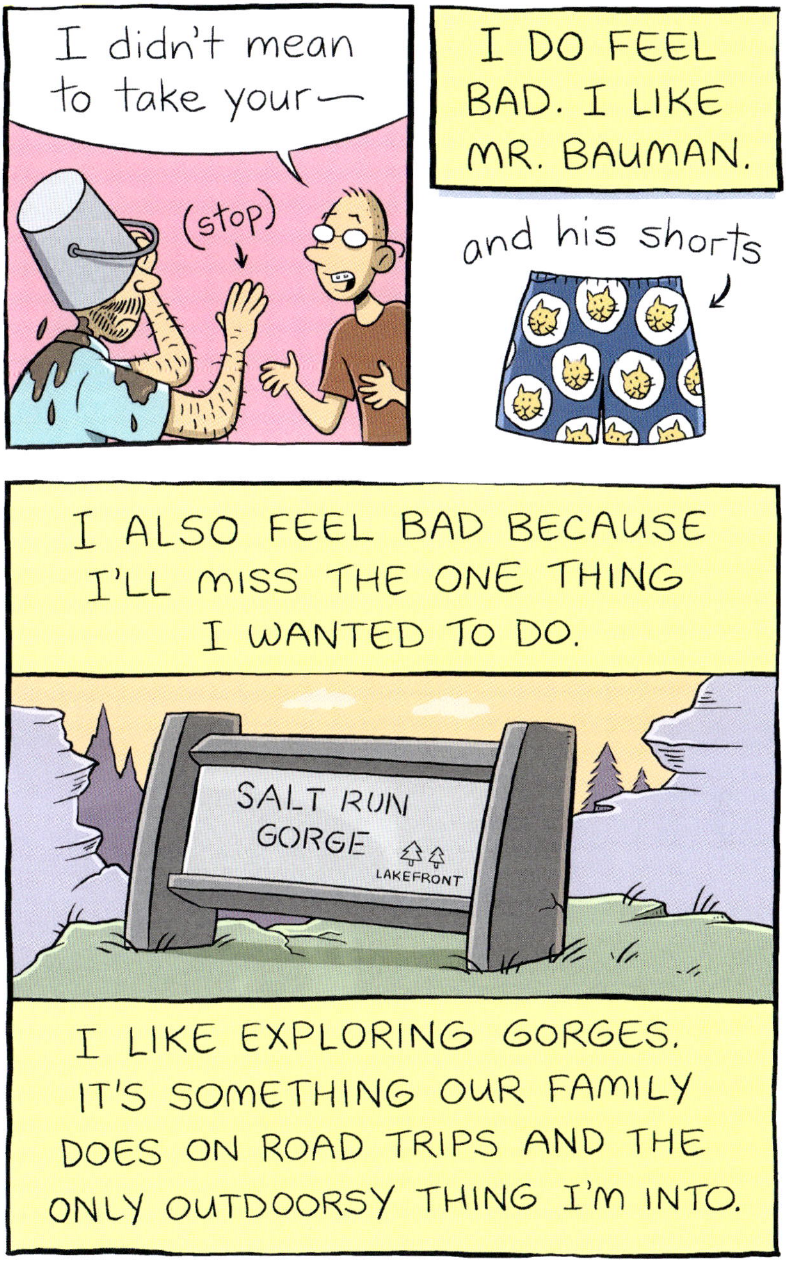
I didn't mean to take your—
(stop)
I DO FEEL BAD. I LIKE MR. BAUMAN.
and his shorts
I ALSO FEEL BAD BECAUSE I'LL MISS THE ONE THING I WANTED TO DO.
SALT RUN GORGE
LAKEFRONT
I LIKE EXPLORING GORGES. IT'S SOMETHING OUR FAMILY DOES ON ROAD TRIPS AND THE ONLY OUTDOORSY THING I'M INTO.

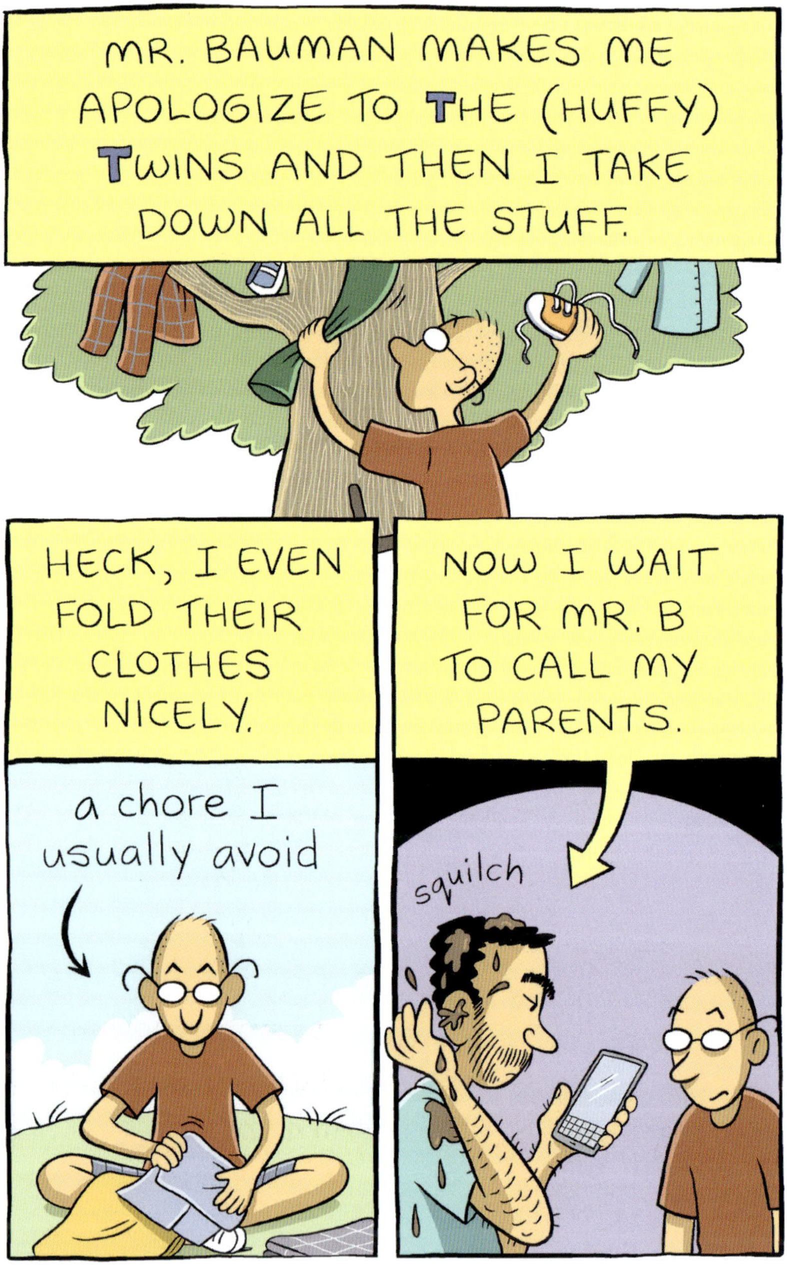
MR. BAUMAN MAKES ME APOLOGIZE TO THE (HUFFY) TWINS AND THEN I TAKE DOWN ALL THE STUFF.
HECK, I EVEN FOLD THEIR CLOTHES NICELY.
a chore I usually avoid
NOW I WAIT FOR MR. B TO CALL MY PARENTS.
squilch

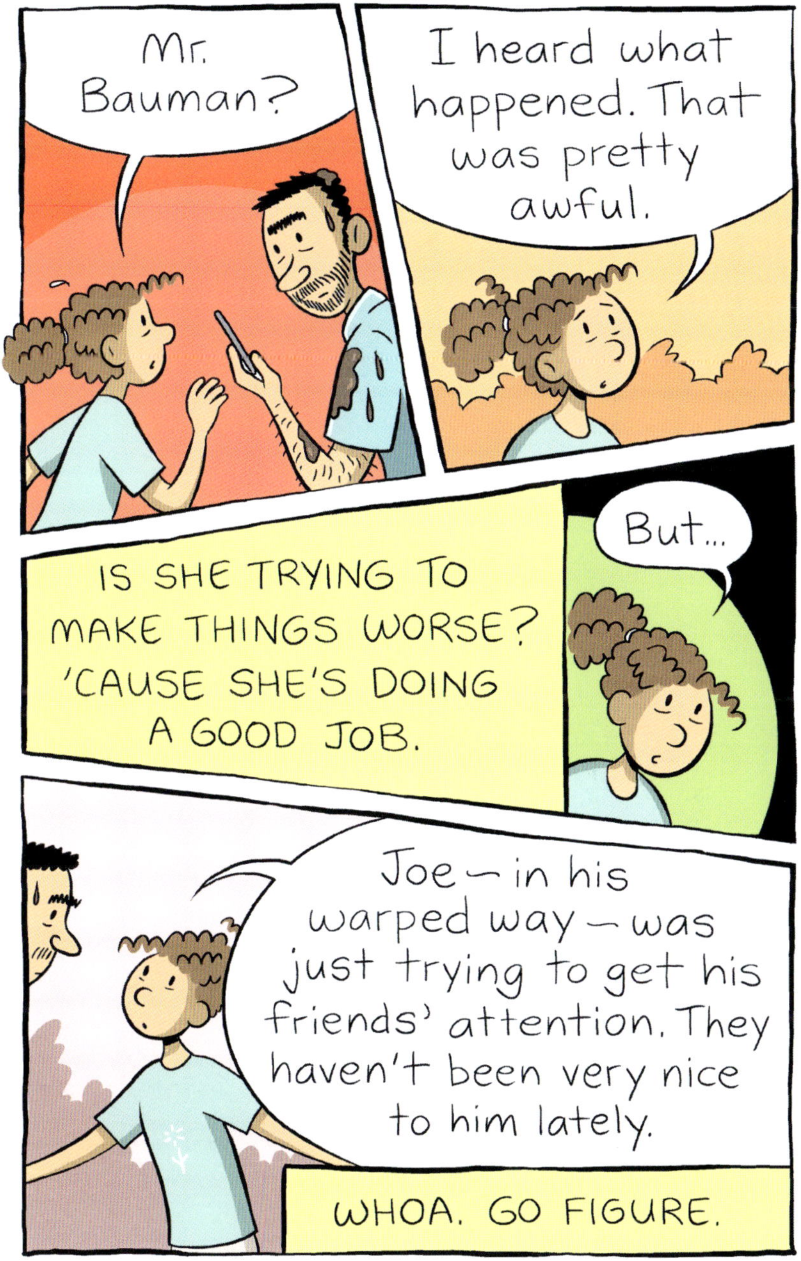
Mr. Bauman?
I heard what happened. That was pretty awful.
IS SHE TRYING TO MAKE THINGS WORSE? 'CAUSE SHE'S DOING A GOOD JOB.
But...
Joe—in his warped way—was just trying to get his friends' attention. They haven't been very nice to him lately.
WHOA. GO FIGURE.

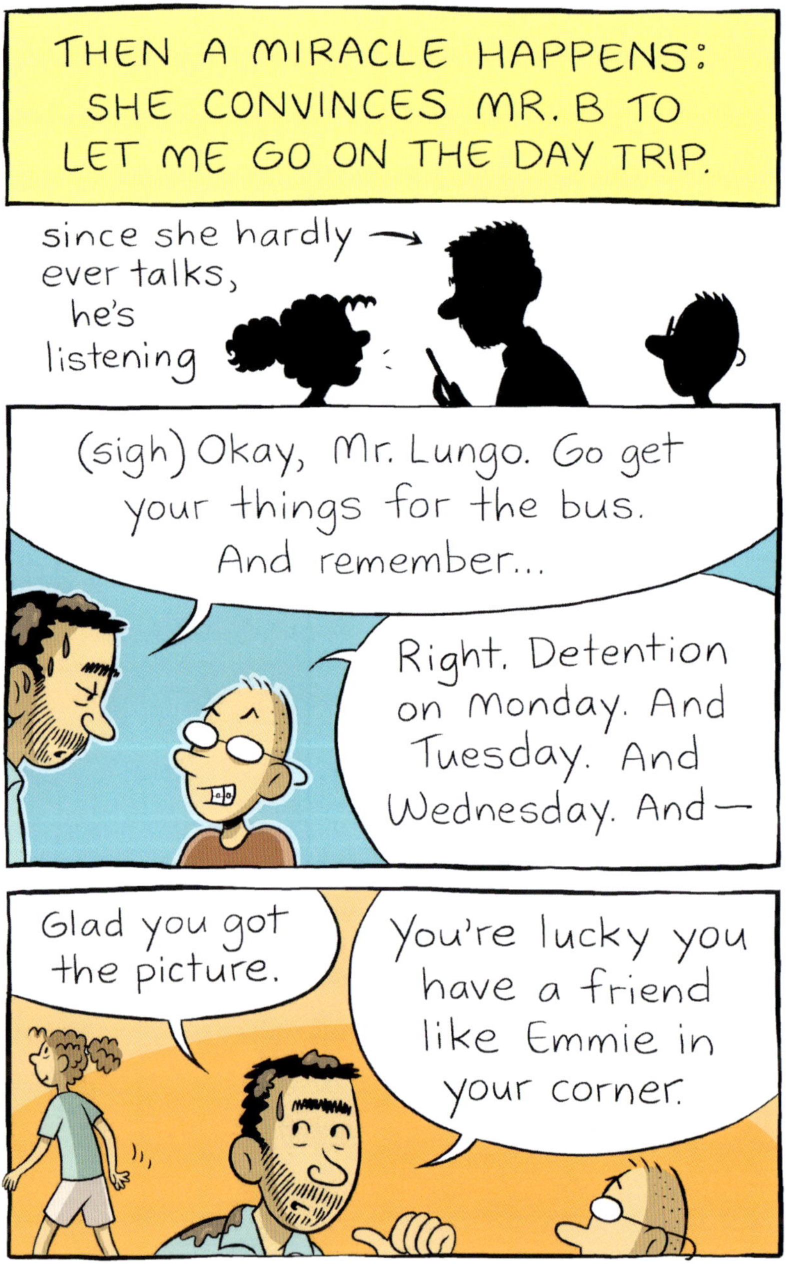
THEN A MIRACLE HAPPENS: SHE CONVINCES MR. B TO LET ME GO ON THE DAY TRIP.
since she hardly ever talks, he's listening
(sigh) Okay, Mr. Lungo. Go get your things for the bus. And remember...
Right. Detention on Monday. And Tuesday. And Wednesday. And—
Glad you got the picture.
You're lucky you have a friend like Emmie in your corner.

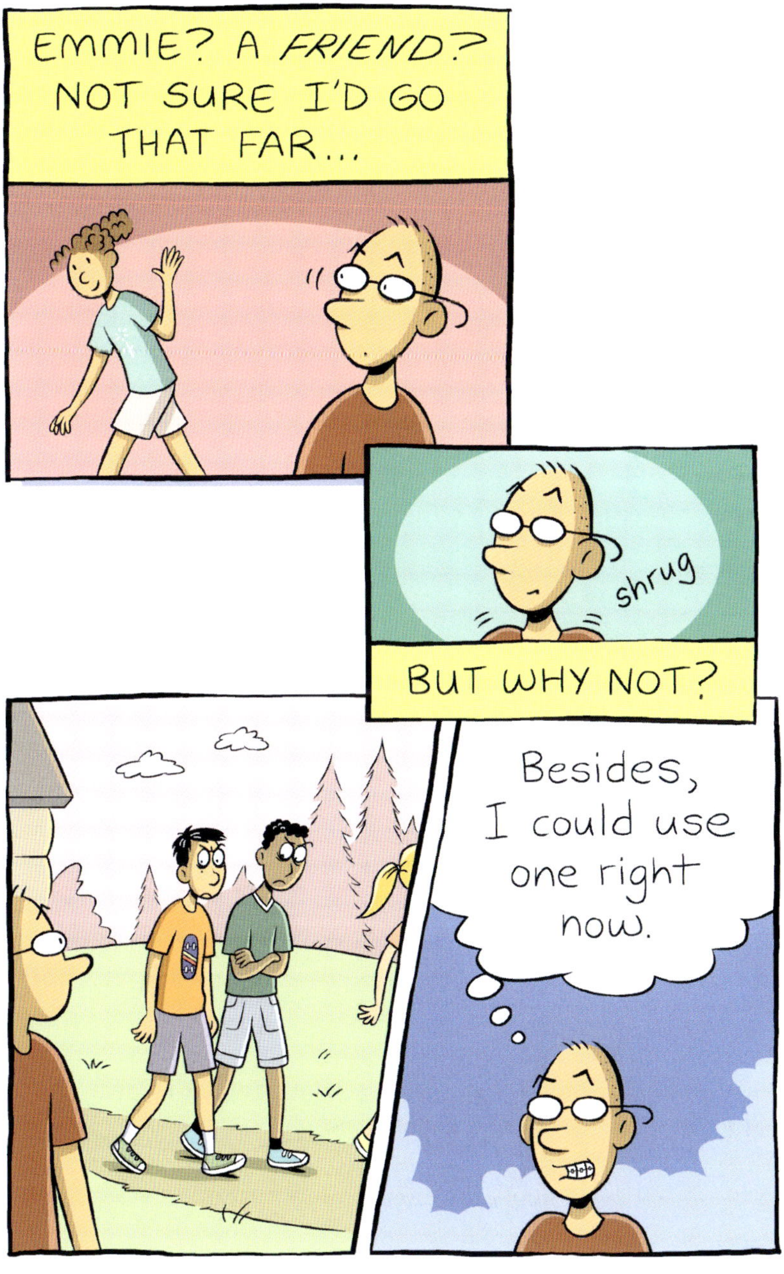
EMMIE? A *FRIEND*?
NOT SURE I'D GO THAT FAR...
shrug
BUT WHY NOT?
Besides, I could use one right now.

EMMIE

For the first time, Joe kinda clings to me.

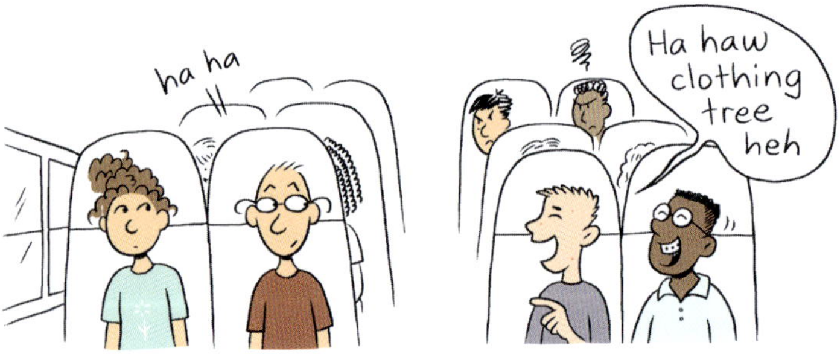

ha ha
Ha haw clothing tree heh

Can't imagine why.

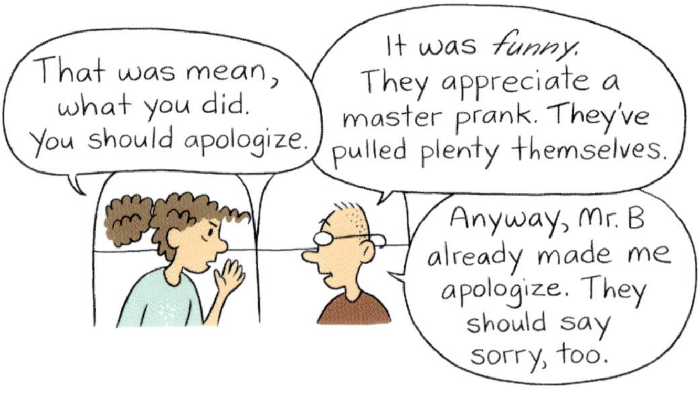

That was mean, what you did. You should apologize.
It was *funny*. They appreciate a master prank. They've pulled plenty themselves.
Anyway, Mr. B already made me apologize. They should say sorry, too.

I just roll my eyes.

Aside from Tyler and Anthony giving Joe death-laser glares, there's something else I've noticed:

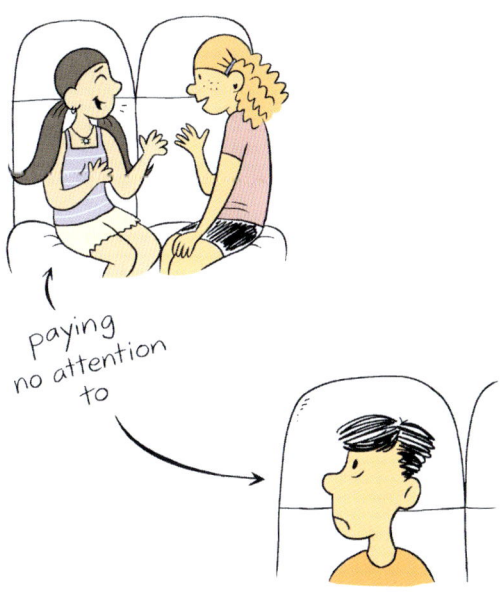

paying no attention to

I wonder what happened. I hate to admit it, but whatever **did** happen . . .

...I'm kinda happy about it.

← feeling guilty-not-guilty

We get to the park in fifteen minutes. Mr. Bauman, Coach Durdle, and the counselors file us out and lead the way. First, we hike through the gorge. It takes a while. It's chillier here, so I'm glad I brought my hoodie. The teachers point out some cool stuff along the way, like the many, many rock layers and some history about the Native American people who originally lived here.

We keep going.

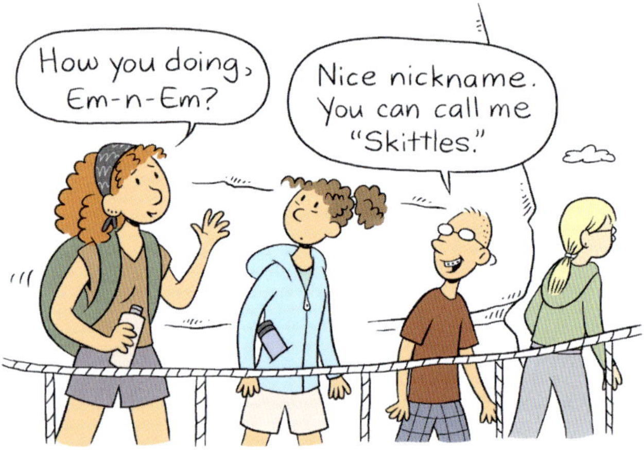
How you doing, Em-n-Em?
Nice nickname. You can call me "Skittles."

I snort and just mutter:

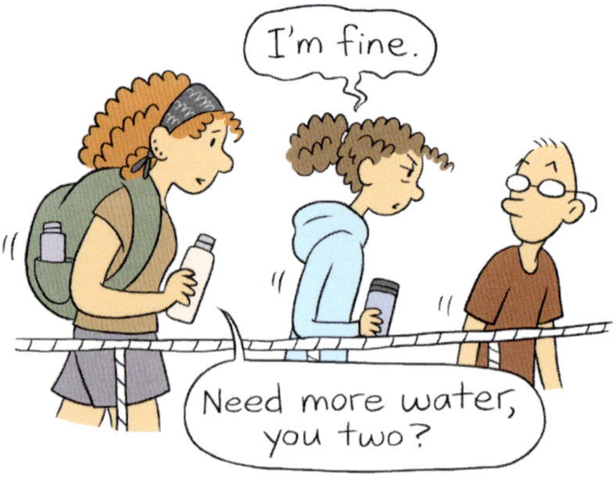
I'm fine.
Need more water, you two?

Joe and I shake our heads. I don't make eye contact with Trina. I'm still grumpy, and I don't wanna talk about it. Not here. I can tell

Trina senses something is up, but she doesn't say anything.

Instead, she rushes to catch up with Ciera, whose powerful calves propel her ahead of the pack.

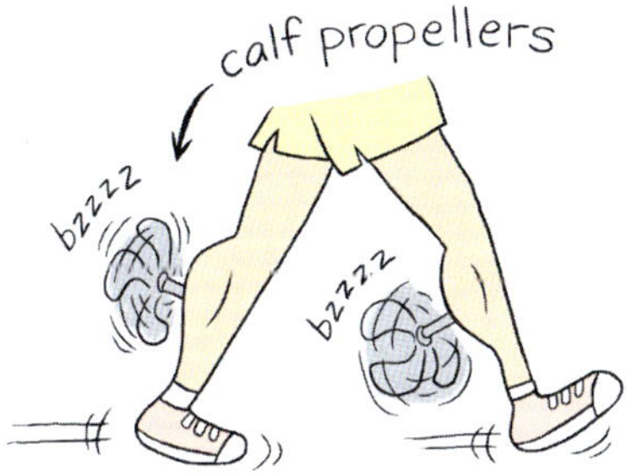
calf propellers
bzzzz
bzzzz

We come to a larger clearing lined with dramatic cliffsides. In the middle of the clearing, Coach Durdle motions for us to gather around a big, flat boulder that's fenced off with netting.

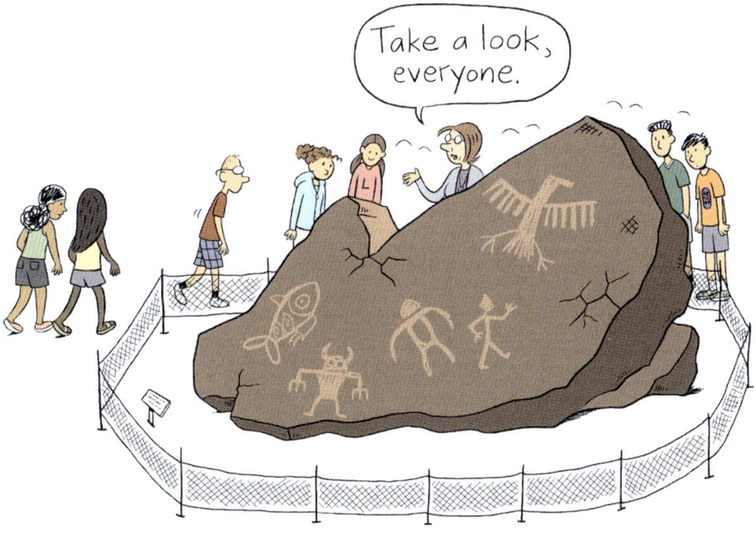
Take a look, everyone.

We inch closer. Drawings are etched into the rock. There is a bird (an eagle, I think), a fish, and a few stick figures. There's also what looks like a person with horns.

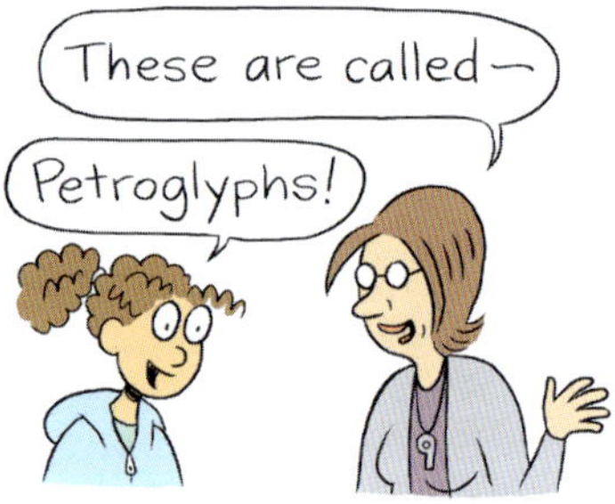
These are called—
Petroglyphs!

I clap my hand over my mouth and feel my cheeks burn. I can't believe I blurted that out.

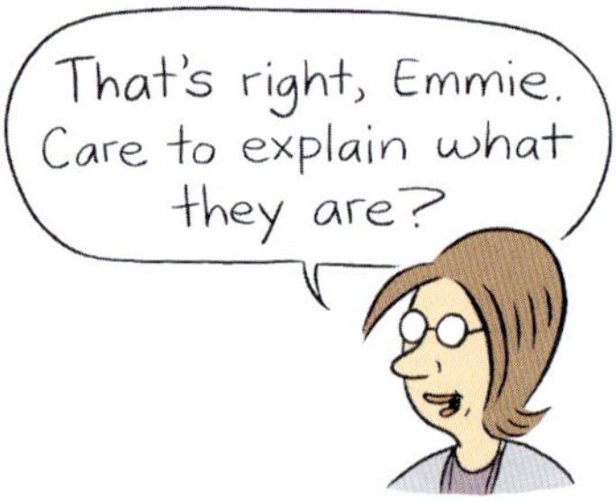
That's right, Emmie. Care to explain what they are?

I want to say no, but everyone is watching.

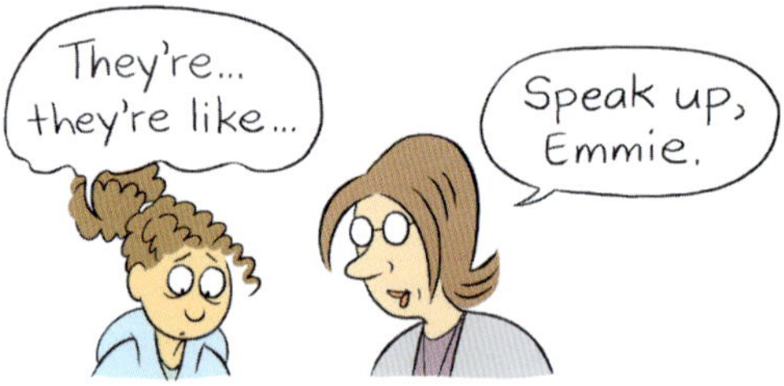
They're... they're like...
Speak up, Emmie.

I gulp.

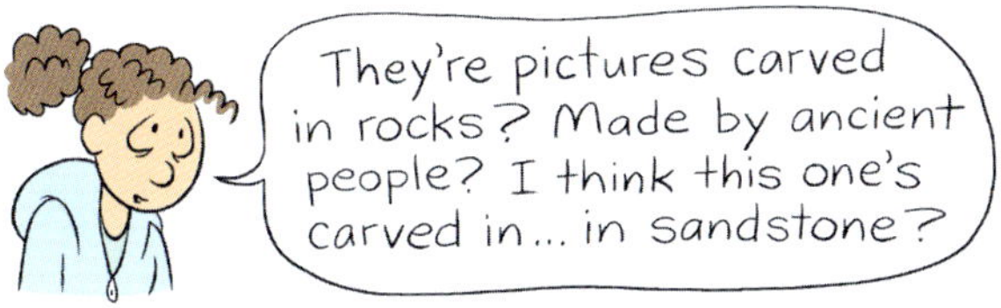
They're pictures carved in rocks? Made by ancient people? I think this one's carved in... in sandstone?

I don't know why, but I automatically glance up at Tyler, who's looking at me like I grew horns myself.

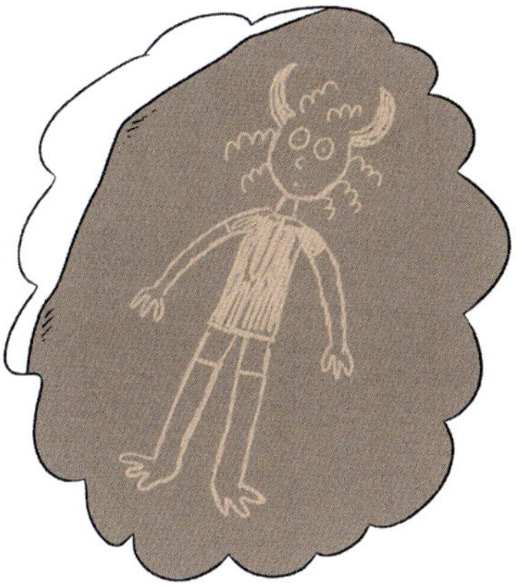

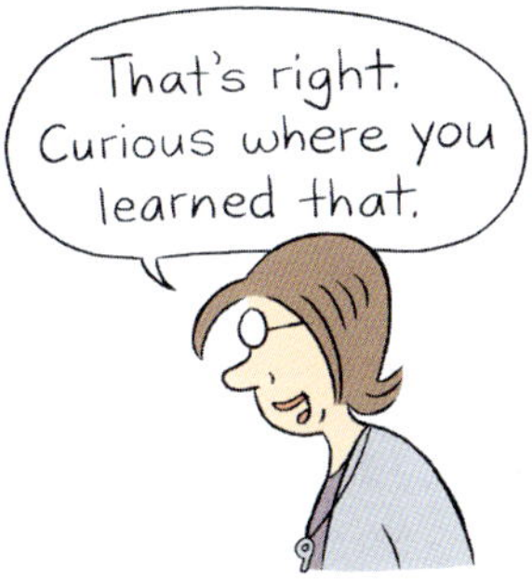
That's right. Curious where you learned that.

I know I'm bright red now.

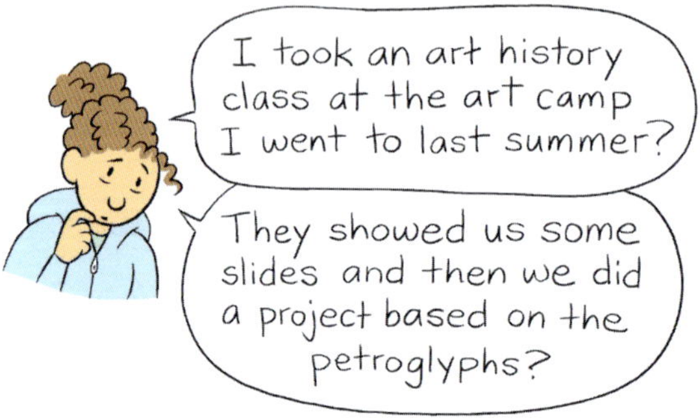
I took an art history class at the art camp I went to last summer?
They showed us some slides and then we did a project based on the petroglyphs?

When I'm nervous, I sound like I'm asking questions. The more I try to stop, the more I do it. But no one seems to care.

And now, as I look up, Tyler's looking back, kinda impressed. The way he looked at me before the whole BG thing.

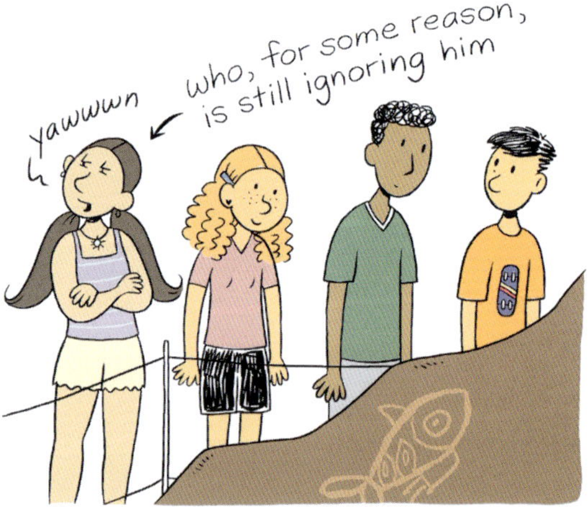
yawwwn
who, for some reason, is still ignoring him

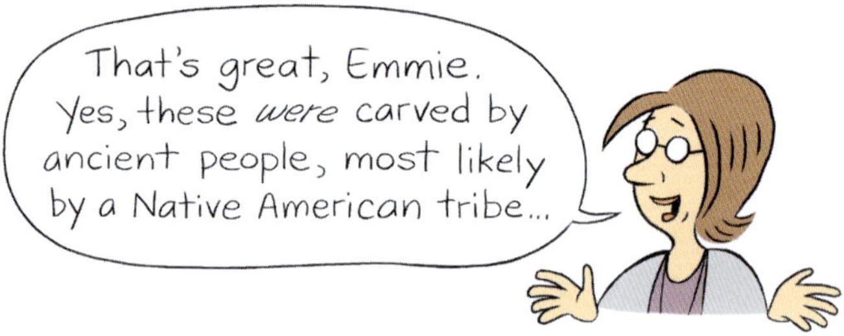
That's great, Emmie. Yes, these *were* carved by ancient people, most likely by a Native American tribe...

I catch Trina smiling at me, too, but I look away.

Coach continues explaining the carvings, and then we return to the trail. Eventually it leads us back to the parking lot. After taking some drinks and snacks from the coolers, we wait to get on the bus to head back to the camp.

(And then, soon, home!)

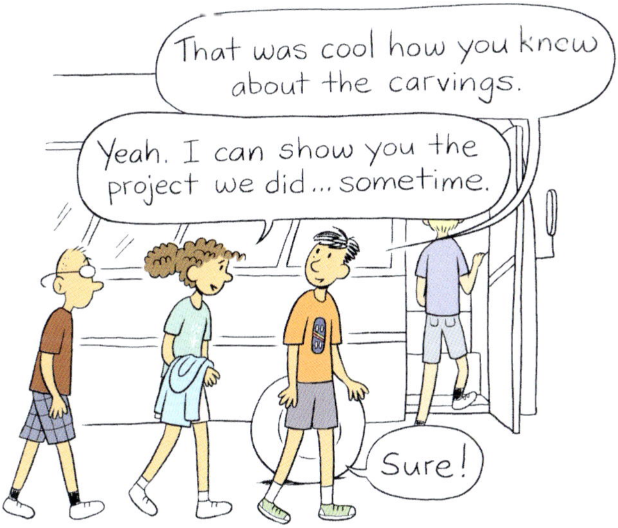
That was cool how you knew about the carvings.
Yeah. I can show you the project we did... sometime.
Sure!

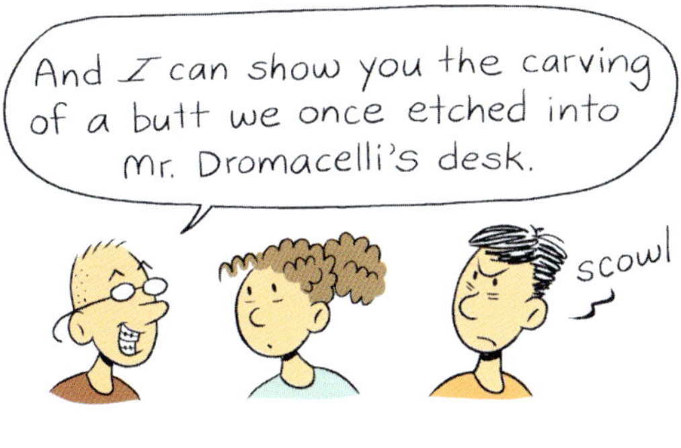
And I can show you the carving of a butt we once etched into Mr. Dromacelli's desk.
scowl

Joe and I sit down as the bus starts.

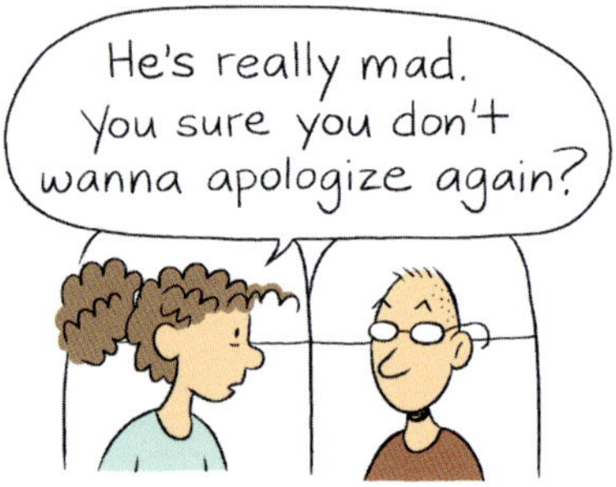
He's really mad. You sure you don't wanna apologize again?

For once Joe is quiet. Then he shrugs.

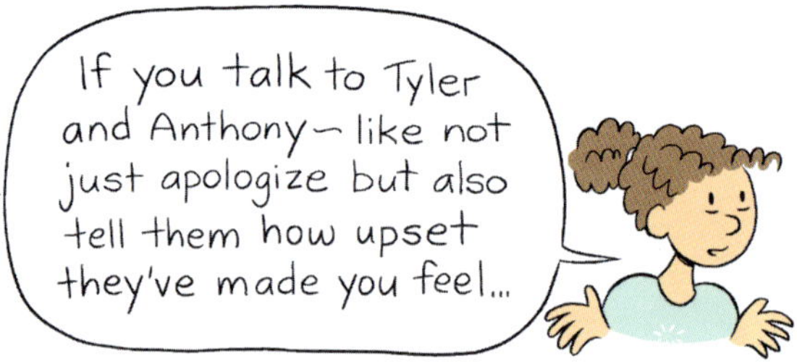
If you talk to Tyler and Anthony—like not just apologize but also tell them how upset they've made you feel...

Joe rolls his eyes.

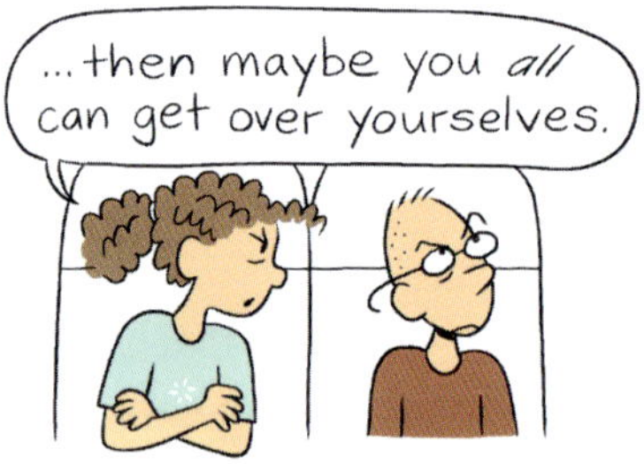
...then maybe you *all* can get over yourselves.

He doesn't say anything, just shrugs again. I'm learning that in Joe-speech . . .

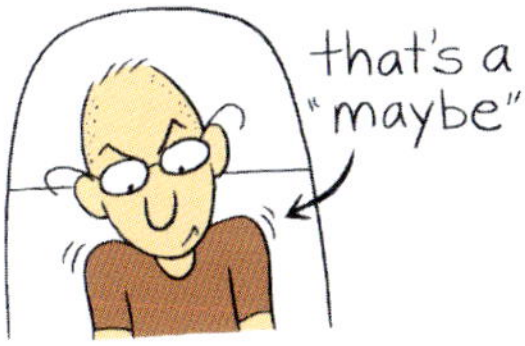
that's a "maybe"

I glance back at Tyler (while trying not to look like I'm glancing). I notice him glancing at BG (while trying not to look like he's glancing). She's chatting with her bus buddy and is clearly avoiding Tyler.

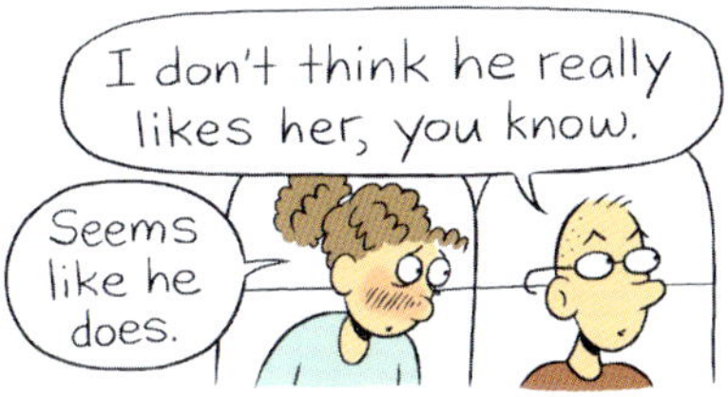
I don't think he really likes her, you know.
Seems like he does.

I think about what they were doing behind the tree.

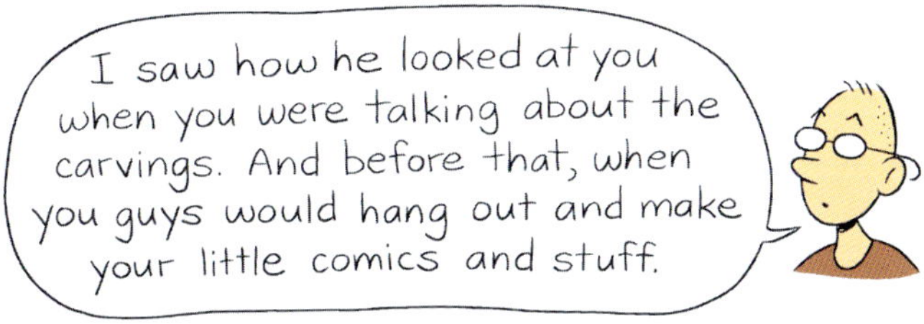
I saw how he looked at you when you were talking about the carvings. And before that, when you guys would hang out and make your little comics and stuff.

I ignore the "little comics" remark.

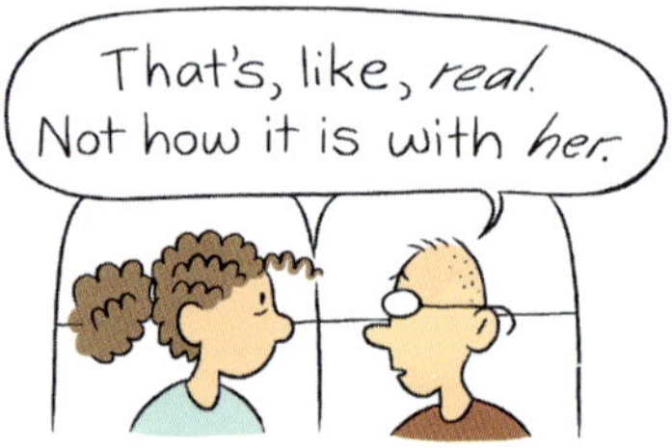
That's, like, *real.* Not how it is with *her.*

Now I'm confused.

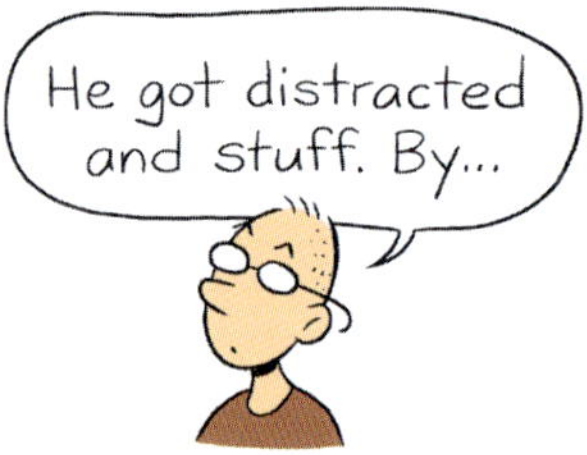
He got distracted and stuff. By...

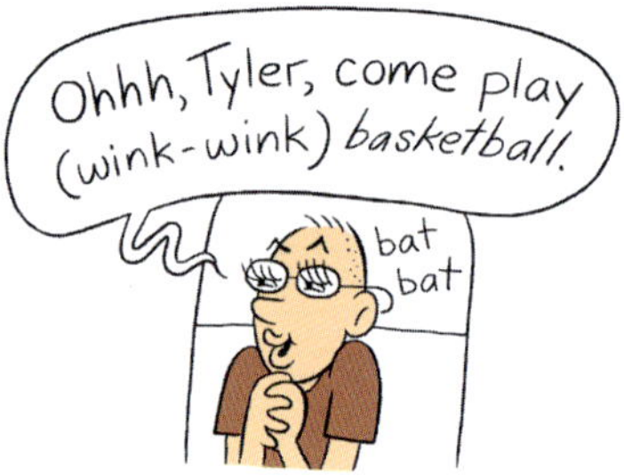
Ohhh, Tyler, come play (wink-wink) *basketball.*
bat bat

I burst out laughing. I can't help it.

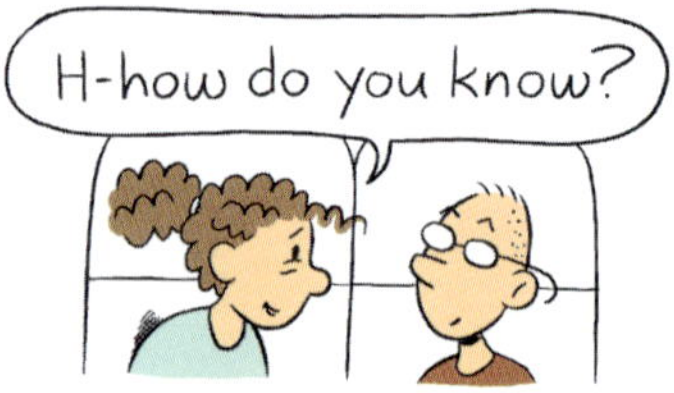
H-how do you know?

Before he has a chance to say anything else, the bus stops, and everyone excitedly pushes their way out.

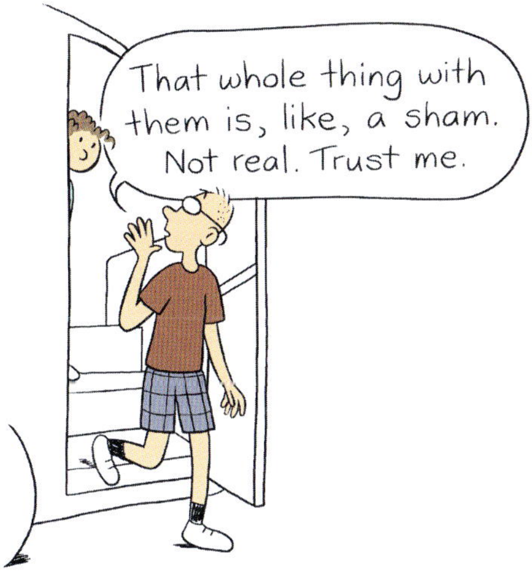
That whole thing with them is, like, a sham. Not real. Trust me.

I nod, unsure. But for some reason—against all odds (and history)—I take his word.

I don't know why.

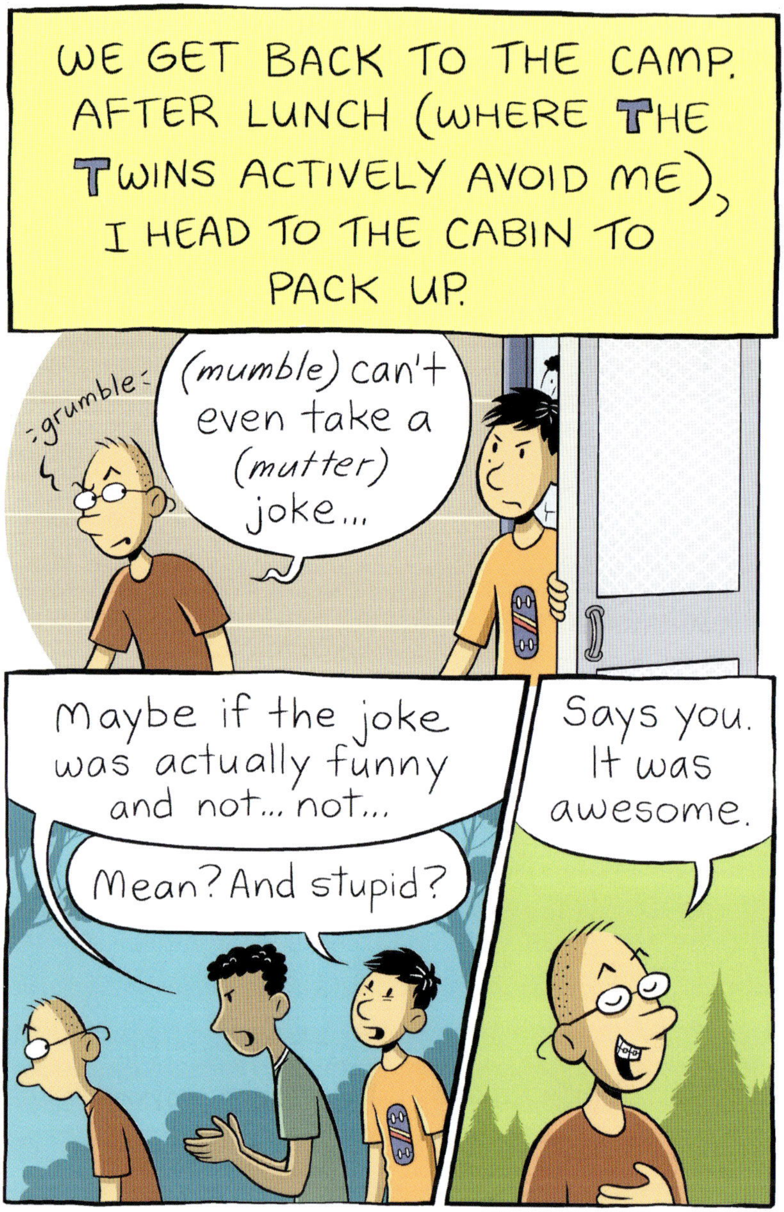
WE GET BACK TO THE CAMP. AFTER LUNCH (WHERE THE TWINS ACTIVELY AVOID ME), I HEAD TO THE CABIN TO PACK UP.
grumble
(mumble) can't even take a (mutter) joke...
Maybe if the joke was actually funny and not... not...
Mean? And stupid?
Says you. It was awesome.

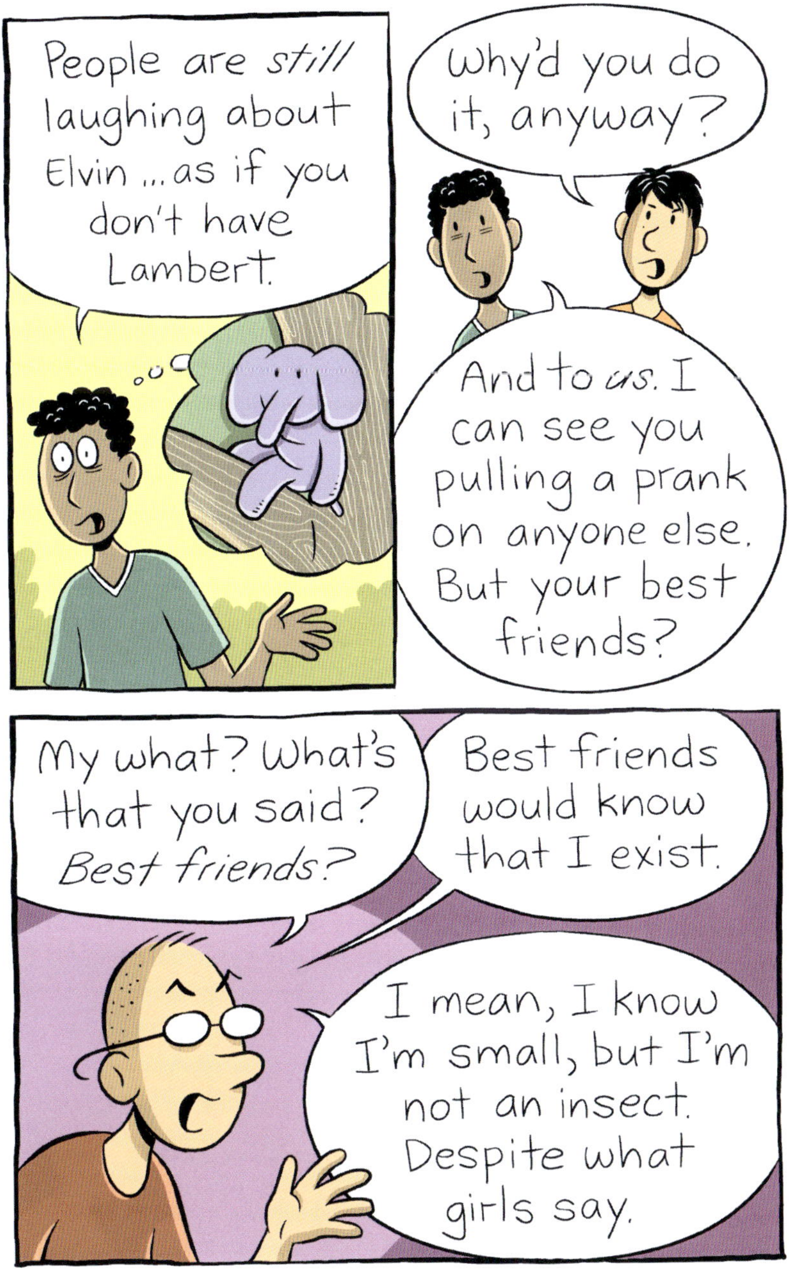
People are *still* laughing about Elvin ... as if you don't have Lambert.
Why'd you do it, anyway?
And to *us*. I can see you pulling a prank on anyone else. But your best friends?
My what? What's that you said? *Best friends?*
Best friends would know that I exist.
I mean, I know I'm small, but I'm not an insect. Despite what girls say.

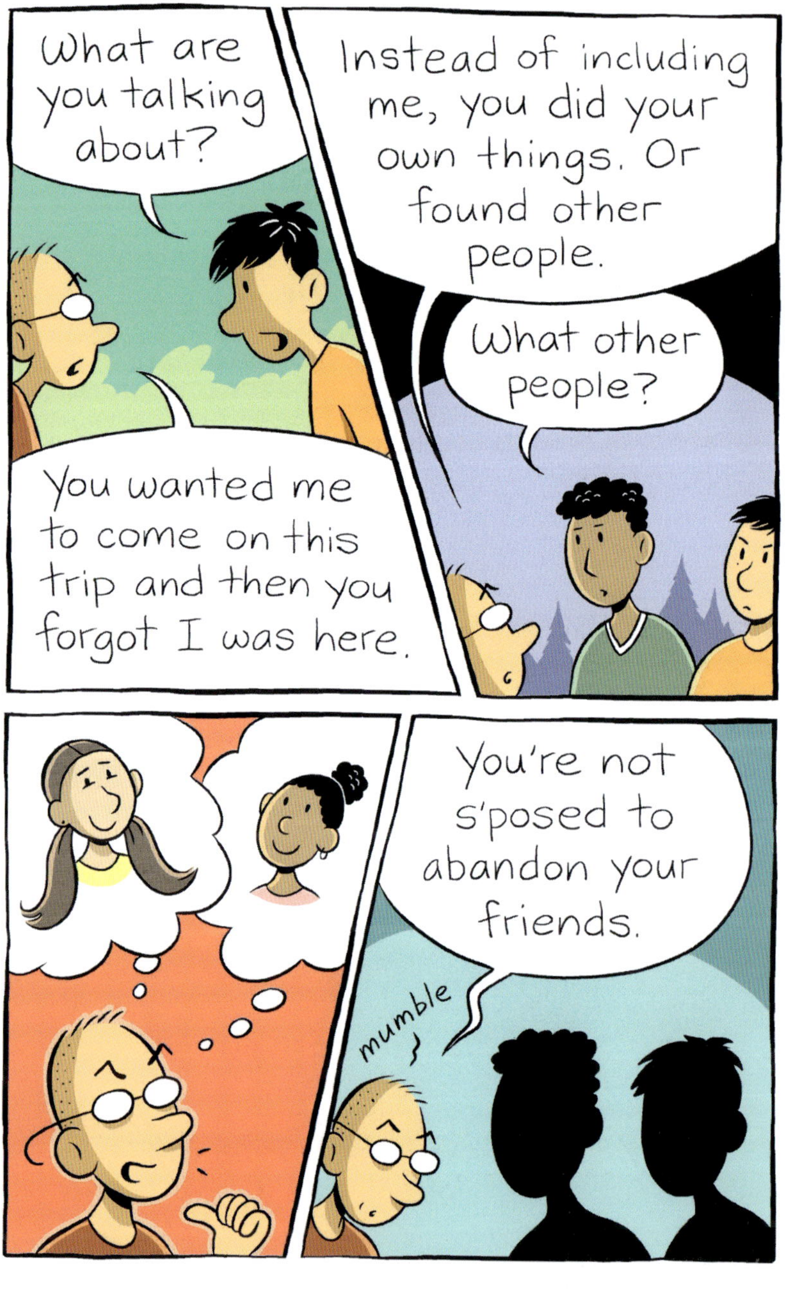
What are you talking about?
You wanted me to come on this trip and then you forgot I was here.
Instead of including me, you did your own things. Or found other people.
What other people?
You're not s'posed to abandon your friends.
mumble

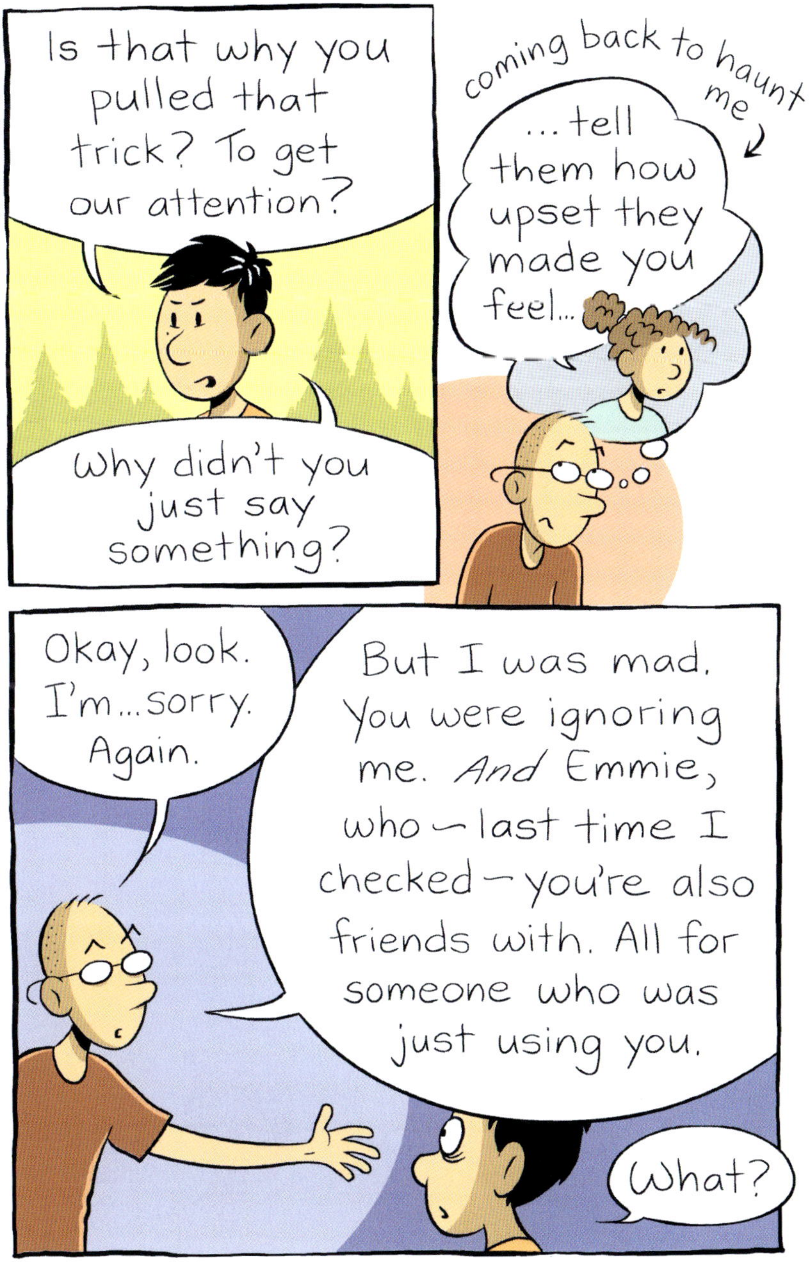
Is that why you pulled that trick? To get our attention?
Why didn't you just say something?
coming back to haunt me
...tell them how upset they made you feel...
Okay, look. I'm...sorry. Again.
But I was mad. You were ignoring me. *And* Emmie, who—last time I checked—you're also friends with. All for someone who was just using you.
What?

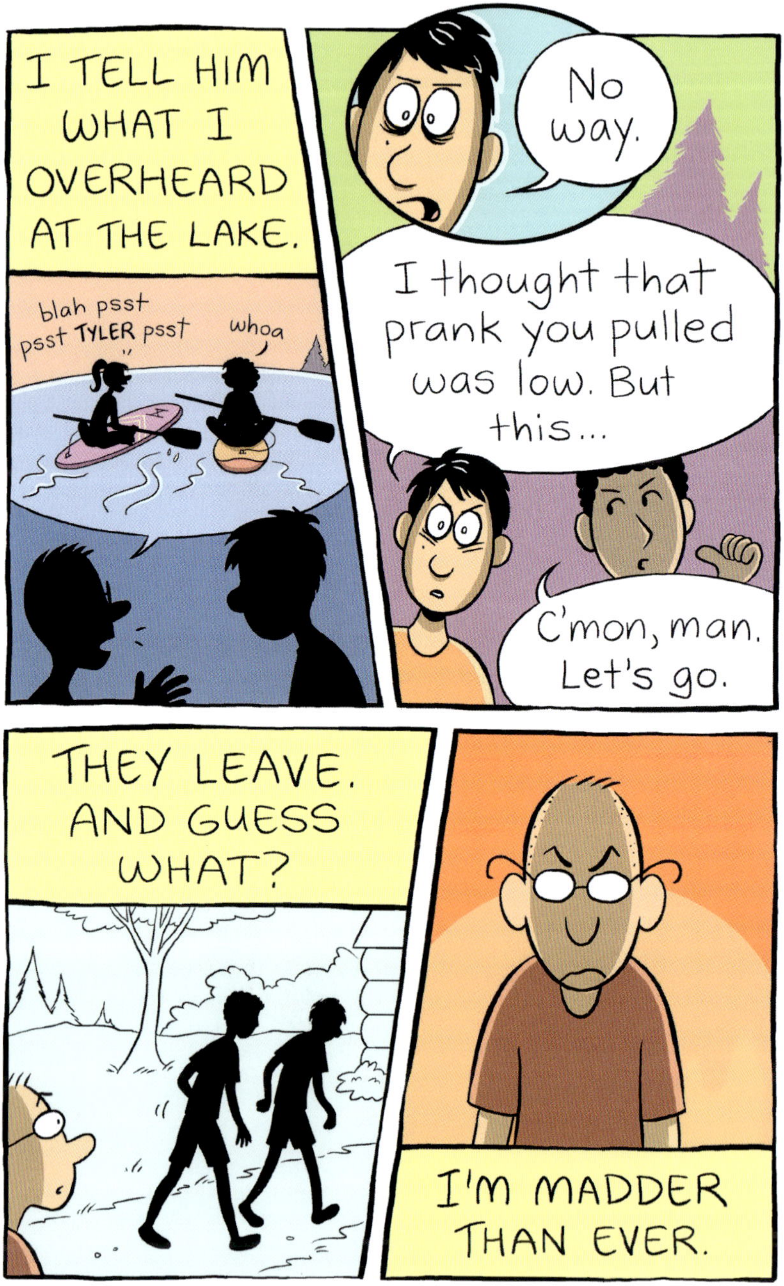
I TELL HIM WHAT I OVERHEARD AT THE LAKE.
blah psst psst TYLER psst
whoa
No way.
I thought that prank you pulled was low. But this...
C'mon, man. Let's go.
THEY LEAVE. AND GUESS WHAT?
I'M MADDER THAN EVER.

EMMIE

Packing up. Celia and Grace are chattering next to me. They just got back from taking selfies by the lake with the Gossip Girls. Now they're actively ignoring me (big surprise) while they pack.

narrowing down 500 pics in 5 minutes

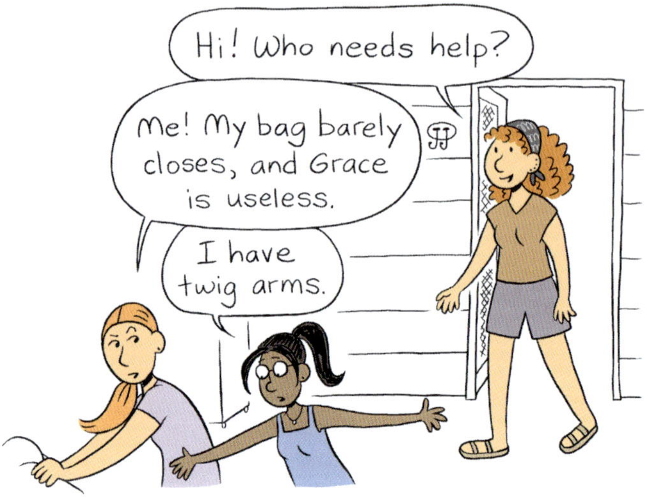
Hi! Who needs help?
Me! My bag barely closes, and Grace is useless.
I have twig arms.

Trina holds the bursting bag closed (how many outfits are *in* there?) while Celia zips it up, literally breaking into a sweat.

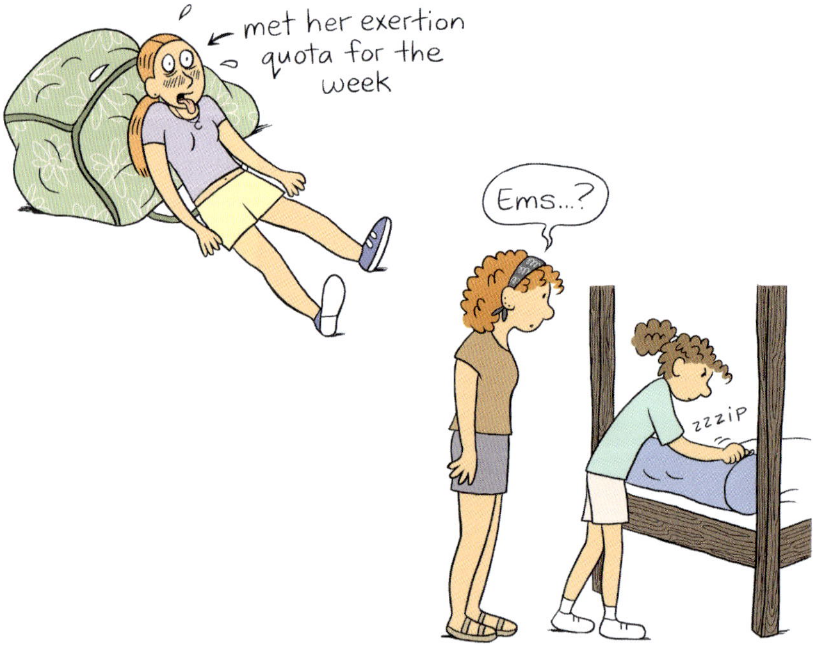
met her exertion quota for the week
Ems...?
zzzip

I don't say anything. I'm still fuming that Trina has avoided me all weekend in favor of my catty bunkmates and the Queen of Calves. Celia and Grace look over, curious. I don't think they're used to seeing me mad. Or any emotion, really, other than my standard one:

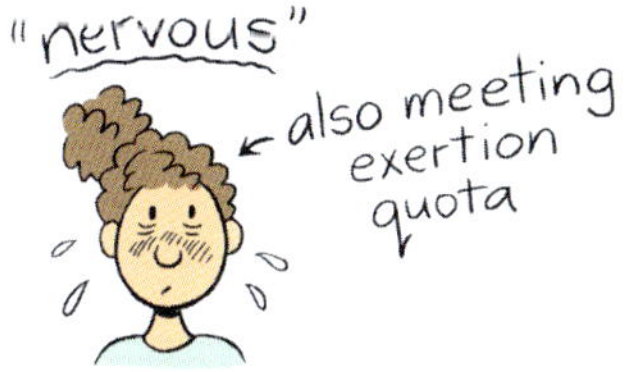
"nervous"
also meeting exertion quota

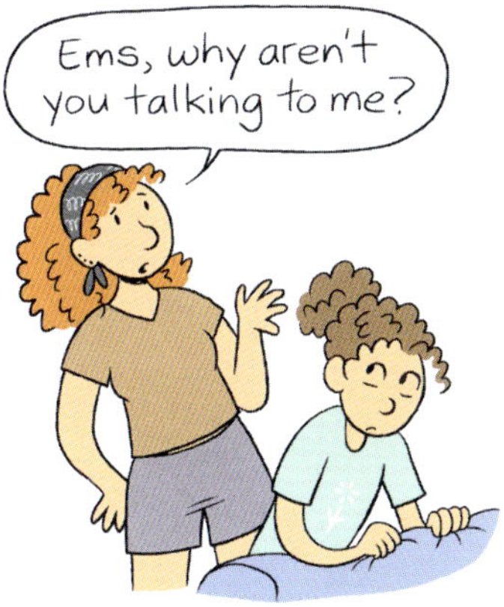
Ems, why aren't you talking to me?

I finally glance up, ready to torture her with my angry glare and continued silence (angry-silence, not shy-silence). But she just looks confused and hurt.

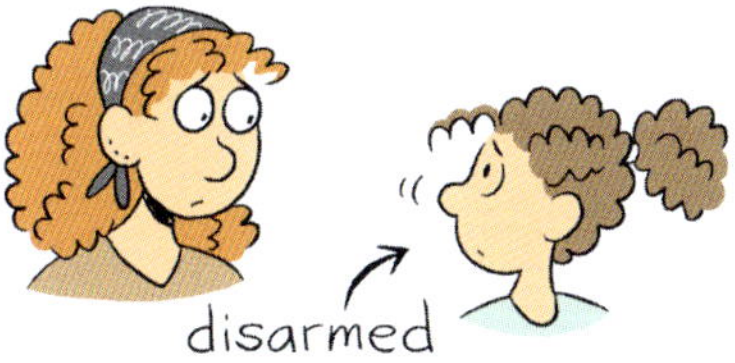
disarmed

I've been preaching to Joe about talking to Tyler and Anthony, and here I am ignoring my own advice.

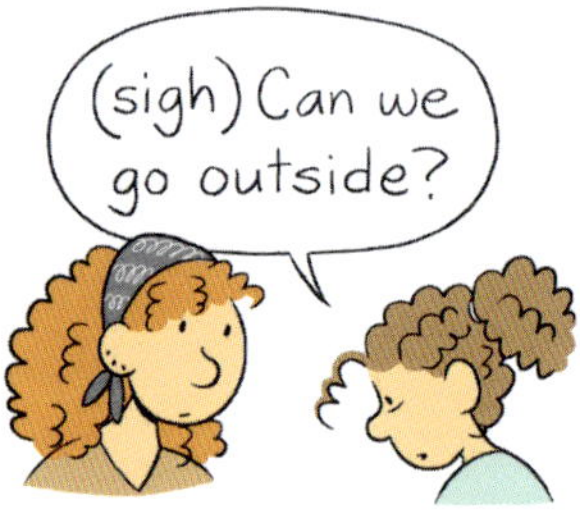
(sigh) Can we go outside?

She follows me to the porch.

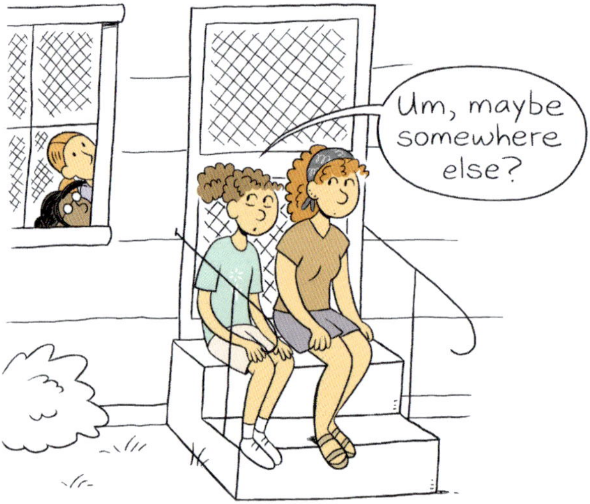
Um, maybe somewhere else?

We walk to the art shack and sit on a bench inside. It only takes a moment's hesitation before I word-vomit. I blab about all my embarrassing incidents, how much I miss Bri and Sarah, about

Tyler's new crush, and how I've been completely snubbed by Trina, who had promised we'd have "seester time" this weekend. Basically, I just spill about how I feel—kinda lost and abandoned.

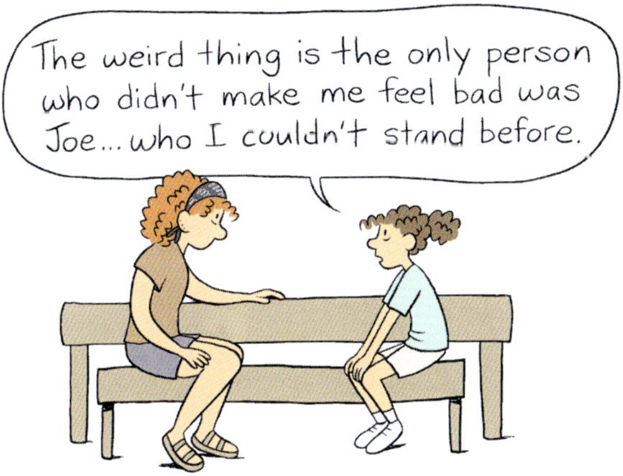
The weird thing is the only person who didn't make me feel bad was Joe... who I couldn't stand before.

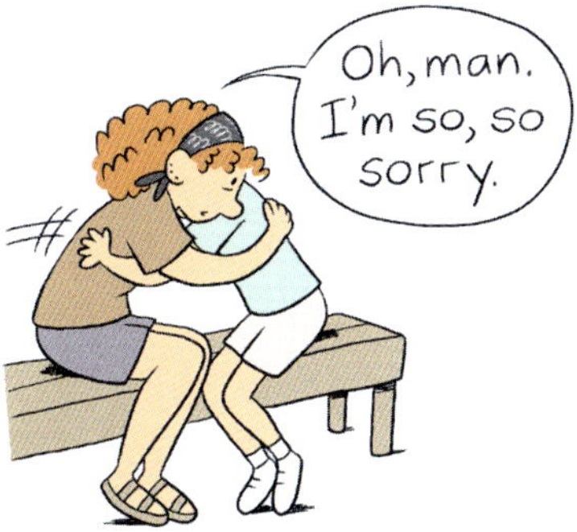
Oh, man. I'm so, so sorry.

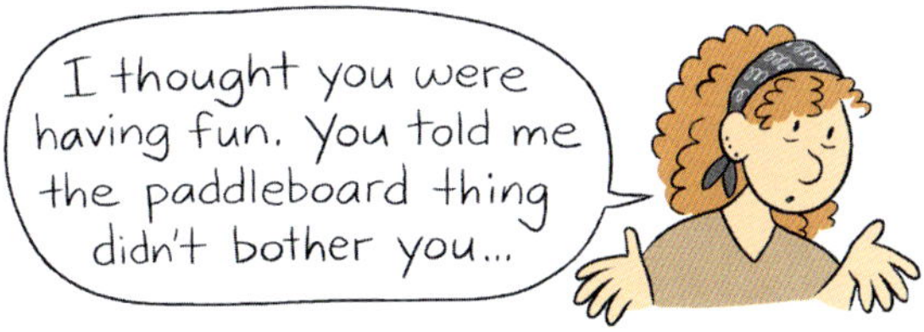
I thought you were having fun. You told me the paddleboard thing didn't bother you...

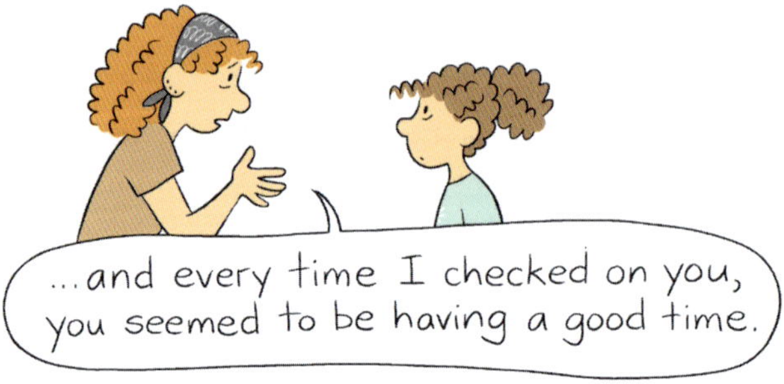
...and every time I checked on you, you seemed to be having a good time.

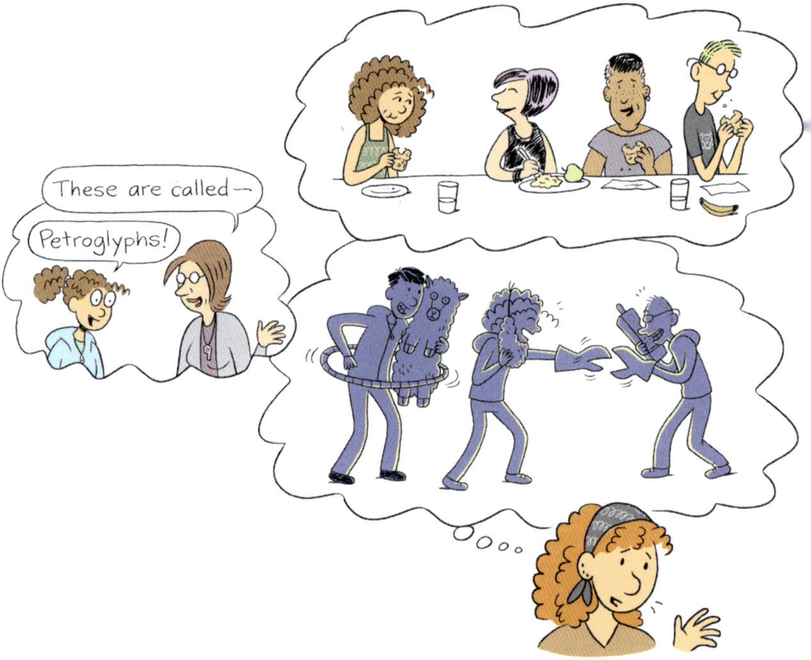
These are called—
Petroglyphs!

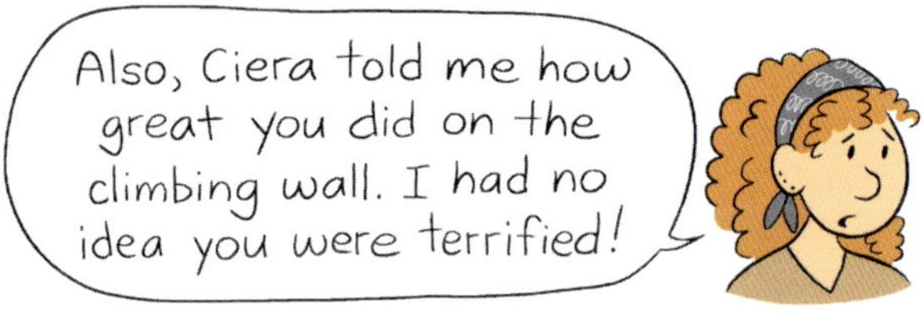
Also, Ciera told me how great you did on the climbing wall. I had no idea you were terrified!

I guess she saw and heard things differently. I also forgot how much I try to hide my feelings. I shouldn't blame her for not reading my mind.

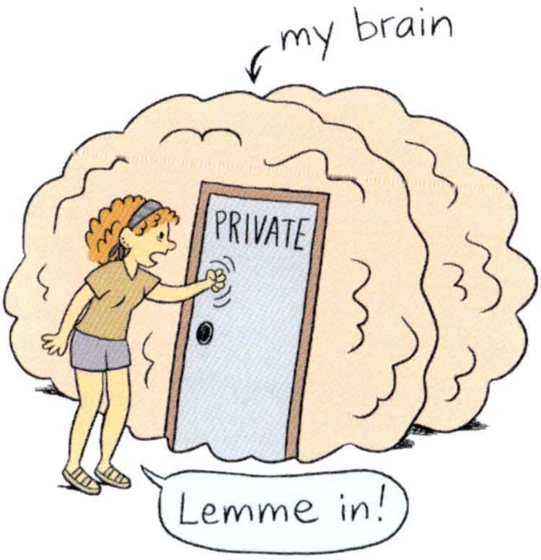
my brain
PRIVATE
Lemme in!

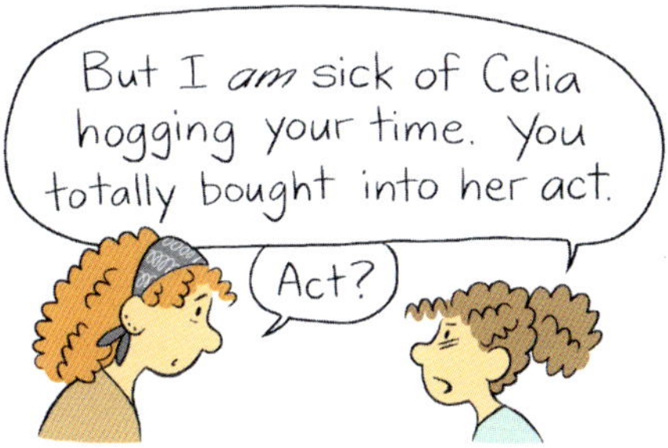
But I *am* sick of Celia hogging your time. You totally bought into her act.
Act?

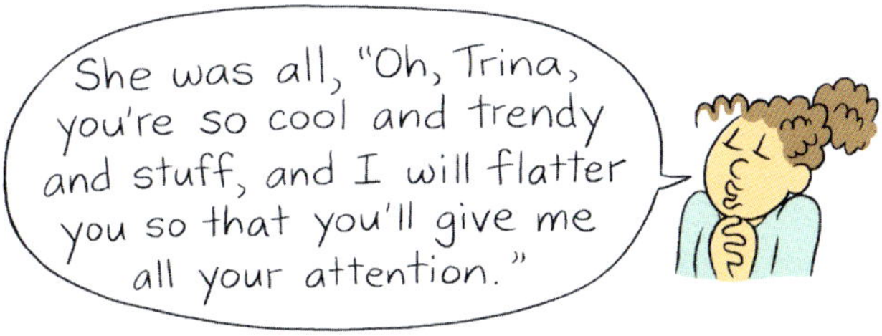
She was all, "Oh, Trina, you're so cool and trendy and stuff, and I will flatter you so that you'll give me all your attention."

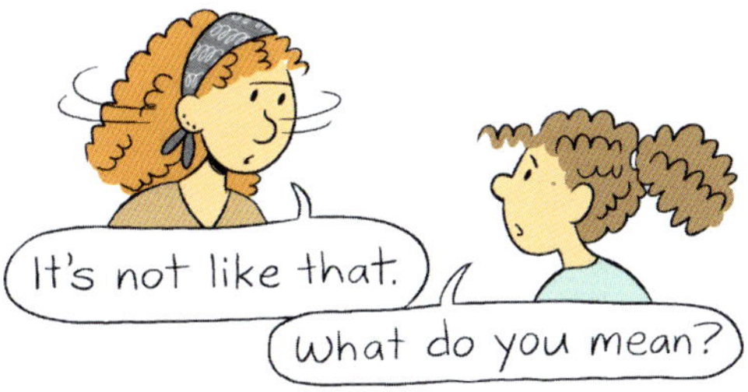
It's not like that.
What do you mean?

"I don't know why Cee latched on to me. Maybe she sees some of herself in me. All that false confidence and stuff."

heh

"Also... I caught her crying in the cabin by herself Friday night, before the campfire."

"We started talking. She's been having a rough time at home, Ems."

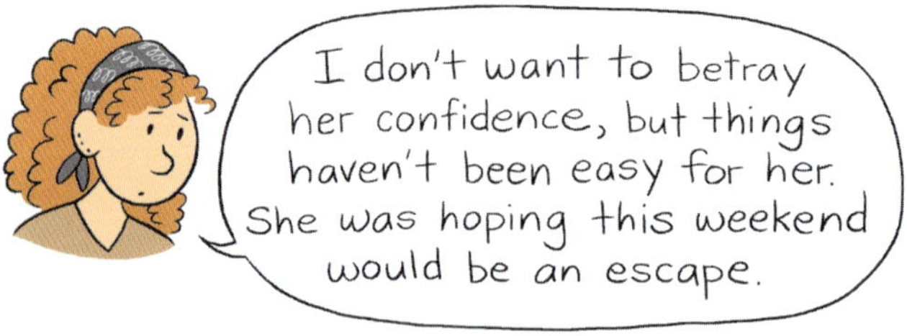

"I don't want to betray her confidence, but things haven't been easy for her. She was hoping this weekend would be an escape."

I'm floored. Cool, collected Queen Cee?

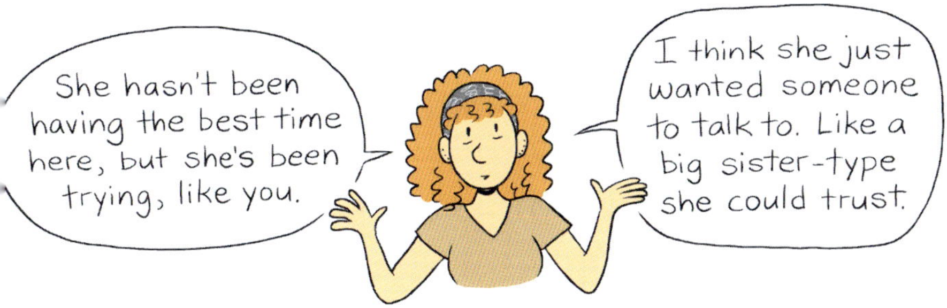
She hasn't been having the best time here, but she's been trying, like you.
I think she just wanted someone to talk to. Like a big sister-type she could trust.

I think about all the times I've confided in Trina. Something I take for granted, I guess.

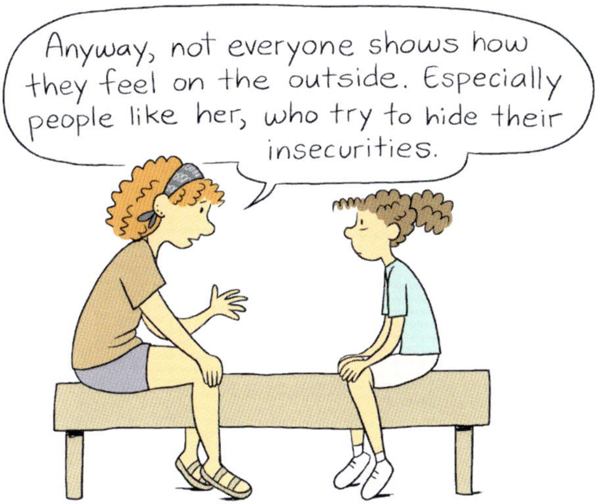
Anyway, not everyone shows how they feel on the outside. Especially people like her, who try to hide their insecurities.

Wow.

As if she **can** read my mind, she says:

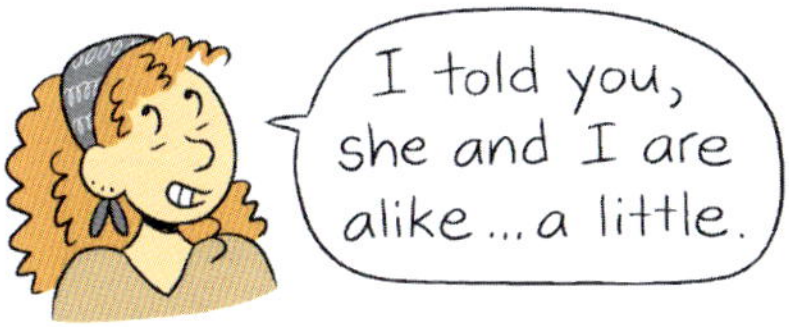
I told you, she and I are alike ... a little.

I don't believe my sister is anything like mean old Celia, but I get her point. Trina told me she often tries to act more confident than she feels—like she owes it to everyone to be super cheerful and together. And how hard it can be when she's not up to it.

We hug it out and head back to the cabin. I finish packing. Celia (kinda shyly) walks over to Trina, holding some nail polish bottles and a tiny brush.

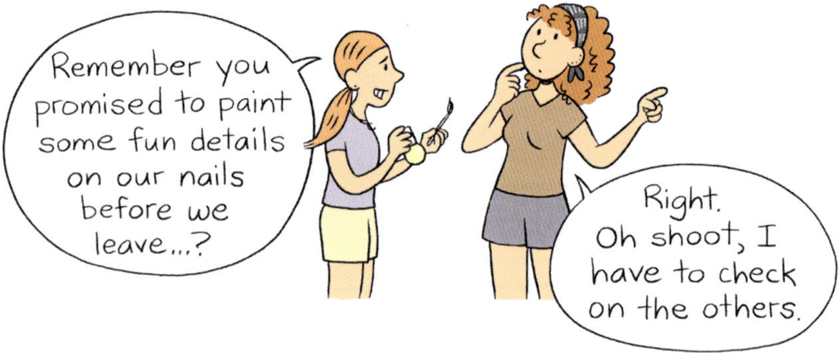
Remember you promised to paint some fun details on our nails before we leave...?
Right. Oh shoot, I have to check on the others.

She gestures to the next-door cabin of girls she's in charge of.

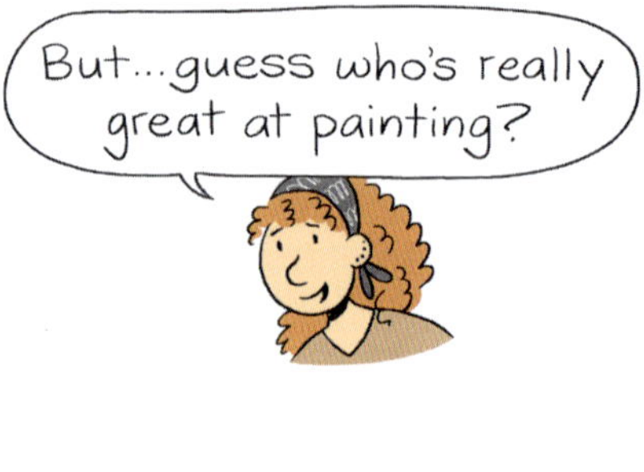
But...guess who's really great at painting?

Oh God, no.

Celia and Grace look like they'd rather peel off their own nails and eat them than have me paint theirs. But I guess they don't want to seem rude in front of Trina (for a change), so they just shrug.

Can you do daisies?

Hesitantly, I nod.

See you at the buses in twenty.

Grace puts on music from her phone playlist as we sit on the floor. Celia holds still while I carefully paint daisies, roses, and even a dragonfly on her nails. On Grace's, I paint little bees. When I'm done, they blow on their fingertips and look really pleased.

You're so good. Where'd you learn to paint?
I dunno. I've always loved it. I grew up taking art lessons and stuff.

You should start a side hustle. The girls at school would pay you for this.

I'm blown away. Was that a **compliment**?

I'd be happy to get paid in art supplies. Or maybe ice cream sundaes.

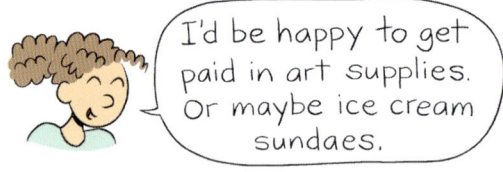

They giggle. Is this all in my head?

We hear kids heading to the buses outside, so we finish up, grab our bags, and head out.

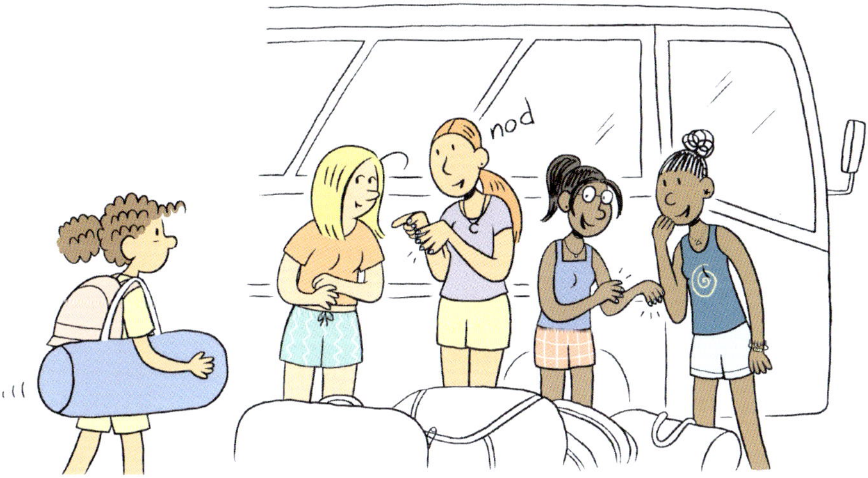
nod

Huh.
Maybe this weekend wasn't all bad.

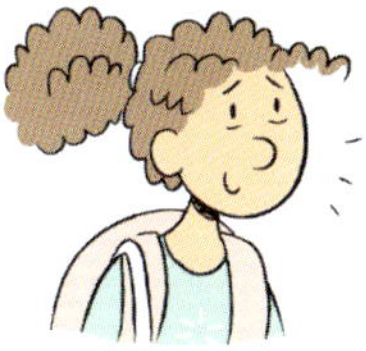

Maybe.

Joe

I'M STILL TICKED OFF. BUT NOW IT'S MOSTLY AIMED AT:

I'M MAD AT MYSELF FOR THE PRANK, FOR NOT SAYING SOMETHING SOONER ABOUT BASKETBALL GIRL, AND FOR NOT TELLING MY FRIENDS WHAT'S ON MY MIND, PERIOD.

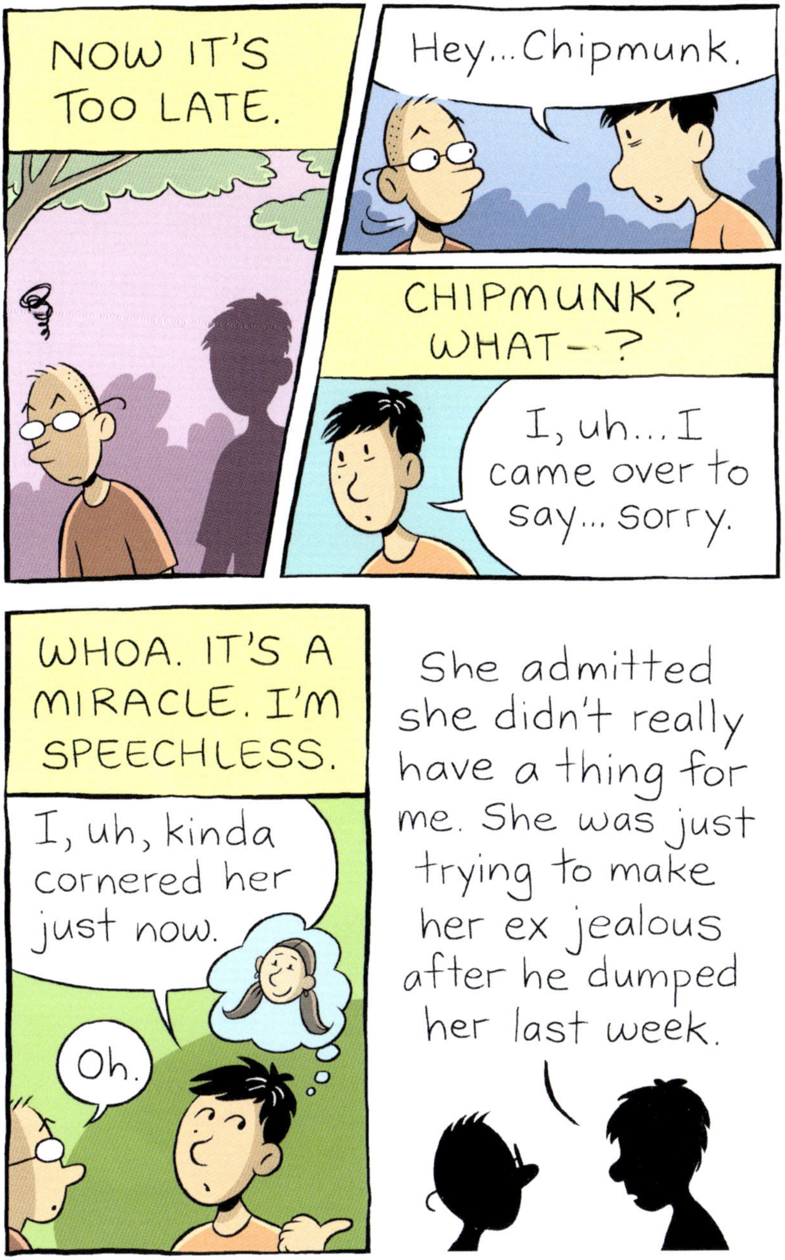
NOW IT'S TOO LATE.
Hey...Chipmunk.
CHIPMUNK? WHAT—?
I, uh... I came over to say... sorry.
WHOA. IT'S A MIRACLE. I'M SPEECHLESS.
I, uh, kinda cornered her just now.
Oh.
She admitted she didn't really have a thing for me. She was just trying to make her ex jealous after he dumped her last week.

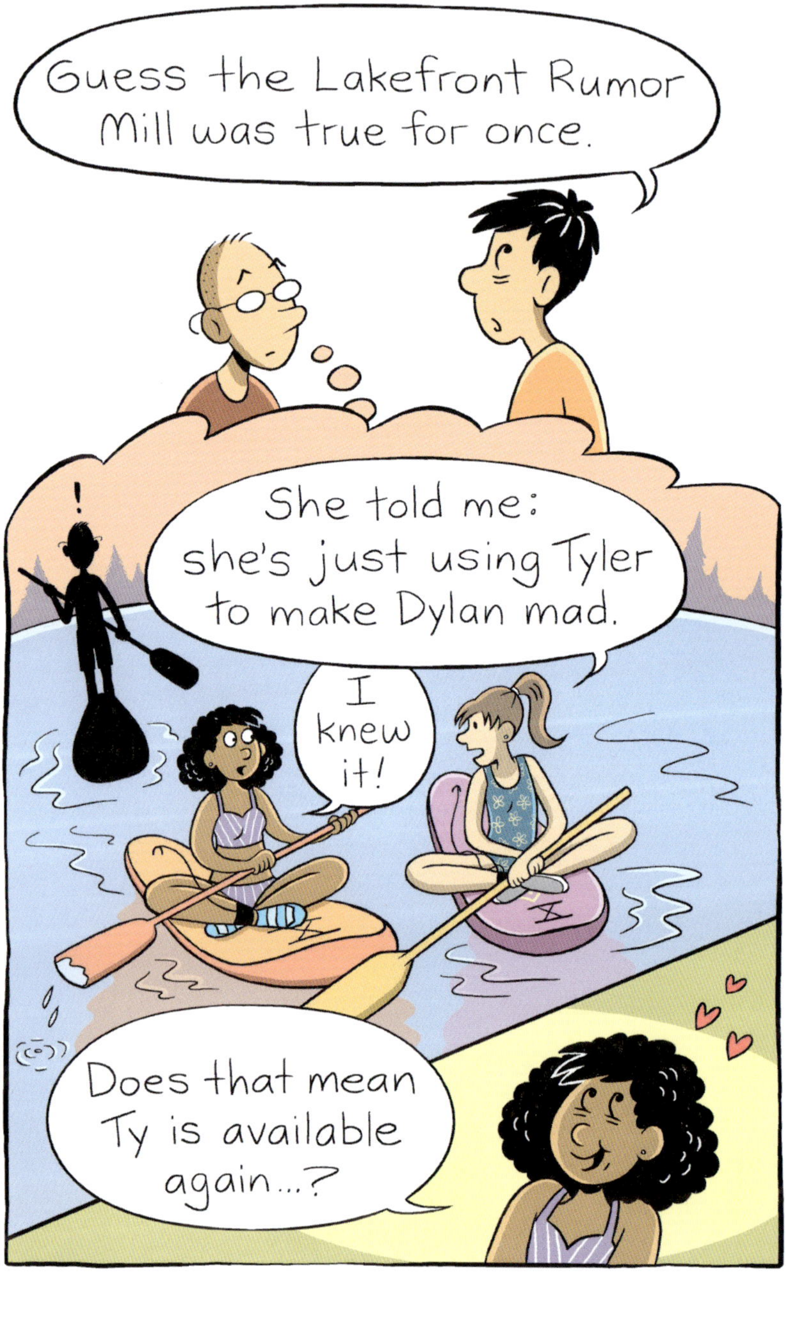
Guess the Lakefront Rumor Mill was true for once.
She told me: she's just using Tyler to make Dylan mad.
I knew it!
Does that mean Ty is available again...?

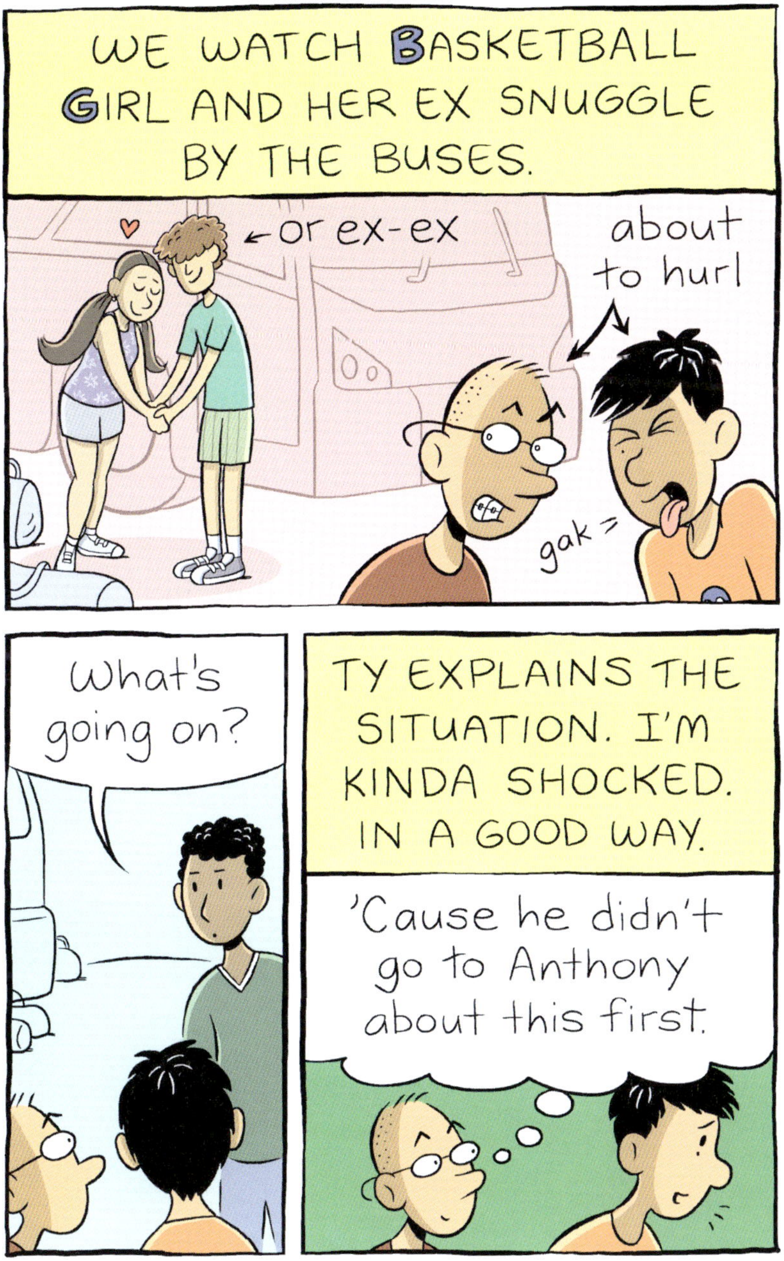
WE WATCH BASKETBALL GIRL AND HER EX SNUGGLE BY THE BUSES.
← or ex-ex
about to hurl
gak
What's going on?
TY EXPLAINS THE SITUATION. I'M KINDA SHOCKED. IN A GOOD WAY.
'Cause he didn't go to Anthony about this first.

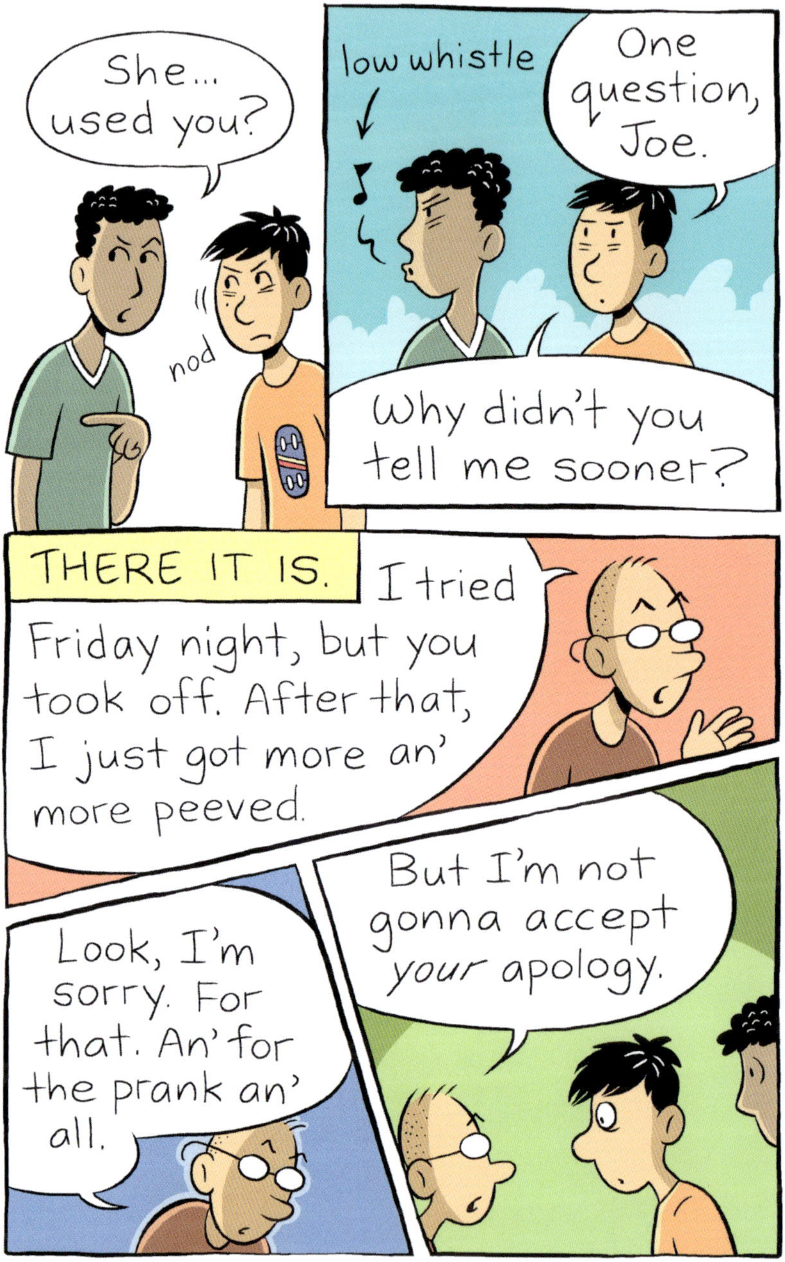
She... used you?
nod
low whistle
One question, Joe.
Why didn't you tell me sooner?
THERE IT IS.
I tried Friday night, but you took off. After that, I just got more an' more peeved.
Look, I'm sorry. For that. An' for the prank an' all.
But I'm not gonna accept *your* apology.

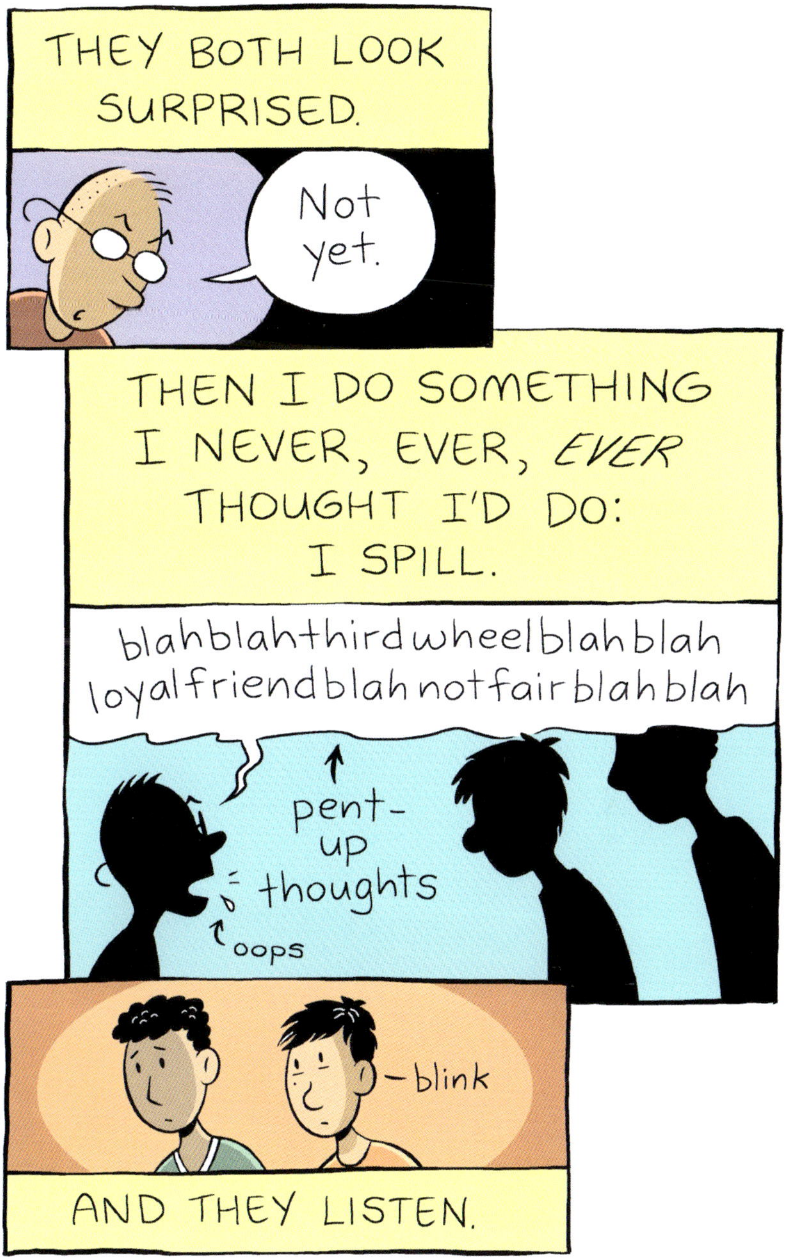
THEY BOTH LOOK SURPRISED.
Not yet.
THEN I DO SOMETHING I NEVER, EVER, *EVER* THOUGHT I'D DO: I SPILL.
blahblahthirdwheelblahblah loyalfriendblahnotfairblahblah
pent-up thoughts
oops
blink
AND THEY LISTEN.

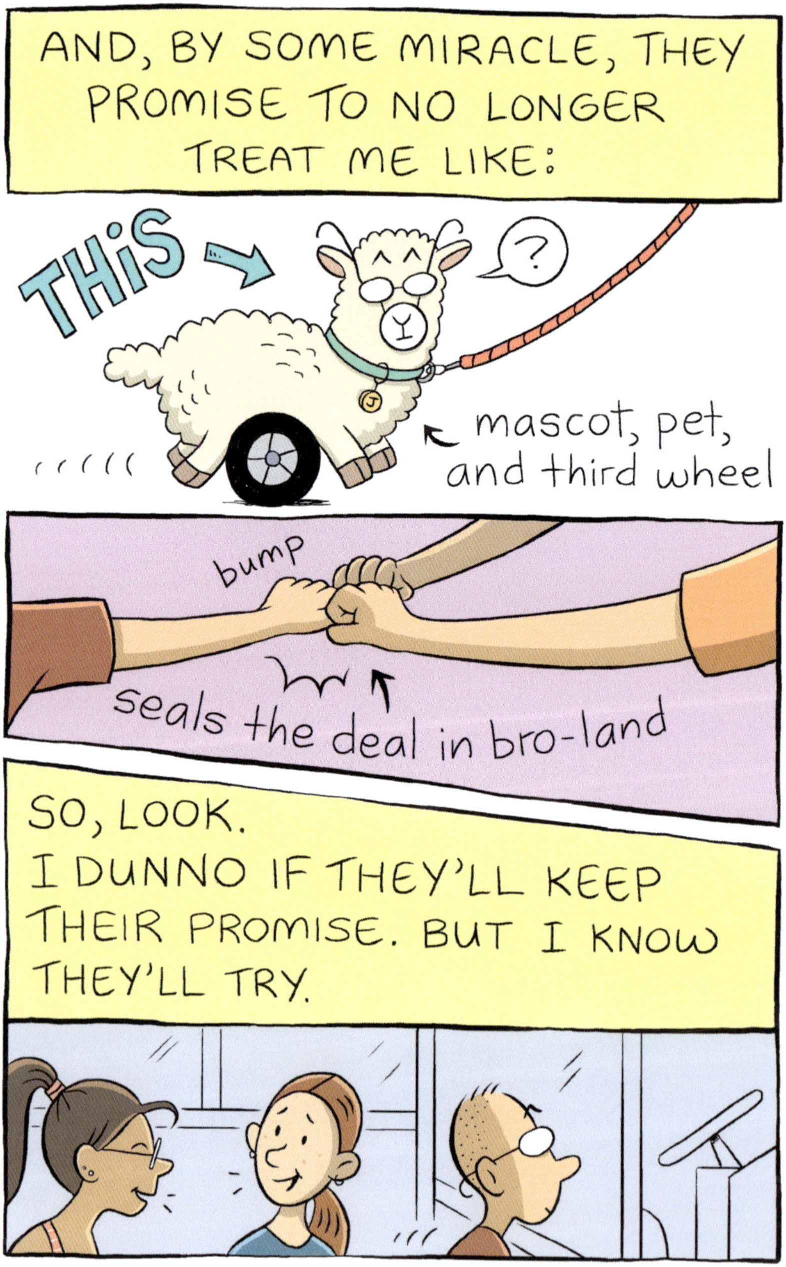

AND, BY SOME MIRACLE, THEY PROMISE TO NO LONGER TREAT ME LIKE:
THIS
?
mascot, pet, and third wheel
bump
seals the deal in bro-land
SO, LOOK.
I DUNNO IF THEY'LL KEEP THEIR PROMISE. BUT I KNOW THEY'LL TRY.

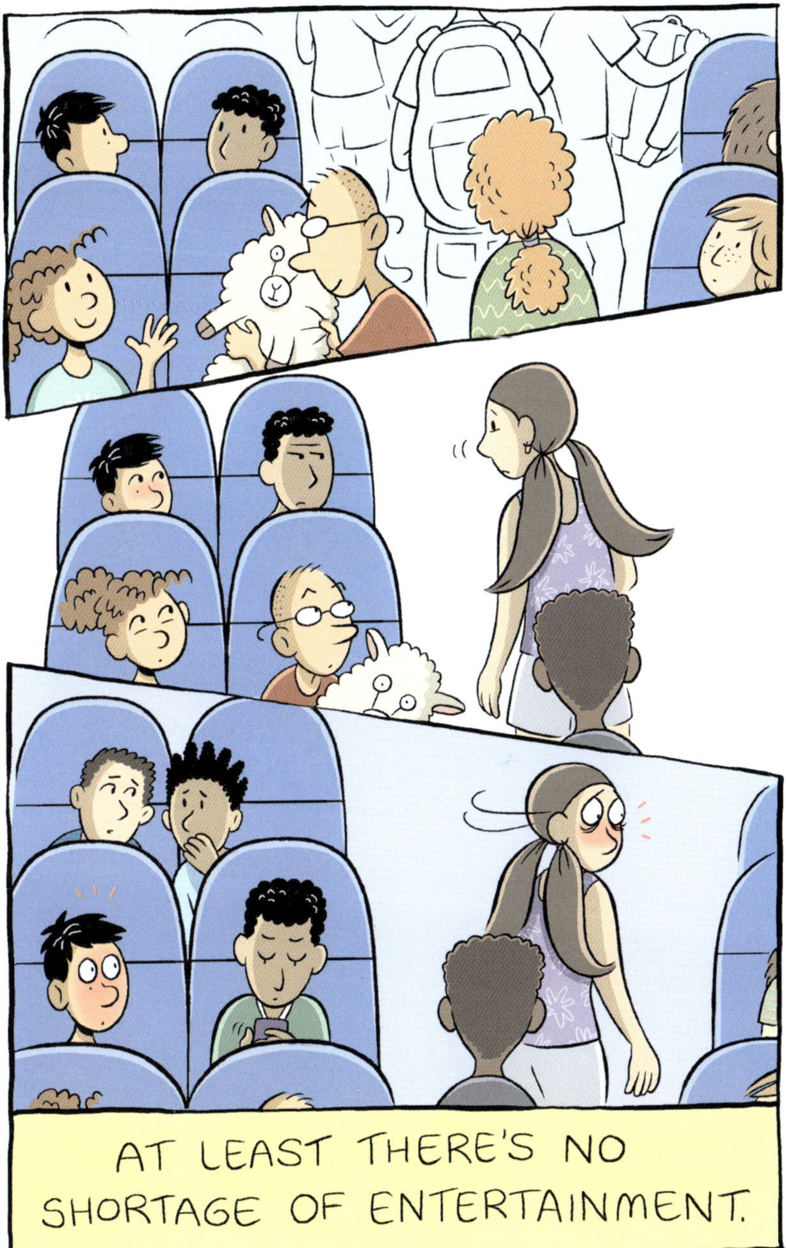
AT LEAST THERE'S NO SHORTAGE OF ENTERTAINMENT.

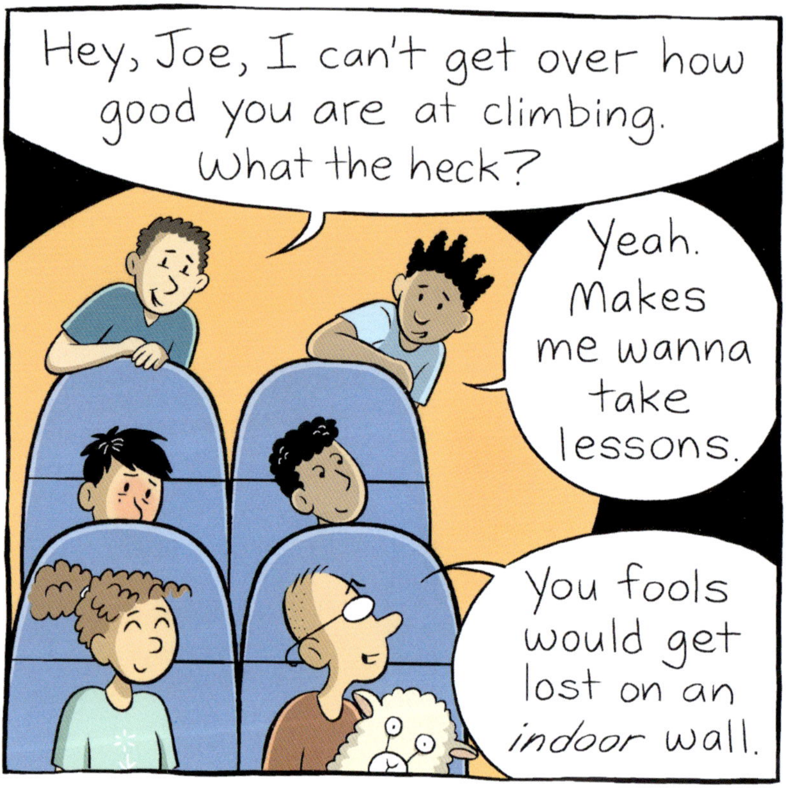
Hey, Joe, I can't get over how good you are at climbing. What the heck?
Yeah. Makes me wanna take lessons.
You fools would get lost on an *indoor* wall.

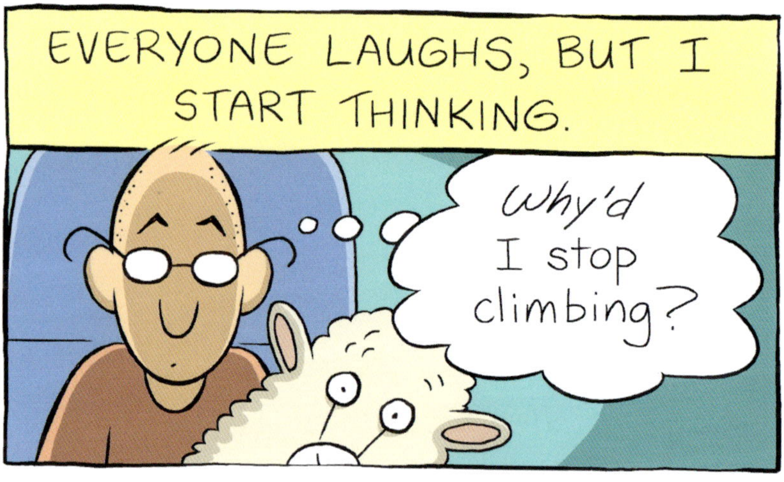
EVERYONE LAUGHS, BUT I START THINKING.
Why'd I stop climbing?

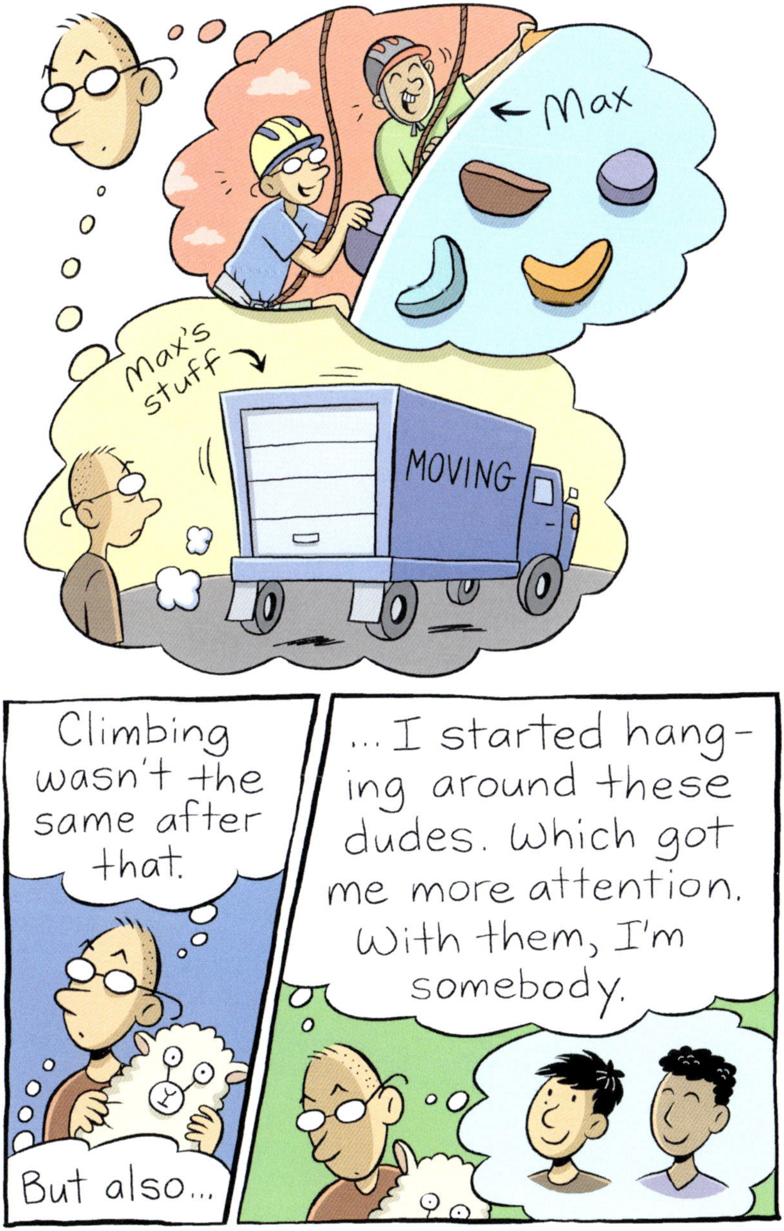
Max
Max's stuff
MOVING
Climbing wasn't the same after that.
But also...
...I started hang-ing around these dudes. Which got me more attention. With them, I'm somebody.

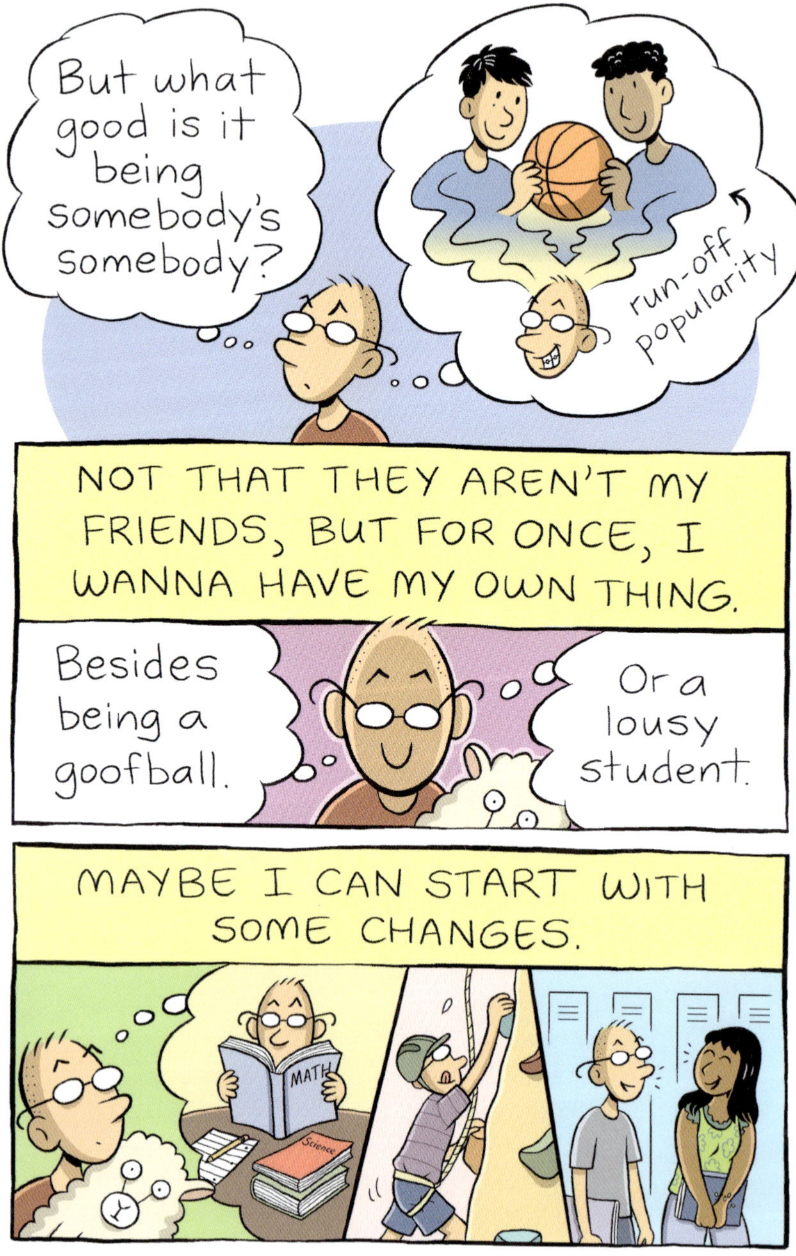
But what good is it being somebody's somebody?
run-off popularity
NOT THAT THEY AREN'T MY FRIENDS, BUT FOR ONCE, I WANNA HAVE MY OWN THING.
Besides being a goofball.
Or a lousy student.
MAYBE I CAN START WITH SOME CHANGES.
MATH
Science

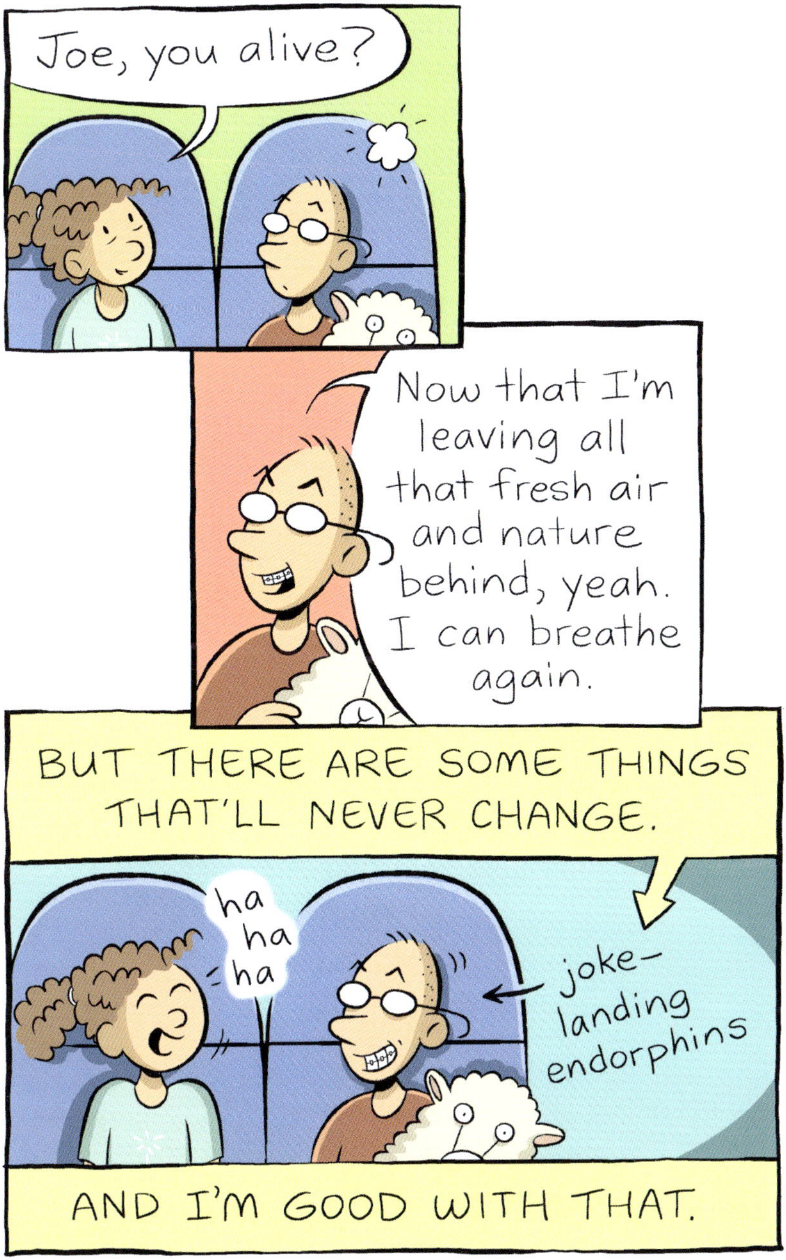
Joe, you alive?
Now that I'm leaving all that fresh air and nature behind, yeah. I can breathe again.
BUT THERE ARE SOME THINGS THAT'LL NEVER CHANGE.
ha ha ha
joke-landing endorphins
AND I'M GOOD WITH THAT.

EMMIE

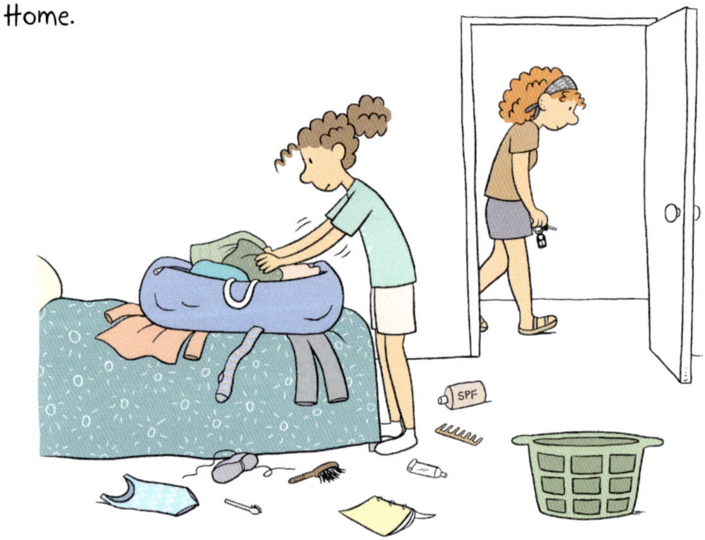
Home.
SPF

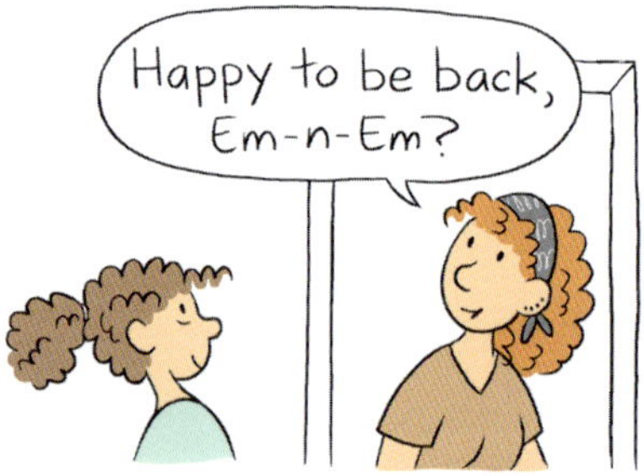
Happy to be back, Em-n-Em?

I nod. I'm relieved to see my bed, my desk, my lamp, my art supplies, and all my "friends."

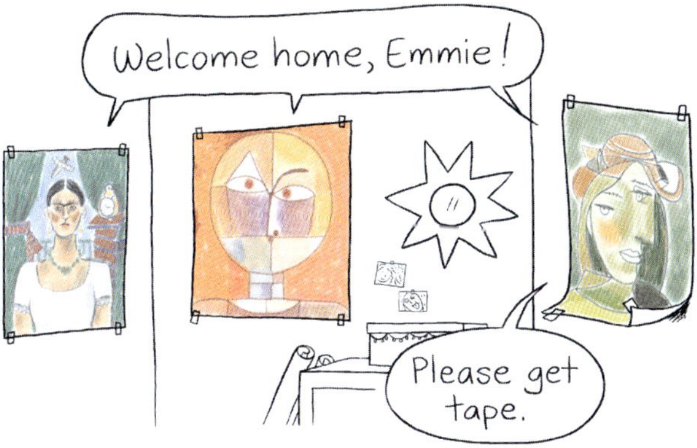
Welcome home, Emmie!
Please get tape.

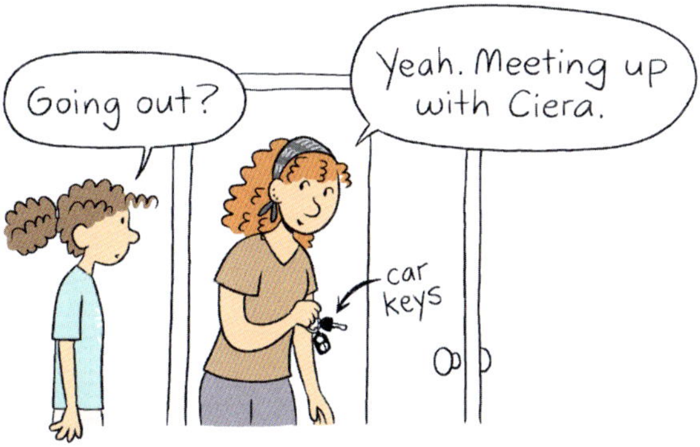
Going out?
Yeah. Meeting up with Ciera.
car keys

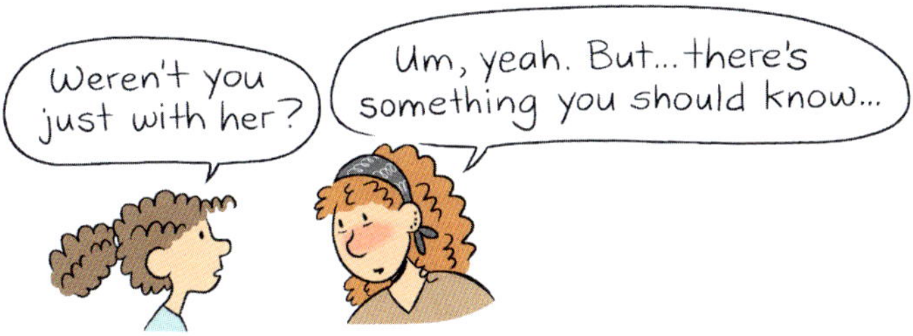
Weren't you just with her?
Um, yeah. But... there's something you should know...

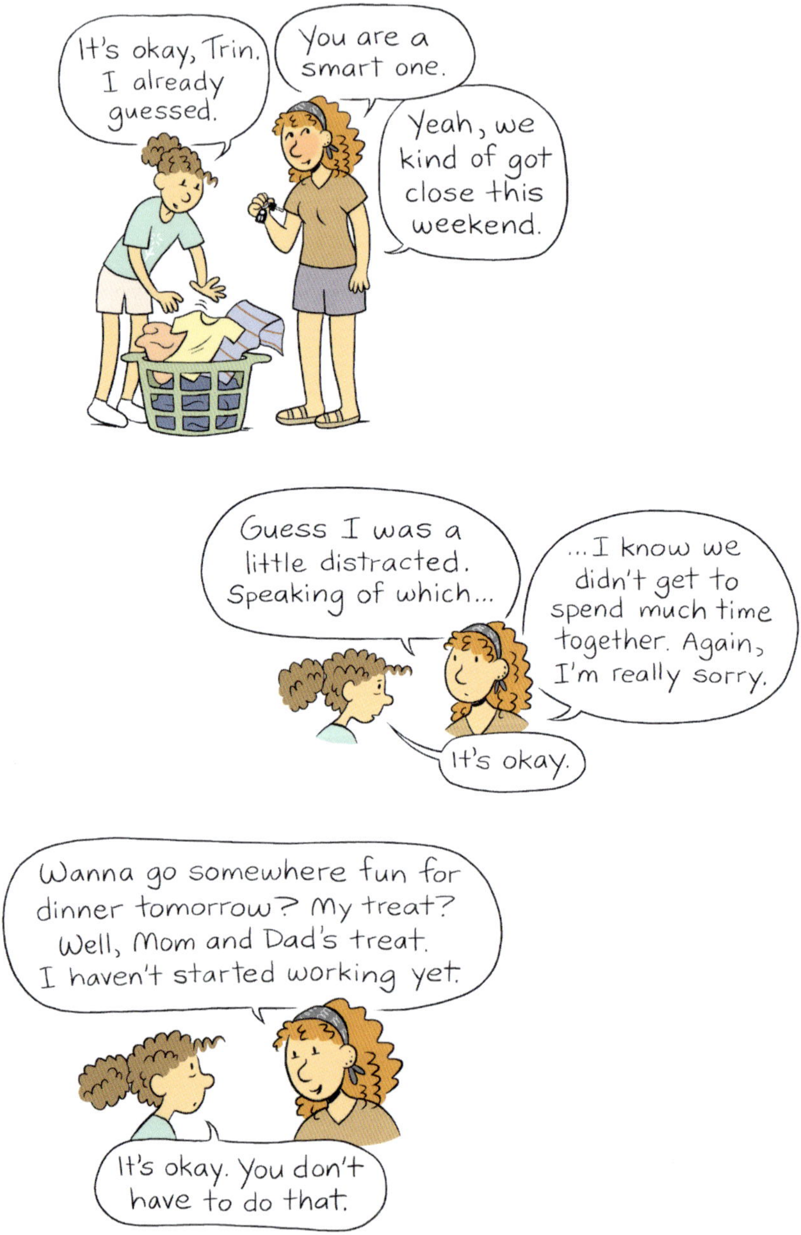
It's okay, Trin. I already guessed.
You are a smart one.
Yeah, we kind of got close this weekend.
Guess I was a little distracted. Speaking of which...
...I know we didn't get to spend much time together. Again, I'm really sorry.
It's okay.
Wanna go somewhere fun for dinner tomorrow? My treat? Well, Mom and Dad's treat. I haven't started working yet.
It's okay. You don't have to do that.

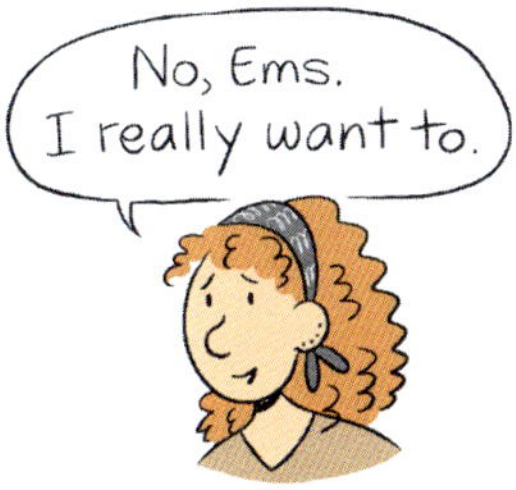
No, Ems.
I really want to.

I look at her. She's sincere. If there's one thing I know, it's when my brother or sister is lying.

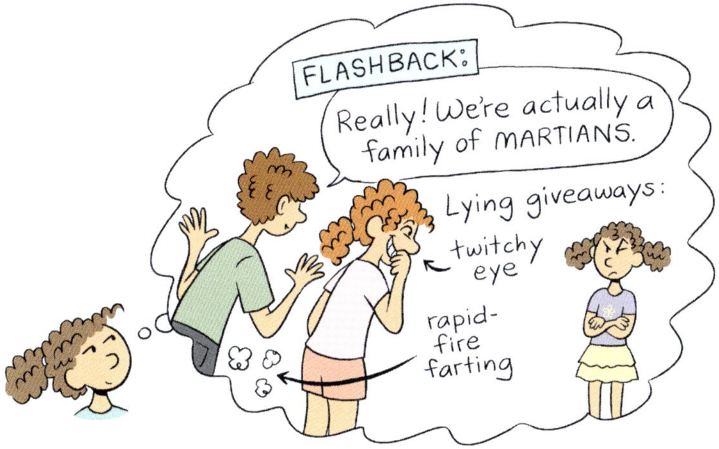
FLASHBACK:
Really! We're actually a family of MARTIANS.
Lying giveaways:
twitchy eye
rapid-fire farting

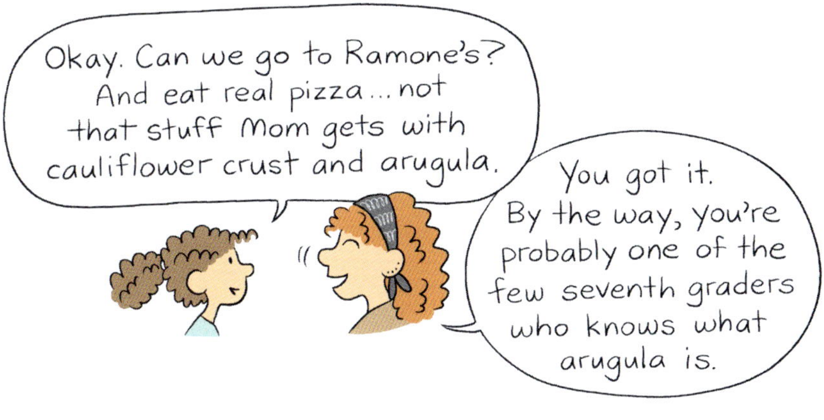
Okay. Can we go to Ramone's? And eat real pizza... not that stuff Mom gets with cauliflower crust and arugula.
You got it. By the way, you're probably one of the few seventh graders who knows what arugula is.

I giggle.

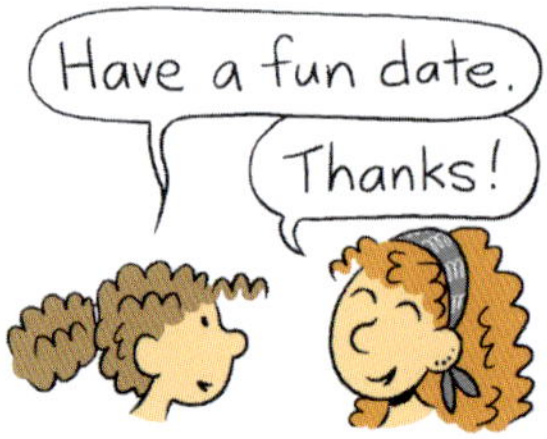
Have a fun date.
Thanks!

She gives me a side-hug and leaves.

After I finish unpacking, I FaceTime Bri and Sarah and fill them in on everything that happened over the weekend. I keep my promise and avoid telling Sarah about Joe's crush. But, wow, it's hard.

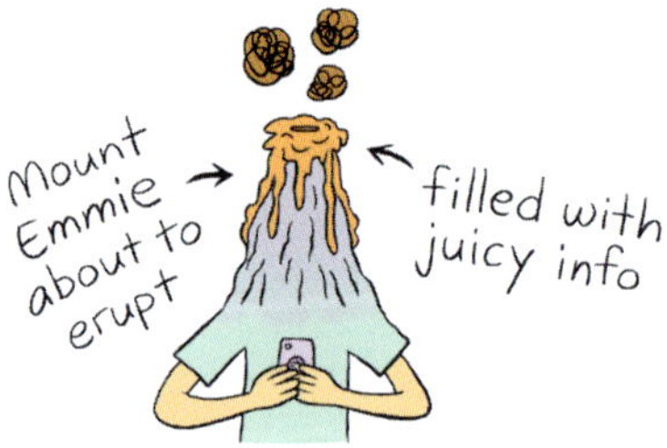
Mount Emmie about to erupt
filled with juicy info

Bri is already feeling better and jokingly promises never to leave my side again.

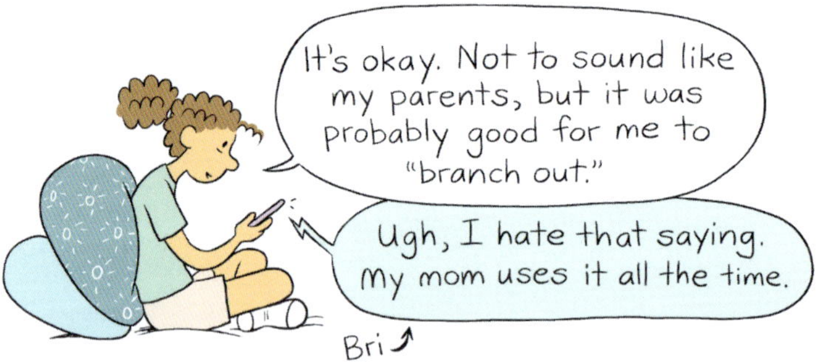
It's okay. Not to sound like my parents, but it was probably good for me to "branch out."
Ugh, I hate that saying. My mom uses it all the time.
Bri

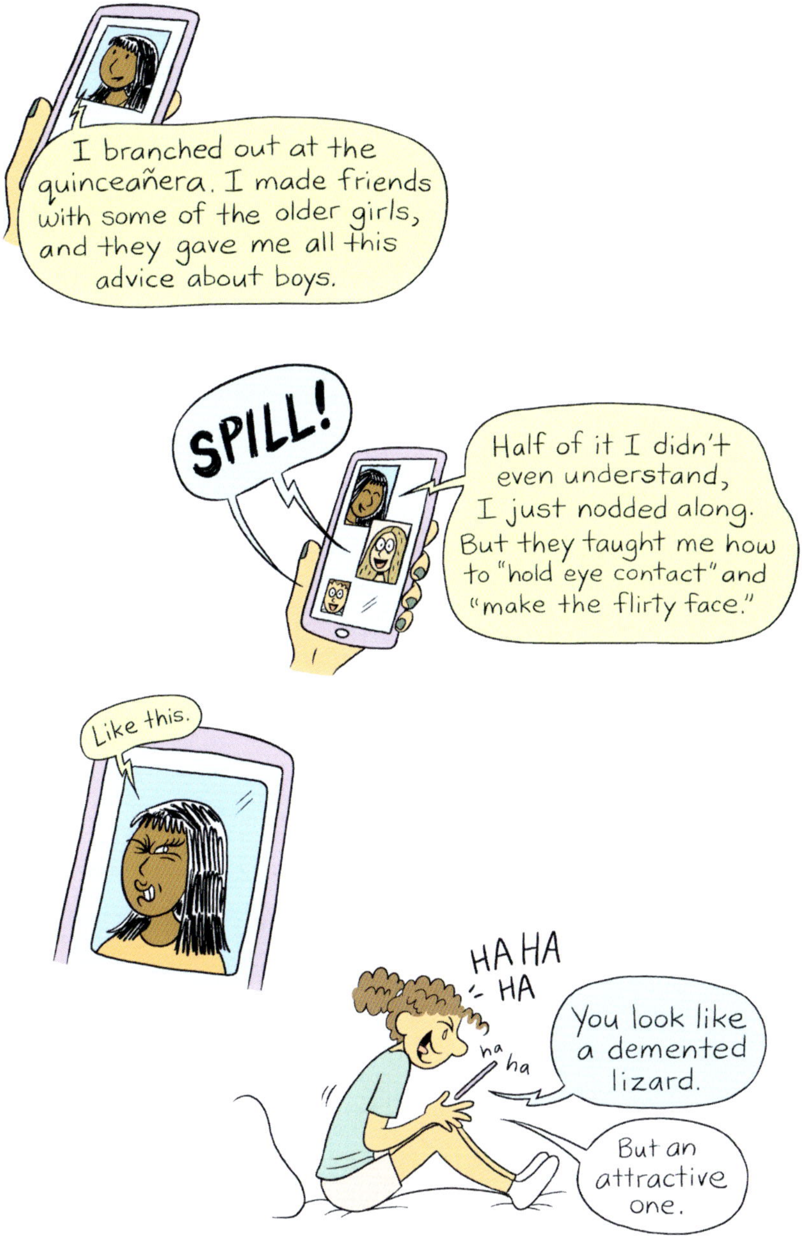
I branched out at the quinceañera. I made friends with some of the older girls, and they gave me all this advice about boys.
SPILL!
Half of it I didn't even understand, I just nodded along. But they taught me how to "hold eye contact" and "make the flirty face."
Like this.
HA HA HA
ha ha
You look like a demented lizard.
But an attractive one.

We laugh some more. Just as we end the call, my phone buzzes and I practically drop it in some old paint water.

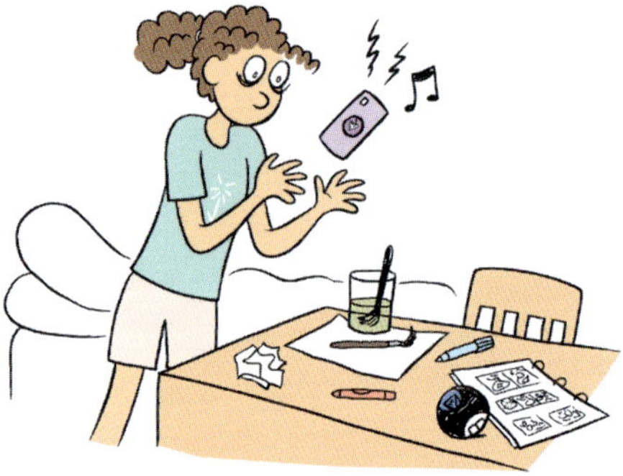

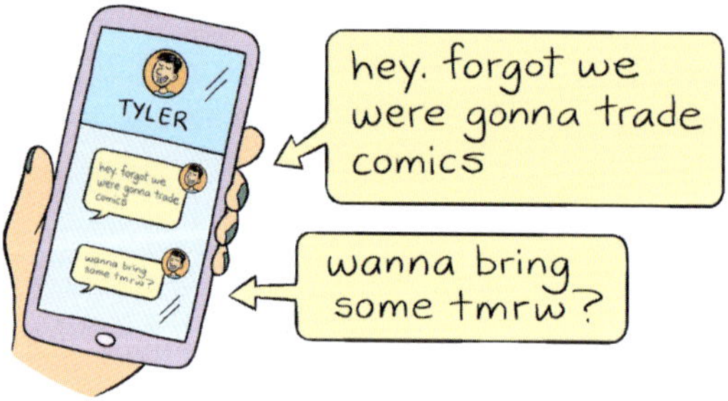
TYLER
hey. forgot we were gonna trade comics
wanna bring some tmrw?

My heart starts pounding. Tyler texting me isn't unusual, as we're friends. Trading comics isn't unusual, either, as our collections have grown. But it's the first time he's back to really "talking" to me since before the weekend.

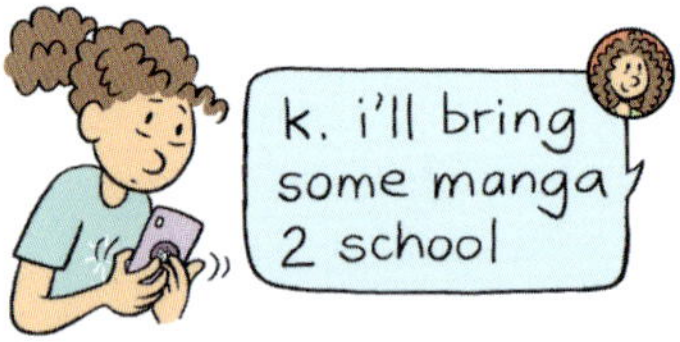
k. i'll bring some manga 2 school

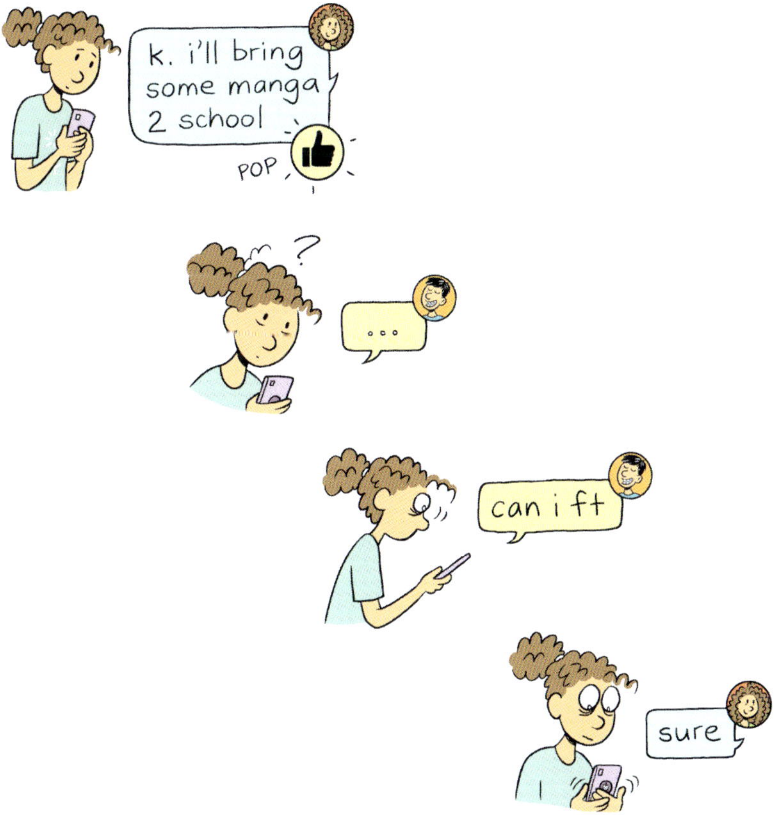
k. i'll bring some manga 2 school
POP
...
can i ft
sure

FaceTime?? I quickly finger-comb my out-of-control curls while I wait a few seconds (that seem like minutes . . . or **weeks**) until the telltale video ringtone sounds.

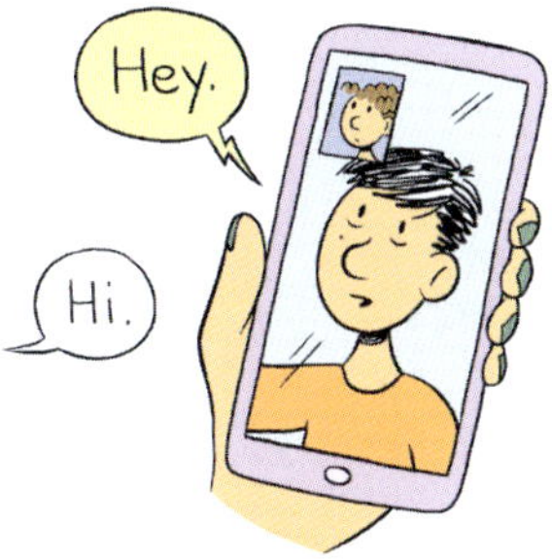
Hey.
Hi.

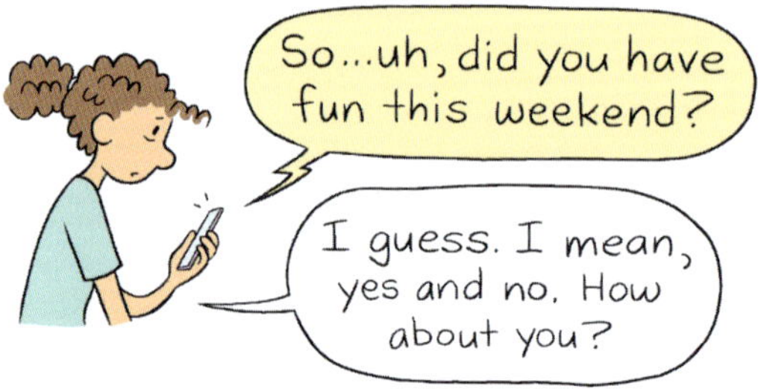
So...uh, did you have fun this weekend?
I guess. I mean, yes and no. How about you?

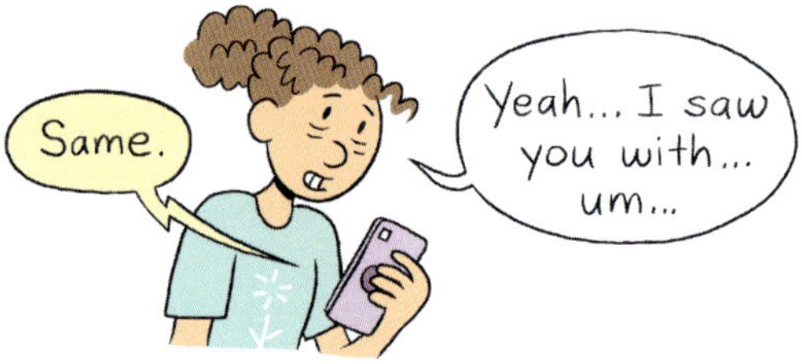
Same.
Yeah... I saw you with... um...

My voice trails off.

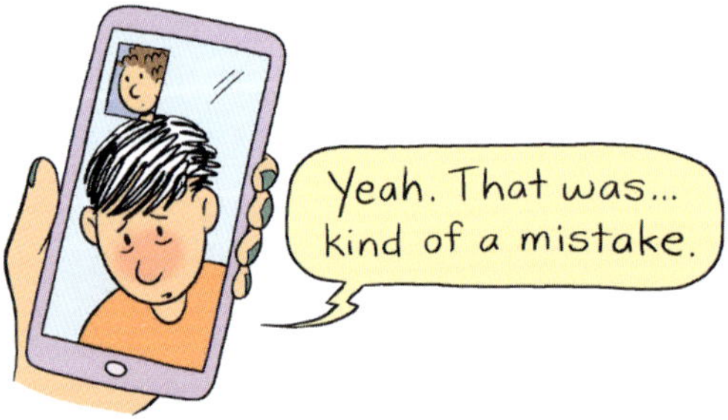
Yeah. That was... kind of a mistake.

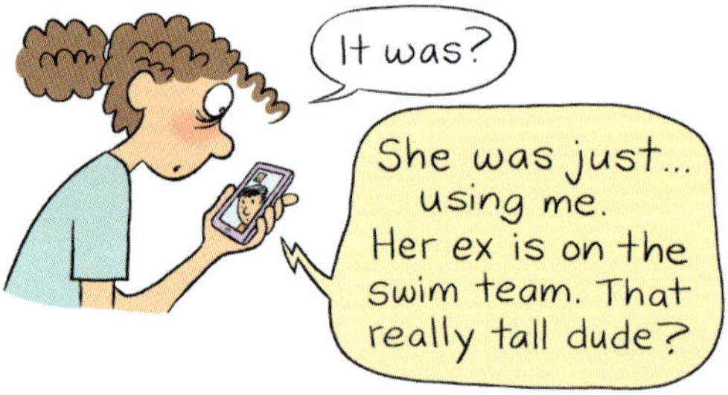
It was?
She was just... using me.
Her ex is on the swim team. That really tall dude?

I instantly know who he's talking about: a popular (and really, really tall) seventh grader with a square face and big, poofy hair that he usually shaves off before swim season.

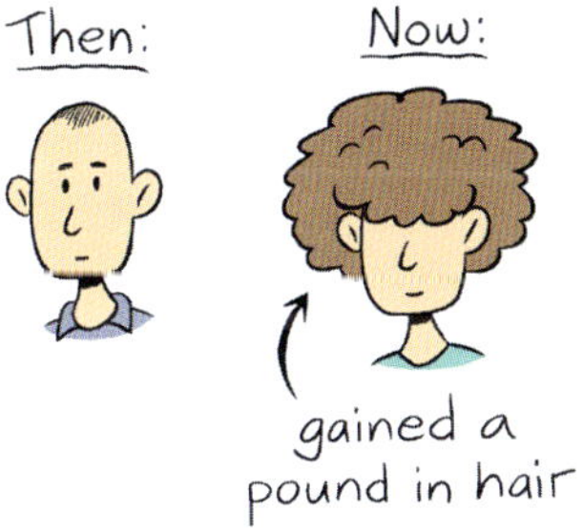
Then:
Now:
gained a pound in hair

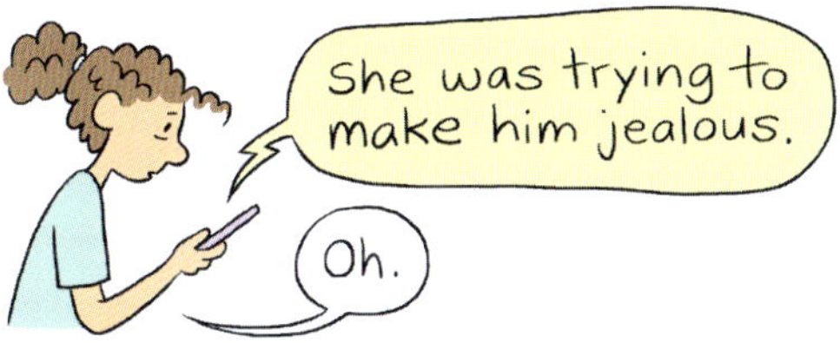
She was trying to make him jealous.
Oh.

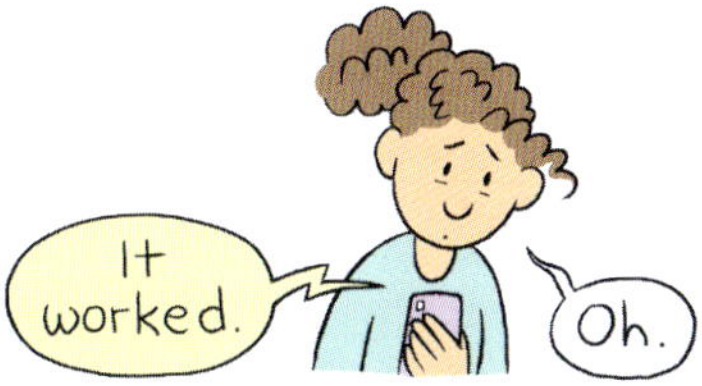
It worked.
Oh.

Pause.

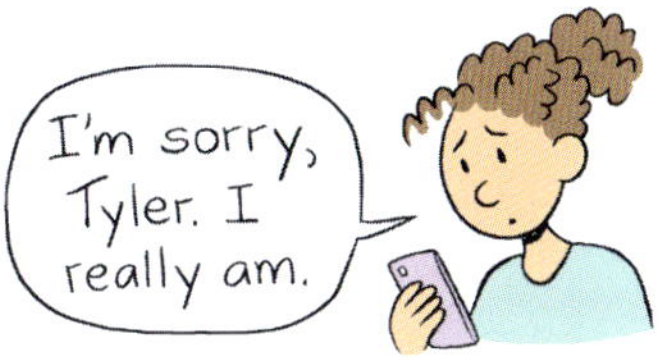
I'm sorry, Tyler. I really am.

I do mean it. Because, crush or no crush, Tyler is my friend.

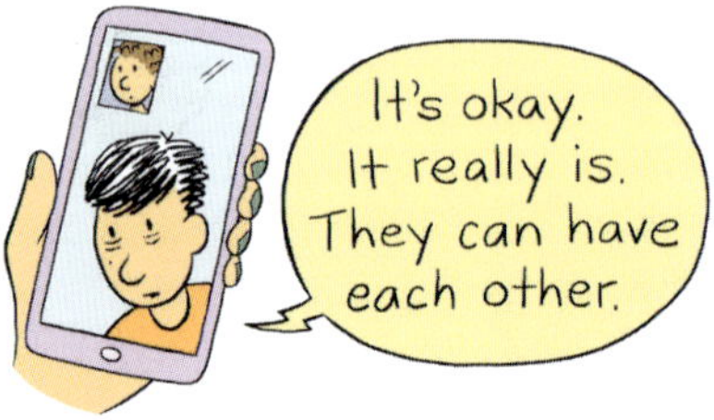
It's okay. It really is. They can have each other.

Another pause.

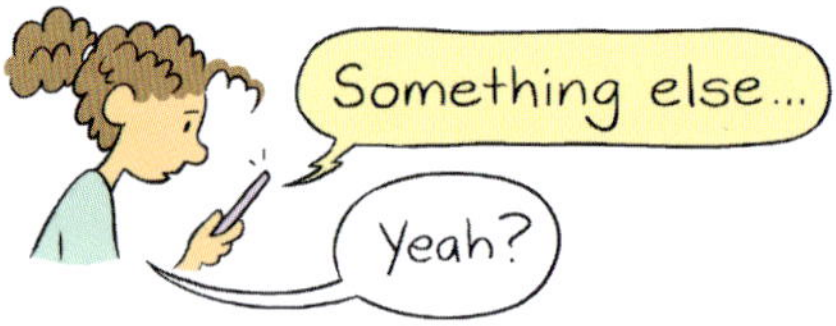
Something else...
Yeah?

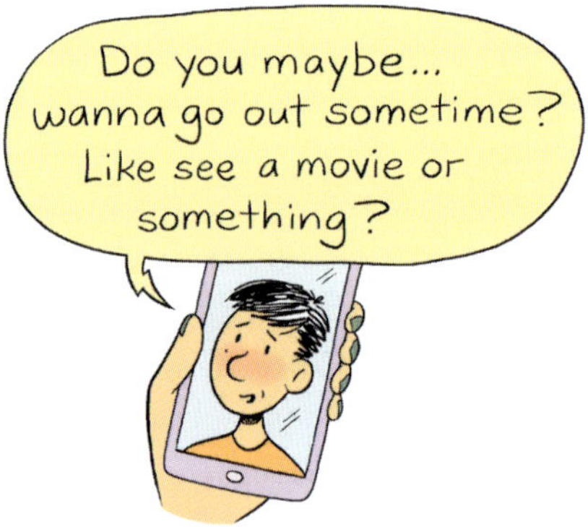
Do you maybe... wanna go out sometime? Like see a movie or something?

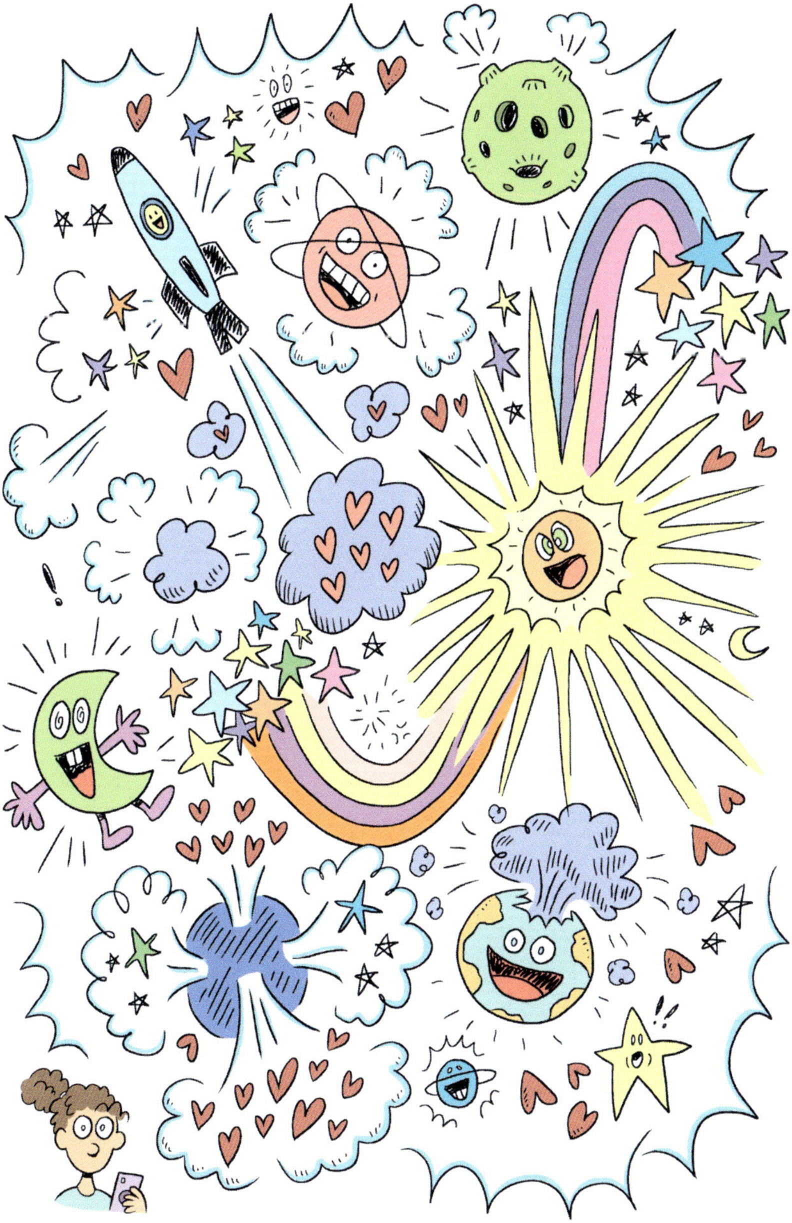

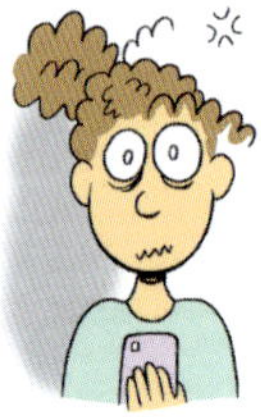

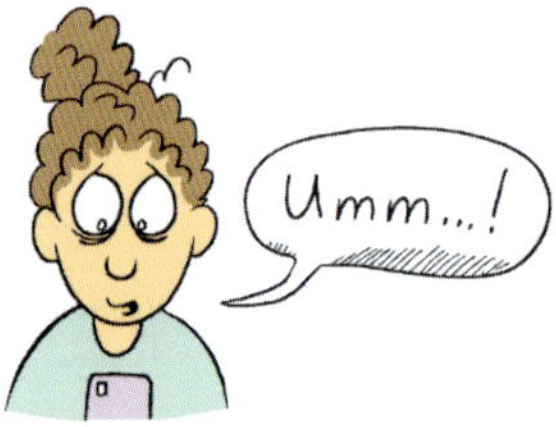
Umm...!

OMG. This is happening. It's really happening.
But . . .

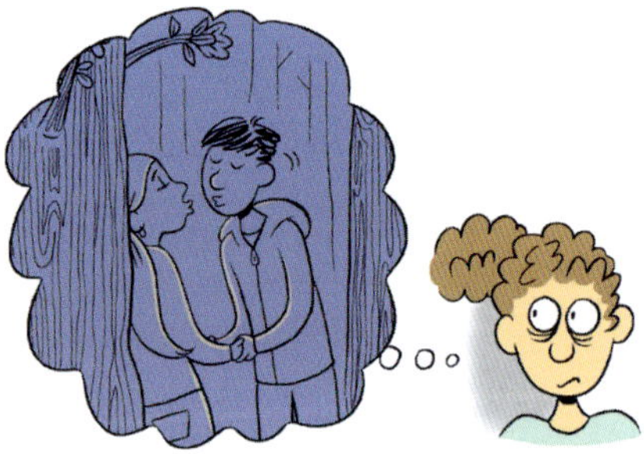

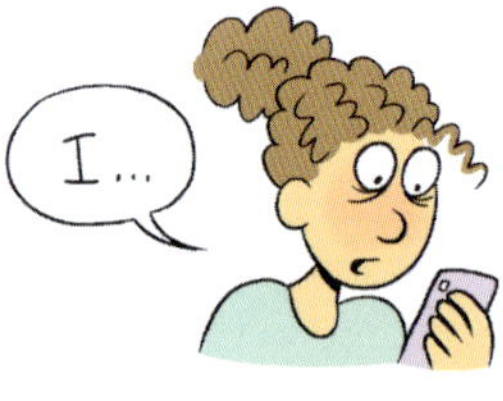
I...

OMG. OMG.
I can't believe what I'm about to say.

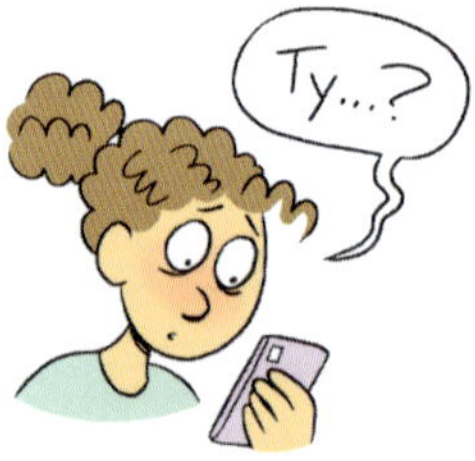
Ty...?

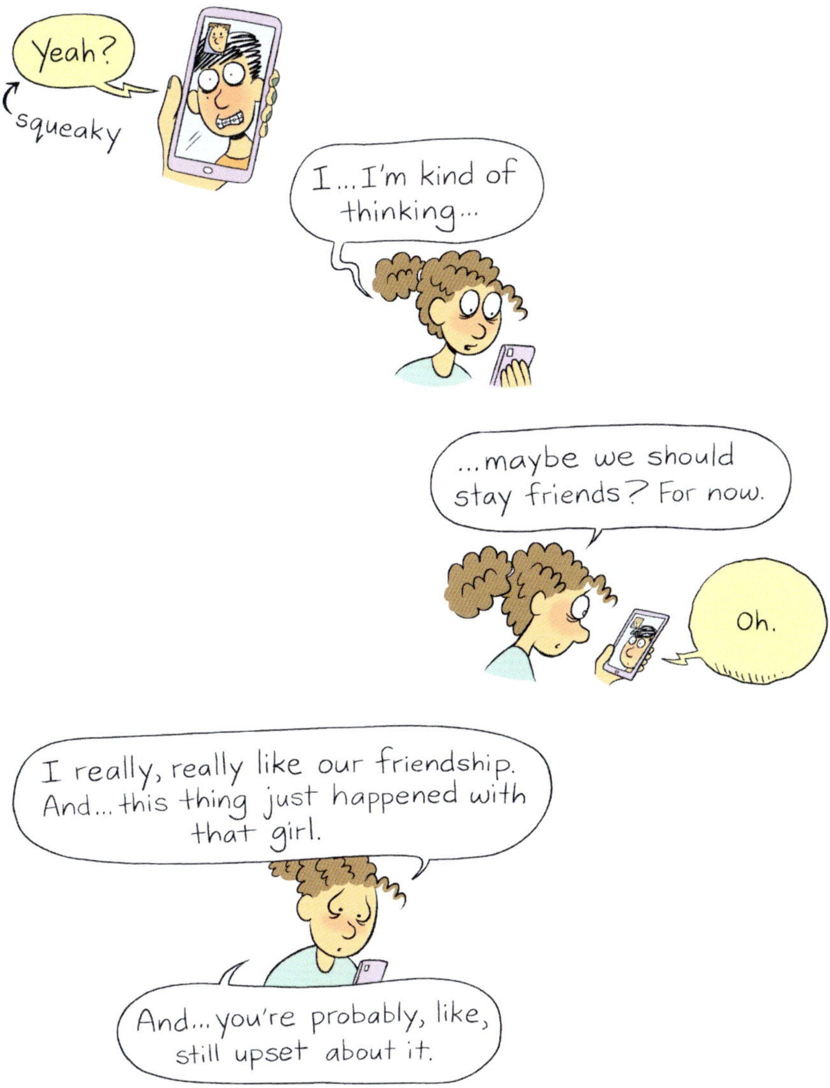
Yeah?
squeaky
I... I'm kind of thinking...
...maybe we should stay friends? For now.
Oh.
I really, really like our friendship. And... this thing just happened with that girl.
And... you're probably, like, still upset about it.

I notice I've stopped sounding like I'm asking questions. A miracle.

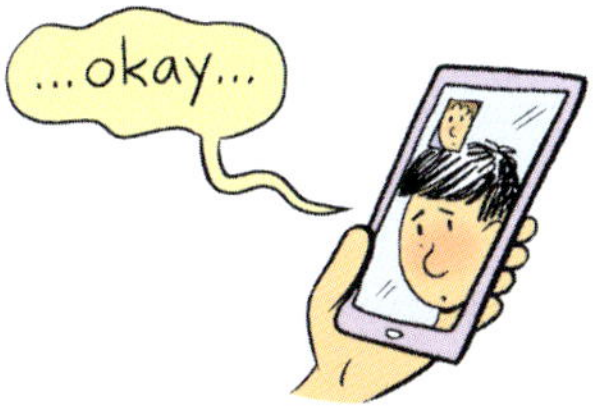
...okay...

He sounds like he's strangling. Before I upset him even more, I quickly say:

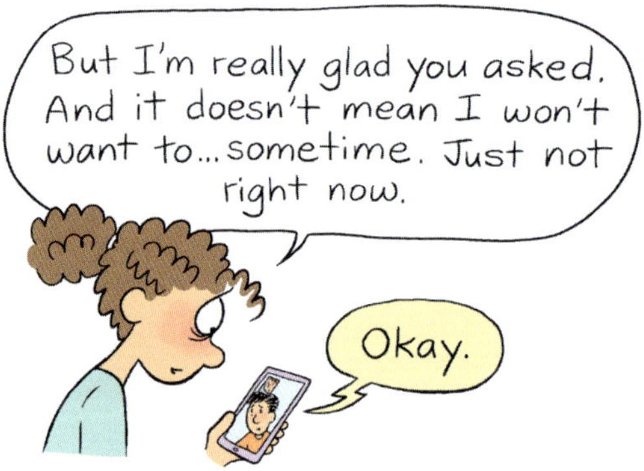
But I'm really glad you asked. And it doesn't mean I won't want to... sometime. Just not right now.
Okay.

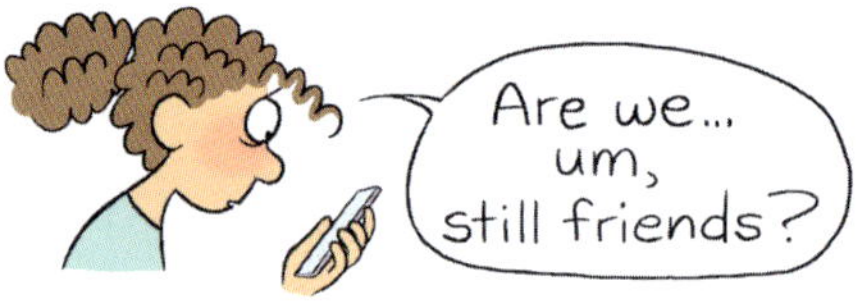
Are we... um, still friends?

He hesitates. But then . . .

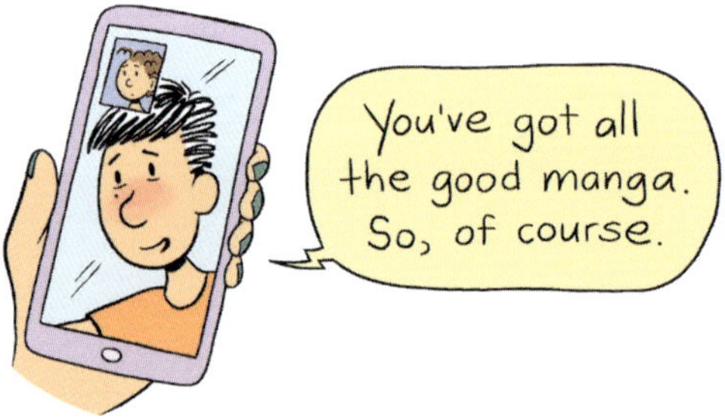
You've got all the good manga. So, of course.

I laugh.

That breaks the tension. I tell him about the comics I'll bring to school tomorrow, and he asks what I'd like to borrow. Then he jokes a little about Joe and my "buddy" situation and tells me he feels bad I got stuck with him.

Actually, it worked out. Here's a shocker: I like him. Underneath all of the... *that.*

He's a good guy. An' a good buddy. Sometimes Anthony and I forget that. We've gotta ... do better, I guess.

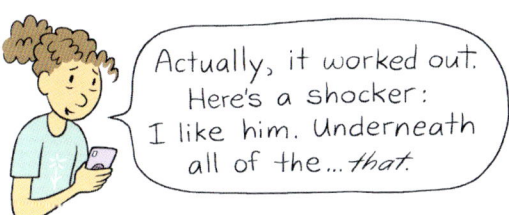

I'm glad to hear it.

We end the call and I just sit there, staring at my poster of **Senecio** by Paul Klee.

Fool!

That's for sure. I can also imagine Bri's and Sarah's reactions:

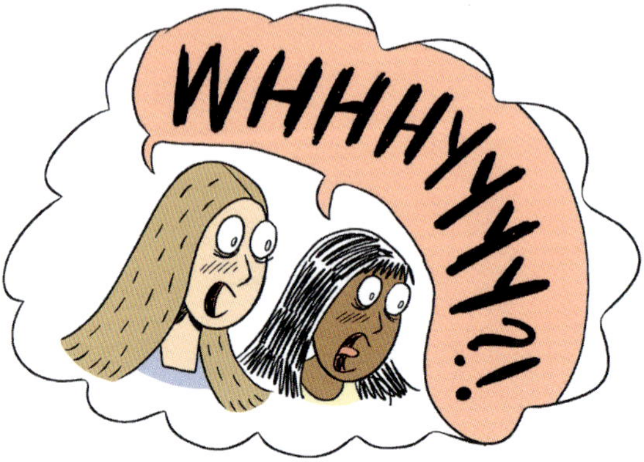
WHHHYYYYY?!

I hope I didn't confuse Tyler. I really meant what I said. Trina once confided that she's been with people who've used her to get over someone else. I don't think Tyler is trying to do that, but I do think he's still kinda upset. And I don't wanna be a "rebound girl."

But mostly . . .

. . . it comes down to what Joe told me after wall climbing, during our creek walk:

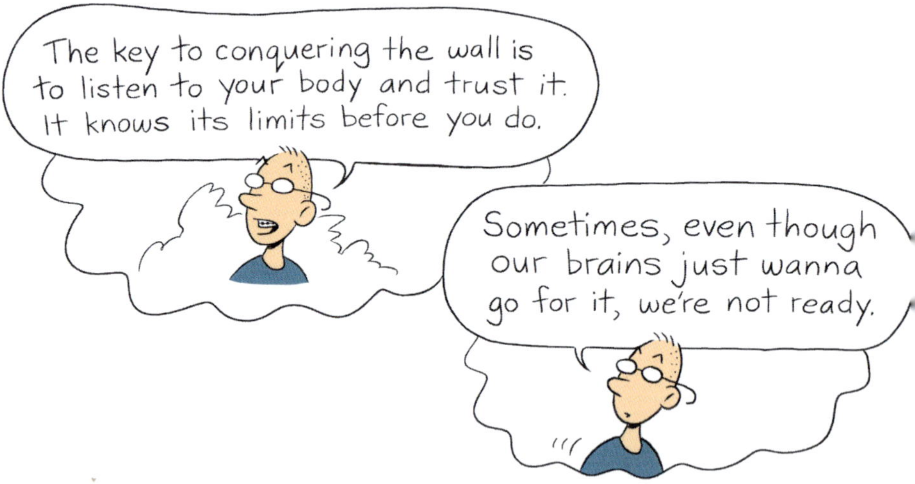
The key to conquering the wall is to listen to your body and trust it. It knows its limits before you do.
Sometimes, even though our brains just wanna go for it, we're not ready.

When Tyler asked me out, I flashed to that awful memory of him and BG about to kiss.

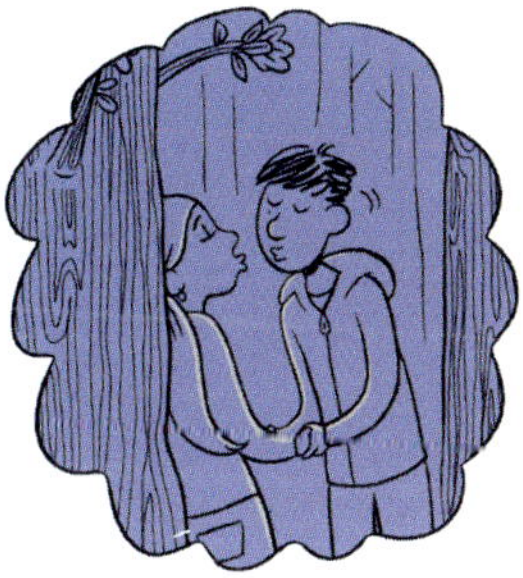

I tried to listen to my body. Really listen.

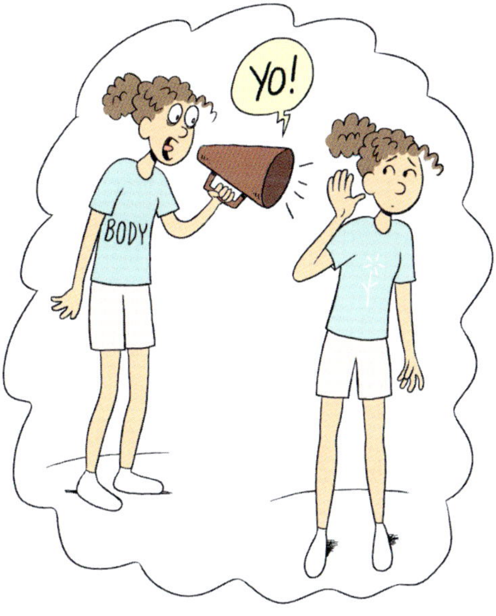
YO!
BODY

And my body told me it's not ready for dating. Or kissing. **Especially** kissing. I thought I was, but it scared me to think of being in BG's place.

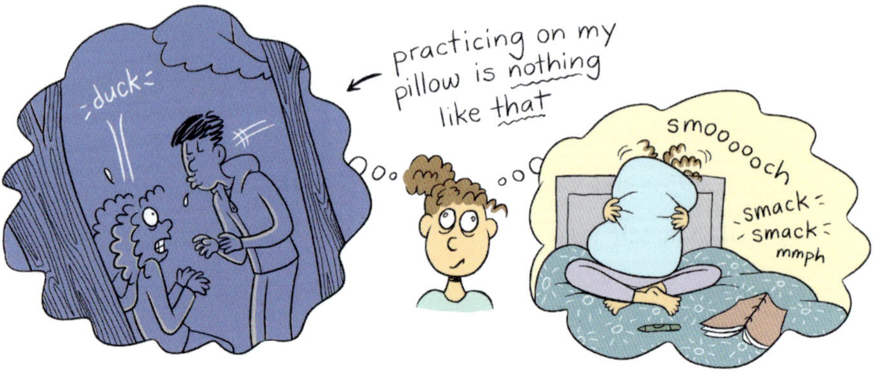
duck
practicing on my pillow is nothing like that
smooooooch
smack
smack
mmph

So, yeah, I think **both** Tyler and I need to be ready for all that. And I don't think either of us is.

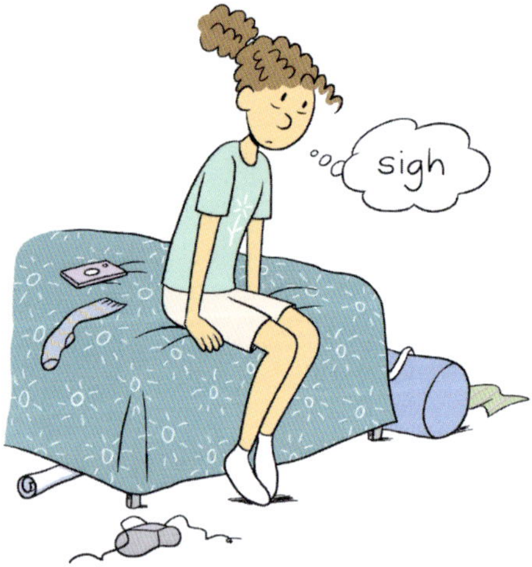
sigh

I get up and head down to the basement, where we keep all our games and books.

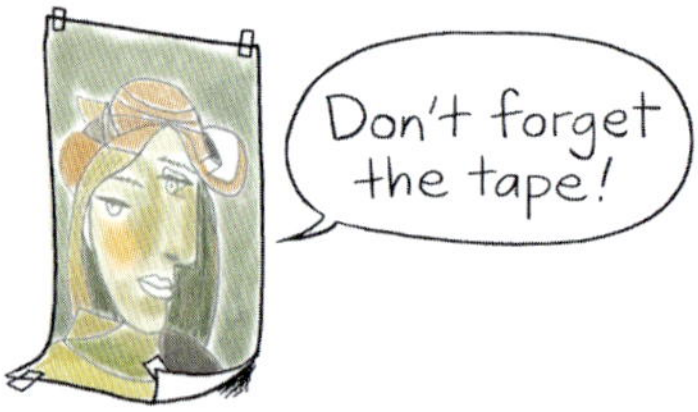
Don't forget the tape!

I think about how this wasn't the class trip I imagined, but I still feel better for it. I'm proud I was able to try some new things. I'm proud Joe and I got to help each other. And I'm proud that I listened to myself (and that Tyler and I are still friends—fingers crossed). I can't wait to tell Trina all about this.

But that's later.

First, I need to find some manga.

EPILOGUE
EMMIE

Back at school.

Before homeroom, I stand in front of the lockers with Bri and Sarah. We chat away.

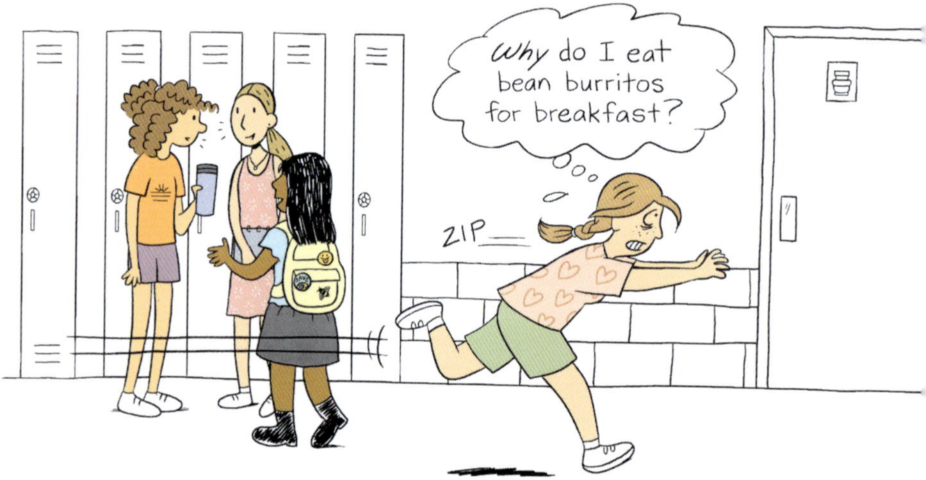

Why do I eat bean burritos for breakfast?
ZIP

I spot Joe walking in. He usually gets to school before Anthony and Tyler. I have a plan in place.

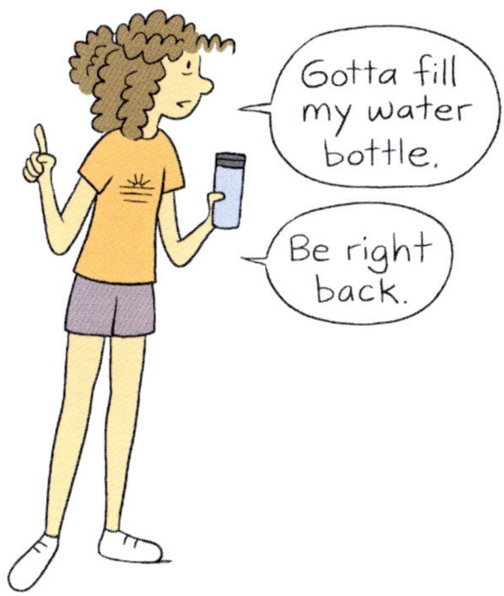
Gotta fill my water bottle.
Be right back.

I head to the water fountain (one of the few working ones), which **happens** to be right by Joe's locker.

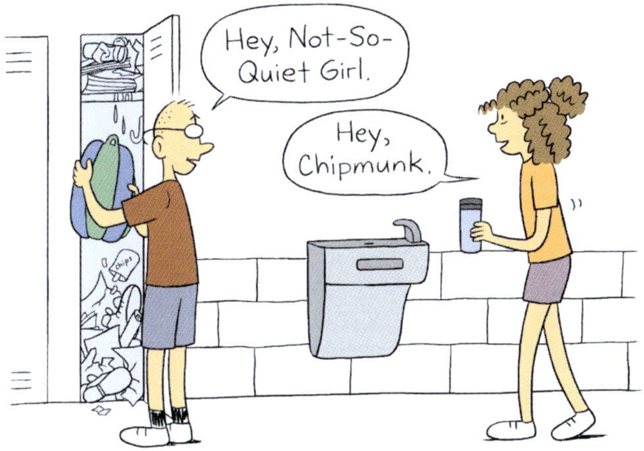
Hey, Not-So-Quiet Girl.
Hey, Chipmunk.

That was a little bold. I start to turn red. Luckily, Joe grins.

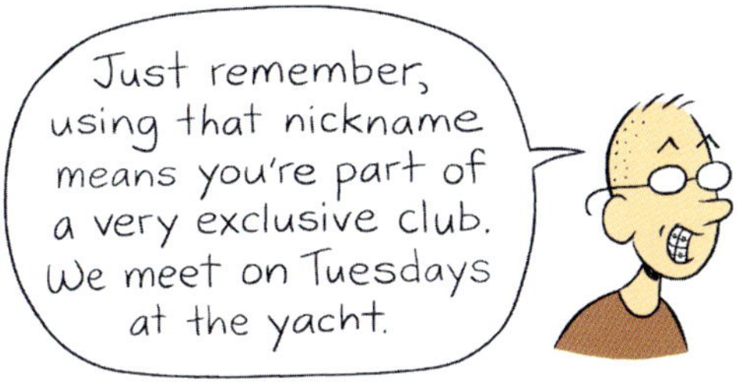
Just remember, using that nickname means you're part of a very exclusive club. We meet on Tuesdays at the yacht.

I smile. His jokes are getting (well . . . slightly) better. At least, he's not using people as punch lines.

Have you ever thought of doing stand-up ... for real?

To my surprise, he looks a little embarrassed. Then he shrugs. **Maybe.**

Thought about it. I might try improv club next year. Dev was telling me about it in the cabin.

That's a great idea.

Yeah? My parents will be happy. They're tired of me lying around. Or being my test audience.

I laugh. Genuinely.

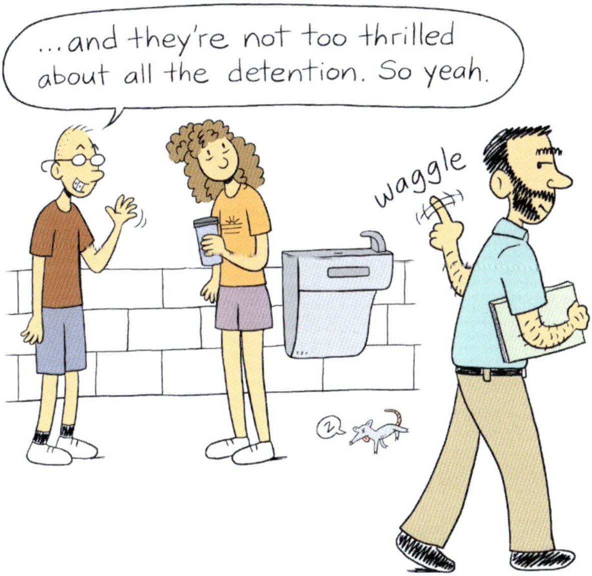
...and they're not too thrilled about all the detention. So yeah.
waggle

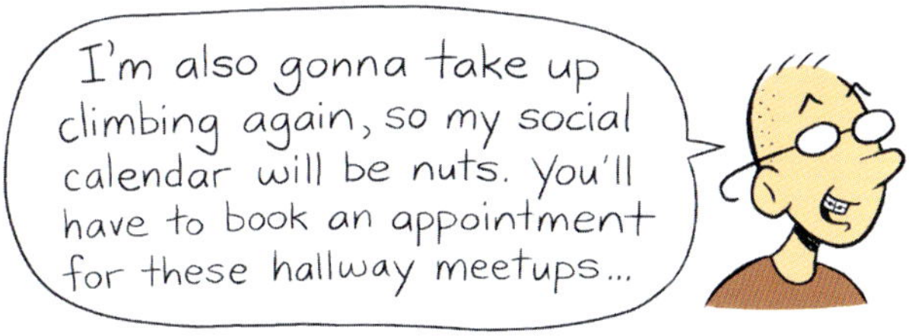
I'm also gonna take up climbing again, so my social calendar will be nuts. You'll have to book an appointment for these hallway meetups...

His voice trails off as he notices Sarah glancing our way.

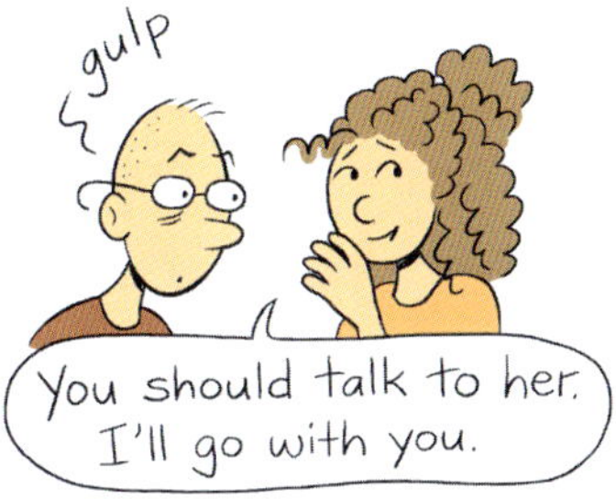
gulp
You should talk to her. I'll go with you.

He starts to protest, but then Bri and Sarah head our way.

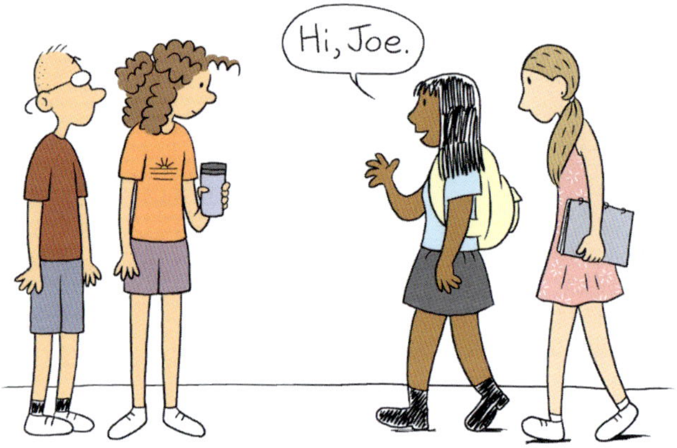
Hi, Joe.

I forgot that Sarah and Joe are kinda friendly, ever since the night of the Student Showcase. But they haven't talked much since.

Bri's not a fan, but then, until this weekend, neither was I.

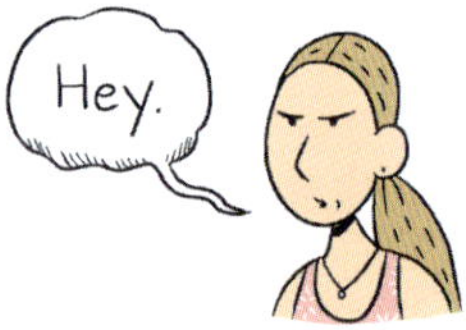
Hey.

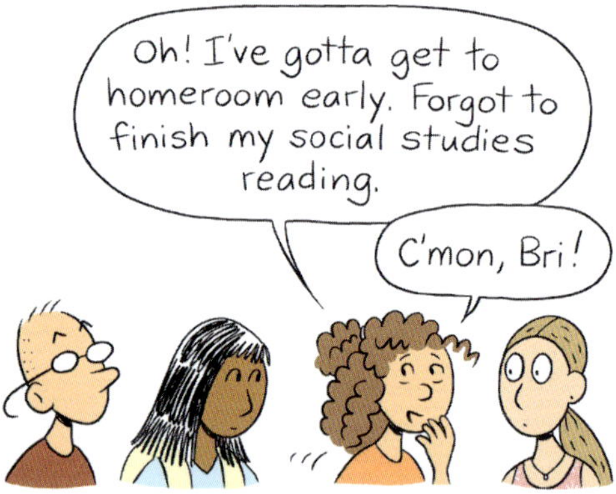
Oh! I've gotta get to homeroom early. Forgot to finish my social studies reading.
C'mon, Bri!

Before Bri can say anything, I grab her arm and pull her down the hall.

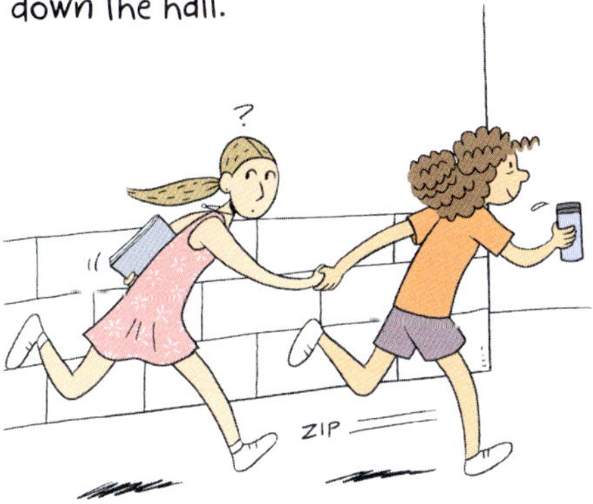
?
ZIP

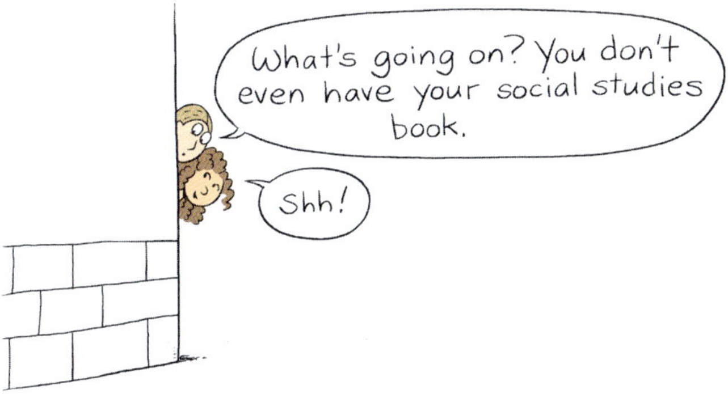
What's going on? You don't even have your social studies book.
Shh!

We watch as Joe and Sarah talk. Like, a lot. And it doesn't even look awkward. After a moment, Sarah bursts out laughing, and Joe looks really pleased.

We watch for another minute or two. And then . . .

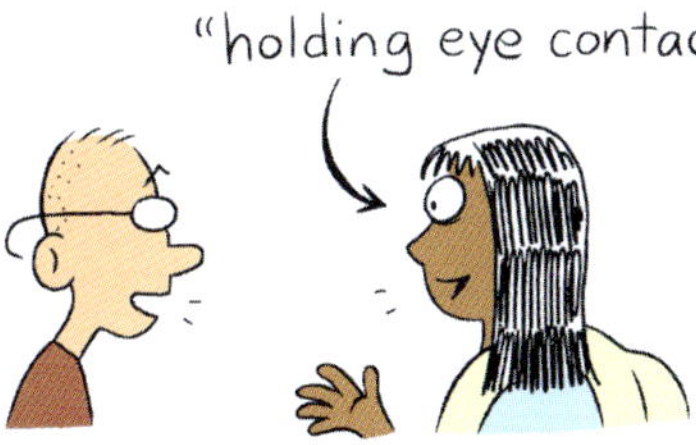
"holding eye contact"

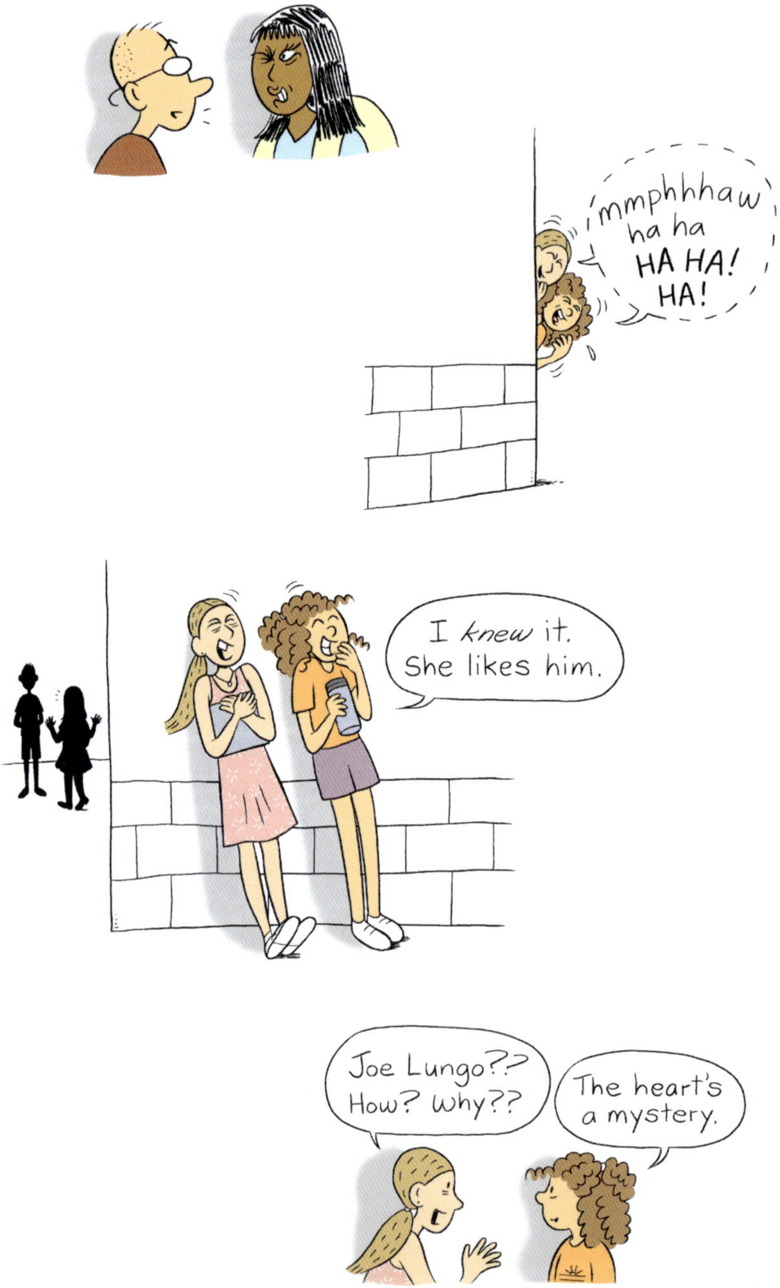

mmphhhaw ha ha HA HA! HA!
I *knew* it. She likes him.
Joe Lungo?? How? Why??
The heart's a mystery.

The bell rings and we start walking to homeroom together.

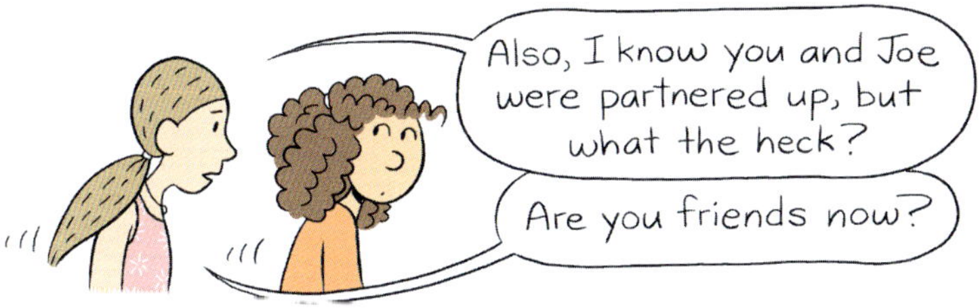
Also, I know you and Joe were partnered up, but what the heck?
Are you friends now?

I glance back and spot Joe and Sarah walking to their homerooms behind us. They are still talking and laughing. I catch Joe's eye when Sarah isn't looking, and he gives me a quick thumbs-up. I give one back.

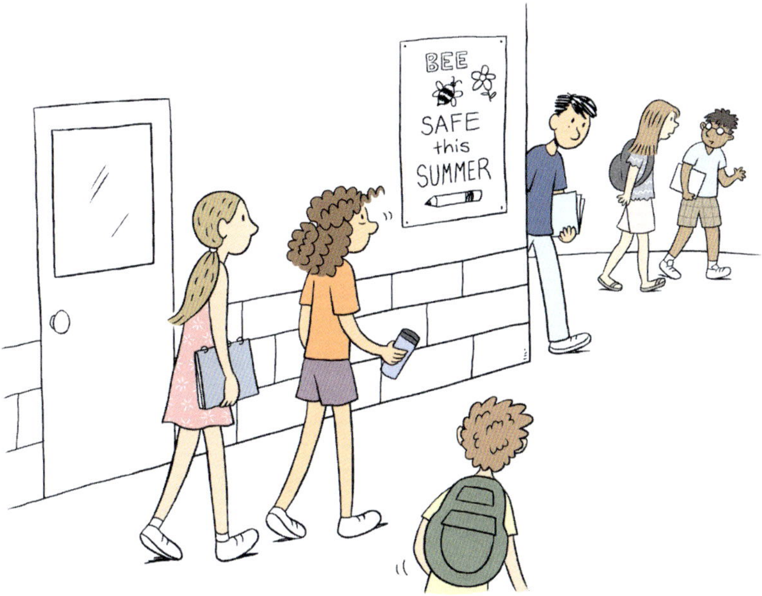
BEE
SAFE
this
SUMMER

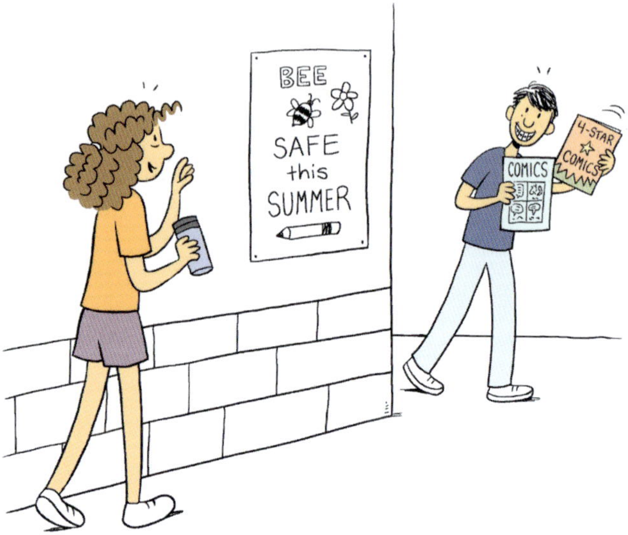
BEE
SAFE
this
SUMMER
COMICS
4-STAR
COMICS

I blush, thinking of Tyler asking me out.
Then I turn back to Bri.

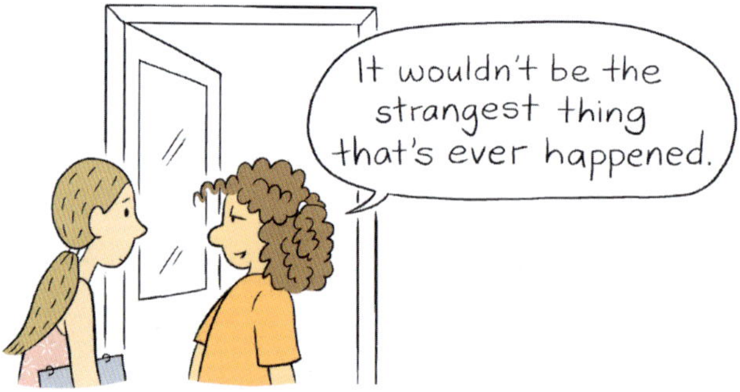
It wouldn't be the strangest thing that's ever happened.

ACKNOWLEDGMENTS

It was so much fun bringing Emmie back into the spotlight for this story. And Joe! How readers clamored for him (and how could I resist?). Thank you to those who wrote to me with your requests for that fun little imp.

When writing, one of my main goals is to show that there's usually more to someone than meets the eye. The world can always use more empathy (and laughter—something Joe understands). I hope that comes across in **Entirely Emmie** as well as the rest of the series.

A huge thank-you goes out to the following people who helped bring this **entirely** fun story to life:

Donna Bray, the mastermind behind this unlikely pairing of Emmie and Joe, and who has always been an absolute joy to work with (miss you!).

Amy Cloud, also an absolute joy to work with and who completely vibes with the heart and soul of this series. Thank you for taking on E&F!

Dan Lazar, who makes every client feel like his one and only.

Always grateful for that razor-sharp mind and endless support.

Laura Mock and Amy Ryan, for being ongoing artistic superheroes with an endless supply of talent.

Taylan Salvati, Sabrina Abballe, Jon Howard, Gwen Morton, Patty Rosati, Kerry Moynagh, and the rest of the hardworking, talented, and ever-supportive team at HarperCollins.

My family: Mike, Mollie, and Nikki, as well as my mom and siblings: Meral, Brad, and Tina (and their awesome families). And, of course, all my wonderful friends. Thanks for always supporting this "comics" life that tends to consume me (in a good way, right?). Love you all.

Rosie, my cute slacker coworker. Glad to finally immortalize you in a book—even if I aged you up half a (dog's) life.

Last but not least, my readers. Thank you for immersing yourselves in these books. You're why I write 'em and love doing so!

(rare alert moment for my coworker)